THE SUMMIT

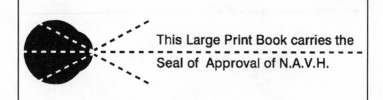

This Large Print Book carries the
Seal of Approval of N.A.V.H.

THE SUMMIT

KAT MARTIN

THORNDIKE PRESS
A part of Gale, Cengage Learning

Detroit • New York • San Francisco • New Haven, Conn • Waterville, Maine • London

GALE
CENGAGE Learning™

LIBRARY OF CONGRESS CATALOGING-IN-PUBLICATION DATA

Martin, Kat.
   The summit / by Kat Martin.
     p. cm. — (Thorndike Press large print romance)
   ISBN-13: 978-1-4104-0333-9 (alk. paper)
   ISBN-10: 1-4104-0333-5 (alk. paper)
   1. Mediums — Fiction. 2. Missing children — Fiction.
   3. Psychic ability — Fiction. 4. Washington (State) — Fiction.
   5. Large type books. I. Title.
   PS3563.A7246S86 2008
   813'.54—dc22   2007041837

Published in 2008 by arrangement with Harlequin Books S.A.

Printed in the United States of America
1 2 3 4 5 6 7 12 11 10 09 08

To those who attack the mountains,
who live for the joy of ascending a
peak, live for the challenge, the thrill of
conquest.
And to those among us who fight so
hard to protect and preserve the last
wild places in this magnificent land
God has given us.
Keep up the fight!

ONE

Autumn Sommers tossed and turned, an icy fear creeping over her. Goose flesh rose over her skin and moisture popped out on her forehead at the vivid, frightening images expanding into the corners of her mind.

A little girl raced across the freshly mown front lawn of her suburban home, laughing as she played kickball with her friends — a child five or six years old with delicate features, big blue eyes and softly curling long blond hair.

"Get the ball, Molly!" a little red-haired boy shouted. All of the children were around the same age.

But Molly's curious blue eyes were fixed on the man standing on the sidewalk holding a fuzzy black-and-white puppy. Ignoring the ball, which rolled past her short legs into the shrubs at the edge of the yard, she hurried toward the man.

"Molly!" Angry, the little boy raced after

the ball, picked it up and gave it a sturdy kick back toward the other children, who squealed with delight and chased after it.

Molly saw only the adorable little puppy.

"You like Cuffy?" the man asked as she reached up to pet the dog with gentle, adoring strokes. "I have another puppy just like him. His name is Nicky, but somehow he got lost. I was hoping you might help me find him."

Lying in bed, Autumn shifted restlessly beneath the covers. "No . . ." she muttered, but the little girl couldn't hear her. She moved her head from side to side, trying to warn the child not to go with the man, but little Molly was already walking away, the puppy held snuggly in her arms.

"Don't . . . go . . ." Autumn whispered, but the little girl just kept walking. Still clutching the puppy, the child climbed into the car and the man closed the door. He made his way to the driver's side, slid behind the wheel and started the engine. An instant later, the vehicle rolled quietly down the street.

"Molly!" shouted the red-haired boy, running toward the disappearing auto. "You aren't supposed to go off with strangers!"

"Molly!" One of the girls clamped her small hands on her hips. "You're not supposed to leave the yard!" She turned to the red-haired boy. "She's really gonna be in trouble."

Worried now, the boy stared down the empty tree-lined street. "Come on! We've got to go tell her mom!" The children started running toward the pathway that led to the house.

When the boy reached up and slammed the knocker down hard on the door, Autumn awakened from the dream.

Her heart was thundering in her chest. Staring up at the ceiling, she blinked several times as the dream slipped away. Then she dragged in a couple of calming breaths; the dream was over. Yet she remembered it clearly and was still unnerved by what she had seen.

With a sigh, Autumn glanced at the glowing red numbers on the digital clock beside her bed. It was almost 6:00 a.m., her usual time to get up. She was a fifth-grade schoolteacher at Lewis and Clark Elementary, though the summer break had just started and she was off work until the first of September. She punched off the alarm before it buzzed and swung her legs to the side of the bed.

Grabbing her quilted pink robe from the foot of the bed, she raked back her short auburn hair. It was naturally wavy; she only had to shower and towel herself dry and her hair fell into soft russet curls around her face. For her busy athletic lifestyle it suited her perfectly.

Autumn thought of the dream as she headed for the bathroom of her twelfth-floor condo. Were the images she had seen a result of something she had watched on TV? Maybe something she had read in the newspapers? And if they were, why had she experienced the same dream three nights in a row?

The shower beckoned, steam rising tantalizingly up inside its glass doors. She stepped beneath the soothing spray, then spent several minutes soaping and washing her hair, indulging herself in the warm, caressing water.

A few more minutes spent in front of the mirror to apply a light touch of make-up and fluff out her hair, then she headed back into the bedroom to dress for the day. In jeans and a T-shirt, she went into the living room, a cozy, sunny area with sliding glass doors at one end leading out onto a balcony overlooking downtown Seattle.

With her father's help, she had purchased the condo five years ago, just before real estate values had gone completely out of sight. She would have preferred one of the small Victorian homes near the Old Town district, but the condo was all she could really afford.

As a compromise to living a high-rise life-style, she had furnished the interior with antiques and hung lacy curtains at the windows. She had pulled up the carpet in the living room and replaced it with hard-wood floors, then covered them with floral rugs and painted one of the walls a soft shade of rose. The bedroom was done in a floral print and she had bought a canopy bed.

The apartment was homey, nothing like the house in her dream, which, she had noticed last night, appeared to be a large custom-built, beige stucco tract home with fancy brick trim. She had only gotten a glimpse or at least remembered only enough to get the feeling the area was fairly exclusive, the children nicely dressed and obviously well cared for.

Autumn sighed as she grabbed her purse and headed for the elevator in the hall. She was meeting her best friend, Terri Markham, at Starbucks for coffee before she headed over to her summer job at Pike's Gym. One of the things she liked best about living in the city was that everything was in walking distance: museums, theaters, libraries and dozens of restaurants and cafés.

The grammar school where she taught was only a few blocks away, the gym just up the hill and Starbucks — her favorite — sat down on the corner.

Terri was waiting when she arrived, twenty-seven years old, the same age as Autumn, a brunette who was slightly taller and more voluptuously built than her own petite, five-foot-three-inch frame. Both women were single, both career women. Terri was a legal secretary at one of the big law firms in town. They had met five years ago, introduced by mutual acquaintances. They say opposites attract and maybe that explained the friendship that had grown between them.

Autumn pushed open the glass door leading into the coffee shop. Terri shot to her feet and waved from the back of the room.

"Over here!" she called out.

Autumn wove her way through the tables that were packed with morning coffee drinkers and sat down in one of the small wrought-iron chairs, gratefully accepting the double-shot, non-fat latte that Terri shoved toward her.

"Thanks. Next time it's my turn." Autumn took a sip of the hot foamy brew that was her favorite morning drink and saw her friend frown above the rim of her paper cup.

"I thought you were staying home last night," Terri said.

"I did." Autumn sighed, catching the concern in Terri's glance. "But I didn't sleep very well, if that's what you're getting at."

"Honey, those dark circles are a dead giveaway." She grinned. "I didn't get a whole lot of sleep, myself, but I bet I had a lot more fun."

Autumn rolled her eyes. Everything about the two women was different. Where Autumn was interested in sports and loved being out of doors, Terri was obsessed with shopping and the latest fashions. And when it came to men, they couldn't have been more opposite.

"I thought you stopped seeing Ray." Autumn took a sip of her coffee. "You said he was dull and boring."

"I wasn't with Ray. I'm through with Ray. Last night at O'Shaunessy's I met this really hot guy named Todd Sizemore. We really clicked, you know. We had this, like, incredible karma or something."

Autumn shook her head. "As I recall, you said you were going to reform. No more one-night stands. You said from now on you were going to get to know the guy, make sure he wasn't just some deadbeat."

"Todd's not a deadbeat — he's a lawyer. And the guy is terrific in bed."

Terri always thought the guys were great in bed the first time they made love. It was after she got to know them that the problems began. Autumn's emotions were too fragile to handle casual sex, but Terri was far more outgoing and spontaneous. She dated as many men as she could fit into her busy schedule and slept with whomever she pleased.

Autumn rarely dated. Except for her two teaching jobs — one at the grammar school and the other at exclusive Pike's Gym where she gave classes in rock climbing, her passion in life — she was kind of shy.

"So I know why *I* didn't get any sleep," Terri said. "What about you? You didn't have that weird dream again, did you?"

Autumn ran a short, neatly manicured nail around the rim of her cup. "Actually, I did."

After the second time it happened, she had told Terri about the dream, hoping her friend might have seen or read something that explained the occurrence.

"Was it the same? A little girl named Molly gets into a car and the guy drives away?"

"Unfortunately, yes."

14

"That's weird. Most people have recurring dreams about falling off a cliff or drowning or something."

"I know." She looked up, a tight feeling moving through her chest. "There's something I've never told you, Terri. I hoped I wouldn't have the dream again then I wouldn't have to worry about it."

Her friend leaned across the table, shoulder-length dark brown hair swinging forward with the movement. "So what haven't you told me?"

"This same thing happened to me once before — when I was a sophomore in high school. I began having this nightmare about a car wreck. My two best friends were in the car. And another kid, a new kid at school. I dreamed the new guy got drunk at a party and drove the car into a tree. It killed all three of them."

Terri's blue eyes widened. "Wow, that really was a nightmare."

"Back then I didn't say anything. I mean . . . it was a dream. Right? I was only fifteen. I thought if I mentioned it, everyone would make fun of me. I knew they wouldn't believe me. I didn't believe it myself."

"Please don't tell me your dream came true."

Autumn's chest squeezed. She never

15

talked about the nightmare. She felt too guilty. She should have done something — said something — and she had never forgiven herself.

"It happened exactly the way I dreamed. The new guy, Tim Wiseman, invited my friends Jeff and Jolie to a party. Tim was a year older and apparently there was liquor there. I guess they all got a little drunk, which Jeff and Jolie had never done before. On the way home, Tim was driving. It was raining and the streets were wet and slick. Tim took a curve too fast and the car slid into a tree. He and Jeff both died instantly. Jolie died a couple of days later."

Terri stared at her in horror. "Oh my God . . ."

Autumn glanced away, remembering the devastation and overwhelming grief she had felt back then. "I should have said something, done something before it was too late. If I had, my friends might still be alive."

Terri reached over and captured Autumn's hand. "It wasn't your fault. Like you said, you were only fifteen and even if you'd said something, no one would have believed you."

"That's what I tell myself."

"Has it happened again anytime since then?"

"Not until now. The first time, before my friends died, my mom had been killed two years earlier in a car wreck, so I figured maybe that's why I dreamed the dream, but now I don't think that was it. I keep hoping this isn't the same, but what if it is? What if there's a little girl out there somewhere who's about to be kidnapped?"

"Even if there is, this isn't like before. You knew those kids. You don't have any idea who this little girl might be. Even if she exists, you don't know where to find her."

"Maybe. But if I knew the people in the dream before, maybe this little girl is someone else I know. I'm going to check the school records, take a look at student photos. Maybe the face or name will click."

"I suppose it's worth a try."

"That's what I figure."

"You know I'll help in any way I can."

"Thanks, Terri."

"Maybe you won't dream it again."

Autumn just nodded, hoping that was true. But she couldn't help remembering how vivid the dream was and how clearly she could recall it.

She finished her coffee as she got up from her chair. "I'd better get going. Class starts at nine and I've still got to change into my climbing clothes."

17

Terri smiled. "Maybe this summer you'll meet someone interesting in class. With all those hard bodies around, there's got to be someone."

Autumn ignored the remark and waved as she headed for the door. Terri was always trying to help her find the right man, but Autumn steered clear of most men. Since high school, she'd had nothing but disastrous relationships. In college she had fallen in love with Steven Elliot, a fellow student at Washington University. She and Steve had dated seriously their sophomore through senior years. Autumn was madly in love with him and they talked a lot about marriage and kids.

It seemed her future was set until that afternoon just before graduation when Steve told her he wanted to end the relationship.

"I just don't love you, Autumn," he had said. "I thought I did, but I don't. I never mean to hurt you, but I have to get on with my life. I hope things work out for you." He had left her standing in the quad, crying like an idiot, hating herself for having fallen in love with him.

She had gone on to graduate, then continued school long enough to get her teaching degree, but it had taken years to get over losing Steve.

Standing on the corner, she pulled her sweater a little closer against the breeze and waited till the stoplight changed to green. She crossed from Second Avenue to Third then continued toward Pike Street. The sun was out today but the air was damp and clouds had begun to gather on the horizon. Seattle got more than its share of rain but Autumn never minded. She had grown up in Burlington, a little town north of the city. The beautiful pines and nearby ocean were worth the clouds and rain.

As she walked the few blocks up the hill, Autumn enjoyed the feel of the wind tugging at her hair. Up ahead, the McKenzie building took up half a block. It was an old six-story structure that had been expensively remodeled and now served as headquarters for McKenzie Enterprises, a chain of upper-end sporting-goods stores. Pike's Gym occupied the second floor. A few other tenants rented space, and there were shops and boutiques on the first floor along the street.

On her teacher's salary, Autumn couldn't afford the exclusive gym's pricey fees, but she earned an annual membership in exchange for teaching summer rock-climbing classes. It was actually a lot of fun, she had discovered, teaching the skills she had begun to learn as a child from her father.

The double glass doors of the building appeared and Autumn walked into the sleek, marble-floored lobby, past Jimmy the security guard, who recognized her, nodded and waved, then she took the elevator up to the second floor.

A wall of glass revealed the gym and Autumn pushed through the door.

"Hey, Autumn!" It was Bruce Ahern, a muscle jock who worked out at least four hours a day and was already lifting weights. Blond and sun-tanned year-round, he was a nice guy who was always friendly but never pressed her for a date, and instead seemed content just to enjoy her friendship.

"Hi, Bruce. How's it going?"

"Same ol', same ol'." He grinned, carving a dimple into his cheek. Then he hoisted a barbell loaded with a ridiculous amount of iron and began his bicep routine.

Autumn kept walking along the blue-and-gray carpeted floor, passing walls of mirrors. In the bicycle room, long rows of TVs entertained the men and women pumping away on bikes that went nowhere. Eighties music played in the background. Sometimes it was country; sometimes hard rock or hip hop. The staff was very fair about the gym's musical selections.

Making her way into the women's dressing room, Autumn headed for her private locker where she kept her climbing clothes. She pulled on stretchy black pants, perfect for climbing — not tight, but not so baggy they got in the way — a black T-shirt and a pair of soft leather climbing shoes that closed with Velcro tabs.

Once she finished changing, she stored her purse and street clothes in the locker and left to teach her second class of the summer.

Two

The headquarters of McKenzie Enterprises took up the entire sixth floor of the building. The president's office looked out over the city streets all the way across the bay.

Seated behind his oversized mahogany desk, Ben McKenzie studied one of the half-dozen files stacked in front of him. His large, private office was done in dark wood accented with brushed chrome and deep dark burgundy carpets. There was a wall of windows behind his desk and a built-in bar in one of the sleek mahogany cabinets that lined one wall.

The intercom buzzed and Ben hit the button, allowing the voice of his secretary and personal assistant, Jennifer Conklin, to flow into the room.

"Your nine o'clock appointment is here," she said. "Kurt Fisher with A-1 Sports."

"Thanks, Jenn, send him in." Ben rose from his leather chair and shot the cuffs on the crisp white shirt beneath the jacket of his navy-blue suit. His clothes were expensive and perfectly tailored to fit his tall frame, but he had earned every dime it took to pay for them and he was a man who appreciated quality and design.

He glanced toward the door. He wasn't sure what Fisher wanted, but the man was head of acquisitions for A-1 Sports, a successful chain of low-end retail sporting-goods stores, so the conversation might prove interesting. With seventy-six stores around the country — and more popping up every day — A-1 posed tough competition for McKenzie's more expensive, higher-quality merchandise, but so far his stores were holding their own.

The door swung open and Ben caught a glimpse of Jenn's light-brown hair as she waited for Fisher to walk into the room. She was thirty-seven-years-old, married with two kids and had been with him for the last seven years, ever since he had incorporated the company. Jenn closed the door behind Fisher — slim, forty-something, with a reputation for being an aggressive, don't-take-no-for-an-answer kind of guy willing to do whatever it took to reach his financial goals, which by the look of his flashy Armani tie were extremely high.

"Would you like a cup of coffee?" Ben asked. At six-foot-two, he was taller than Fisher, wider through the chest and shoulders, more athletically built. Though they both had dark brown hair, Ben's was thicker and slightly curly.

"No thanks. I'm fine." Fisher seated himself in one of the black leather chairs in front of the desk. Ben unbuttoned his suit coat and sat down across from him.

"So what can I do for you this morning, Kurt?" Ben smiled. He was always polite but he didn't believe in wasting time.

Fisher lifted his leather briefcase onto his lap, popped the latches and pulled out a manila folder. "I think it's more like what I can do for you."

He set the folder on Ben's desk and shoved it forward. "It goes without saying what a fine job you've done in building McKenzie Sporting Goods into the successful company it is today. As you know, A-1 has been equally successful in selling its line of less expensive merchandise. The company is growing by leaps and bounds and we've decided the next logical step is to add stores that sell more expensive, higher quality goods. Stores like yours, Ben."

Ben made no comment, just leaned back in his chair.

Fisher tapped the folder. "This is an offer to purchase your stores, Ben — all of them. I know you'll want to take it to your accountant and lawyer, but you're going to see that the price and terms are more than fair."

Ben didn't bother to open the file, just pushed it back across the desk. "Not interested. McKenzie Enterprises isn't for sale."

Fisher smiled thinly. "Everything's for sale — at the right price."

"Not McKenzie. At least not today." Ben rose from his chair. "Tell your people I appreciate their interest. If I change my mind, they'll be the first to know."

Fisher looked stunned. "You aren't even going to look at it?"

"Like I said, not interested."

Fisher picked up the file, shoved it a little too firmly back into his briefcase and rose from his chair. "A-1 wants your stores, Ben. You can expect to hear from us again."

"The answer will be the same."

Fisher made no reply as he marched rather brusquely toward the door.

"Have a good day," Ben called after him, then smiled to himself as he sat back down. It was a measure of all he'd accomplished that a company as successful as A-1 wanted to buy his stores. Still, he had worked hard to achieve his success and there was still so much more he wanted to accomplish.

From the time he was a kid working for his dad at McKenzie Mercantile, his family's rural mid-west department store, he knew business was what he wanted to do with his life. He had studied hard, been determined to go to college, excelled at nearly every high-school sport and been the president of his senior class.

The effort had won him a scholarship to the University of Michigan, and the sports he had loved helped him zero in on which direction to take. Nike had recruited him to work in a management position right out of college but after a few years he realized he wanted to work for himself.

His mom passed away when he was twenty-four, then his dad died and left him the family business. Ben sold the mercantile, moved to the Pacific Northwest and opened his first sporting-goods store.

He smiled. He was as good at business as he always thought he would be and the rest, as they say, was history. He now owned twenty-one stores and had invested his earnings wisely in both the stock market and real estate. His financial portfolio had a net worth of twenty-five million and it was growing every day.

He had the life he had always wanted.

At least, he had until six years ago. That was the year he lost his daughter, Molly . . . the same year his wife divorced him, the year that had left him devastated and grieving and on the brink of losing his sanity.

He'd survived — barely — by burying himself in his work. McKenzie Sporting Goods had saved his life and he wasn't about to sell it.

Not now, nor anytime soon.

Standing in front of the climbing wall in an area in the southeast section of the gym, Autumn looked at her half-dozen students, two women and four men.

"Any questions?"

Today was the second in a series of basic rock-climbing classes that would take place over the summer. Once the group had progressed far enough, there would be actual forays into the nearby Cascade Mountains. They would do some bouldering then progress to top-roping: safe, easy ways to build confidence and improve their skills. Maybe they would even do some more difficult technical climbing.

In her first session, she had addressed the general nature of the sport, some of its history and topics to be discussed in future lessons: getting your body in shape and the right nutrition, choosing the proper clothing; mountain hazards; climb rating systems; and the proper equipment and how to use it.

This morning they were discussing weather forecasts and navigation, which included the use of USGS maps and GPS instrumentation.

"I use my GPS all the time," said Matthew Gould, a tall, string bean of a guy with shaggy brown hair. "Are you saying I'm better off hauling out a map? That's kind of old-fashioned, isn't it?"

"A GPS is an invaluable piece of equipment — I won't argue with that — and some of the newer devices are pretty fantastic. But for the most part the information on a USGS map is far more extensive than what's on the equipment most people own. The maps show vegetation, rivers, streams, snowfields and glaciers, as well as roads, trails and less tangible features, like boundaries and section lines. Learn to read them well and it may save your butt when the rest of your planning goes south."

A few chuckles rumbled from the group.

"There are sample maps on the counter over there. I know most of you are hikers so you probably already have some experience using them. Take a look at the maps and go over what we've discussed. See if you understand everything that's printed on them. If you need any help, I'm right here."

The students rose from their places on the floor and ambled to the counter. Autumn stayed for questions, then once her students had left, changed into her shorts and went into the weight room to do her morning routine.

She usually worked out before class but sometimes she went to the gym in the evenings. It didn't really matter, as long as she got her workout done. As a climber it was essential to stay in shape. Her small frame was solid and compact, with strong muscles in her arms, legs and thighs. But her breasts were nicely rounded — one of her most feminine features — and she was proud of the way she looked in a pair of shorts or a bikini.

She usually did a ninety-minute routine four or five days a week, which gave her weekends off to climb or to simply relax and enjoy herself.

Today, as soon as she had finished on the StairMaster and the Nautilus machines, she showered, dressed and set out to see if she could find the mysterious little girl who had appeared in her dreams.

She had decided to begin at the school, which wasn't far away. Summer school was in session, though she hadn't offered to teach. The summer was hers and she loved every minute of it. Shoving through the door of the main office building, a flat-roofed, two-story brick structure, she walked over to speak to her friend, Lisa Gregory, who worked as office manager.

"Hi, Lise, sorry to bother you, but I was hoping you might do me a favor." Lisa was in her thirties, a pretty woman with short brown hair who was efficient and always friendly.

"What kind of favor?"

"I need to get into the school's computer files. I want to take a look at photos of the girls between five and seven years old."

"What for?"

"I'm trying to find a particular child. I know what she looks like, but not her name. I'm not even sure she's a student at Lewis and Clark."

"Do I dare ask why you're doing this?"

"I wish you wouldn't. Even if I told you, you wouldn't believe it. But it's important I find her, whoever she is. Will you help me? You're way better at this computer stuff than I am."

"Sure. As long as it doesn't get me into

trouble."

They walked into the back room and Lisa sat down at one of the office computers. The school was proud of its cutting-edge technology. Everything was computerized and updated every year.

"What else do you know besides her age?" Lisa asked as she typed in the information. "Maybe we can narrow the search."

"I know she's blond and blue-eyed. I think her first name is Molly. Besides my guess at her age, I'm afraid that's just about it."

"Every little bit helps." Lisa input the information, hit the search button and waited for the results to come up. There were several pages of photos of students who fit at least some of the criteria and Autumn studied each girl's face. Some she had seen on the playground but none of the others looked familiar, none were named Molly and none resembled the little girl she had seen in her dreams.

"Does your information go backward?" Autumn asked. "Maybe she was a student here last year but her family moved somewhere else."

"We have the names and photos. We'll have to adjust for age, though, if you think she's only six. She would have been five then."

Autumn sighed. "I suppose she could be younger now or maybe she could be older, I don't know." In fact, she had no idea if the little girl actually existed.

"I'll bring up the photos for the past three years and you can see if you recognize her."

"Thanks, Lise."

But a search of the pictures led nowhere and after a thorough examination of each possible child, Autumn ignored a kink in the back of her neck and straightened away from the screen.

"Well, that's it," Lisa said.

"I really appreciate your help, even if we didn't find her."

Lisa slid her chair back from the computer. "So tell me why you're looking for this girl."

Autumn studied her friend, trying to decide whether or not to tell her the truth. She sighed. "I've been having dreams about her. It's weird because it's the same dream over and over. In the dream, a man she doesn't know convinces her to get in his car and drives away with her. The dream doesn't go any further but I get the feeling something bad is going to happen. I was thinking maybe I should try to find her, warn her parents. Of course, it's just a dream and it probably isn't even real."

Lisa stuck a pencil into the light-brown hair over her ear. "But it might be. You see that stuff on TV all the time."

Autumn relaxed and smiled. "That's kind of what I thought. Thanks for understanding."

"No problem. Good luck — one way or the other."

Autumn nodded and headed for the door. All the way back to her apartment, she searched the face of every little girl she passed, thinking maybe she had seen the child on the street, but none of the small faces looked familiar.

She was tired by the time she got home.

And no closer to discovering who the little girl was than she had been before.

That night Autumn had the dream. It was exactly the same as the past three nights, though each time she noticed more details. Tonight she saw that the man with the puppy was blond and fair, with a friendly smile and eyes that crinkled at the corners.

And the little red-haired boy was named Robbie. She heard one of the other children call him that. But just as before, as the little blond girl climbed into the car and the vehicle drove away, Autumn jerked awake and the warning on her lips died as she re-

33

alized none of it was real.

Leaning back against the white wrought-iron headboard of her canopy bed, Autumn raked a hand through her sweat-damp auburn hair. She tried to tell herself she hadn't really seen anything bad — only a little girl getting into someone's car — but she couldn't imagine why a man would take a child he didn't seem to know away from her friends and family unless he had some evil intent.

It was two in the morning. Autumn lay back on her pillow and tried to fall asleep, but an hour ticked past and then another. Exhaustion finally overcame her and she drifted into a restless sleep.

THREE

It was Tuesday. Autumn didn't have a climbing class this morning. Figuring a good solid workout might clear her head, revive her tired body and rejuvenate her lagging spirits, she headed for the gym. Afterward, she planned to call Joe Duffy, a fellow climber and friend who worked for the Seattle police.

As soon as she got back to her apartment, a little before noon, she left a message for Joe. Joe was a detective in the burglary division but she figured he might be able to help her. She wanted to ask him if there was a way she could look at the list of registered pedophiles living in the Seattle area to see if she recognized the blond man in the dream.

She was trying to think of what she might say to him without mentioning the dream when the phone in her apartment began to ring.

It was Joe, returning her call. "Hey, hot

stuff, what can I do for you?"

"I need a favor, Joe." Now for the lie, which she told very poorly. ". . . Um . . . just before school let out for the summer, I saw a guy loitering near the playground. At the time I didn't think anything about it, but I was wondering if maybe you could arrange for me to take a look at your files . . . you know, the ones that show photos of known pedophiles in the area. I just want to be on the safe side, make sure he wasn't one of them."

"Sure. I'll tell the sergeant you want to take a look at the mug book. When do you want to come down?"

"How about this afternoon?"

"You got it. Stop by anytime after . . . say two o'clock. That should give the guys time to get the stuff ready."

It was two-fifteen when she walked into the modern structure on Virginia Street that housed the west precinct of the Seattle police department. She gave Joe's name to the desk sergeant who sent her down the hall. Joe, a ruddy complexioned, dark-haired man who claimed to be at least half Irish, was waiting.

"Hey Autumn, good to see you."

"You too, Joe."

"This is a little out of my area, but one of

the guys got the stuff together. It's all on computer these days but we've also got photos — easier for lay people to use." Joe led her into a room and she sat down at a table with several albums stacked on top. She opened the first and began to thumb through pages of pictures. There were some very rough-looking men in the books — guys with earrings and beards and long, scraggly hair — while others looked completely harmless. She figured those were probably the ones to really worry about.

She spent nearly two hours going through the photo albums, but no face jumped out at her or even looked vaguely familiar. Twice she had tried and come up empty, she thought as she left the building.

In a way she was glad.

It's just a dream, that's all. Even if it isn't, you've done everything you can think of to stop it from happening.

She tried to convince herself, but still it bothered her. So much so she took an Ambien that night and slept straight through till morning.

For the first time in days, Autumn awakened fully rested. She said a little thank you that the pill had worked and the nightmare hadn't come and prayed it would never come again. Deciding to forego her morning workout, she lay back against the pillow and slept for a little longer, just to indulge herself.

She had a climbing class today and a couple of private lessons in the afternoon, which made her some extra money, then she planned to meet Terri at the gym that evening, after her friend got off work. Terri was a legal secretary at Hughes, Jones, Weinstein and Meyers, one of the city's most prestigious law firms. She wasn't a member at Pike's Gym but occasionally worked out using one of the guest passes Autumn got as part of her teaching deal. Terri wasn't much on exercise, but she liked looking at the men.

At six o'clock, Autumn headed for the gym, hoping to get the serious part of her workout done before Terri arrived and they wound up sitting at one of the tables in the health bar drinking smoothies.

She had just finished using the thigh machine, stretching and working muscles that were invaluable in climbing, when she spotted her friend. Terri was wearing tight black leotards and a pink-and-black midrift top and she looked terrific. She had a fabulous figure and she showed it off whenever she could.

"Hi ya'll!" Terri waved and walked toward her. She was born in Virginia but raised out west and her southern accent was mostly gone, surfacing only on occasion just for fun.

"I see you're ready to sweat," Autumn teased, knowing that was the last thing Terri wanted.

"Sure thing, honey. I'll just go put my bag in a locker and be right back." She disappeared for a few minutes, turning several male heads as she walked past. While she was gone, Josh Kendall, Autumn's climbing partner, walked into the gym.

"Hey, Autumn, how's it hangin'?"

Autumn smiled at Josh's favorite expression and gave her usual reply. "By the thumbs, Josh, how about you?" They had met during a four-man climb up in the Cascade Mountains two years ago. Josh was long and lanky, with sandy hair and a slightly freckled face. He wasn't killer handsome, but good-looking in a sort of nerdy way.

"We still going up next weekend?" he asked.

"You bet. I've really been looking forward to it. I can't wait to tackle Castle Rock."

"Yeah, me too."

A climbing partner had to be someone

you could trust with your life because that was literally what you had to do. Autumn had admired Josh's skill and he had respected hers so they had decided to make a climb together. Their styles turned out to be extremely compatible. They were both certified guides and in the summer they headed for the mountains whenever they weren't giving classes or doing private coaching.

They were friends. Close friends. Climbing together had a way of doing that. Autumn felt safe with Josh — in more ways than one. She knew he had no interest in her beyond their climbing partnership. It was Terri he wanted, Terri who snagged his attention whenever she walked into a room. Considering she saw him only as a friend and it didn't look like that was going to change anytime soon, Autumn felt sorry for him.

Josh's gaze darted away from her to the shapely brunette sauntering toward him. Terri's hips swayed provocatively, her gaze moving over the guys with the bulging muscles who were working out on the weight machines.

"Hi, Terri," Josh said, his smile a little too bright.

"Hi, Josh."

"How's it going?" he asked.

"Fine. Great, in fact." She turned away from him as if he weren't there and leaned over to whisper in Autumn's ear. "See that hunk over there working on the bicep machine?"

Autumn glanced that way. "I see him." She had noticed him a couple of times before, but hadn't really paid much attention.

"Well, what's his name, honey? Is he married?"

"How would I know?"

Terri rolled her eyes. "Lord, you are impossible."

They both stared at *the hunk* whose arms bulged with nicely shaped muscle as he strained on the weight machine. Josh made a noise in his throat, returning their attention to him.

"Well, I . . . um . . . guess I better get going. I'll see you next weekend, Autumn."

"Call me the end of the week and we'll go over our trip plans."

"Sounds good."

"So, Josh . . . you wouldn't happen to know that guy over there in the corner?" Terri asked.

Josh turned that way. "I don't know him but I've seen his picture in the newspaper.

41

He owns this building. That's Ben Mc-Kenzie."

Terri's dark eyebrows shot up. "Is that so?"

Terri was openly salivating and Josh looked like he wanted to slash his wrists. "Like I said, I better get going." With a last longing glance at Terri, he headed for the climbing gym.

Terri surveyed the room, the long rows of white-and-black exercise machines, rows of treadmills each with its own TV, and racks of heavy chrome barbells at the far end in front of a wall of mirrors.

"I'm ready if you are," she said. "Why don't we start over there?" She pointed toward the area where Ben McKenzie was now lying back on a black vinyl bench hoisting a barbell loaded with weights.

Autumn gave him a long, assessing glance. Terri was right. The man was amazing. Not only drop-dead gorgeous, but with a lean, athletic body that looked as if it were sculpted more from sports than lifting weights in a gym. He had thick dark-brown hair, nicely trimmed, a square jaw and dark brown eyes. He was wearing shorts and Reeboks. A tank top stretched over his powerful chest and she caught a glimpse of curly dark-brown chest hair.

"Nice, huh?" Terri said.

"Very nice."

"Probably married with at least four kids."

"At least."

Terri sighed. "Wouldn't it be great if he wasn't?"

"I thought you were madly in lust with Todd."

Terri cast her a glance. "I was thinking of *you*."

Autumn laughed. "*Sure* you were."

Terri just smiled. They started out in the bike room, riding only long enough to get Terri warmed up a little but not break into a sweat. From there they moved on to the Nautilus machines.

"I really was thinking of you," Terri said as she shoved the handles in the air, working her arms and shoulders. "Now that I've hooked up with Todd, I'm not looking for anyone else."

At least for now, that was probably true. Terri really was a good friend and she was always on the lookout for a man for Autumn. "Even if *the hunk* was single, a guy like that would have a horde of women chasing after him from dawn to dusk."

"All too true," Terri agreed regretfully.

They worked out for almost an hour — a record for Terri — then retired to the snack bar for thick berry smoothies. Terri planned to stay at home that night and order pizza. Todd, of course, was coming by to join her.

Autumn left the gym, went home and made herself a plate of leftovers from the chicken she had roasted for herself on Sunday. She carried her plate into the living room and curled up on the overstuffed sofa in front of the TV.

She had a class tomorrow morning so she went to bed early. She considered taking an Ambien, but didn't like taking any sort of drug and she could hardly take sleeping pills forever.

Instead, she hoped the glass of white wine she'd had with her makeshift supper would help her fall asleep — and that tonight she wouldn't dream.

It was raining, the air heavy with mist. Inside the house, it was warm, the kitchen steamy from the pot boiling on the stove. A group of three women moved together with practiced ease, working to prepare the evening meal. They were a family, Autumn thought somewhere in the depths of her mind. All of them were blond and fair, girls and women of various ages, the oldest, a woman in her late thirties, all of them pretty.

Autumn watched the women chop vegetables and roll out biscuit dough. They didn't say much as they did their jobs and began to take down cups and dishes to set the kitchen table.

Autumn might have kept dreaming if the youngest of the women, a girl of eleven or twelve, hadn't turned just then and looked straight at her. Autumn knew that face. She recognized the pretty oval shape, the soft blue eyes and long silky lashes, the pale blond hair drifting like corn silk around her narrow shoulders.

Those eyes were staring into hers and the pain in them jolted Autumn from a deep, hypnotic sleep.

Heart pounding, palms sweating, she bolted upright in bed. It was her! The girl named Molly! It was the little girl she had dreamed about before, only she was no longer a child but a girl approaching her teens. Autumn knew it deep in her bones.

Trembling, she swung her legs to the side of the bed. It was nearly two-thirty but she was wide awake, her mouth dry and her heart beating too fast. Images of the dream rolled around in her head. Straightening her pink silk nightie, she padded into the bathroom and turned on the tap, shakily filled the glass next to the sink with water and took a long, calming drink.

Her mind spun, replaying the images she

had seen. If this was the same girl — and Autumn was convinced it was — she was somewhere around eleven or twelve. How could that be?

She tried to recall the first series of dreams, when the child was much younger. Was there something in the dream that hinted at the time frame? Nothing she could recall. Still, if the child was five or six then and eleven or twelve now, the abduction — if that's what it had been — would have had to have happened at least six years ago.

The whole thing was crazy. Certainly tonight's dream was nothing at all like the nightmare she'd had in her teens and yet . . .

There was no use trying to sleep. Instead, she walked into the kitchen, poured herself a glass of milk and carried it over to the sofa. Pulling the soft wool afghan her grandmother had crocheted off the back of the couch, Autumn covered her legs, leaned back and let her mind sift through the dream.

Maybe the dream tonight was actually that. A real dream where everything's just a fantasy.

Or maybe neither of them were real.

Autumn finished her milk and stretched out on the sofa. If she continued to dream, maybe she would see the girl as a full-grown woman, happy wherever she had finally ended up, and Autumn could stop worrying about her.

Maybe she was wrong and — unlike before — nothing bad had happened or was going to. Warm beneath the comforter, she finally fell asleep. When she did, she began to dream.

Three women worked in the kitchen, the little girl no longer a child, but taller, beginning to develop breasts, showing the first signs of becoming a woman. And when she looked at Autumn there was always so much pain in her eyes, Autumn awakened from the dream.

She lay there on the sofa, heart thumping madly, exhausted and even more worried. This was no simple dream. This was a message — just like it had been when she was fifteen.

She couldn't ignore it the way she had before. She refused to sit around and let something terrible happen again. Dear God, if only she knew what to do.

FOUR

It was early morning, almost time to get up. As Autumn lay awake on the sofa staring up at the ceiling, memories of the dream played over and over in her head. If this was the same blond child, the little girl named Molly from the first dream, maybe she was among the millions of children who went missing and were never found. Maybe she was reaching out, asking Autumn for help.

But if that's true, why now? Why didn't the dreams begin years earlier? So far it appeared she didn't even know the girl. It was all so utterly confusing.

Tired to the bone and still thinking of the dream, she tossed back the afghan and headed for the bathroom to shower and dress for the gym. She needed some physical exertion, something to clear her head. Hopefully, her climbing class would take her mind off the girl. After lunch she had a couple of private lessons and around five-thirty she was supposed to meet Terri for drinks at O'Shaunessy's Bar and Grill, an upscale local hangout that was one of Terri's favorite see-and-be scenes.

The day passed swiftly. Autumn arrived at the bar right on time but Terri, as usual, was running a little late. By the time she got there, Autumn was sipping a nice chilled glass of Kendall Jackson chardonnay and beginning to relax.

Terri was smiling as she wove her way through the crowd at the bar and sitting at tables. She walked up and hung her purse on the back of one of the stools around the tiny table and waved one of the cocktail waitresses over.

"I'm desperate for a Cosmo, Rita. After a day like today, I really deserve one."

"Will do, hon." Rita sashayed away, tray propped on her shoulder, wide hips swaying, and returned just a few minutes later with the drink. Terri was a regular and always got good service and Autumn enjoyed the lively little pub as well.

Terri took a sip from her frosty, long-stemmed martini glass. "So how was your day, girlfriend? Mine totally sucked."

Autumn sipped her wine. "My day was fine. Last night was the pits."

Terri rolled her eyes. "Don't even tell me.

The dream, right?"

"Yes . . . and no."

"Okay, tell me."

"I had a different dream about the same person."

"What?"

She nodded. "No kids playing ball in the yard, no little boy named Robbie. This time, the girl was five or six years older . . . maybe eleven or twelve. I don't think she was a teenager yet."

"Wow, that's weird. And you still think these dreams are real?"

"I'm probably crazy, but yes. I think maybe little Molly got into that car and the man drove away with her, like in the dream. But he didn't kill her — he couldn't have if she's older in the second dream. I think maybe he just took her off with him somewhere."

"Maybe you'll just keep dreaming about her until she's all grown up and everything will be fine."

"I thought of that. I suppose it's possible, but . . ."

"But what?"

"But I don't think that's going to happen. I think . . . I don't know but . . . I think Molly is trying to send me some kind of message. I think she's asking me for help."

50

Terri fixed her with a stare. "That's a pretty far stretch, don't you think? If she *is* trying to reach you, why did she wait until now? Why didn't she send you this supposed message five or six years ago?"

Autumn hooked a curl behind her ear. "I don't know."

"You have to admit this is all pretty crazy."

"No kidding." She trailed her finger through the condensation on her wine glass. "If it weren't for what happened in high school, I'd ignore the whole damned thing."

Terri frowned. "The car accident . . . right? I see what you mean."

"The weird thing is — what caused it to happen back then? And why is it happening now?"

Terri ignored the question since neither of them had an answer. "You know what I think you should do? I think you should go through old newspapers to see if a little girl was abducted five or six years ago. If there was and her name was Molly —"

"You're right!" Autumn sat up straighter on the stool. "I should have thought of that myself. I'd have to make certain assumptions. I may have guessed her age wrong, so I'd need to do a spread of several years. I've got to assume I'm somehow connected or this wouldn't be happening, so I'll start

51

looking here in Seattle."

"It might not work but it's worth a try."

"It's a great idea." If Autumn's hunch was right, it was absolutely worth a try.

Terri looked up just then and broke into a smile. "Todd just walked in. Isn't he gorgeous?"

Todd was definitely a pretty boy, tall and blond, sort of the Brad Pitt type. But Autumn couldn't help wondering if there was any substance behind that pretty face.

Terri introduced her and the three of them chatted for a while. Todd held his own. He seemed to be polite and intelligent. Still, it was too soon to make a judgment.

Autumn stood up from her stool. "Listen, I'd better get going. I've got classes in the morning. Nice meeting you, Todd."

"You too, Autumn."

Terri cast her a meaningful glance. "Keep me posted on your . . . research, will you?"

"Will do." Autumn left the bar and headed down the street for home. The sun was just setting over the water and glimpses of the sea appeared between the buildings. Pretty as it was, the neighborhood she lived in wasn't the most desirable. Transients haunted the bus stop not far away and drug deals were made on the streets, but the condo was affordable and only blocks from museums and theaters. And all of the downtown was improving a little at a time. She loved Seattle. She couldn't think of anywhere she would rather live.

By the time she reached her building and took the elevator up to her condo, dusk was setting in. She baked a pork chop, cooking it on a rack so there would be less grease, and settled in to watch a little TV. The sitcoms were always cheery. She watched a few of those, then started yawning and decided to go to bed.

She purposely avoided the Ambien, hoping if she dreamed she might get more information, though a good night's sleep was certainly a temptation.

Instead, she drifted into slumber and again that night she had the dream.

Since it was a good long way from her apartment to the *Seattle Times* on John Street, Autumn decided to phone before she made the trip. The receptionist at the *Times* told her that archival information could be found at the library, not the newspaper, so she made a second call and discovered that the Central Library on nearby Fourth Avenue was where she needed to go. There were old newspapers there, she was told, dating back to the late eighteen-hundreds.

A number of newspapers covered the Seattle area, but the *Times* was the largest. Autumn figured if a child had been abducted in the city or in any of the surrounding towns, the *Seattle Times* would probably have covered the story.

It occurred to her that she was a person who usually followed the news, in print and on TV, so she should have seen something if it had happened anywhere near. Still, she traveled as often as she could so she might have been out of town or maybe she had just somehow missed it.

The lady at the information booth walked up the counter. She had silver hair and wore too much powder and circles of pink rouge on her cheeks.

"May I help you?"

"I'd like to take a look through your newspaper archives. I need to search for children who might have been reported missing. I need to go back at least seven years." That should be long enough to cover the period, since she wasn't really sure of Molly's age.

"All right. If you'll please follow me."

Autumn trailed along behind the older woman into a back room filled with equipment.

"Everything from more recent times is stored on microfilm. You'll find copies of every paper printed and an index by subject matter. Just type in *missing children* and it should bring up what you need."

"Thank you."

Autumn sat down and set to work, going back five years, thinking little Molly might have been six then and eleven now. Since Autumn had been living in Seattle, she figured she might have seen or met her during that time.

There were stacks of articles. Unfortunately, nothing looked remotely like it had anything to do with a little girl named Molly. There were several children mentioned, missing then found. One was lost in the mountains and rescued by local search teams.

She tried four years back, found a story about a pedophile named Gerald Meeks who had been arrested for molesting and killing several young children, but Molly's name — thank God — was not among those mentioned.

The year 2001, six years back, would make the child six then and twelve now, which was Autumn's strongest suspicion. She was paging through the summer issues, reading snippets here and there, when an article popped up. The headline read, *Issaquah Girl Reported Missing.* The paper was dated June 30, 2001 and the disappearance had happened the day before the paper went to press.

A six year old girl disappeared from her home late yesterday afternoon, the article read. *According to reports, the child was playing ball in her yard with friends when an unknown man appeared on the sidewalk.*

The article went on to describe the incident and included a description of the missing girl: long blond hair, blue eyes, wearing jeans, sneakers and a purple T-shirt with a picture of Barney the dinosaur on the front.

There was even a photo, one Autumn recognized the instant she saw it. And the name beneath the picture read *Molly Lynn McKenzie.*

Autumn's chest squeezed so hard it was difficult to breathe. Her heart was pumping, trying to beat its way through her chest. *The child was real. The dream was real. The kidnapping had really occurred.*

Autumn felt light-headed. She reread the date. That summer she had been staying with her dad in Burlington before starting her teaching job in Seattle. She probably would have seen the article, which would have been carried in all the local papers, but in June she was in Europe — a graduation gift to herself — traveling with a group of climbers.

McKenzie? McKenzie? Why did the name sound familiar?

It hit her like a bolt of lightning — she had heard the name only a few days ago. Josh had mentioned it when she and Terri were working out at the gym.

Autumn quickly scanned the article and there it was: Molly Lynn McKenzie was the daughter of sporting goods retailer Ben McKenzie and his wife, Joanne, residents of Issaquah, Washington, a town in the foothills just east of Seattle.

Pieces of the puzzle began falling together. She had noticed McKenzie at the gym only recently. She tried to think back. As nearly as she could recall, the first time was some-where around the time she had started to dream about Molly.

She studied the screen, frantically pressed the button to skip forward in time. Article after article had been written about little Molly — interviews with her parents, the desperate search to find her. As she skimmed the pages, Autumn prayed the child had been found. Yet deep inside, she was certain the little girl had not.

According to the *Times,* the search had continued for weeks, though the articles became more and more scarce. As far as

Autumn could tell, no clue to the child's disappearance was ever discovered.

An image of handsome Ben McKenzie popped into her head. How devastated he and his wife must have been to lose their little girl. Her chest ached. She couldn't begin to imagine the pain, the terrible grief they must have suffered. She had to talk to Ben McKenzie, find out as much as she could about what had happened.

If Molly was still missing . . .

She printed the newspaper articles, paid for the copies and left the building. She had to see Ben McKenzie and perhaps speak to his wife. She needed to know if anything had been discovered about Molly during the past six years. As soon as she got home, she would call McKenzie's office and make an appointment to see him.

God only knew what she was going to say.

Ben ended the conference call he had been having with his financial VP, George Murphy, and Russ Petrone, a real estate broker in Issaquah. The town was Ben's home when he moved to the area, the place he had opened his first store.

According to Russ, a long-time friend who had sold him and Joanne their home then helped him lease the building for McKenzie

Sporting Goods, that store was about to be put in jeopardy. Apparently his competitor, A-1 Sports, had been nosing around, sniffing out property within a two-block range of his Issaquah location, one of the top-selling stores in the chain. Rumor had it that A-1 had located a piece of real estate just across the street and was seriously interested in making a purchase.

Ben swore as he hung up the phone and leaned back in his black leather chair. *Son-ofabitch!* He didn't believe for a moment that A-1 wanted to operate a store in the area. But he believed completely that they would do it if they thought it would urge him to sell them the McKenzie chain. With their lower prices, A-1 was tough competition. People were suckers when it came to getting something for less, even if it meant sacrificing quality.

In the world of sports, cheap products not only didn't last, they could actually be dangerous.

A-1 was definitely a problem, one Ben was determined to solve.

His intercom buzzed. "Your five-thirty is here," Jenn said.

"Remind me who it is."

"A woman named Autumn Sommers. She said it was a personal matter. You said to schedule her at the end of the day."

He tried to remember the name but it didn't ring a bell. He had dated any number of women since his divorce, though none of them seriously. He wasn't interested in a long-term relationship and he always made that clear from the start. But he enjoyed women and he liked sex. And the women he dated seemed to have no complaints. "Go ahead and send her in."

He stood up as the door opened, saw a petite young woman in her twenties, pretty but not gorgeous like the models and movie starlets he occasionally spent time with. He preferred them blond and buxom and this one was petite and dark-haired, though she seemed to have a very nice pair of breasts.

She wasn't really his type and he was almost positive he had never been out with her. That was something of a relief.

"My assistant says you wanted to see me on a personal matter. I don't believe we've met, Ms. Summers. What can I do for you?" He motioned for her to have a seat in front of his desk, but she walked over to the window and looked out across the city. He could tell she was nervous. He wondered why.

"Spectacular view," she said. "I live close to here but my condo looks over the city, not out at the water."

"It's a very lovely view. Now as I said, what can I do for you?"

She turned to face him, but still didn't take a seat so neither did he.

"You can start by calling me Autumn, though you're right we haven't met. I've seen you at Pike's Gym a couple of times. I didn't even know who you were until a few days ago."

He didn't remember seeing her, but she wasn't really the sort to catch a man's eye . . . not at first glance, at any rate. "Autumn Summers. Interesting name."

"It's *Sommers* with an *O*. My parents thought it was cute." She walked back his way and sat down and Ben sat down across from her. There was something intriguing about her. She had big green eyes that tilted up at the corners, a heart-shaped face and thick, short, softly curling hair that was almost red but not quite. In the overhead light, there were streaks of russet and gold — autumn colors, just like her name.

"So who are you, Autumn Sommers, and why are you here?"

She took a deep breath and released it slowly, as if she searched for exactly what to say. "I'm a fifth-grade teacher at Lewis and Clark Elementary School. I'm here to talk

61

to you about your daughter."

"Katie?"

Her russet brows inched up. They were perfectly formed, he noticed, adding a nice symmetry to her face.

"You have a daughter named Katie?" she asked.

"Yes. That's her photo over there."

"She's lovely. How old is she?"

"Ten." He was beginning to get annoyed. His time was valuable. Only his daughter took precedence over work. "You're a teacher. I figured Katie was the reason you were here."

"I'm here because of your other daughter. Molly."

For an instant, Ben couldn't breathe. No one had mentioned his older daughter in years. He wouldn't allow it, couldn't stand the shock it brought whenever he heard her name. The swift jolt of memories, the harsh stab of pain.

He stood up. "My daughter Molly is dead. She was abducted from our home six years ago. What the hell are you doing here?"

"I know about the abduction. I read the articles in the newspaper archives. As far as I can tell, they never found any trace of her and if that's the case —"

"Molly's dead!" Ben rounded the desk,

his hands balling into fists as he tried to hang on to his temper. "Gerald Meeks killed her — along with God knows how many other children before he was captured and sentenced to life in prison. Now get out of my office!"

In an effort to avoid his wrath, Autumn slipped out of her chair and took a few steps backward as he advanced. "Please . . . I don't believe Molly was murdered. I think she may still be alive and if she is, she needs your help."

His insides contracted into a painful knot. Just talking about Molly made his stomach roll.

"Are you telling me you've seen her? Because if you are, I don't believe you." It had taken him years to convince himself but he had finally accepted the fact she was dead and no one was going to dredge up the awful heartbreak again.

"I haven't seen her . . . not exactly, but —"

"Why the hell did you come here? What are you, some kind of charlatan? Or maybe you're some kind of nut. Either way I want you out of here." He walked past her and jerked open the tall mahogany door. "Ms. Sommers's business here is finished," he said to Jenn. "See her down to the lobby, will you? Make sure she leaves the building. Make sure she doesn't return."

"But I teach classes at the climbing gym," she said quickly. "I'm also a member of the club. I'm there almost every day of the week."

"Fine." He fixed his eyes on Jenn, who was glaring at Autumn Sommers like a she-wolf protecting her cub. "See that she has access to the building, but not to any of the offices above the second floor."

"I'll take care of it," Jenn said. "Come with me, Ms. Sommers."

"I didn't come here to cause trouble. I wanted to talk to you or your wife —"

Ben's temper snapped. "Joanne and I have been divorced for nearly four years. You call her, you bother my family in any way, I'll get a restraining order against you. Now get out!"

The woman said no more, just cast him a pitying glance and walked ahead of Jenn toward the elevator. Ben didn't release the breath he had been holding till the elevator door slid closed and Autumn Sommers disappeared.

He didn't know how long he stood there staring into space. Long enough for Jenn to return from her trip to the lobby.

"You all right, boss?" She had always been

protective.

"I'm fine. I just . . . the woman's some kind of nutcase. Or maybe she was trying to extort money from me or something. I don't think she'll show up here again."

At least he hoped not. His brief encounter with Autumn Summers — Sommers with an *O*, he mentally corrected — had his stomach churning with acid. He'd have to pop a Pepcid before he'd be able to eat.

"You want me to have her checked out?" Jenn asked.

"Let it go for now. Like I said, I don't think she'll be back." The woman was gone, but the memories were stirring. They were hovering in his head, threatening to come to life. He couldn't afford to let that happen.

The best solution was to put his mind on something else . . . something that had nothing to do with his family or the past or involved his emotions.

Ben walked back into his office, sat down at his desk, opened the file on the Issaquah store, picked up the phone and went to work.

FIVE

Autumn trembled as she walked the few blocks to her apartment. She had known her meeting with Ben McKenzie wouldn't be easy, but she hadn't expected to be tossed out of the man's office into the street!

The jerk wouldn't even talk to her, wouldn't give her the least chance to explain. She remembered the article she had uncovered about Gerald Meeks, a pedophile and serial killer who had been active in the Seattle area. He had been arrested and eventually convicted.

First thing in the morning, she was going back to the library to run Meeks's name. Maybe she would find a reference to Molly, something that would explain Ben McKenzie's belief that Meeks had killed her.

If she found proof that Molly was dead, she would drop the whole thing. She would take a sleeping pill every night until she stopped dreaming about the girl. Even if it took the rest of her life.

The following morning she dressed and headed for the gym. She would have to wait until afternoon to go back to the newspaper files. She worked out, then began her climbing class. In the last session, they had talked about getting the body in shape and discussed proper nutrition, then she'd spent the rest of the lesson getting her students familiar with the climbing wall.

Today she discussed proper clothing and equipment then demonstrated some climbing techniques. Throughout the class, Autumn was careful to keep her mind focused on her students and helping them learn the best and safest methods for addressing the climb. She didn't allow her mind to stray toward little Molly McKenzie and what might have happened to her at the hands of Gerald Meeks.

Autumn suppressed a shudder, but the thought remained in the back of her head. As soon as class was over, she changed into street clothes and left for the library.

Running through the microfilm, she approached the search as she had before. Dozens of articles on Meeks surfaced in the newspaper files, from his arrest, all the way through his long, drawn-out trial. In the end, he had been sentenced to life in prison.

Autumn paused as Molly McKenzie's name popped up in one of the articles. It appeared again in several more.

Though Meeks has only confessed to the murders of the two children whose bodies were found in what appeared to be his dumping ground at the bottom of a ravine, it is believed he is also responsible for the death of six-year-old Molly McKenzie, who also went missing in the area around that time.

Apparently Meeks never admitted to the crime, but he never denied it either. One article mentioned that the description of the man given to police by witness only vaguely matched that of Gerald Meeks, but the age of the witnesses, all of whom were children under the age of seven, and the disparity of the descriptions were a factor in concluding that Meeks was the man responsible for Molly's abduction and murder.

In a later paper, Autumn saw again that efforts were made to get Meeks to give up information about the location of Molly's body. Though he seemed to be the man responsible, Meeks never confessed and he never gave the police the location of the victim's grave.

Because he didn't kill her!

The thought arose and wouldn't go away. The photos of Gerald Meeks convinced

Autumn further. Though as near as she could guess, he was about the same height as the man in her dreams, he was thinner and had brown hair, a gaunt man with the sunken eyes of a predator, not the warm, friendly eyes of the man in her dream.

Also, according to the information, Meeks had used chloroform to render his victims helpless before dragging them into his car.

Not like Molly, who, according to her dream, had been lured away by a man with a puppy.

More determined than ever, Autumn vowed to convince Ben McKenzie to at least hear her out.

But how to reach him?

She was no longer welcome in his office. She could try to speak to his ex-wife, but that might involve their younger daughter, Katie. It wouldn't be fair to a child who must have already suffered a very great deal. And Autumn believed that if she approached the family, McKenzie would go after that restraining order.

Besides, Autumn was convinced Ben McKenzie was the link. She had never seen or met his ex-wife and she had only started dreaming about Molly after she had noticed Ben at the gym.

What to do?

It wouldn't be easy but maybe if she tried again, McKenzie would at least hear her out.

Since the gym was the most likely place to find him, she headed there first thing the following morning. She didn't usually work out on weekends, but she needed information and made a beeline straight for the sign-in desk.

To get into the gym, you had to flash a tag with a bar code over a lighted glass plate. The bar code reader analyzed the code and checked to see if your membership was paid up and active. Autumn knew Mike Logan, one of the staff guys who worked behind the desk. He was sitting a few feet away, inputting something into his computer.

"Hi, Mike."

Mike looked her way, saw her and smiled. "Hey, sweet cheeks." He jogged over to the counter in his white shirt and shorts, his dark hair neatly combed. The uniform was a requirement. All the guys on the staff looked like they just came off the tennis court at Wimbledon. The women dressed the same, in a white knit shirt and shorts with Pike's Gym embroidered in black letters on the pocket. The climbing instructors were the exception. To attack the wall, they needed to wear more flexible clothes.

"Listen, Mike, I've got a problem. I was hoping you might be able to help me."

"Name it."

She pointed to the bar code reader. "That machine keeps track of everyone who goes in and out, right?"

"Right."

"I presume the information goes into a computer. Can you pull up a person by name, see what times he checks in each day?"

"Sure."

"I need to know the days and times for Ben McKenzie."

"Whoa! Wait a minute, Autumn. Ben's our landlord. I don't think he'd appreciate someone nosing into his business."

"It's no big deal," she lied. Again. "I just want to talk to him. It's about his daughter." *Not the live one. The one he thinks is dead.*

"Why don't you just go up to his office?"

"It's kind of personal. I'd rather make it less formal. Besides, I've seen him here before. He'll just think my bumping into him is a coincidence."

"I don't know . . ."

"Come on, Mike. Didn't I give you a couple of free climbing lessons last month?"

"Yeah, but . . . you sure you aren't stalking him or something?"

She cast him a *you've-got-to-be-kidding-me* look. Everyone knew she hardly ever dated and mostly avoided men in general. She had even heard a rumor she was gay, which was definitely news to her.

"Okay, okay. Hang on a minute. I'll print out his sheet for the past two months and you can take a look at it. Just don't mention my name, okay?"

"Cross my heart."

It didn't take long to figure out Ben's schedule. He came in every weekday and never on weekends, usually got there even earlier than she did. There were gaps, of course, several missing days clumped together. She figured those days he was probably away on business. In the past few weeks, he had started working out in the evenings on Tuesday and Thursday nights.

Autumn tapped the page. "Thanks, Mike. This is great." She grinned. "I'll destroy the incriminating evidence as soon as I'm done with it."

Mike looked relieved. He was a good guy. She didn't blame him for not wanting to risk his job and she had no intention of betraying his trust. She studied the list, trying to decide the best approach.

She remembered how furious McKenzie

had been in his office and decided not to confront him at the gym, where there would be people around. Instead she would wait outside, hoping she could speak to him alone.

At seven-forty-five Tuesday evening, Autumn parked herself on Pike Street in a little coffee shop with a clear view of the McKenzie building. According to the log, Ben was a man who adhered to a very strict schedule. He went into the gym at seven p.m., probably coming straight from his sixth-floor office, and though she had no way of knowing what time he left, she figured he probably worked out for at least an hour.

Eight o'clock came but no Ben. At eight-thirty on the nose, he walked out the door, dressed in slacks and a shirt unbuttoned at the throat, sleeves rolled up, his coat and tie draped over one arm.

Autumn set her white porcelain coffee cup down in its saucer and scrambled for the door. She caught up with Ben at the corner, stood there beside him a moment before he realized she was there.

"Mr. McKenzie?"

His head turned. His square jaw hardened. "You!"

"Please don't be angry. I have to speak to

you. I know you don't want to talk to me. I know how painful thinking about Molly must be, but you have to listen."

Several people walked up and stood next to them, waiting for the light to change. Ben took one look at them, gripped her arm and dragged her back against the wall of a nearby building.

"What the hell do you want? Money? Do you think you've found some way to extort me for cash? Because it isn't going to work."

"I don't want your money! I just want you to listen to me!"

He took a steadying breath, let it out slowly. The set of his jaw said he was fighting for control. "You've got three minutes."

Her mind spun, frantic to think where to begin. "I've been having this dream," she started. "It isn't a regular dream, not like the kind we all have every night. This is different, so real it's as if it's actually happening. And it's the same dream every night."

"This is bullshit. Everyone dreams."

"This isn't just any dream. This is a dream about Molly." Even in the faint yellow light shining down from the street lamp she could see his face go pale.

She hurried on, afraid he would walk away. "Of course, I didn't know who she was at first. In my dream, I saw this little girl get into a car with a man she didn't know and I was afraid for her. I thought this was something that hadn't happened yet but was about to and maybe I could find out who the little girl was and somehow prevent it."

He checked his watch. "You're time is up, lady. I'm leaving and if you try to talk to me again, I'll have you arrested for stalking."

Tears welled in her eyes. "You don't understand. I think Molly is still alive. Please . . . won't you at least hear me out?"

But Ben was already walking away, his broad shoulders slumped forward, perhaps against the breeze but Autumn thought it was the weight of his terrible memories.

Dear God, she had to reach him. Ben McKenzie was Molly's father and Autumn believed he was the key that had set the dreams in motion. With his help, maybe they could find her.

She wiped the tears from her cheeks, hating herself for crying. Dammit, why wouldn't he at least give her a chance?

But in her heart, she understood. She knew that every time she brought up Molly's name, the old pain surfaced. She needed proof — something that would convince Ben McKenzie there was at least a chance his daughter was still alive.

She went to bed that night, her mind still churning. She dreamed the kitchen dream again, saw the pain in Molly's face. By morning, she knew what she had to do.

Ben cancelled his late-night date with Delores Delgato, an exotic, Hispanic fashion model with the Allure Agency who had just finished a photo shoot down at the wharf. He had met Dee through a mutual friend when he was in L.A. on business and they had gone out a few times.

This week Delores was here in Seattle and tonight was the last night of her magazine shoot. She had called wanting to celebrate. At the time it had sounded like a good idea.

But after his encounter with Autumn Sommers, Ben wasn't in the mood to be sociable. He wasn't even in the mood to get laid.

He walked the few blocks to his penthouse apartment on the top floor of the Bay Towers in the trendy Belltown neighborhood. He had purchased the luxury condo last year. He could afford it and as he grew more and more successful the extra security the building provided had become a necessity.

He used his passcard to access his private elevator and rode to the twentieth floor. As he walked into the marble-floored entry, the lights of the city shone through the wall of windows in the living room. Down the hall to the left, there was a powder room and two bedrooms, each with a private marble bath. The master suite and bath and his home office were down the opposite hall.

Ben headed that way. As soon as he walked into the office, he picked up the phone on his desk. All the way home, he told himself the call could wait until morning, but he knew he wouldn't sleep if he left this business unfinished.

His mind strayed to the woman who had accosted him on the sidewalk. It was her tears that had gotten to him. Either the woman was a hell of an actress, a magnificent con, or she really believed the crap she was spewing about Molly.

He dialed Pete Rossi's cell number and heard the man's gruff voice on the other end. "Yeah?"

"I've got a job for you, Pete."

"Must be important for you to call this time of night."

"I want you to find out everything you can about a woman named Autumn Sommers. She says she's a fifth grade teacher at Lewis and Clark Elementary. She also teaches a rock-climbing class at Pike's Gym."

"Not exactly your usual type."

"Hardly. I have no idea if any of what she's told me is true. I'd appreciate knowing as much as you can by tomorrow."

"Not in a hurry, are you?" Pete said sarcastically.

"Can you handle it?"

"I'll talk to you before the end of the day."

Ben hung up the phone and ran a hand through his thick dark hair. There was no use stewing over Autumn Sommers, at least not until he had more information. Walking to the wet bar, he poured himself a snifter of Courvoisier and sat down in the deep leather chair behind his desk.

He swirled the brandy in his glass and took a drink, then felt the liquid burn down his throat and the slight relaxation of his muscles. He tried not to think of Autumn Sommers, but her heart-shaped face and deep green eyes popped into his head.

Who the hell are you? he thought, his mind beginning to churn with questions again.

And what the hell do you want?

"You have *got* to be kidding." Terri eyed her across the small round table at Starbucks.

"I'm not kidding. I called the prison directly. They told me Gerald Meeks was recently moved to the Federal Correctional

78

Institution in Sheridan, Oregon. Apparently, the guy's been a model prisoner. Sheridan is just south of Portland, so it's not all that far. I spoke to a man named Deavers and he submitted my name to Meeks requesting a visit. Apparently, Meeks agreed to see me."

"I can't believe this. You're telling me this guy Meeks agreed to meet with Seattle's resident psychic?"

"I'm not a psychic. I'm not anything except a woman stuck with a dream that won't go away. And Meeks thinks he's meeting with a friend of the McKenzie family who's trying to help them gain some kind of closure. That's what I told Mr. Deavers."

"Cute . . . like you're the family's personal shrink or something. You'd better hope Ben McKenzie doesn't get wind of this."

Autumn swallowed, remembering the dark rage on McKenzie's face when she had mentioned his daughter's name.

"I guess Meeks doesn't get many visitors. Mr. Deavers thinks that's the reason he agreed to see me."

"When are you going?"

"I'm driving down to Sheridan early Saturday morning. It's about sixty miles south of Portland. I'm meeting with Meeks late in the afternoon."

"I thought you and Josh were supposed to

go climbing."

"I had to cancel. I think Josh found someone else to go with him."

Terri pinned her with a disbelieving stare. "So you're actually going into a federal prison to see this guy."

Autumn nodded. "On the way back, I'm spending the night in Portland with Sandy Harrison. You remember — my roommate in college? I'll be driving back to Seattle on Sunday."

Terri sipped her latte through the hole in the plastic lid of her cup. "I've heard those places are pretty awful."

Autumn suppressed a shiver. "I don't even want to know." Going into a federal penitentiary wasn't going to be any picnic but Autumn was determined to find out if Meeks knew anything about the McKenzie girl. "I have to do this, Terri. If I come up empty-handed, I'll let the whole thing drop."

Terri cast her a look that said *what a crock of bull.* She knew Autumn could be a real bloodhound when she was set on something. *This* was a major something.

"Call me when you get back," Terri said, rising from her chair. "I'll worry until you do."

"I'll let you know how it goes." Autumn grabbed her paper cup in one hand and slung her small brown leather purse over her shoulder with the other. "Wish me luck."

Terri nodded. "I have a feeling you're going to need it."

Six

According to plan, very early Saturday morning, Autumn pulled her red Ford Escape out of its narrow space in the garage beneath her apartment building and drove the small SUV toward the Freeway 5 on-ramp, heading for Portland. The traffic wasn't that bad. Most people left the city on Friday night and she was getting out of town long before the Saturday shoppers hit the road.

It was a four-hour drive to Portland. Once she got there, she turned onto Highway 18 for the sixty-mile drive to the Sheridan correctional facility. On the seat beside her sat four pages — single-spaced — of visitor regulations.

Autumn had read them thoroughly, making sure not to wear anything khaki — expressively forbidden since the prisoners wore khaki pants and shirts — or anything metal on her person.

Her nerves began to build as she drove into the lot in front of the tile-roofed main building, parked in a visitor's space, got out and locked her SUV. Then she took a deep breath and headed for the entrance marked Visitors. Inside the lobby, security cameras were everywhere, watching every inch of the building.

Autumn walked to the information counter and a woman in a white uniform shirt and pants walked over at her approach.

"Name, please."

"Autumn Sommers . . . with an 'O'."

The guard, a bulky matron with heavy breasts and short black hair, looked down at the pages on her clipboard. "Your name's on the list. You're here on a special pass to see Gerald Meeks?"

"That's right."

"You'll still have to go through security check-in just like any other visitor."

"I was told I would."

"Follow me."

The matron led her along a linoleum floor waxed to a polished sheen, toward a door that led to the check-in area. There were even more cameras inside and three male guards who looked as if they took their jobs in deadly earnest.

Visiting hours ended at three o'clock and

it was almost two now, so most of the inmate visitors had already checked in. Still there were a couple of beefy guys dressed like bikers with stringy hair and tattoos in line behind a heavyset Hispanic woman who was accompanied by a chubby girl of about fourteen.

As Autumn took her place at the rear of the line, the bikers' attention swung from the girl and they eyed her as if they had just been served a fresh piece of meat. Autumn's nose wrinkled at the sour smell of body odor and the foul breath of the man standing beside her, his lecherous gaze creeping rudely over her breasts.

"Nice tits," he said to his buddy.

"Nice ass," the other man said.

"Keep a civil tongue," ordered the guard, "or you won't be seeing your good-for-nothing brother."

The men said no more but the curl of their lips and their heavy-lidded gazes made it clear what they were thinking. Wishing she were anywhere but in that room, Autumn fixed her attention on the guard and set her purse on the conveyor belt that carried it beneath an X-ray machine like the ones at the airports. She was asked to remove her shoes and jacket, which also went through the machine.

She had read in the regulations that visitors were subject to random drug tests and prayed she wouldn't be chosen. But she only had to walk through a metal detector — which thankfully didn't go off — and make her way to the opposite end of the conveyor belt.

"First door to your left down the hall," said one of the guards as she picked up her purse and slung it over her shoulder.

Eager to escape, she walked out the exit door, made a left and spotted a door with a small window in it. When she opened the door, she saw that it wasn't the main visiting area, but a narrow room that accommodated only four inmates at a time. It was set up much the way she had seen on TV, with the prisoner seated on one side of the glass and the visitor on the other.

Three of the four spaces were currently in use. An obese woman with dirty, coarse black hair sat on one of the stools talking to a huge, dark-skinned man with earrings in both ears. There was a skinny white guy talking to his girlfriend, who looked like she was on drugs but couldn't be because they wouldn't have let her in.

The third guy was talking to a man in a cheap striped suit who seemed to be trying to conduct some sort of business, though

Autumn couldn't imagine what. The entire scene was depressing and she began to think coming here was the worst idea she'd ever had.

Then the door on the opposite side of the glass swung open and Gerald Meeks walked in. He was wearing the khaki inmate's uniform and looked exactly like his picture — thin to the point of being gaunt with hollow, sunken eyes. His hair was a faded brown, not blond like the man in her dreams.

He took a seat across from her. When he looked into her face, Autumn shivered.

"Take it easy, lady. You're way too old to interest me."

She sat up a little straighter. She had come here to talk to the man. She wasn't about to let him intimidate her.

"Thank you for seeing me," she said.

"I don't get many visitors. I figured it might help pass the time."

"I came here to ask you some questions about Molly McKenzie."

He smiled, a thin slash across the lower half of his face. "A lot of people have asked me about her. What makes you think I've got something new to say?"

"I don't know . . . I was hoping . . . It's been six years since Molly disappeared.

86

You've been locked up for most of that time. I thought maybe by now you might be more forthcoming where Molly is concerned."

"What's it to you, one way or the other?"

"I'm a . . . friend of the family. I'm just trying to find out if Molly is really dead."

Dark eyes bored into her. "You don't think so? Everyone else is sure I killed her."

"Did you?"

He didn't answer for the longest time. "It took guts for you to come. The guys in here would eat you up with a spoon if they had the chance. They'll all be jealous when I tell 'em what my visitor looked like." Those sunken eyes moved over her, making her skin crawl. "I bet you were a real pretty little thing, Autumn Sommers, when you were a little girl. Those bright green eyes and all that silky red-gold hair. If I'd seen you back then —"

"I came here to talk about Molly," Autumn interrupted, ignoring the sick feeling in her stomach and the suddenly too-fast pounding of her heart.

Gerald Meeks looked her in the eye. "I would have told 'em, but they wouldn't have listened if I had, so I just kept quiet."

"Told them what?"

"You want the truth? I never laid eyes on Molly McKenzie. I didn't kill her. I wasn't anywhere near her. I just figured . . . let 'em keep guessing, what do I care? Kind of gave me a chuckle in the middle of the night, those cops all thinkin' it was me."

For several seconds Autumn just sat there. Of course, there was no way to know for sure if Gerald Meeks was telling the truth, but Autumn believed him completely.

From what she had read, after his arrest Meeks had bragged about the murders he had committed but he had never mentioned little Molly.

"Thank you for your candor, Mr. Meeks."

"My . . . pleasure . . ." Meeks rose and so did she. She could feel his eyes on her all the way to the door.

Relief washed over her as the door closed behind her and she headed back down the hall. She returned to the screening area to be re-checked before being allowed to leave.

As she pushed through the doors of the main building and walked out into the sunshine, she took a deep breath of clean Oregon air. Though no one had physically touched her, she felt as if she needed a long, hot shower. She couldn't wait till she got to her friend Sandy's house so she could bathe and put on fresh clothes.

It was ridiculous. The facility was clean and well cared for but that didn't change the way she felt. In truth, it was a dismal experience, but the trip had been worth it.

Autumn was even more convinced that Molly McKenzie was alive and reaching out to her for help.

She had to see Ben. This time Autumn had something to tell him that might make him listen. Or at least she hoped he would.

Sitting in the Coffee Bean Café across the street from the McKenzie building after work on Monday night, she felt like the stalker he believed her to be. She had no idea what time he might leave his office, but she had arrived at five-thirty, determined to wait until midnight if she had to.

Fortunately, Ben walked through the glass lobby doors onto the sidewalk at six-thirty. Autumn waited until he reached the corner, then slipped out of the café and followed him down the street, careful to keep her distance and stay in the shadows. She shuddered to think what McKenzie might do if he realized she was there.

She had no idea where he might be going, but she was hoping to find a place where she could corner him, make him listen without creating a scene. She kept pace with him — she didn't want to lose him — but didn't get too close.

She wondered where he was headed. Wherever it was, he walked with purpose as he always seemed to do, his long legs carrying him rapidly down the street. Another few blocks and she saw him go into a little Italian restaurant called Luigi's. She had been there a couple of times and had enjoyed the food and the quiet atmosphere.

She was wearing black slacks and a black V-neck sweater so she wouldn't stand out in the darkness, nice enough clothes that she wouldn't look out of place in Luigi's. She walked into the bar and stood just out of sight until she spotted him at a quiet booth at the back of the main dining room.

No one was with him. Perhaps he was waiting for someone. McKenzie wouldn't want to make a scene in a nice place like this. It was the perfect time to approach.

Autumn crossed the room and slid into the booth beside him.

"Don't yell and don't get mad. What I have to tell you will only take a minute."

His jaw clamped down. He looked like the top of his head might blow off any minute. "Get out of here or I'm going to have you thrown out."

"I went to see Gerald Meeks. I talked to him and he told me he didn't kill Molly. I think he would be willing to tell you the same thing if you went there and asked him yourself."

Something shifted in his features. "You went to the federal penitentiary to see Gerald Meeks?"

"Meeks was transferred to the facility in Sheridan, Oregon for good behavior. I drove down on Saturday."

He sat back in the booth, his face an unreadable mask. "I hired a detective to check you out. You really are a teacher. In fact you have an extremely good reputation at the school where you work."

"I'm not crazy. And I swear I'm not after your money."

"So what do you want?"

"I think your daughter Molly is alive. I've seen her in my dreams. I don't know where she is, but I think she is reaching out to me for help."

"Why you? And if she really is alive, why would she wait until now?"

"I haven't figured that part out. I think it has something to do with you . . . with me seeing you at the gym. I probably wouldn't believe any of this myself except . . ."

"Except what?"

"This happened to me once before. I had a dream about my two best friends — the same dream over and over. In the dream,

91

Jeff and Jolie and a third kid were killed in a car accident. I was only fifteen. I didn't believe it would actually happen and I thought that even if I said something, no one would believe me, that they would just make fun of me."

"What happened?"

"They went to a party and their car went off the road into a tree, just like in my dream. All three of them were killed."

A long silence followed.

"I'm sorry," Ben said.

"I can't ignore it this time. I won't. In my dream, I saw your daughter taken that day from in front of your house but the man I saw wasn't Gerald Meeks. I've seen Molly as she is now, six years older, a lovely young girl approaching her teens. It's her, Ben — the same pale blond hair, the same big blue eyes. She's alive. I know it."

He swallowed and glanced away. When he looked at her again, the pain in his eyes made an ache throb in her chest.

"Do you have any idea how hard this is for me? Can you begin to know the way I suffered when Molly was abducted? If I believe you, all that pain will surface again, all the terrible grief. If you're wrong or even if you're right and I can't find her — I don't think I can survive that kind of pain again."

Autumn didn't know what to say. She knew what she was asking, knew the terrible price Ben McKenzie would pay if she was wrong. But there was a lost young girl to think of. A child who seemed desperate for her help.

"We have to try. I lost three friends the last time. There was pain there, too, Ben."

"If you're wrong, I swear to God —"

"I could be. I won't lie about it. This has only happened to me once before. But the dreams are so clear, so real. I see her face — the same face I saw in the newspapers. I hear the little boy, Robbie, calling her name."

His head whipped toward her. "Robbie? Robbie Hines?"

"I don't know his last name. They were playing together in the yard that day."

He tightened his hand into a fist to keep it from trembling. "Robbie was there that day. It wasn't in the papers."

"Red hair and freckles?"

"That's him."

"You have to help me, Ben. You have no other choice."

He took a deep breath and slowly released it. "I need to sleep on this. Pete came up with your address and phone number. Unless I regain my senses, I'll be in touch with

93

you soon."

Autumn gave him a tentative smile, fighting to hold back tears. "Thank you."

She started to get up from the booth as an exotic, olive-skinned woman walked up to the table. She was tall and elegantly thin, her skin silky smooth, the most beautiful woman Autumn had ever seen.

"Sorry I am late, *querido,* but the limo got tied up in traffic." Her nearly black eyes swung to Autumn. "I see you have kept yourself entertained."

"Autumn Sommers this is Delores Delgato."

"Pleased to meet you," Autumn said. "I didn't mean to interfere with your evening, Ms. Delgato. I just needed to speak to Mr. McKenzie about a personal matter."

"That is all right, *chica.* If it hadn't been you it would have been someone else."

Ben frowned.

"I look forward to your call," Autumn said to him, feeling awkward and desperate to escape.

Ben just nodded. As Autumn turned to walk away, he helped Delores Delgato remove her burgundy cashmere jacket then seated her beside him in the booth.

Winding her way through the tables toward the front door, Autumn stepped out into the crisp Seattle night air. She had accomplished her goal: convinced Ben McKenzie to listen and perhaps begin to believe her at least a little.

From now on, she didn't think he would be able to turn away. Molly was his daughter. From the pain Autumn had seen in his face, it was obvious how much he loved her. If Molly was alive, he would have to try to find her.

He would have no other choice.

Ben endured his evening with Delores, all the while wishing the night would end. His mind was on Autumn Sommers and on Molly and whether or not he dared to believe she might still be alive.

Though Delores made it clear she expected him to join her in her suite at the Fairmont Olympic Hotel, he declined. Sometime over the past few days, sex with the exotic model had lost its appeal. Like most of the women he dated, Delores required a lot of attention. Currently his attention was fixed somewhere else.

Leaving Delores fuming in the grandiose lobby of the five-star hotel, he walked the few blocks to his penthouse. The answering machine in his office was blinking. Next to it, a stack of papers waited in the fax machine.

He played back the phone messages, including one from Pete Rossi explaining the fax: more information Pete had collected on Autumn Sommers. Ben lifted the pages out of the machine, walked over and sank down in his butter-soft leather chair.

He skimmed through Pete's report, the high points of which the detective had given him over the phone.

Autumn Kathleen Sommers. Born June 3, 1980 to Kathleen L. and Maxwell M. Sommers.

Kathleen Sommers had died in 1993 when Autumn was thirteen. Max Sommers, a fireman, had raised her. He was retired now, giving him more time to devote to his hobby, rock climbing. It was Max who had sparked his daughter's interest in the sport. At twenty-seven she was a certified member of the American Mountain Guides Association and apparently an extremely qualified climber.

According to the report, Autumn had gone to the University of Seattle — partly on scholarship, partly school loans — graduated at the top of her class and then went on to get her teaching degree.

In a subparagraph, her relationship with a

guy in college named Steven Elliot was mentioned and two other men with whom she'd had brief affairs, neither of them recent. Pete was extremely thorough.

Ben almost smiled. From the looks of the report, Autumn hadn't dated a lot. He didn't believe for a minute she hadn't been asked.

There was something about Autumn Sommers, something that reached out and snagged a man's interest. She might not be a buxom blonde with a movie star face, or an exotic, olive-skinned brunette, but with her silky russet curls, green cat-eyes and tight little body, in a different sort of way the woman was sexy as hell.

Ben ignored the unwanted shot of desire that came with the thought, just as he had the surprising physical attraction he had felt for her the moment she had walked into his office. He had clamped down hard on it then, certain she was some kind of crazy. But tonight, when he had seen the quick flash of tears in her eyes, he had felt the pull again.

Autumn was different from the women he dated. She seemed more passionate about life, more vital. If he was honest with himself and circumstances were different, he wouldn't mind taking Autumn Sommers to bed.

It wasn't going to happen. Though Pete's report showed nothing out of the ordinary, past or present, it didn't mean he could trust her. She could be the world's smoothest charlatan or simply a nutcase who believed what she was telling him was real.

He made a note to call Pete in the morning to have him check whether Autumn had really made a trip to the prison in Sheridan, find out if she had actually talked to Meeks. In fact, if she had, he would have Pete go up there himself, see if he could confirm what Meeks had said about Molly.

The name whispered though his head as he hadn't allowed it to in years. What if Molly were actually alive? She'd be twelve years old on August first. If she *was* alive, what horrors had she suffered in the years since she had been taken? Had she been abused? Molested? Brutalized in some terrible way?

God, he couldn't bear to think that she was being mistreated. It was one of the reasons, after the long, hopeless search, he had grasped onto the theory that she had been murdered by Meeks. Better to think her dead than alive and suffering.

But the Sommers woman had raised that

possibility and he realized that whatever had happened to Molly over the years didn't matter. If she was alive, he just wanted her home, back where he could take care of her and heal whatever wounds she might have suffered.

A memory arose of the last day he had seen her, standing in the door to his study.

"Daddy! Daddy will you come out to my dollhouse and play with me?"

He was busy. There was always so much to do. But he always made time for Molly.

"All right, angel, what shall we play?" Scooping her up in his arms, he carried her toward the door leading out to the backyard.

"Let's have a tea party!" Molly said, hugging his neck. A make-believe tea party was her favorite pastime.

"Okay, but you have to pour."

Molly giggled and rested her head on his shoulder.

Ben closed his eyes against the memory. During the first years after his daughter's disappearance, he had thought of that day a thousand times. But in the past several years, he had learned to block the memories. They were simply too painful, too destructive.

Now, because of Autumn Sommers, the memory had returned. Ben ignored the burning behind his eyes, leaned back in his chair and fought not to give in to his grief.

SEVEN

Autumn didn't hear from Ben on Tuesday. He didn't call on Wednesday. By Thursday night, she was resigned — if he didn't get in touch with her by Friday afternoon, she was going to brave his secretary's wrath, go up to his office and force her way in to see him.

Autumn sighed as she pushed through the door leading into the climbing gym. At least for the past few days she hadn't been dreaming. Well, except for Monday, the last time she had seen Ben.

Four of her students were already there. As she set her notes on the table, the other two walked in. She was ready to begin the day's lesson when a tall male figure strode through the door dressed in khaki shorts and a dark green T-shirt with the picture of a kayak plunging through white water and COULONGE GORGE printed on the front.

Autumn tried not to admire Ben Mc-

Kenzie's wide shoulders and powerful biceps and the long bands of muscle in his suntanned legs. He was wearing a pair of Reeboks but carried rubber-soled climbing shoes in one hand.

Autumn spoke to him as he walked toward her. "Mr. McKenzie. I've been hoping to hear from you. Unfortunately, we're about to start our lesson. Perhaps after —"

"I signed up for your class at the front desk. I've bought the book you recommended and studied the first few chapters . . . the parts of the class I've missed. I'll be joining your sessions from now on."

Her mind was spinning. He hadn't called all week and now he was here? "Could I speak to you for a moment outside?"

"Of course."

He set his shoes on the floor and followed her.

As soon as the door was closed, Autumn spun to face him. "All right, McKenzie, what's going on? I've been waiting to hear from you all week but you never called. Now you join my class? I'd like to know why."

Ben shrugged those wide shoulders. "I'm in the sporting goods business. I like hiking, canoeing, kayaking, just about everything. We sell some of the finest climbing gear money can buy but I've never tried the sport. I figured this was a good opportunity."

She clamped her hands on her hips. "Fine. Now, what's the real reason you're here?"

Ben's gaze locked with hers. "You really want to know? I'll tell you. You came to me with some cock-and-bull story about Molly. I don't know you from Adam but just because you say so, I'm supposed to believe she's alive after all these years and you think that together we can find her. If I'm crazy enough to believe you, it will turn my life upside down. There's a chance my family will hear about it. And if they do, *they'll* suffer. You say you need my help? Here's the deal. I'm not committing to anything until I know who the hell you are."

She opened her mouth but Ben cut her off.

"I'm not talking about the standard things — that you're a twenty-seven-year-old schoolteacher or that your father is a retired fireman who lives in Burlington. I mean who you are in here." He set a fist over his heart. "I need to believe you're telling me the truth — not just what you *believe* is the truth. You want something from me, Autumn? Well, I want something from you."

"How did you know about my father? Did you have me investigated like some kind of criminal?"

"You didn't think I would?"

Of course he would. With his money and connections, it wouldn't be that hard to do. "So exactly what is it you want?"

"I want time to get to know you, find out if you're for real. Once I'm satisfied, you'll have my complete cooperation."

"What about Molly? Every day lost is a day we could be looking for her."

"Molly's been gone six years. Odds are she's dead, just like the police believe. I have to think of Katie and Joanne. If this all starts again, questions will be asked, word will get back to them sooner or later. Neither of them or anyone else in my family deserves to suffer through all that again."

It was a very good argument. His family had to come first and he had no real reason to believe her. He had to be certain he could trust her. If the situation were reversed, she would feel exactly the same.

"All right, we'll do it your way. If that means you'll be learning to climb, then I guess that's what you'll do." She gave him a challenging smile. "You might even discover you like it. It's an extremely exciting sport."

Ben just nodded. "Then I guess we had better get started. Your students are waiting."

Autumn studied him a moment more. Not for the first time, it occurred to her what a handsome man Ben McKenzie was. Solid jaw, nicely formed lips, straight nose and dark brown eyes that seemed to take in more than you meant for them to see. He was tall and bronzed and extremely fit. She didn't like the little curl of heat that slid into her stomach when he looked at her the way he was now.

Autumn steeled herself. She had seen the kind of women Ben McKenzie dated. Delores Delgato was on the cover of this month's *Vogue* magazine. Autumn wasn't anywhere close to their league, and that was just fine with her. She was a failure where men were concerned. She wasn't about to be taken in by a guy like Ben.

Ben watched Autumn at work. As soon as they had entered the climbing gym, her entire concentration fixed on the students who had come to her to learn.

"Before we begin, we have a new student. This is Ben McKenzie. You might recognize the name, since he's in the sporting goods business and the owner of this building."

Several people nodded.

Ben followed her gaze toward the women in the group. "Ben, meet Courtney Roland

and Winnie Caruthers." A tall rangy blonde and an attractive brunette with muscular arms and legs. "This is Ian Camden and Bruce Lansky." Ian blond, early twenties; Bruce dark-haired and at least fifteen years older. "And these two guys are Matt Gould and Ned Wheaton." Matt was tall with shaggy brown hair. Ned was a lanky, good-looking black man with a shaved head and small silver earrings.

"Good to meet you," Ben said to the group.

"All right, let's get to work," said Autumn.

He could see she took her job seriously as she led her students over to one of the tables and began to go through the gear spread out on the top.

"We've been talking about equipment in general. As you can see, I use mostly Black Diamond. It happens to be my personal favorite, but there are other companies that make good products as well." She flicked a glance his way. "Maybe Ben can give us his opinion."

"We don't sell anything in our stores that isn't top of the line and our staff is knowledgeable and helpful. I know we sell Black Diamond, so it must be good. Since I'm new to the sport, for the present I'll defer to Autumn on the subject."

For an instant Autumn's green eyes moved over his face and he felt a tug of awareness low in his groin. She looked back down at the equipment. "What you see here are the basics: harness, carabiners, camalots, wired hexes, stoppers, a helmet, a chalk bag and a couple of different types of belay devices."

The group gathered round as she went over each of the different items. She held up a bundle of rope. "This line is static — no give. It's used for jugging up or rappelling down a mountain." She held up another bundle. "This is a seventy-meter bundle of climbing rope. It's a light, strong, dynamic line with low impact force — designed so that if you fall, there's enough give to help your body absorb the shock when you hit the end." She gave them a few moments to examine the items and answered a couple of questions.

"You've all got climbing slippers," she said. "Go ahead and put them on. And if you have your own harness, put that on. If not, we've got some here for you to use."

The group suited up. Autumn was wearing trim-fitting khaki shorts with oversize pockets and a sleeveless, orange, scoop-neck top that said I LEAD, YOU FOLLOW. Since Ben had anticipated needing them, he had picked up a pair of leather-topped, rubber-soled climbing shoes at his down-town store. He sat down on a bench to put them on, making a mental note to follow Autumn's suggestions for the rest of the gear he would need.

He had told her the truth. He had been seriously thinking of giving the sport a try and this presented the perfect opportunity.

Far more important, this gave him some time. He wasn't ready to involve himself in what was surely a wild-goose chase that could cause more misery for him and his family. Then again, as crazy as the whole thing sounded, after the lengths she had gone to, he wasn't prepared to discount the slim possibility that Autumn Sommers might actually have some sort of bizarre psychic connection to his daughter and there was a chance Molly was still alive.

He had to ferret out the truth about Autumn and the only way to do that was to spend some time with her.

He looked down at the gear on the table. He would check with the guys in the climbing department but he had a feeling Autumn knew as much about choosing the right gear as they did. Maybe more.

"I'll go first," she said. "That way you can watch the way I take the wall." She looked over at Ned. "You've handled a line before,

Ned. How about working the rope for me?"

"No problem." There was a length of rope looped over a bar at the top of the wall. Ned, apparently the most experienced student in the group, ran one end of the line through the belay device on his harness while Autumn tied a double figure-eight into hers, securing the rope to the belt around her waist.

"When I come down, it'll be your turn," she said to the group. Her gaze ran over the cluster of students until she came to him. "I think today we'll start with Ben."

Autumn's eyes locked with his and Ben almost smiled. She was testing him. He could see it in those tilted cat-eyes. She didn't like the ground rules he had set, but she had no choice except to go along with them. He took a look at the wall. It was forty feet high. Some walls went to eighty.

The floor in front was protected by a thick foam-rubber vinyl-covered mat but it wouldn't be enough to prevent injury if the climber took a fall from the top. Autumn coated her small hands with the dry, white, resin-like climber's chalk and headed for the wall.

Autumn's sure hands and small feet searched and found the tiny niches and crevices in the holds as she made her way up the wall with skill and a fluid grace.

Ben found himself watching with fascination the movement of the muscles in her arms and legs and the way her buttocks tightened under her shorts as she moved higher and higher up the wall. Her waist was small, her breasts nicely rounded. His groin clenched almost painfully and he muttered a curse.

The last thing he needed was any sort of physical attraction to Autumn Sommers. He had no idea who she really was or if any of what she had told him was real.

He fixed his concentration on Autumn who had reached the top of the wall and was now smoothly riding the rope Ned held back down to the bottom. She was good. That much was clear. She made the sport look easy and he knew damned well it wasn't.

Once she returned to solid ground, she centered those green eyes directly on him. "Your turn, Ben."

EIGHT

Class was finally over. Thinking that everyone had left the gym, Autumn began to bag her gear, concentrating on stowing everything properly.

"I enjoyed your class today."

She looked over her shoulder to find Ben McKenzie just a few feet away. "I didn't realize you were still here. I thought you'd be anxious to get back to work."

"I am. I wanted to ask if you were busy tonight."

Autumn eyed him warily. "Not really." Not unless watching an old movie on Turner Classics was busy. "Why?"

"I told you before — I need time to get to know you. I'll come by your place after I leave the office . . . say six-thirty? We'll go over to my downtown store and you can help me pick out the climbing gear I'm going to need. It shouldn't take all that long."

She didn't want to go with him. He made

her nervous in a way she couldn't quite explain. But she needed his help and she couldn't think of a reason to say no. "All right."

Ben left her to finish her task and she carried her gear back to her locker. She had a couple of private lessons that afternoon then afterward stopped in at Barnes and Noble to pick up a few new paperback books, since she felt at a loss if she ran out of something to read.

Ben arrived in her lobby at six-thirty, but insisted on coming up instead of letting her come down to meet him.

"I want to see where you live," he said over the intercom. "A person's home says a lot about them."

She didn't like the idea. She didn't want Ben McKenzie barging into her home — her life — but she didn't see any other way to get his help. Without it, Molly would never have a chance to be found.

She was nervous as she opened the door. She loved her cozy apartment, but Ben McKenzie was rich and used to living in far higher style. Since their discussion at Luigi's on Monday, she had gone back to the library and run his name. Over the past few years, article after article had appeared in the society section, showing Ben at benefits, plays and opening night concerts — escorting some of the most glamorous women in the world. Apparently, he was wildly successful in his business endeavors and equally successful with women.

He stepped through the open door, his eyes darting into the compact kitchen with its sparkling white countertops and cheerful white-and-rose flowered wallpaper, moving past the breakfast bar that separated the area from the living room. "So this is the place you call home."

She managed a smile. "This is it. Would you like a glass of wine or something else? I keep a bottle of Jack Daniels up in the cupboard for my dad. He isn't really supposed to drink, but he's pretty hard-headed about it and I figure a little whiskey once in a while isn't really going to hurt him."

"Wine sounds good."

"Red or white?"

He eyed her with interest. "White is good for right now."

She pulled out two stemmed wine glasses, took an opened bottle out of the fridge and filled the glasses with chardonnay.

Ben took a sip and savored it slowly. "Not bad. Local vintner?"

"Columbia Crest. This is an estate vintage. I guess you figured I'd pour it out of a box?"

He laughed. "Not at all. You don't strike me as quite that down-home."

He lifted his glass off the breakfast bar and wandered toward the windows overlooking the city, pausing here and there to consider an antique Victorian clock, a porcelain figurine, a hundred-year-old green glass plate she had fallen instantly in love with and bought for practically nothing at a garage sale. The molded ceilings drew his eye, the sheer lace curtains, the floral rugs on the hardwood floors.

"The place is amazingly feminine," he said. "I have to admit I'm a little surprised."

Her posture tightened defensively. "I like sports. That doesn't mean I'm not a woman."

Those brown eyes drifted over her, seemed to warm with appreciation. She was wearing dark-gray, low-slung bell-bottom pants, a pair of black heeled boots and a deep pink sweater that hugged her curves.

"No," he said. "You are definitely a woman." His rich baritone rolled through her, sent a curl of warmth into her stomach. Autumn forced herself to ignore it and took a steadying sip of her wine.

Ben glanced into the bedroom, saw the canopied bed with its white eyelet bedspread and matching dust ruffle. "Very pretty.

That's where you've been having your dreams?"

She nodded.

"Any lately?"

"Last Monday, after I spoke to you."

"None since then?"

"No."

"So you think there's a connection between me and the dreams."

"I think it's the most likely explanation."

He wandered into her bedroom, went into her bathroom and eventually returned to the living room.

"You know," she said, "it's rude to enter a woman's bedroom uninvited."

The edge of his mouth faintly curved. "From the look in your eye, I imagine I'd be waiting a good long while." The amusement faded. "You know my terms. I find out what I need to know or I'm out of this."

Autumn shook her head. "I don't think you're going to back out. I don't think your conscience will let you. Just like mine won't let me."

He said nothing for a while. "Nevertheless. Until I believe I can trust you, I'm going to stick to you like I'm your shadow."

Autumn set her glass down a little too hard, making the crystal ring. "What if I say no? What if I just tell you to go away and forget the whole thing?"

"You won't. You just said your conscience won't let you."

Autumn bit her lip. He was right — but so was she. They were in this together, whether they liked it or not. She would do what she had to in order to make this easier for both of them.

They sat at the counter and talked for a while: a little about her family, her father and what sort of parent he was as she grew up but mostly about climbing.

"You did okay for your first time," Autumn said, speaking of his morning effort on the wall.

"I climbed like a buffoon and you know it. I fell three times before I got to the top. Damn good thing I was wearing a harness."

"But you got there. You stuck with it. Most people would have quit. And you have the lean muscles and flexible strength to make a good climber."

He smiled. "It was challenging. I think I'm going to like it."

And Autumn thought that in time — if he was serious about learning the sport — he could become very good. He was strong, limber and athletic. And he had a certain grace of movement that few men had.

They finished their wine and set the

glasses down.

"Time to go," Ben said, rising from his stool. "Better get your jacket. It's always cold in the evenings this time of year."

She looked up at him. He was there to learn about her but she had just learned something about him. There was a protective streak in Ben McKenzie. She retrieved her navy-blue jacket from the closet in the entry; Ben took it from her and held it out so she could put it on.

"Thank you." She smiled, then remembering he had also helped Delores Delgato out of her expensive cashmere jacket that night at Luigi's, the smile slipped away.

Get a grip, she warned herself, wishing she had never dreamed about Molly, never managed to get herself in this position. But she had agreed to spend time with Ben McKenzie, one of the wealthiest, most desirable bachelors in Seattle.

She wasn't a fool. Ben was handsome and powerful. And with that lean, hard-muscled body one of the most sexually attractive men she had ever met. She had to be careful, had to keep her distance, keep her mind fixed on her goal.

Think of Molly, she told herself and then walked past him as he held open her apartment door.

The store was posh. Two stories high with a loft that displayed expensive sports clothing. The main floor was sectioned into areas pertaining to different sports, each decorated with huge photos of extreme athletes competing in their areas of expertise: ultimate skiing in deep, untouched powder, snowboarding down triple black-diamond slopes, biking, motocross, hiking, hang gliding. Climbing was no exception. There was a fantastic picture of a climber on an overhang thousands of feet in the air — stuck like a fly, completely horizontal against the magnificent mountain vistas.

"All right," Ben said, leading her in that direction. "Just pick out whatever you think I need and don't worry about the cost." He grinned. "I get one helluva discount."

Autumn ignored the odd little flutter that grin caused and set to work, studying each piece of gear. It took a while, but it was kind of fun, the vicarious thrill of getting to buy anything you wanted no matter the cost. She helped him choose the best harness for his size, strength and level of ability. Climbing rope, carabiners, hexes, cams, as well as an ultralight tent and sleeping bag, and waterproof bags to pack all the stuff in.

Ben insisted on picking out some clothes: lightweight and durable with lots of pockets. He was carrying two armloads of merchandise by the time they left the store.

"Let's catch a cab," he said. "I want to drop this off at my condo then we'll go get something to eat."

Fresh nerves assailed her. "I think I'll just go on back home."

Ben fixed her with a glare. "You know the drill. The sooner I'm satisfied you're for real, the sooner we can get on with the search — assuming there's going to be one."

Autumn sighed. "Fine, we'll go to dinner." She waited for Ben in the taxi while he carried the bags up to his condo on the twentieth floor.

"You're welcome to come up," he said, but Autumn declined and instead waited for his return.

The wind whipped her hair and the air was damp but invigorating as they stepped out of the cab in front of Solstice not far from Pioneer Square, one of Seattle's newer, currently hip cafés. The place was full on Friday night, but the owner knew Ben and they were quickly led to a cozy table at the rear of the restaurant where they each ordered a glass of wine — red this time.

"You like wine, I gather," Ben said, lifting his glass and studying the deep burgundy cabernet. It was a twelve-dollar glass he'd insisted she try. And he was right; it was fantastic.

"I got interested through a friend of mine in college. Washington has some amazingly good vineyards."

He studied her over the rim of his glass. "This friend . . . his name wouldn't be Steven Elliot?"

Autumn stiffened. It annoyed her that he knew so much more about her than she knew about him and yet she could hardly fault him for being cautious. "I can see your report was thorough."

"You and Steven . . . the two of you were serious?"

"I was. Steve moved on to greener pastures."

He swirled the dark liquid in his glass. "You like wine. What else do you like?"

She managed a smile. "I like good food — and climbing, of course — and on occasion I like to play dress-up."

"Dress-up?"

Her smile turned sincere. "Long sequined gowns and tuxedos. I don't get much opportunity but one of my climbing partners is the son of a wealthy computer magnate.

His dad presses him to go to an occasional formal event. I go with him when he needs a date."

"Apparently my report wasn't as thorough as I thought. Are you seeing this guy on a regular basis?"

"I told you, he's my climbing partner. Josh is just a very good friend." Autumn hadn't noticed the tension in Ben's shoulders until it began to ease.

"All right, you like to play dress-up. How about tomorrow night? I've been invited to a black-tie benefit for the Seattle Symphony. I wasn't going to go, but —"

Autumn swiftly shook her head. "You're making this far too personal and that isn't a good idea. Besides, I'm planning to go climbing with Josh."

"We're talking about my daughter. That's about as personal as it gets. I want to know what makes you tick. I think tomorrow night — you in an evening gown, me in a tux — is a *very* good idea."

She was already tired of the game. Ben was sophisticated and charming, the sort of guy who enjoyed casual sex and one-night stands. Autumn wasn't that way and the more time she spent with him, the harder it was not to be aware of him as a man.

She might be a failure at male-female

relationships but she was still a woman. There were times her body ached for the touch of a man but she couldn't afford to start thinking that way about Ben.

"Tell me about the dreams," Ben said softly, changing the subject.

Autumn felt a sweep of relief. This was the topic she wanted to discuss, the reason she was sitting here with Ben McKenzie. "They started some weeks back . . . I think it was shortly after I saw you at the gym. Or maybe even that night, but I don't really remember."

She looked up as the waiter arrived, a tall woman wearing a crisp black apron over her white blouse and black slacks. Both of them gave her their orders: a medium-rare filet for Ben with Roquefort sauce on the side; homemade tortellini with a sun-dried to-mato cream sauce for Autumn.

While they were waiting for their meals, she described in detail her recurring dreams of the day Molly had been abducted, the children playing in the yard and the little red-haired boy named Robbie. She told Ben about the man and how he had convinced Molly to go with him in his car to help him find his lost puppy.

"How old a guy was he?"

"Late thirties, maybe a little younger.

Blond hair. Kind of a nice-looking man. I remember he had friendly eyes."

One of Ben's dark eyebrows went up, sending a hint of embarrassment into Autumn's cheeks. "I know it sounds crazy, but his eyes kind of crinkled when he smiled and I remember thinking that you couldn't trust a person just because he looked harmless."

Ben cast her a meaningful glance. "That much is certainly true."

Autumn's flush deepened, but she forced herself to go on. "The man gave Molly this little black and white puppy to hold. He said its name was Cuffy. He said he had another puppy named Nicky but Nicky had gotten lost. He asked Molly to help him find it."

Ben's jaw turned to granite and the warmth in his eyes disappeared. "I swear, if you are making all of this up —"

"You know some of it's true. They were playing ball in the yard. I read that later in the newspaper. You told me yourself the little boy's name was Robbie. That wasn't in any of the papers I read but you told me yourself he was there that day in the yard."

Ben took a drink of his wine and she thought that he was working to stay in control. The waiter arrived with their salads but neither of them started to eat.

"Tell me about the second dream . . . the one where Molly is older."

Just to give herself some time, Autumn took a sip of her wine then set the glass back down. "I didn't recognize her at first. She was with two women, both of them blond and fair. They were working in the kitchen, preparing a meal . . . supper, I think. They were all very solemn. None of them laughing. It bothered me even in my sleep."

"Go on."

"The women were talking, but I couldn't hear what they were saying. That happened in the first dream, but as the nights progressed, the dream became more clear. Maybe if it keeps happening, eventually I'll know what's being said."

He picked up his fork, but didn't take a bite. He kept his dark gaze centered on her face. "How did you know the girl in the second dream was Molly?"

"Like I said, I didn't recognize her at first, but once I got a look at her, I didn't have the slightest doubt. She has these huge blue eyes and her eyebrows arch up in this sweetly feminine way. She has your nose, you know — only smaller, of course. I'd like to see a picture of your wife —"

"Ex-wife," he corrected.

"Yes, well, I'd like to see if I can pick out

Molly's features in her."

He leaned toward her. "That's it? That's all you saw? Three women working in a kitchen?"

She didn't want to tell him; it was bound to be painful. But if they were going to have any chance of success she had to be completely truthful.

"There was something else . . . something that convinced me I had to look for her, try to find her."

"Say it. I can tell you don't want to."

She released a slow breath. "In the dream — for an instant — Molly turns and looks straight at me. There is so much pain in her eyes . . . so much despair. It seems to run soul-deep. It's as if she is begging for my help."

Ben just sat there, his chest squeezing like a thousand-pound boulder sat on top of it. What if Autumn Sommers was telling the truth? If he closed his eyes, he could see Molly's big blue eyes looking at him from beneath the sweet, pale arch of her brows. If Molly was alive, was she being beaten, abused? Or was she just desperately unhappy, living in a place she didn't belong — being raised by strangers who weren't her family and didn't really love her?

If she still lived, did she remember her real parents? She had been old enough and yet maybe, over the years, those memories had slowly faded.

Ben shoved his salad away without taking a bite. "Here's what I'm going to do. Tomorrow I'll talk to Pete Rossi, the private detective I hired to investigate you."

Two days ago, Pete had called him in response to Ben's inquiry about Autumn and Gerald Meeks. According to Pete, Autumn had indeed spoken to Meeks at the federal prison in Sheridan, but Rossi couldn't confirm what Meeks had said. The inmate had refused his request for a visit and probably wouldn't have told him anything anyway.

"I'll ask Rossi to start digging around, see if he can turn up anything new about Molly's disappearance." He hadn't done this yet. He'd wanted more proof that Autumn's crazy dreams were real.

"Did Rossi work on the case when Molly first disappeared?"

"No. I used a different agency. But I think it might be better to start fresh. Look at the whole thing from a different perspective."

"That sounds like a good idea." Autumn gave him such a bright, hopeful smile that Ben found himself oddly disarmed. "So we're going to start looking?"

He leaned back in his chair. "Don't get too excited. I said I'd ask Pete to do a little digging. I'm not about to set this whole thing in motion — not yet."

"But —"

"Cancel your climbing trip and I'll pick you up for the benefit at seven o'clock tomorrow night."

She toyed with her fork, eyeing him across the table. "Are you sure your friends won't think you're lowering your standards? I'm hardly a cover model."

No, she was nothing at all like Delores Delgato or any of the other women he was likely to take to this kind of affair. But she was smart and interesting and — though she didn't seem to know it — sexy as hell. An image of Autumn's tight round behind flexing as she climbed the wall sent a shot of pure lust into his groin. She chewed her bottom lip, which was rosy and full and made him want to run his tongue across it.

Under different circumstances —

Ben cut off the thought. "To tell you the truth, the evening will probably be a whole lot more interesting with you instead of someone who doesn't really want to be there in the first place. Now eat your salad and let's enjoy our meal. We can talk about climbing, if you want. That shouldn't be too personal."

Autumn's small shoulders relaxed and she gave him another smile. It made her seem completely sincere and utterly without guile. He reminded himself he couldn't risk trusting her — not yet. He had to think of Katie and Joanne, his parents and the rest of his family. He refused to see them suffer again.

Time was what he needed. Time to know if Autumn Sommers was telling the truth. And if she was, time to discover whether or not — as impossible as it sounded — her dreams might lead him to Molly.

But how much time did he have?

Ben prayed that his need for caution wouldn't come at Molly's expense.

NINE

Autumn was tired when she got back home. The evening with Ben had been taxing. She knew it was the sexual attraction she felt for him that she didn't want to feel. She tried to tell herself it was only natural with a man as handsome and charming as Ben, but the truth was that Ben seemed to affect her in a different way than other men.

Usually, she had a knack for keeping the opposite sex at arm's length. She let men know early on that she enjoyed their friendship but she wasn't interested in anything more. Most of them accepted it, some were maybe even a little relieved.

Ben was different. There was a look in his eyes that said he saw her as a woman, an object of desire that had nothing at all to do with friendship. It surprised and flattered her. The man dated the most beautiful women in the world. That he would show the slightest interest in her was amazing.

Of course she could be wrong. She could be seeing something that wasn't really there. Or perhaps he was just that way with women in general, seeing each of them as an object to be conquered.

Ronnie Hillson had been that way — charming her, pretending an interest in her that lasted through the month they had dated, then disappearing the day after he took her to bed. At first she believed she must be a really bad lover, but eventually she decided that more likely it was the conquest that had interested Ronnie and she was just too naive to see.

Autumn yawned as she headed for the bedroom, stripping off her sweater along the way. She had called Josh on her cell on the way home from the restaurant to apologize for breaking off their climbing date again.

"Things happen," he'd said. "It's no big deal. Mike Logan's been bugging me to go. I'll ring him up, see if he can get his shit together by tomorrow morning."

"Mike's not ready for Castle Rock."

"Yeah, I know. We'll go somewhere else." She could almost see Josh grin. "Which is good because I wouldn't want to tackle Castle Rock with anyone but you."

"I'm really sorry, Josh."

There was a pause on the end of the line. "You . . . uh . . . seem kind of pre-occupied lately. You'd tell me, wouldn't you, if something was wrong?"

"I'm fine. I've been having a little trouble sleeping is all. I'm sure it will pass. I'll talk to you next week." She'd hung up the phone and found Ben watching her.

"Sounds like your friend, Josh, is worried about you."

"He's a very caring guy."

"You sure it isn't more than that?"

Her head had come up at the odd note in his voice. "Actually, Josh is in love with my best friend, Terri Markham. Unfortunately for Josh, Terri doesn't know he exists."

"Poor guy."

"Yeah. I keep hoping Terri will open her eyes and see how great Josh is."

The taxi had pulled up in front of her building a few minutes later and Ben insisted on escorting her to her door. She didn't invite him in and it was clear he didn't expect her to. She'd said good-bye, then closed the door and leaned against it, surprised to discover how fast her heart was racing.

Damn.

Autumn sighed as she undressed and tossed her clothes on the bed. Feeling any sort of physical attraction to Ben McKenzie was the last thing she wanted. The man was way out of her league and even if he was interested — which he probably wasn't — she'd be a fool to even consider getting involved with him.

Autumn hung up her clothes — determined not to think of him — slipped into her pink shortie nightgown, drew back the covers and crawled into bed.

That night, she dreamed.

Ben spent all day Saturday at his office, working on the problem of A-1 Sports and their threat to his Issaquah store. He made a phone call to Russ Petrone, the real estate broker who'd been keeping him informed, and Russ told him A-1 had officially made an offer on the vacant lot on the corner across the street from his store.

"Sonofabitch."

"The sellers haven't accepted yet, but it looks like they probably will."

"Not good news."

"You said A-1 wants to buy your stores. I got this info without much trouble. I think they want you to know. Probably figure the threat of a competing store so close might be enough to get you to accept their offer."

"I'm sure that's what they're hoping but

I'm not taking the bait, which means they'll have to go one step further."

"You think they'll actually build across the street?"

"I think they'll go that far if they have to. They'll figure if they can drive down the profits on the Issaquah store — maybe even force it to close — I'll be inclined to accept their offer for the chain."

"Anything you want me to do?"

"I want you to talk to the owners of that property. Keep it quiet, but see if you can find out the terms of A-1's offer. Tell the owners we'll up the price by twenty percent but the sale has to close in three business days. And if they go back to A-1, the deal is no longer on the table."

For their plan to work, A-1 had to buy that particular piece of property. There was nothing else suitable in the downtown area or anywhere close and it didn't look like there would be anytime soon. If Ben could quietly make the purchase and keep the land out of A-1's hands, the company would be out of luck.

"You sure you can close in three days?" Russ asked.

"You make the deal. I'll find the money."

Russ hung up with a promise to call him back with any news and Ben made a call to

Pete Rossi — the second attempt of the day.

"Sorry I didn't get back to you," Pete said. "My cell's been out of range."

"Not a problem. Damn phones don't work half the time."

"After the deal with Meeks, I'm guessing you want me to take another look into your daughter's disappearance."

"Good guess."

"You figure if Gerald Meeks didn't kill her, there's a chance she might still be alive."

"So far you're one step ahead of me."

"So how does the Sommers woman fit in?" Pete asked.

Ben had been careful not to tell Rossi any more than he had to, but he trusted the investigator and if he was going to go on with this, he had to play it straight. "About two weeks ago, Autumn Sommers approached me about Molly. She claimed she was having recurring dreams about her. I know it sounds crazy, but she was determined enough to go see Meeks, which couldn't have been pleasant. And she knows things, Pete, things that weren't in the papers."

He told the investigator about little Robbie Hines in the yard, how the boy wasn't mentioned in the papers, yet Autumn had described him perfectly. "If Meeks really told her he didn't kill Molly, then I can't ignore the possibility that this might be real."

"I've known a few cops who worked with psychics. I used to think it was all a load of crap but according to a couple of the guys, sometimes it worked. If Molly was my daughter, I'd be willing to try just about anything."

"Thanks, Pete."

"I'll call you, whatever I find."

Ben hung up the phone and leaned back in his chair. It was starting again. The whole awful mess was starting all over and he felt helpless to stop it.

The phone rang just then, his private line. He looked at the caller's number and saw that it was Katie. He took a deep breath and picked up the phone, heard her sweet voice and smiled.

"Hi, honey."

"Hi, Daddy. I just called to make sure you didn't forget you were picking me up tomorrow."

"Do I ever forget?"

"Well no, but I just wanted to be sure. We're going out on the boat, right?"

His forty-foot cabin cruiser, *Katydid.* "Yup, and I'm bringing us a picnic lunch. I haven't forgotten." Katie loved boats and anything to do with water. She wanted him to take her kayaking, teach her the sport, but she was only ten and it could be dangerous and he worried she might get hurt. He and Joanne were both overly protective, he knew, but they had already lost one daughter. He wasn't taking any chances on losing another.

"Okay, Dad, I'll see you tomorrow."

"Love you," Ben said. And he did, wildly. He never missed one of his visitation days and always tried to make them special for Katie. But he didn't ask for more time than what the courts had allotted. He knew he should make an effort to be with Katie more often, knew that Joanne wanted him to, but something always seemed to get in the way. He told himself it wasn't how much Katie reminded him of Molly. It wasn't that when he looked at her gleaming blond hair and big blue eyes, an ache rose in his chest.

An image surfaced of his first-born daughter, the one he had believed long dead. He thought of Autumn Sommers and the swirl of uncertainties that were pulling at him with inescapable force and prayed Autumn was as innocent and sincere as she appeared.

Not a woman with her own agenda who might wind up destroying him and the people he loved.

■ ■ ■ ■

Autumn paced her living room, more nervous than she would have imagined. It was ridiculous. So what if Ben McKenzie was the darling of the social set and she was wearing a black and silver sequined gown she had bought on the sale rack at Macy's? It had never bothered her with Josh. Of course Josh wore rented tuxedos.

She took a deep breath and slowly let it out. She'd been tempted to cancel the date. She hadn't slept well last night. After her last dream of Molly, she had placed a pencil and notebook next to the bed, determined to write down each detail exactly as she had seen it. When the dream came and jolted her awake, she had turned on the light next to the bed and started writing, jotting down every image she had seen while it was fresh in her mind.

Unfortunately, she was wide awake by the time she finished and unable to get back to sleep until nearly dawn. She would have cancelled if she hadn't wanted to talk to Ben and go over the details of the dream, which were now a little clearer than before.

Autumn glanced at the antique clock above the sofa, saw that it was a quarter to seven. Time dragged and her nerves spun tighter as each minute slowly ticked past. She thought about opening the bottle of Mumms that Terri had given her for her birthday. Maybe a glass of champagne would calm her nerves.

In the end, she just paced, hoping Ben would arrive on time, staring at the clock and wishing the hands would move faster.

He arrived right on the hour, coming up to her door as he had before, then waiting in the living room while she went to get her black pashmina, meant to serve as her wrap for the night.

He turned to her as they stood in front of the elevator waiting for the doors to open. "By the way, have I told you how stunning you look?" His eyes, the color of finely aged whiskey, moved over her with obvious appreciation.

"You don't have to be kind. As I said, I'm not a cover model."

He caught her shoulder and turned her to face him. "You really don't know, do you?"

"What are you talking about?"

"You don't have to be a cover model to be a beautiful woman, Autumn. You're different, that's all. You have an incredibly pretty face and the most glorious dark-copper hair. You have your own sort of style and you wear it extremely well."

She felt a rush of pleasure she didn't want to feel. He had noticed the way she had styled her hair, and sprinkled in a bit of silver glitter. Long rhinestone earrings dangled from her ears. Her black-and-silver gown was strapless. She had cut off the tiny straps herself, giving it the sleeker appearance she preferred. The slinky black fabric curved down over her hips, then flared out at the bottom, and she had sewn a row of silver sequins around the hem. Though she liked the way the dress had turned out, she was afraid Ben would think it looked cheap.

Apparently he approved.

"You don't have to take a backseat to anyone, Autumn." He smiled as he slid his arm around her waist and urged her into the elevator. "I'm glad you agreed to come."

She was there with him, but finding the right time to talk about Molly wasn't going to be easy. As they climbed into the back of the long black limousine that waited at the curb, she flicked a glance at her escort. Ben looked gorgeous. He was wearing an Italian-cut tuxedo, Armani maybe. She wasn't that good at fashion, but she could tell it was expensive and perfectly suited his lean, hard-muscled frame.

In the limo, he opened a bottle of Dom

Perignon and poured the champagne into stemmed crystal glasses. He handed her a glass and held up his own.

"To successful ventures."

She eyed him over the top of the glass. "To success," she repeated. She started to take a sip, then stopped, understanding his toast meant that he had begun the search. "You spoke to Pete Rossi."

"I told you I would. He's a good man. If there's anything new to find, Pete will find it."

Autumn sipped her champagne and tried to sound casual. "I dreamed about her again last night."

Tension crept into Ben's shoulders. "What did you see?"

Autumn opened her small black beaded purse and took out the copy she had made of the notes she had taken in the middle of the night.

"I wrote everything down. You can look it over whenever you get time."

Ben flicked on the light inside the plush interior of the limo and read each of the lines she had written.

"This is fairly detailed. All three women were attractive, tall and slim, with long blond hair and blue eyes. You say that nothing about them seemed to show a concern for fashion. What does that mean exactly?"

"I'm not sure. But considering they were all fairly young, they were dressed rather simply — not a Tommy Bahama T-shirt in the bunch."

"You guessed their ages . . . Molly twelve — well, almost twelve at any rate. One of them appears to be about fifteen. The other late thirties."

"That's right."

"You say the house was inexpensively furnished — an older stove, a long table in the kitchen beneath an overhanging lamp. The women seemed to be setting the table for dinner." He looked up. "It says you could see mountains out the kitchen window."

"This was the first time I noticed them."

"Mountain peaks or just hills?"

"I'm not sure. I just caught a glimpse. I couldn't tell if they were granite or sandstone or anything else about them. And nothing about them looked familiar."

Ben's dark gaze moved over her face. "You've dreamed every time we've been together."

"Yes."

He seemed to file that information away, went back to studying the rest of the notes she had made, then carefully folded the sheets of paper and stuck them into the inside pocket of his tuxedo jacket.

They reached the location of the benefit, held in a ballroom of the ritzy Fairmont Olympic Hotel. Now that she had given Ben her latest information on the dream, she could relax a little. Maybe even try to enjoy herself.

Well, at least as much as her nerves would let her.

Ben helped her out of the limo and they walked along the red carpet into the hotel, one of the Pacific Northwest's most stunning, with magnificent molded ceilings and Corinthian columns in the lobby and an ornate curving staircase leading up to the Spanish Ballroom on the second floor. Autumn had been there for drinks on special occasions, but this was different. She was a guest here tonight and she was determined to make the most of it.

Ben moved through the lobby like a man who belonged in the elegant surroundings and she clung to his arm.

He leaned toward her. "You said you like to play dress-up. Well, Cinderella, you can't do much better than this."

No, it didn't get any better than this. She was attending a ball with Prince Charming, but just like Cinderella at the end of the night, her coach would turn into a pumpkin and she would return to the real world where she was merely a grammar school teacher.

And Prince Charming would only come looking for her as long as he needed her to help him find his daughter.

Inside the fabulous Spanish Ballroom, they were seated at a round table with six other people, all of them formally and expensively dressed. Ben introduced her, telling them she was a friend of his, a schoolteacher as well as a professional climbing instructor who was currently giving him lessons.

The men looked her over, considered her size and cast her dubious glances, but the women were clearly intrigued. Autumn found herself answering questions about climbing and the skill it required and beginning to actually enjoy herself.

"You see, you're doing just fine," Ben said to her softly. "I knew you would."

"Did you?"

"Yes, I did. You're the only one who seems to doubt your capabilities."

She looked up at him. "Not when it comes to climbing."

"No, not then."

Dinner was served and the speeches

began, thankfully not lasting nearly as long as she had feared. Then the eight-piece orchestra began playing slow, romantic Frank Sinatra–style music — perfect for a Cinderella night.

"Anyone who likes to wear ball gowns must like to dance." Ben shoved back his chair, stood up and offered her his arm. "May I have the pleasure?"

She smiled and accepted. Ben guided her out onto the dance floor and she turned and went into his arms. He looked incredibly handsome tonight. With his dark hair perfectly combed, his solid jaw and tanned complexion, he drew the attention of every woman in the room. She tried to ignore the closeness of his big, hard body, the smooth way he led her in the steps of a waltz, how warm his hand felt wrapped around her own.

"God, you smell good," he said, cutting into her thoughts.

"Michael Kors — perfume not cologne — and it costs a fortune. I know it's a wicked indulgence but I figure I'm worth it."

"Ahh . . ." He bent and pressed his cheek against hers as he stepped into a turn. "What other wicked indulgences do you allow yourself, Autumn Sommers?"

Thinking of the tiny pink butterfly tattooed on the left cheek of her bottom, her face went warm. She looked up to see Ben watching her, a faint smile on his lips.

"All right, let's have it."

"Not a chance."

"I won't rest until I know what it is."

She shook her head. "Not going to happen."

Ben ran a finger along her cheek. "I'll take that as a challenge. I never could resist a challenge."

The formal evening didn't drag the way they usually did. Instead, Ben found himself enjoying himself, smiling at something Autumn said, pleased by the excitement in her pretty green eyes, her obvious pleasure in such a lavish affair. Most of the women he dated had been to dozens of events like this one. They endured but didn't really enjoy them.

Autumn was different.

In fact, the entire evening had been different from the moment he had opened the door to her apartment and seen her in her remodeled evening gown. He knew it wasn't expensive, but somehow she had made it appear as if it were, and the body-hugging style perfectly showed off her small, toned, nicely curved body.

Until tonight he had thought her merely pretty but he had told her the truth — with her shiny dark copper hair, finely arched eyebrows and delicate features, Autumn was a beautiful woman.

As dessert was served — a tower of chocolate curls topped with whipped cream on a bed of pureed raspberry sauce — he found himself staring into those green cat-eyes and had to remind himself to eat. It was amazing. She wasn't even his type.

He reminded himself of that again as he watched her little pink tongue dart out to lick a smudge of whipped cream from her spoon. She wasn't his type and for all he knew, she could be three bricks shy of a load.

They danced again and he held her a little closer than he should have, surprised to discover how well her small frame tucked into his. Desire spilled through him and he was hard before the music really got started, but then he'd been aroused on and off all night.

He couldn't help thinking about the wicked perfume she wore and the even more wicked something she wouldn't tell him about. It would drive him mad until he discovered what it was and yet he damned well knew how dangerous it was to get involved with her on any sort of personal level.

Still there seemed no way to avoid it.

They were riding in the limo on their way back to her condo when he hit her with his latest demand.

"It was a nice evening, wasn't it?" he said casually, easing into the subject he wanted to discuss.

Autumn looked at him and smiled. "I had a wonderful time, Ben. I didn't think I would enjoy myself but I did. I really did feel like Cinderella."

He straightened a little, gearing himself up for the argument he knew would come. "I hope it won't spoil your memory of the evening when I tell you Prince Charming is planning to spend the night."

"What?"

"Not in your bed . . . at least not without an invitation."

"What are you talking about?"

"Look, Autumn, you've had this dream of yours every time we've been together. Odds are you'll dream again tonight. If you do, I want to be there when you wake up."

"No way. I am not letting you stay with me. No way, no how, no sir."

He gave her what he hoped was a disarming smile. "You aren't afraid of me, are you?"

Autumn eyed him with suspicion. "There's such a thing as date rape, you know. Maybe once I let you in —"

"I don't have to rape my women. I don't intend to start with you."

She stared at him for a moment, then blew out a breath. "Look, I'll write it all down, just like I did before. I won't leave anything out."

"Let me stay. When you wake up, I'll be there to help you focus. I'll ask you questions while your mind is fresh. Maybe something important will come out."

She chewed her bottom lip, a habit he had noticed, whenever she was nervous. Her lips were plump and glossy and a soft shade of rose. His groin tightened and a shot of lust hit him like a fist in the stomach. He couldn't remember the last time a woman had turned him on the way this one did.

"Let me stay," he coaxed, wishing he wouldn't be sleeping on the sofa but next to her in that sweetly sexy canopy bed.

"It's a bad idea, Ben."

"All of this is a bad idea. The whole damned thing is totally insane."

"I know it is — but it's happening just the same."

"Then let me stay. If I'm satisfied your dreams are for real, you'll have my complete cooperation. We'll work together, do whatever it takes to find out the truth about Molly."

The limo rolled to a stop. An instant later, the driver jerked open the door. Autumn turned to get out, but Ben caught her arm.

"What's it going to be, Autumn? We keep dancing around this or we set things in motion?"

Autumn released a long, resigned sigh. "All right. You can stay, but you're sleeping on the couch."

Ben wasn't sure it was truly a victory but he nodded. His driver gave him a conspiratorial wink as he stepped out of the car.

Apparently, his reputation preceded him.

If you only knew, Ben thought. He hoped Autumn wouldn't notice the driver's knowing grin.

TEN

Autumn unlocked the door to her condo, her nerves kicking in again. For God's sake, Ben McKenzie was spending the night with her! Well, not exactly *with* her. Not in her bed, at any rate.

The thought sent a sliver of heat into her stomach. Dear God, even on the sofa the man would be far too close for comfort. She found him ridiculously attractive and he would be there in her living room, sleeping just a few feet away.

He's there for good reason, she told herself. *It's really no big deal.* At least it shouldn't be. For one reason or another, Josh had slept on the couch at least four or five times. But Josh wasn't Ben and that was the rub.

Autumn flicked a glance at the tall man standing beside the breakfast bar stripping off his black tuxedo jacket. He tossed it over the back of a chair, then proceeded to remove his black bow tie, unfasten his gold-

and-onyx cufflinks and remove the matching studs that closed the front of his pleated white shirt.

When he started to tug the shirt out of his trousers, Autumn held up a hand. "Wait a minute! What do you think you're doing?"

"I'm taking off my shirt. You don't expect me to sleep in my clothes, do you?"

"I don't know, I . . . I mean, you should have thought to bring something with you or . . . or . . ."

"Look, I didn't plan this. After I read the paper you gave me with the details of your dream, it seemed like a good idea."

She nervously chewed her lip. "Maybe we should try it a different night when we're both better prepared."

Ben unfastened the last of the studs and his white shirt parted, exposing his chest. It was wide and muscled and lightly furred. Autumn's gaze moved over that hard male anatomy and her stomach contracted.

"You're looking at me like you've never seen a man's bare chest before."

"Well, I —"

"There was good ol' Steven Elliot, remember?"

"Steve wasn't built like you." Autumn closed her eyes, wishing she could call back the words.

Ben stood there grinning. "I think I like you, Autumn Sommers. You have an honesty I haven't seen in a woman in years." He frowned. "At least I hope you do." He turned and walked over to the sofa, which wasn't all that big. "You got an extra pillow I can borrow? Maybe a blanket?"

She went into her bedroom and came out with a blanket and pillow and set them down on the end of the couch. When Ben went in to use the bathroom, Autumn gave him one of the extra toothbrushes she kept for emergencies then waited for him to come out.

Noticing she still wore her evening gown, he paused on his way to the sofa. "Unless you're planning to offer me a nightcap, I suggest we both go to bed."

She quickly nodded. A nightcap with a half-naked Ben McKenzie was the last thing she wanted. "If there's anything you need . . ."

Ben cast her a slow, sensuous glance that said exactly what he needed. "Actually there is one more thing." The husky note in his voice threw out warning signals, but she couldn't make herself move.

Ben walked over to where she stood in the bedroom doorway. "A Cinderella night wouldn't be complete without a goodnight kiss."

Before she could protest, he bent his head and settled his mouth very softly over hers. It was supposed to be a sweet, romantic good-night kiss and for a few brief moments it was. He tasted a little like chocolate and champagne and his lips were softer than they appeared and seemed to fit perfectly with hers.

She meant to pull away, to end the moment on a casually romantic note, but instead her lips parted under his, allowing him entrance, and his tongue swept in. A rush of heat slammed into her, then raced out through her limbs. Ben drew her into his arms and before she knew it she was clinging to his neck, kissing him back with the same urgency he was kissing her.

Her legs turned to jelly. Her body felt as limp as overcooked spaghetti and her lips trembled at the pleasure of his skillful mouth and tongue. He seemed to drink her in, to savor the taste of her. He nibbled the corners of her mouth, kissed her one way and then another, then kissed her deeply again.

She was trembling, her nipples aching, her body on fire for him. Her traitorous hands slid inside his shirt and she felt the intriguing texture of muscle over bone. It was the touch of hot bare skin that returned her to sanity.

Autumn jerked away as if she'd been burned, retreated quickly to the safety of her bedroom and firmly closed the door. Leaning back against the wall, she realized her heart was racing as if she had run a thousand miles and her legs were shaking, barely holding her up.

Good Lord, she had never been kissed that way, not by Steve Elliot or that weasel Ronnie Hillson or any other man. No wonder women fell at Ben's feet. Dear God, if he was this good at kissing what would he be like in bed?

Her eyes widened in horror at the thought. She refused to think of Ben in any sort of physical sense. With his reputation as a philanderer and her history of unwise choices where men were concerned, just kissing him was tantamount to a disaster. Autumn took a deep breath and worked to close her mind to any more thoughts of Ben and especially those that might wander in the direction of the bedroom.

On the opposite side of the wall, she could hear him in the living room, fiddling with his blanket and pillow. She knew he wouldn't sleep in his expensive tuxedo pants. She tried not to wonder whether he wore boxers or briefs.

Blowing out a breath, she came away from the wall, twisted her body around enough to unfasten the zipper on her sequined dress and stepped out of it. She took off her lacy black underwear and thigh-high black stockings and put on an oversize T-shirt that read CLIMBERS LIKE GETTING HIGH.

She preferred her pink shortie nightgown, but knowing that Ben McKenzie — the best kisser on the planet — was sleeping on the other side of the wall, she chose the T-shirt instead.

"Don't forget to leave your door open," Ben called from the living room.

Autumn walked over and jerked it open, ready to argue, grateful to discover the light was no longer turned on.

"If you start to dream, I'll be able to hear you," he explained, his deep voice drifting up from the sofa. "You might say something important."

He was right, of course. That was the reason he was there.

"Okay . . . all right, I'll leave it open." Leaving the door ajar, she finished her bathroom routine then went over to the bed, pulled back the covers and stretched out beneath the sheets. It took a while, but it was getting late and as tired as she was, she finally fell asleep.

Ben was sleeping in fits and starts. It had taken him an hour after that blazing kiss to bring his body under control enough to fall asleep. Damn, he hadn't expected the powerful jolt of desire that had swept through him the minute his mouth touched hers. Those ripe, sweet lips and a body that seemed to melt in his arms. She was incredibly responsive and it turned him on like crazy. There was something about Autumn Sommers that reached him in a way no woman had for a very long time.

As he lay awake for the second time that night, he found the thought disturbing. He liked his life the way it was. No entanglements, no emotional involvements. The risk just wasn't worth it. He knew the pain of losing someone you loved and he wasn't about to chance that kind of pain again.

Still, he had to admit the lady had captured his interest. Her mix of outside toughness and inside softness was intriguing. During the course of the evening, they had talked about hiking and camping and their shared love of the outdoors. He had mentioned his love of kayaking, and she said she had always wanted to try the sport.

She was in incredible physical condition, a true athlete, and according to Pete Rossi's report, one of the best climbers in Washington State.

And yet as he lay there looking at the dainty Victorian furnishings in her living room, as he caught the lingering scent of her soft perfume and thought how sexy she looked in an evening gown, there was no mistaking that this was a very feminine woman.

Intriguing. That was the word for Autumn Sommers.

To his perfectly ordered world, maybe even dangerous.

Ben sighed into the darkness. Currently, he was mostly in danger of not getting back to sleep. Though tomorrow was Sunday, he had work to do at the office in the morning and it was his day to pick up Katie. He plumped his pillow and tried to clear his head so that he could get some rest. He had just closed his eyes when he heard the muffled sound of Autumn's voice floating toward him from the other room.

Shooting up off the sofa, he raced through the open bedroom door. Autumn appeared to be sound asleep so he knelt quietly beside the bed. She seemed to be dreaming, her head tossing back and forth on the pillow, her lips moving, mumbling whispered words. He studied her a moment, making certain she was actually asleep and not pretending, assuring himself this wasn't some sort of ploy.

If she was faking, she was damned good. She whispered something else and he moved close enough to hear, heard her say, "No . . . not . . . Ruthie . . . Molly . . ."

He had no idea what she was talking about. Picking up the pad and paper she had put beside the bed, he wrote down the words but didn't wake her. Not yet. Not until she began to drift into a deeper sleep did he reach out to touch her. In the same instant, she opened her eyes and jolted upright in the bed.

"It's all right," Ben said gently. "You were just dreaming. Do you remember?"

She blinked several times, trying to get her bearings, then slowly nodded.

"Tell me what you recall."

Her hand trembled as she pushed back her thick dark hair, shoving the heavy curls away from her face. "They were there in the kitchen . . . Molly and the other two women."

"What were they doing?" he gently prodded.

"The older woman was scolding Molly for

something she had done but I don't know what it was."

"What else?"

"The older woman said something like, 'He'll be home any minute. We need to have everything ready. He doesn't like to be kept waiting.' "

"Go on. What else did you see?"

"I saw the mountains through the window, just like before . . . the simple kitchen with the light hanging down over the long wooden table." She closed her eyes for a moment, concentrating, trying to remember, then shook her head. "That's it. That's all I can recall."

"What about Ruthie?"

She glanced up at him. "Ruthie?"

"It was a name you said before you woke up. You said, 'Not Ruthie . . . Molly.' "

Her eyebrows drew together in concentration. "Not Ruthie . . . ?" She looked up. "Yes . . . now I remember. The older woman called her *Ruthie,* but it was Molly I saw. I don't know why she called her that."

Ben started to frown. "Maybe you have the wrong girl. Maybe you're dreaming about someone else."

Autumn caught his arm. "It's her, Ben, I know it."

"Then why did they call her Ruthie?"

She took a breath and he could almost see the wheels turning in her head. "I need a drink of water. Would you hand me my robe?"

He reached out and caught a handful of quilted pink satin trimmed with lace, dragged it off the foot of the bed and handed it to her.

A corner of his mouth edged up as she slipped the frilly garment over a man-sized T-shirt with CLIMBERS LIKE TO GET HIGH printed on the front.

Intriguing.

She moved past him into the kitchen, opened the refrigerator and took out a chilled bottle of water. She cranked off the lid and took several long swallows, then returned her attention to him.

"Maybe whoever took Molly didn't know her name so he just made one up."

"She would have told him her name," Ben said.

"Then maybe he didn't like the way it sounded or he figured someone might recognize the name so he changed it."

Ben mulled that over. "That's possible. He would have changed her name if he was afraid someone might see something about Molly on the news or read her name in the papers."

Autumn's fingers tightened around the plastic water bottle. "Dammit, I wish I could remember more or that the dream would go further."

"In time, maybe it will."

She looked up at him. "You were right to stay. I wouldn't have remembered the part about Ruthie. At least not tonight." She held out the bottle. "You want a drink?"

He took it from her hand and drank several big swallows. He caught a taste of her on the bottle. Memories of their kiss returned and his body began to stir. He handed back the water and pulled himself under control. "Thanks."

Autumn's gaze ran over his naked chest, moved lower and her cat-eyes rounded. "Boxers."

He couldn't help a grin. "Nice fitted ones, though. Not those big, baggy-legged kind. You thought I looked like a briefs man?"

She blushed. Even in the thin stream of light coming in through the balcony doors in the living room, he could see the slight rose in her cheeks.

"Actually, I never gave it any thought, one way or another."

"Too bad. I was hoping you had."

She flicked him a sideways glance, then turned away. "I've never dreamed more than once in a night, so you can go home if you want or you can stay until morning."

"I'll stay. I'm not much on wrestling the bums on the street this time of night."

She nodded as if that were a wise decision.

"Will you be able to go back to sleep?" he asked.

"It's never easy."

He reached out and ran a finger along her cheek. "I could help with the problem," he couldn't resist saying, letting his guard down a moment since he knew she would refuse.

Autumn backed away. "On second thought, maybe it's better if you wrestle the bums."

Ben just smiled. "Try to get some rest. I'll see you in the morning."

"Are . . . we going to start looking?"

His smile slid away. "Yes."

"We're going to find her, Ben."

He didn't answer. The possibility was too painfully remote. But he had made up his mind and from this moment forward he was committed to the search.

Ben lay down on the sofa, but he didn't fall asleep.

It was odd having a man in the house for

breakfast. Even when Josh had stayed over, Autumn hadn't cooked. They had always gone out to eat instead. For reasons she refused to examine, she felt like cooking this morning.

While Ben was in the shower, Autumn poured two glasses of orange juice, cooked bacon in the microwave, toasted a couple of English muffins, and scrambled some Egg Beaters with onions and tomatoes.

The table was set when he walked into the kitchen wearing the same tuxedo pants he had worn the night before, bare-chested, towel-drying his thick dark hair.

"Something sure smells good."

She tried not to stare but it wasn't that easy. The man had a beautiful V-shaped body that was all lean sinew and powerful muscle in just the right proportions. Of course she saw jocks with far bigger muscles in the gym all the time, but somehow it wasn't the same.

"I hope you like bacon and eggs," she said to him as he dragged on his wrinkled white shirt. "Well . . . bacon and Egg Beaters at any rate. My dad has high cholesterol. He got me started cooking egg substitutes, since they're better for him than eggs and they're also lower in calories."

"I'm not picky, especially when I'm starving." He hadn't bothered with his cufflinks and studs and the shirt hung open as he moved toward the table. "Anything I can do to help?"

"It's almost ready. Go ahead and sit down."

Ben rolled up his shirt sleeves, revealing those terrific forearms and sat down in one of the chairs at the small dining table in the living room. "It was nice of you to make breakfast. I can't remember the last time I've had someone cook for me."

She focused her attention on stirring the eggs. "Didn't your wife like to cook?"

He scoffed. "Jo hated anything to do with the kitchen. She didn't like to clean up the mess . . . or at least that's what she said. We ate out a lot, which was harder after the girls were born."

His expression closed up as he said this last and she knew he wouldn't say more.

"I enjoy cooking," Autumn said pleasantly. "What I make is pretty basic, stuff my dad taught me. I eat at home more often than I go out."

"I guess your dad mostly raised you."

She turned the burner off and reached for a plate. "My mom died when I was thirteen. She was killed in a car accident. Drunk driver swerved onto her side of the road. I

164

guess you probably know that."

He didn't confirm or deny it. "Must have been hard on you."

The loss of her mother was painful to discuss but she needed him to have faith in her and to do that, she had to be forthright, no matter how difficult the subject.

"Her death nearly destroyed me. I was always a little bit shy. After that, I withdrew almost completely. My dad decided I needed something to take my mind off losing my mother so he started to take me climbing. He has high blood pressure now, so climbing's out but we still go hiking once in a while and he exercises regularly to keep himself healthy."

Ben made no comment. He was looking at her in that way she had noticed lately, as if he were trying to figure her out. She set the plates on the table, filled their coffee mugs and sat down in the chair across from him.

"Actually, I'm glad you're here this morning." She took a sip of orange juice. "Now that we're ready to get started, we need some sort of plan."

"A plan," he repeated.

"I've been trying to think where to begin our search; what sorts of things we might do to get things rolling. To start with, I was hoping you'd have a photo of Molly you could lend me. I mean, I have copies of the ones that were printed in the newspapers but I need a real picture, not a copy."

"I've got a couple at home. I'll have to figure out exactly where I put them, but I know they're there someplace."

She paused in the midst of crunching into a strip of bacon. He had put away the photos, as if seeing them was too painful.

"What?" Ben asked, apparently not liking the way she was looking at him. "I said I'd get the picture and I will."

"Great." She bit down on the bacon, crunched a couple of times.

"Why do you want it, anyway?"

She reached for her coffee cup. "I want to have it computer aged. I've seen that done on TV. I want to make absolutely sure the girl in my dream is Molly."

Ben eyed her with renewed suspicion. "But you're fairly certain it is."

"I'm very sure it's her. I just don't want to cut any corners and besides, we'll need it if we're going to start a new search. She's twelve now, not six. We need to be able to show people what she looks like today."

"All right, I'll take care of it. The company has a very sophisticated Web site. That means we've got some really savvy computer geeks working for us. They'll know how to age the photo or find someone who does."

Autumn beamed. "That's great! What else should we do?"

"Well, since you dreamed about the guy who took her, you know what he looks like. Maybe you could go through the mug books down at the police station. See if you recognize a face."

She took a sip of coffee. "I already did that. I have a friend named Joe Duffy who's a detective. I spent an afternoon going over photos of known pedophiles in Seattle and the surrounding areas who fit the description."

"You told this guy Duffy about your dream?"

"I told him there was a man hanging around the school and I wanted to make sure he wasn't any sort of a threat."

Ben smiled. "Very clever."

"I'm not a good liar. I'm amazed Joe actually believed me."

"It was worth a try, even if it didn't pan out."

"What else can you think of?"

"I figure we should re-canvas the area where Molly was taken. In the last six years, maybe someone has remembered something they didn't think was important at the time."

"Good idea. I knew if we put our heads together —"

"Let's not get ahead of ourselves. So far all we have to go on is a dream about a blond guy with a puppy and girl named Ruthie who lives in a house in the mountains."

"Sorry." She toyed with her eggs, then finally took a bite. "So when can we drive out to Issaquah?"

"I'm busy today. I've got some work to do at my office and as soon as I'm finished, I'm taking Katie on a boat trip around the harbor. She loves boats . . . just about anything to do with water."

"I'd like to meet her sometime."

Ben made no reply. He kept his private life private and though Autumn felt a twinge of disappointment that she was excluded, she couldn't really blame him.

"So when can we go out there? We need to get started."

She could see he was still reluctant. She knew he didn't really believe they would find his daughter so the search was bound to be painful. But unlike Ben, Autumn refused to consider the possibility of failure.

"Ben?"

"All right, how does Monday sound?

When do you finish your lessons for the day?"

"I'll be done by two."

"I'll be working in my office. I'll meet you in the lobby at two-fifteen."

He didn't suggest she come up. He didn't want people knowing about the search. He was worried about his family finding out. He had mentioned his ex-wife several times. Autumn wondered if he might still be in love with her. The notion bothered her more than it should have.

As soon as they finished their breakfast, Ben grabbed his tuxedo jacket off the back of the chair, stuffed his cufflinks and studs into one of the pockets and slung the coat over his shoulder. "Thanks for the meal."

"No problem."

He opened the door but didn't leave. There was something in his eyes when he looked at her that made her breath catch.

"That kiss last night . . . I'm afraid this could get complicated."

Autumn hurriedly shook her head. "It won't. I won't let it. Last night was just . . . you know . . . a fantasy. We're working together, that's all. Strictly a means to an end."

Ben stared at her a moment, then nodded. As he stepped out into the hall and closed the door, she couldn't tell if he was relieved or disappointed.

ELEVEN

Right on schedule, Autumn finished her last private lesson, changed into jeans, a white cotton blouse and brown corduroy sport coat, stepped into a pair of loafers and headed for the lobby. Ben was just coming out of the elevator when she got there.

Earlier that morning, she had been a little surprised when Ben arrived at her climbing session, since he had already made his decision to help her. He didn't need to continue the lessons, but the man was an athlete who liked a challenge and climbing was certainly that. It was obvious by how fast he was improving that he had been reading extensively, had perhaps been getting help from some of the guys who worked at his stores.

He seemed determined to learn and he had a natural knack for the sport, scaling the wall this time all the way to the top without falling. She liked the way he moved, liked to watch the muscles working in his arms and legs as he shifted and pulled himself higher.

After class, Josh came in hoping to schedule another weekend trip and she introduced the two men. Their first few moments were spent sizing each other up the way men do, then Ben reminded her of their appointment that afternoon, nodded to Josh and left the climbing gym.

"So what about this weekend?" Josh asked after Ben was gone. "You must be getting the itch to hit the mountains by now."

She thought of Molly and the search she was committed to. "I can't say for sure, Josh. I'm really busy right now."

He tipped his head toward the door. "Busy with him?"

Autumn shook her head. "Not the way you're thinking. We're involved in a project is all."

Josh's gaze remained on her face. "Be careful, Autumn. That guy has a major reputation where women are concerned."

Don't I know.

"You get in too deep with a guy like that you're bound to get hurt."

Her stomach knotted. "You don't have to worry, Josh. But thanks anyway."

That had been two hours ago. Now it was two-fifteen and Autumn stood in the lobby waiting for Ben. She spotted him walking toward her in that purposeful way of his, as if time were a valuable commodity and he didn't want to waste it.

"My car's in the underground parking. Let's go." He urged her back toward the elevator he had just walked out of, climbed in and hit the button: Lower Level 1. His car was waiting in the valet area when they got there, a gorgeous silver Mercedes.

"Beautiful car," she said.

"I like it."

She surveyed the sleek, expensive automobile. "Nice as it is, somehow I thought you might be a little more energy conscious."

He flicked her a glance. "So what do you drive?"

"A Ford Escape hybrid. It gets thirty-six miles per gallon."

He patted the roof of his car. "This little beauty is an E-320 CDI. It tops out at about a hundred and sixty." He grinned. "It gets thirty-seven miles to the gallon — sometimes better. Let's go."

Autumn bit back a smile. It seemed to her that a guy in Ben's line of work ought to be environmentally conscious and for some ridiculous reason, she was inordinately happy to see that he was. He held open her door while she slid into the dark-gray leather seat, then rounded the car and climbed in.

They left Seattle and drove east on Interstate 90, heading toward the mountains. Autumn asked how his Sunday outing with Katie had gone.

He smiled. "It was a great day on the water."

"What kind of boat do you have?"

"Forty-foot Raptor. It's Australian-built. I'll admit it guzzles diesel big-time, but not as bad as some and it's one of the safest boats you can buy. Besides, I don't really use it that often."

Talk about boats led into a discussion of kayaking, Ben's favorite sport, but as the car drew closer to his old Issaquah neighborhood, the conversation became more and more sparse and his expression more and more grim.

"You have a store out here, don't you?" Autumn said, trying to lighten the mood. "It seems like I've driven past it."

They had exited the freeway and were weaving their way through the central area of town. Originally, it had been named Gilman, she had read, and was settled during a coalmining boom.

"The store's right up here on the left," Ben said.

Autumn spotted the sign, MCKENZIE SPORTING GOODS, above the door of a two-story brick building with dark-green canopies over the windows.

Ben pointed to a vacant lot across the street. "We just made a deal on that piece of land on the corner."

"You're expanding?"

He shook his head. "Just trying to stay ahead of the competition." As they continued through town, he explained about A-1 Sports and how they were trying to force him to sell his entire chain of sporting-goods stores.

"They don't know about the lot deal yet," he said. "Kurt Fisher's going to be fit to be tied." He explained about A-1's VP of acquisitions and how hard the man had been pushing to make the purchase.

By the time Ben finished, they were pulling up in front of a big gray stucco-and-stone tract house at the end of the block, but it was the beige house three doors down with the fancy brick trim that Autumn recognized instantly.

"This isn't your house. That's it down there. I saw it in my dream."

Ben's gaze zeroed in on her. "You sure?"

"Absolutely." It was clear he had purposely stopped in the wrong place just to see if she

175

would realize it wasn't the house where Molly had been taken.

"I have to be sure, Autumn. Or at least as sure as I possibly can be."

"It's all right." She glanced around. "What about your wife? If we talk to the neighbors, she's bound to find out."

"Six months after Molly was abducted, we moved out of the neighborhood. Neither of us wanted to live here anymore. There were just too many painful memories."

"I don't think I would have stayed either."

"Joanne and Katie still live in the house we moved into. It's here in Issaquah in one of the more upscale areas. Unfortunately, by the time we got settled, our marriage was basically over. We blamed each other for what happened to Molly, though deep down I don't think either of us really believed it was anyone's fault. Just one of those tragic things that happen. I was hoping if we started over, maybe things would work out. Mostly it was my fault they didn't."

"Why is that?"

"I started working longer and longer hours. I just didn't want to be home. Maybe I should have tried harder, but the truth is, our marriage wasn't that strong to begin with. If it hadn't been for the girls . . ."

He let the sentence trail off and Autumn

didn't press him for more. Trust was a two-way street. It was clear Ben was still hurting, even after all these years. Maybe in time he would trust her enough to share more of his feelings. They might even turn out to be friends.

That was what she wanted from a man, she told herself, *friendship, nothing more.* If she wanted to keep from getting hurt, it was crucial her relationship with Ben go no further.

They climbed out of the car and started walking toward the house next door to the one he and his family once had owned. A gray-haired woman in her seventies wearing a loose-fitting flowered pantsuit answered the knock at the door.

"Why, Ben McKenzie. What a surprise. What on earth are you doing out here?"

"Hello, Mrs. Biggs. It's nice to see you. This is Autumn Sommers. She's a friend of mine."

"It's nice to meet you," the older woman said, then returned her attention to Ben. "Still handsome as ever, I see. How long has it been . . . nearly six years, isn't it? Not since your poor dear little Molly —"

"That's what we wanted to talk to you about," Autumn cut in, ending the painful words.

"We were hoping you might remember something about that day," Ben added. "Something you didn't think of at the time."

She let out a pity-filled sigh. "Like I told the police, I was sitting in the family room watching TV when it happened. I can't recall which show it was, but —"

"Did you see anyone suspicious hanging around the neighborhood before it happened?" Ben asked. "Someone sitting in a parked car or maybe just driving around?"

"Not that I recall."

"Is there anything at all you remember that was a little out of the ordinary? Something that might have occurred before or after the abduction?"

Mrs. Biggs shook her gray-haired head. "Nothing that seemed unusual. I remember Mr. Bothwell's cat died the day before. He was surely broken up about that cat."

Ben took a breath and slowly released it.

Autumn caught his arm. "Well, thank you anyway, Mrs. Biggs." With a little tug, she urged him away from the door. Beneath his tan, his face looked paler than it had when they arrived. Until Mrs. Biggs had opened that door, Autumn hadn't really understood how difficult this was going to be for Ben.

Still, they were there and Autumn was determined.

They spent the next hour knocking on doors in the neighborhood, getting the same responses the police had gotten six years ago.

No one had seen anything.

"So much for canvassing the neighbors," Ben said darkly. His shoulders were stiff with tension and his jaw looked hard.

"It happened really fast, Ben. The neighbors were inside or out in their backyards."

"Yeah, I know."

"It was worth a try."

He nodded wearily.

"We need to talk to the children," she said. "The kids who were playing with Molly that day. I know that's the last thing you want to do, but we have to, Ben."

He clenched his jaw, but nodded. "There were only three of them besides Molly. They were all close to Molly's age and all of them went to the same grammar school. As far as I know, none of them have moved from the area."

"You know where they live?"

"They were all from this neighborhood or close by. I talked to them a number of times after Molly was taken. I kept hoping the kids would think of something that might help us find her, but they were all so little. I'm not sure how much they'll remember this many years later."

"I remember a lot of things from my childhood. Maybe one of them will, too."

"It's worth a try."

They climbed back into his car, drove to the first child's house a few blocks away and parked at the curb. This time of day even the kids in summer school would probably be at home or playing somewhere nearby.

Mrs. Sidwell, the mother of one of the girls in the yard that day, was sympathetic and polite. She warned Ben not to press Emily too hard.

"I don't know how much she remembers, you know? I think mostly she remembers all the excitement afterward with the police and all. And how sad everyone was."

Ben promised he would be careful.

Though the girl was now six years older, Autumn recognized her as one of the children in her dream. Dark-haired and dark-eyed with a dimple in her cheek. Unfortunately, Emily didn't remember anything more than she had told the police at the time of the abduction.

"I'm sorry, Mr. McKenzie," she said. "I was awful little then. I wish I'd been paying more attention."

"We all wish that, Emmie."

The other little girl, Megan Turner, began

to cry when Ben asked if she remembered Molly.

"I remember her," the twelve-year-old said, wiping away the wetness on her cheeks. "We were best friends. I never forgot her and I never will."

Ben swallowed hard. "I'll never forget her either," he said softly. "She's right here in my heart." He placed a fist over his heart and Autumn's throat closed up.

Megan put her arms around Ben's neck and gave him a hug and Ben hugged her back so sweetly Autumn had to look away.

Megan moved out of his embrace. She was tall for her age, her light brown hair cut shoulder-length and curled under. "Why are you asking me about Molly after all this time?"

When Ben seemed to grope for words, Autumn answered for him. "We're just trying to tie up some loose ends. We thought you might be able to help in some way."

"I wish I could. But all I remember about that day was a white car going around the corner at the end of the block with Molly inside, then everyone shouting and going crazy."

According to the newspapers, the car was pretty much all that the children had seen. Their descriptions of the man who had taken Molly had been so varied as to render them totally useless.

And Gerald Meeks had been driving a white Toyota at the time he was arrested.

There had been plenty of evidence against him in the other murder cases and there was, of course, his confession to those crimes. Though there was no blood evidence in the car and no DNA except his own, the white car seen during the abduction was one more reason to believe Meeks had murdered little Molly.

They returned to the front of Megan's house, Ben looking so exhausted and grim Autumn suggested they speak to the last child, Robbie Hines, another day.

"We're here," Ben said darkly. "Let's get it done."

When they pulled up in front of Robbie's house, the garage door was open and an old car — nineteen-fifty-something — sat on blocks with the hood open. A red-haired youth leaned into the engine, a grease rag stuffed into the back pocket of a pair of baggy jeans.

He turned at their approach and Autumn saw an older version of the boy who had been in her dream.

"Mr. McKenzie . . ." Robbie said. "It's nice to see you."

"Hi, Robbie."

Robbie looked a little older than the girls . . . maybe thirteen now, with short-cropped red hair combed up on the sides and a face full of freckles.

"Hello, Robbie." She gave him a smile. "My name is Autumn Sommers. I'm a friend of Ben's. We were hoping you might answer a couple of questions about Molly."

"That was a long time ago," Robbie said, obviously not interested in stirring up the past anymore than Ben was.

"We just want to know if there's anything about that day you might have remembered later, in the years since it happened."

Robbie looked uneasy. "They caught the guy, right? The guy's in prison?"

"He's in prison," Ben said. "We're just trying to tie up a few loose ends."

"He coming up for parole or something?"

Ben flicked Autumn a glance. "Meeks never confessed to killing her, Robbie. We just want to see if we might have missed something . . . anything at all."

Robbie jerked the rag from his pocket and wiped his greasy hands. "You know, there is something . . . I mean, I didn't know anything about cars when I was seven, but now . . . well, classic cars are a hobby of mine and my dad's."

"Go on," Ben urged.

"The car I saw that day . . . back then I didn't know what it was, but now I know it was a Chevy Super Sport. A Chevelle, the one with the big 396 engine. I've seen a dozen of them at car shows over the years. It wasn't fixed up or anything so it just looked like a plain old white car to me back then."

Autumn looked up at Ben. Inside her chest, her pulse was beating faster. Meeks had been driving a Toyota.

"I didn't think it mattered or I would have said something to the cops when I first figured it out. But Molly was . . . you know . . . dead. And the guy who killed her was in jail."

"I'm just glad you noticed it," Ben said. "I want you to tell me everything you can about that car."

For the next fifteen minutes, Robbie launched into a dissertation on collectible cars and the Chevy Chevelle in particular. "The day Molly was taken is burned into my brain . . . everyone crying, and talking to the cops and all the stuff that happened after. I can still close my eyes and see that car. That's how I recognized it when I saw one like it at the car show. A Super Sport like that . . . it's a real classic, worth some money even in poor condition."

Ben squeezed his shoulder. "Thanks, Robbie. You've really been a big help."

Robbie walked beside them out to Ben's Mercedes. "I think of her sometimes, you know. I guess I always will."

Ben nodded. "Yeah."

They climbed into the car and Ben started the engine. Autumn noticed the way his hands gripped the wheel and when she turned she saw that Robbie watched them until the car disappeared out of sight.

"Well, it's a lead," Autumn said into the quiet that had settled inside the car.

"Yes, it is. And if Robbie Hines is right, Gerald Meeks had nothing at all to do with Molly's disappearance."

Autumn's gaze snagged his in the mirror. "Which means my dreams might be real. If they are, Molly could still be alive."

TWELVE

"All right, girlfriend — you are dating *the hunk!* You have got to tell all!"

Autumn and Terri perched on stools at a tall round table in their usual spot at the back of O'Shaunessy's. It was Tuesday, six o'clock. Terri had just gotten off work, as had most of the patrons chatting noisily in the pub.

"We aren't dating," Autumn told her. "We're working together to find his daughter."

"But you said you went out with him Saturday night. The man took you to the Olympic Hotel, for God's sake."

Autumn had mentioned the evening with Ben and told her friend that she had agreed to give Ben time to get to know her, to hopefully come to trust her. And it seemed to have worked.

She hadn't told Terri that Ben had spent the night. Her friend would never believe that nothing had happened . . . well, almost nothing. There was, after all, that mind-shattering kiss.

"You're blushing. Oh, my God — what happened after the benefit? Don't tell me you slept with him!"

"Don't be ridiculous. You know why Ben and I are spending time together. It was your idea for me to talk to him in the first place."

Terri eyed her shrewdly. "You'd tell me, wouldn't you — if you had sex with him?"

"No. But I didn't. All he did was kiss me good night." There, it was out in the open. She hated to lie to her best friend.

Terri's eyes widened. "Well, come on — what was it like? A long, slow, dreamy, kiss, or a hot, burning, tongue-sucking orgy of a kiss?"

The color deepened in Autumn's cheeks. "It was just a kiss, that's all. Nothing out of the ordinary." *You liar! It was the hottest, wettest, sexiest kiss you've ever had and you will probably never forget it.* "Ben isn't my type and in case you haven't read the society pages lately, I am definitely not his. But right now we need each other. There's a chance his daughter is alive and if she is we need to find her."

"You're getting pretty involved in this,"

Terri said.

"I know I am. But I think Molly's reaching out to me. I can't turn my back on her. Besides, it wouldn't be fair to Ben. I dragged him into this. You can't imagine how painful this whole thing is for him. I'm not about to abandon him now."

Terri swirled the swizzle stick through the Cosmo she was drinking. "Just be careful. I *have* read the papers and we both know the guy is a heartbreaker. You can tell that much just by looking at him."

It was true and it was something Autumn didn't intend to forget.

"So what's the latest with Todd?" she asked, trying for a change of subject.

"Todd is a jerk. I never should have gone out with him."

Sooner or later, they all became jerks, at least in Terri's opinion. Autumn wondered if her friend would ever figure out what she actually wanted in a man. Then again, maybe she and Terri weren't really so different. For one reason or another, neither of them wanted to get into a serious relationship. They just approached the problem in an opposite manner. Terri slept with them and dumped them. Autumn rarely went out at all.

Across the table, Terri glanced up as a

lanky, familiar figure walked through the front door of the bar. "Look, here comes Josh." Her blue eyes rounded. "Oh, my God, *the hunk* is with him."

Autumn's head jerked toward the men crossing the bar in their direction, one of whom was Ben. "For heaven's sake, stop calling him that," she whispered to Terri.

Josh smiled as they reached the table. "Hey, Autumn . . . Terri."

"Hi, Josh," Autumn said. Terri smiled briefly at Josh then her predatory gaze fixed on Ben and a lump of ice settled in Autumn's stomach. She worked to keep the smile on her face. "Ben, this is my friend, Terri Markham."

"Nice to meet you, Terri," Ben said casually.

"You, too," said Terri and to Autumn's utter amazement she didn't ooze a single drop of her abundant female charm in Ben's direction.

"I tried to call you on your cell," Ben said, "but you didn't pick up. Then I saw Josh coming out of the gym as I was leaving the office. He thought you might be down here with Terri."

Autumn dug into her purse and pulled out her cell phone. "It's so loud in here I guess I didn't hear it ring." She stuck the phone back into her bag, suddenly realizing that if Ben was looking for her, it must have something to do with Molly.

"What is it? Did you find out something?"

He caught her elbow, urging her up off the stool. "Excuse us a minute, will you?"

"Sure," said Josh, who looked at Terri as if he had just received a gift.

Ben led Autumn out the front door and a little ways down the block. She hadn't realized he was carrying something in his hand until he held out a rolled-up sheet of paper.

"My guys got this for me. Take a look and see what you think."

Autumn carefully unrolled the paper. For several long moments, she just stared. It was the computer-aged photo of Molly. "It looks like her, I mean the way she is now, but . . ."

"But what?"

"But in my dream, her hair's longer, almost to her waist, and her lips don't seem as full, or maybe it's just that in the dream she isn't smiling, the way she is here." She studied the photo. "And there's something different about her eyes . . . In my dream, they don't seem as sparkly as they look here."

"She was happy the day the photo was taken. Joanne had bought her a pretty new dress and she was excited to have her picture taken in it."

There was something in his tone that made her look up at him. There was an odd glitter in his eyes and she saw that his jaw looked tight.

"You say she looks different," he said. "But this *is* the girl in your dreams? You still think it's Molly?"

"It's her, Ben."

He nodded. "I've got Pete Rossi working on finding the car. I looked up the make and model on the Internet and Robbie was right — it's a classic, pretty hard to find. The DMV has very good records. I'm thinking we start with Washington State, check the records six years back and compare them with those today. Rossi's an ex-cop. He's got connections with the force. He says he can get what we need."

Autumn nodded. "Starting in this area sounds good, though if I'd stolen someone's child, I might take her out of state, just to keep anyone from finding her."

"Even so, odds are good the guy was from somewhere around here. He must have seen Molly someplace, then found out where she lived."

"So we track down the car and — if we're lucky — maybe the guy still owns it."

"There's always a chance."

"But if he does," Autumn said, "I'm the only one who knows what he looks like. I've been thinking about this, Ben, and I think we need to do a sketch. You know, one of those composite-type drawings. They do it all the time on TV. That way we'll all know who we're looking for."

"Not a bad idea. Maybe the guy will turn out to be someone I saw in the neighborhood or somewhere else. If not, we can use it when we canvas car owners. I'll get Pete to find us a sketch artist, someone the cops have used."

"Maybe we should talk to the police ourselves."

"We don't have anything to give them. A dream and a thirteen-year-old kid who thinks he might have figured out what kind of car the kidnapper was driving six years ago."

"And the fact Gerald Meeks says he didn't kill Molly."

"Which Meeks told you but refused to tell anyone else." He sighed. "We need something concrete. When we find it, I'll talk to Doug Watkins. He was the lead detective on the case when Molly was first abducted."

"I thought the FBI handled kidnapping cases."

"They were involved. The guy who worked the case has since left the bureau and the two of us mostly butted heads anyway."

"But you think this detective might help?"

"Maybe . . . if we have something new to give him. But Watkins is a realist. He's not going to buy into this dream theory without any proof and the department's not going to want to spend money on an old case with no new evidence."

His gaze locked with hers. "You were with me yesterday morning. Did you dream about Molly last night?"

She moistened her lips, a little intimidated by that iron-hard stare. "Yes."

"Did you notice anything new? Anything different?"

"It was a long day and I was tired. The dream was kind of fuzzy."

"I want to stay at your house tonight. If you dream, I want to be there when you wake up." When she opened her mouth to argue, he held up his hand. "It helped the last time. I want to try it again."

Autumn shook her head. "We can't do that, Ben."

He knew she was thinking about the kiss and the edge of his mouth faintly curved. "I promise I won't attack you. I won't even kiss you goodnight . . . not unless you want me to."

She fought not to tremble. A memory of his mouth moving over hers sent a curl of heat into her belly. Of course she wanted him to kiss her — at least the insane part of her that still thought of sex craved it like a flower craved rain. The rational part of her pea-sized brain was terrified that it would happen.

"I'm not your type, Ben. You know it and so do I. And frankly, you're not my type either."

Ben looked amused. "I didn't know you had a type. The few guys you've dated all seemed pretty different."

Her hackles went up. Was there anything about her private life he hadn't read in his damn report? "Who I date is none of your business and you can bet that any man I might be interested in would not be one who specializes in cover models and one-night stands."

"Wait a minute! First — you're just as beautiful as any of the women I've dated, whether you see yourself that way or not, and second — I don't specialize in one-night stands."

"Just women who aren't interested in

anything remotely resembling a relationship."

"Are you saying you *are* interested?"

She bit her lip. The last thing she wanted was to get involved with a man and especially not a heartbreaker like Ben. "No, but —"

"I want to stay the night. No strings, *no sex*, strictly business. You talked me into looking for Molly. Now I'm committed to doing everything in my power to find her. I thought that's the way you felt, too."

"I do, I just . . ." She took a deep breath. Ben was a man who rarely took no for an answer. It was the reason he was so successful in business — and with women. In this case, he also had right on his side. Molly was his daughter and he would do anything to find her. Autumn could hardly fault him for that.

Still, she was already on dangerously thin ice where Ben was concerned. She would have to be extremely careful.

She released the breath she hadn't realized she had been holding. "All right. You win. But bring something to sleep in this time."

He grinned. "I sleep naked. In deference to you, I left on my boxers last time."

Her face heated up. "I'm trying to forget."

He reached out and touched her cheek.

"Are you? Because I'm trying like hell to forget how sexy you looked in that ridiculous over-sized T-shirt. So far it hasn't worked."

Autumn's jaw dropped. The nightshirt was the least sexy thing she owned. Her stomach fluttered as if it were full of feathers and her mouth went dry. "You're scaring me, Ben."

"Yeah, well, you're scaring me too. Let's just keep focused on Molly."

She was scaring him? She thought of Delores Delgato, the beautiful, exotic model. Now *there* was a woman who could frighten a man, though Ben didn't seem the least bit threatened.

She cast him a glance but couldn't read his expression and returned her thoughts to Molly. Maybe if Ben was there when she dreamed, another clue would surface.

"Okay. Then I'll see you tonight. What time?"

"I've got plenty of work to do at the office. How 'bout I show up around nine?"

She nodded. She almost weakened and suggested she cook him dinner — before sanity returned like a flashing neon sign, pointing out what a bad idea that was.

"See you then," she said.

"Yeah," he said softly. "See you then."

Ben worked late, then went home, stuffed his shaving kit and a change of clothes into a small canvas satchel and walked down Second Avenue to Autumn's condo. The air was warm and damp, the first days of summer were beginning to settle in. He inhaled the salty sea air and caught a glimpse here and there of the lights along the waterfront reflecting against the sea. A blue and gold taxi honked at the car in front of him but Ben barely noticed, preoccupied as he was with his earlier conversation with Autumn.

You're scaring me, Ben.

Yeah, well, you're scaring me too.

The words had just popped out, but as soon as he'd said them, he realized they were true. Intriguing little Autumn Sommers scared the holy bejeezus out of him. He wasn't quite sure why.

He only knew that when he had checked his calendar this afternoon and discovered he had a date Friday night with Beverly Styles, a woman he spent time with on occasion, the notion seemed so repugnant he had actually picked up the phone to call and cancel.

He couldn't, he'd realized. It was an

important affair for Bev and her father, Sam, a long-time friend and business associate Ben admired and respected. He would have to go, but he would try to end the evening as early as possible and he didn't intend to ask her out again.

Maybe it was just that finding Molly came first and doing that meant spending time with Autumn. Maybe it was just that Autumn was so different from any of the women he had dated since he and Joanne had divorced.

Hell, she was *way* different from the woman he had married.

Joanne came from an old-money, high-society family and that, along with her good looks and expensive education, had attracted him. Even after they were married, they'd led fairly separate lives. Ben worked long hours, Joanne was involved with her mother in charity events and spent her days at the country club.

After the girls were born, she was even busier and so was he, though on weekends they always made time for their children. At least Ben had until Molly disappeared from his life. After that, the less time he spent at home the better.

He sighed as he strode along the sidewalk toward Autumn's cozy apartment and reminded himself that nothing had changed. He still worked the same long hours. There still wasn't time in his busy schedule for a serious relationship with a woman. And he really didn't want one.

But whenever the unwanted notion crept in, he thought of Autumn in her ridiculous T-shirt, her strong legs and small feet showing beneath the hem. He remembered her sleekly toned body climbing the wall at the gym, the tight round cheeks of her bottom flexing in a way that made him hard just watching her.

He was in lust — of that he was sure.

He told himself he couldn't allow himself to feel anything more than that. He imagined what Autumn would say if he told her how much he wanted to take her to bed and he almost smiled. She was hardly the type for casual sex. He didn't have to read a report to know that.

He resigned himself to being on his best behavior as he knocked on her door and Autumn pulled it open. She was wearing a soft fleece jogging suit in a pretty apricot shade; her auburn hair curled casually around her face. She smiled and he remembered how soft her lips felt moving under his and his body tightened. When she looked up at him, lamplight glittered on the red, gold and mink-brown strands of her hair and he wanted to run his fingers through it.

"Come on in," she said and he did the damnedest thing. He reached out, hauled her into his arms and very thoroughly kissed her.

It was a long, deep, demanding kiss that had her swaying toward him with only a token protest. Then he stepped back and walked past her as if nothing out of the ordinary had occurred.

Autumn just stood there, her hand coming up to her lips.

"I brought my own pillow," Ben said lightly. "Yours was too hard." Parts of his anatomy were far harder, but he didn't say that to Autumn.

"You promised you wouldn't kiss me," she said tartly, still holding open the door.

"I said I wouldn't kiss you goodnight. That was a hello kiss."

Autumn closed the door. "You can't just waltz in here and . . . and . . ."

"Actually, I didn't plan to. I planned to be extremely well-behaved. You just looked so delectable I couldn't resist." He tossed the pillow down on the sofa and set his overnight bag on the floor.

"You have dozens of women, Ben. Why are you doing this to me?"

"I'm not doing anything. I kissed you, okay? It isn't a federal offense. You want to watch some TV?"

She stomped off into the bedroom. He wasn't sure why her reaction amused him but it did. When she came back out, she was once more in charge.

"This is my home." She marched over and stood right in front of him. "Therefore, I have some say in what happens here."

"Yeah . . . so?"

"So if I want you to kiss me, I'll let you know."

The corner of his mouth edged up. "I don't think you will. I think you want me to kiss you right now, but you won't say so because you're afraid of what will happen if I do."

"I'm not afraid of you or any other man!"

"Then why is it you never date? Why is it, the only men in your life are *friends?* Did Steven Elliot really hurt you that badly? Or maybe it was that guy, Ronnie Hillson. Any full-grown man who still calls himself *Ronnie* has to be a nitwit."

She was standing so close he could see the pupils of her eyes flare. When she swung, he almost didn't see the blow coming until it was too late. Thankfully, he caught her wrist before her hand connected with his cheek.

"You bastard! My private life is none of your business!"

He told himself to let go. He couldn't believe he had goaded her the way he had. He never did that to a woman. He always treated them with complete respect. And kept them at a distance.

"You're too good for a guy like that, Autumn," he said softly, gentling his hold on her wrist. "Hillson didn't deserve you and neither did that fool, Steve Elliot." And then he eased her closer and very tenderly kissed her.

For an instant, she resisted. Then a soft little sigh came from her throat and she was kissing him back. God, she tasted like apples — or maybe it was pears — and her mouth felt like silk under his. He went achingly hard inside his jeans and a jolt of pure lust tore through him.

You can't do this, he told himself but he just kept kissing her. He couldn't seem to stop. His hands sifted through her hair and silky curls wrapped around his fingers.

"God, I want you," he said against her cheek and then he kissed her again and drove his tongue into her mouth and felt hers slide over his. "I don't know what it is but I can't stop thinking about you."

Autumn trembled. "We can't . . . please, Ben . . . please don't do this to me."

He swallowed, then took a long, deep, shuddering breath. It took sheer force of will to pull away. At the loss of her warmth, his body clenched as if he'd jumped into an icy stream and he saw that Autumn was trembling. He pulled her against his chest and wrapped his arms around her.

"I swear I didn't come here for this. I can't figure out what's going on between us but something sure as hell is."

Her tremors began to lessen, but she didn't pull away. "It's just stress," she said softly. "Both of us are worried about finding Molly."

"I don't think it's stress." He kissed the top of her head and she turned to look up at him, her green eyes wide and uncertain.

"It must be. It has to be." Tentatively, she reached out and touched his face. "I wish you were someone else. Any man but Ben McKenzie." And then she kissed him full on the lips.

Her tongue was in his mouth an instant later and he thought how small and sleek it felt gliding over his. Her breasts pressed into his chest, soft and full and yet her nipples were diamond hard. His body clenched so hard he throbbed and desire poured through him.

He deepened the kiss and his hand found the hem of her zippered fleece jacket and slid beneath the fabric. She wasn't wearing a bra, he realized as his fingers curled over the apple-round fullness of her breast, testing the size and shape, the texture of her skin.

Ben groaned and Autumn trembled. She went up on her tiptoes to press herself more fully into his hand and he thought what a passionate creature she was and what a shame it was that she worked so hard to hide it.

He slid down the zipper on the front of her jacket and eased it off her shoulders. She had lovely breasts — the kind that tipped up — and her nipples were the color of pale pink roses.

He wanted her. Lowering his head, he took one tight bud into his mouth and Autumn's small hands slid into his hair. She arched her back, giving him better access, then jerked in a breath as he bit down on the end, began to suckle and taste her, circle the tip with his tongue.

She caught the hem of his pullover and tugged it up and over his head, leaving him bare-chested. Her lips pressed against his skin and his heart pounded. His groin contracted and his erection throbbed painfully against the fly of his jeans.

He hadn't been this turned on since he was a kid. He told himself it was just that she was so different, that she had caught his interest in a way few women ever had. He pulled the cord on her pants and eased them down over her hips. She was wearing a pair of tiny apricot thong panties that barely covered the russet curls between her legs and a shot of heat went straight to his groin.

In the antique mirror on the wall, he caught a glimpse of them standing there half-naked. The apricot thong rode between the cheeks of her bottom and his erection throbbed. He'd been itching to hold those tight globes since the day he'd first watched her climb the wall and he did that now, cupping the roundness, pulling her against his arousal, letting her feel how hard he was.

Autumn made a soft little whimpering sound that made him go harder still and in the mirror he watched them clinging to each other. It was such an erotic image it was all he could do not to drag her down on the carpet and bury himself as deep as he possibly could.

He watched a moment more, enjoying the

way his big body wrapped around her petite, feminine frame, then something in the mirror caught his eye. He moved his hand a little and there — tattooed on a pale, perfect globe — was the tiny image of a pink butterfly.

It was her *wicked secret,* he realized and the knowledge released something primitive inside him.

"I've got to have you," he said, kissing her fiercely as he lifted her into his arms and strode toward the bedroom, determined to satisfy this need he couldn't explain. "I have to have you *now.*" She clung to his shoulders as he settled her on the mattress and started to unzip his jeans.

When Autumn looked up at him, he couldn't miss the panic in her eyes. "What . . . what are we doing?"

"Something both of us seem to want very badly." Worried she was about to bolt, he leaned down and kissed her, taking his time, stirring the passion he knew was there. When she was pliant in his arms, he finally let her go, kicked off his shoes and stepped out of his jeans and the rest of his clothes.

She was staring at his erection, gaping as if she had never seen a man with a hard-on before, when the phone next to the bed began to ring.

His body clenched so hard he shook and Ben foully cursed.

The line rang again before Autumn jerked her gaze away and reached for the receiver.

She raked back her thick auburn hair with a shaky hand. "Hello . . . Myra is that you?" She sat bolt upright. "Slow down. Tell me what's wrong." There was conversation on the other end of the line. "Is he going to be all right? Yes, yes, I know you'll stay with him. I'm on my way. I'll get there as quickly as I can."

Her eyes were huge green pools as she hung up the phone and looked up at him. "My dad had a heart attack. I have to go." She shot off the bed and raced into the living room, frantically searching for her clothes.

His own clothes were scattered all over the floor. He pulled on his boxers and jeans, then found and put on the rest of his garments. Autumn was dressed and searching for her car keys by the time he finished.

She grabbed her purse and picked the keys up off the kitchen counter.

"I'm sorry, Ben . . . about everything. I don't know what happened, I just . . ." She shook her head. "I have to go."

Ben reached out and plucked the keys from her fingers. "You're in no shape to drive. Get your jacket and I'll drive you to the hospital."

"You don't have to do that — I'm fine. Besides, I've already made a mess of the evening. There's no need for you to —"

"Bullshit. You didn't make a mess of anything. Sooner or later, we'll finish what we started here tonight, but for now you've got more important matters on your mind. Now get your jacket and let's go."

For a moment, he thought she would argue. Instead, she hurried over to the closet, dragged a lightweight jacket off a hanger and started for the door. They took her car, since his was still parked at his apartment. Some of her climbing gear was in the passenger seat. She tossed it into the back with the rest of the stuff she carried and threw their jackets in the backseat.

Ben took the wheel and they headed out of town. He drove the little red SUV up on the Interstate and headed north. The roads were fairly easy to travel this time of night; it was a little over an hour's drive to Burlington. Autumn sat statue-still all the way, her eyes focused on the white line appearing ahead of them. It was clear she wouldn't be dreaming about Molly tonight. They'd be lucky if either of them got any sleep.

Under different circumstances, Ben might

have smiled. He would have kept her up late anyway, making slow, passionate love to her.

That wasn't going to happen tonight.

Worse yet, there was something in Autumn's expression that made him suspect it never would.

Thirteen

Autumn directed Ben to take the 230 Exit off Interstate 5 toward Burlington, then they headed up the North Cascades Highway to United General Hospital.

"You go on in," Ben said as they pulled into the parking lot. "I'll take care of the car and find you."

She nodded, cracked open the car door and took off for the entrance at a run. The woman at the reception desk pointed her toward the door of the emergency waiting room, where she found Myra Hammond, her father's long-time girlfriend, pacing impatiently just outside the entrance.

"Autumn! Thank God you're here!" A woman in her late fifties with silver hair tinted blond, Myra was slightly overweight but always well dressed and attractive. "Your father's inside but they won't let me in because I'm not a member of his immediate family."

"Is he going to be all right?" Autumn asked just as Ben joined them.

"I think so. The doctor came out a little while ago and said he was doing okay, but I'm still worried."

Autumn introduced Ben to Myra as a friend from Seattle, the person who had driven her up, making it sound as if they were only distantly acquainted. As if she hadn't been half naked with him a little over an hour ago, hadn't been on the verge of having wild, erotic sex with him — would have if the phone hadn't rung, saving her from the consequences of her wild, unbridled lust.

"What happened?" she asked.

"Well, he started having these pains in his chest and then he couldn't seem to catch his breath. I got scared and called 911. I think he was worried too, because he really didn't argue all that much. The ambulance brought him here and they've been running tests on him ever since."

"So you were over at his house when it happened?"

"We had an early supper and watched a little TV."

"Do you have any idea what might have caused this? Was he doing something overly stressful?"

Myra looked away, then down at her feet. "Well . . . I guess you could say that. You see, there wasn't anything good on TV and after a while . . . well, things got started between us and we wound up in bed, then your dad's chest started hurting and he couldn't seem to breathe and . . . well, you know the rest."

Autumn stared at Myra as if she had never seen the woman before. "Are you telling me you and my father were having sex when this happened?" Her voice rose a notch. It was ridiculous. Her father was an adult. He and Myra had been seeing each other for years. Her father could certainly have sex with the woman if he wanted.

"It isn't a crime, you know."

From the corner of her eye, she saw amusement curve Ben's lips.

Autumn kept her attention fixed on Myra. "But his heart . . . Dad has a heart condition, for heaven's sake. He isn't supposed to overexert himself."

Myra's silver-blond eyebrows went up. "He's supposed to get plenty of exercise, isn't he?"

"Well, yes, but —"

"He isn't supposed to drink, but he likes a glass of whiskey in the evenings and you don't seem to mind that."

"I do mind, but you know how stubborn he is."

Myra nodded sagely. "Well, there's something he likes even more than his glass of Jack."

Autumn's eyes widened.

"So how's he doing?" Ben interjected diplomatically, ending what was becoming a very disturbing conversation.

"Like I said, I think he's going to be okay. The doctor says he's feeling much better but they want to do a few more tests."

Ben turned to Autumn. "Why don't you go see what you can find out and Myra and I will wait for you here."

"Good idea." She should have done that already, she realized as she made her way through the doors into the emergency room waiting area, but she wasn't thinking all that clearly — *hadn't been all evening,* she reminded herself.

The emergency room doctor joined her at the front desk, a young-looking, dark-haired man wearing tortoise-shell glasses. His name was Leonard Jackson.

"Mr. Sommers is doing very well," Dr. Jackson said. "I think he may have suffered a case of acute indigestion. That combined with bit of overexertion brought on what appeared to be a heart attack. We'll keep him a day or two for observation just to make sure, but I think he's going to be fine."

She nearly sagged with relief.

"You can see him for a few minutes but don't stay too long."

Ignoring the antiseptic hospital smell she had always hated, Autumn went into a curtained enclosure in the middle of a row of six others. She found her father awake and grumbling.

"I told her it was nothing. Can't believe she went and called you too." He wasn't a tall man but his shoulders and legs were muscled from climbing for so many years and he didn't have the usual sixty-year-old's paunch. His high blood pressure and two-hundred-seventy-plus cholesterol had come as a surprise, linked to a bad gene somewhere in the family, the doctors said. So far Max had refused to take any of the prescription medications available, certain the drugs were worse than the high cholesterol.

Autumn wasn't sure she disagreed. "Myra was worried about you, Dad. She cares for you a very great deal."

He looked her straight in the face. "Ought to marry her, I guess. Make an honest woman of her."

Surprise jolted through her. Had Max just said the *M* word? Autumn couldn't believe it. His marriage to her mother had been a total disaster. Max Sommers had sworn he would never remarry and was constantly sending her e-mails with those dumb jokes about married men. Though he'd been seeing Myra for years, it never occurred to her that he might actually marry the woman.

Autumn looked at him lying there, paler than usual, his salt-and-pepper hair hanging over his forehead. "You aren't serious, are you? About marrying Myra, I mean?"

He gave a faint shrug. "At least she could have come in here with me. I mean, hell, we're almost living together."

He was serious. She couldn't believe it. She took a steadying breath. "I realize you have your own life, Dad. Whatever you decide is fine with me, but there is one thing you need to consider."

"What's that?"

"Your heart, Dad. You really think you and Myra should be . . . well . . . behaving the way you were with your high blood pressure and all?"

He grunted. "If I'm gonna die, I'm gonna die. Till that happens, I'm gonna live. You might try a little of that yourself."

She stiffened. Max was always pressing her to live her life, not be afraid of it. He had never pressured her to get married, but he believed she should experience life the way he always had. The way he had done when her mother had been alive.

One thing was certain. Max Sommers had been a rounder.

And he had never been faithful.

If she were honest with herself, she would have to admit her father's casual relationships with women was one of the reasons she kept men at a distance. She was afraid of what would happen if she fell in love with a man and wasn't woman enough to keep him from straying. Exactly what had happened with Steve.

Going up a mountain, she wasn't afraid, she was in control. But where men were concerned . . .

She thought about the way she had lost control tonight with Ben and felt her face heating up. How could she criticize her father when she and Ben had been doing the exact same thing?

"All right," she said to Max, "we'll leave the subject alone for now. I just don't want anything to happen to you."

Whatever problems her dad had with women, to her he'd been the best father in the world and Autumn loved him deeply.

He reached over and caught her hand. "Doc says I'm gonna be fine so there's no need for you to worry. I want you to send Myra home and go on back home yourself."

"You know very well that isn't going to happen. Myra won't leave and neither will I."

He didn't look pleased. "You drive down by yourself?"

"No . . . I . . . a friend drove me down."

"Josh?"

"No, a man named Ben McKenzie."

One of her father's bushy salt and pepper eyebrows went up. "McKenzie? Not the sporting-goods guy?"

She nodded, her mouth feeling suddenly dry. "He's a student in one of my climbing classes."

"That so? How long you been seein' him?"

"We aren't dating, Dad. We're just friends."

He frowned. "Another one of your man *friends?* From what it looks like in the papers, McKenzie doesn't have women friends." Max studied her hard. "You be careful with that fella, you hear?" Then the corners of his mouth curled up. "On the other hand, maybe it's time you *were* a little less careful. Maybe you ought to get rid of that bunch of neutered males you hang around with and find yourself a real man. Take a lesson from me and Myra."

Autumn's cheeks were burning. Her father's eyes closed for a moment and he relaxed against the pillow. It was obvious the events of the evening and all the talking had worn him out. A nurse appeared and shooed her out of the curtained-off area, telling her that in the next couple of hours Max would be moved into a private room. Dr. Jackson suggested that she and Myra go home but Autumn refused.

"We're staying," she said, certain Myra would agree.

"Suit yourself," said the doctor. "But visiting hours don't start till eight in the morning."

She returned to the waiting room and relayed to Myra the conversation she'd had with her dad. "He wants us to go home, Myra, but —"

"I'm staying right here," the older woman said firmly. "At least till I see him in the morning."

That became the plan and to her surprise, Ben seemed not to mind. He stretched out on a couple of chairs in the waiting room and fell asleep. He didn't wake up until morning.

Autumn couldn't help thinking that at least she was safe from Ben — and herself — for one more night.

"I want to meet him," her father grumbled. "He brought you down here, didn't he? Stayed up half the night just 'cause you were too stubborn to leave. Least you can do is introduce us."

Autumn bit back a frustrated curse. Since there was no talking Max out of it, she led Ben into the hospital room. His dark hair was mussed, a shadow of beard shaded his jaw and his clothes were rumpled.

"So you're Ben McKenzie."

"Nice to meet you, Mr. Sommers. Glad you're feeling better."

Her father eyed him warily. "Bought some gear from your store down in Seattle," he said. "Good quality merchandise. Still works just like new."

"We only carry the best. I'm glad you approve."

"My daughter says she's teaching you to climb," Max said.

"That's right. She's a very good instructor."

"So what are you teachin' *her?*"

Autumn's eyes widened. "Dad!"

"I think that's her business, don't you? Hers and mine. Just like last night was your business."

Max chuckled, assessed Ben a moment, then gave him a slow, man-to-man smile. "I like a plain-speakin' fella. Good to meet you, McKenzie."

Ben nodded. "You, too, Mr. Sommers."

"It's Max. Take her home, will ya? She's got enough to do without worrying over me. Besides, I got a woman of my own to take care of me."

"I met Myra," Ben said. "She seems like a keeper."

"Took me a while to figure that out." Max winked at Autumn. "But that's just what I intend to do."

Autumn bent over and kissed his cheek, then stepped outside the room and said her farewells to Myra.

"You'll call me if there's any sort of problem."

"You know I will," promised Myra.

Autumn gave her a hug, wondering how she could have missed the deepening affection between Myra and her father, and left the hospital with Ben.

"I can't believe he's thinking of getting married."

"Why shouldn't he? He's only about sixty, isn't he? That isn't all that old these days."

"He swore he would never remarry. He

was a great father, but he was a terrible husband. He and my mother fought like cats and dogs. They were fighting the night she died. It was the reason she left the house. Maybe if she hadn't been so upset, she would have been paying more attention while she was driving. Maybe she wouldn't have gotten killed."

Sitting behind the wheel of her Escape as they drove down Interstate 5, Ben flicked her a sideways glance. "You don't think the accident was your father's fault, do you?"

It was a question she'd asked herself more than once. "I guess I did for a while. Then I realized it might have happened anyway. Maybe some other night or a year down the road, or something else might have happened."

"That's right. There are lots of maybes in the world. Maybe if I'd been home the afternoon Molly was abducted instead of down at the office working, she would still be here. But it was a workday, just like any other. There was no way to predict what would happen."

"No . . . I guess there never is." She looked over at Ben, whose vision remained on the road as he continued toward the city. Both of them were tired and unkempt and she

221

couldn't remember the last time she had eaten.

"I talked to Pete Rossi this morning," Ben said. "I called him from the hospital. Pete's got the information we need on those car owners."

"How many are there?"

"According to the Washington State DMV, thirty-three."

"You still don't think we should go to the police? If the man who took Molly still owns the car, she might be living right there in his house. The police could interview the car owners faster than one man working alone. Once I've got that sketch completed, they'll know who to look for."

"First, the police department isn't about to expend that kind of manpower without more to go on than a boy who might have remembered the make of a car he saw when he was seven years old and a woman who saw the kidnapper in her dreams. Second, if the cops get involved, the guy might grab Molly and bolt before we even get close."

He caught her eye in the mirror. "But we do need that sketch. Pete's got an artist lined up for this afternoon, if you think you can make it."

"I'll make it. What time?"

"Three o'clock at your apartment."

"I'll be there."

They drove the rest of the way into the city without much more conversation. Autumn was exhausted and Ben's mind was on Molly and the DMV list Pete had retrieved for him.

They had almost reached the exit for the downtown area when his deep voice cut through the silence.

"I've been thinking about our search. In your dream, you see Molly in a house in the mountains and there are two other blond women with her."

"That's right. Are you thinking that one of the addresses on the DMV list might wind up being the house in the mountains or one of the women might come to the door or something?" She had considered that herself.

Ben nodded. "I'll be working on the list with Pete. I'll make sure he has that information. If anything fits, we'll talk to the people ourselves."

"With school out for the summer, I've got a lot of extra time. I could make some of those calls. And I'm sure I'd recognize the guy or the women if I saw them."

"If the man still has Molly, he could be dangerous. No way I'm letting you go on

223

your own. It would be great if you came with me though. You might pick up something I miss."

She could handle the calls by herself, she was sure, but she remembered Ben's protective streak and she could see by the set of his jaw that he wasn't going to cave on this. His hopes were building, she realized. He was starting to believe they might actually find his daughter.

Autumn looked over at Ben. He was talking about Molly as if she were alive. She wasn't sure when he'd begun to believe that might be so, but it made her chest feel tight.

God, what if I'm wrong and Molly is dead?

She squeezed her eyes shut, refusing to think about it.

"We haven't talked about last night," Ben said softly, signaling then easing the car onto the off-ramp leading downtown. With his unshaven jaw and dark, unkempt hair, he looked like he ought to be riding a Harley instead of driving a hybrid. She ignored a little shiver of awareness, tried to block the memory of heated kisses and naked bodies and worked to sound nonchalant.

"What's there to talk about? I told you it was a bad idea for you to spend the night and I was right."

"It wasn't a bad idea. Making love was

the best idea either of us has had since all of this craziness started."

"It's not going to happen, Ben. It was a case of temporary insanity on my part. If you need someone to satisfy your sexual appetite, call Delores Delgato."

He slammed on the brakes so hard and swerved toward the curb so fast the seat belt jerked across her chest.

"Dammit, I don't need someone to satisfy my appetite. Can't you understand — it's you I want, not Delores Delgato. It's that amazing body of yours that turns me on, that crazy little pink butterfly that makes me want to drag you into bed and not let you out until both of us are too exhausted to move."

Autumn stared into his angry face — too stunned to speak.

"Is that understood?"

She swallowed and nodded.

"All right then." He put the car back in drive and carefully pulled out into the morning traffic. Autumn still said nothing, but her heart was thumping, trying to pound its way out of her chest.

Was it possible Ben felt more for her than just lust?

Even if it were true, he wasn't the kind of man to be happy with one woman for any length of time.

And what about her?

God in heaven, what did she feel for him?

Fourteen

After her sleepless night in Burlington and the drive back home with Ben, Autumn missed her Wednesday-morning climbing class. Earlier, she had phoned Josh from the hospital, explained the situation with her dad and asked him to fill in for her.

Like the good friend he had been since she met him, Josh agreed. "Just let me know if you need me to do anything else," he'd said.

"Thanks, Josh."

"Are we still planning to take your class on that bouldering trip on Saturday?"

"Are you kidding? I think they'd go without me if I tried to back out."

"Good. I'll see you then."

The Fourth of July weekend was coming up and the class was ready for its first outing. Plans had been made and she wasn't about to disappoint her students. She wasn't sure whether Ben would be going but she found herself hoping he would. He was a very good student, but he needed to get actual climbing experience out-of-doors.

She was thinking about the trip when Ben drove her little Ford up in front of his Bay Towers apartment. He shoved the car into park and got out, then waited while Autumn rounded the car and slid behind the wheel.

"I left my overnight bag at your condo last night. I'll come by later and pick it up."

She didn't want to think what the consequences of that might be. "Are you seeing Pete Rossi this morning?"

"One o'clock this afternoon. And don't forget your three o'clock meeting with the sketch artist."

"I won't forget."

"I'll bring the DMV info over when I come to get my stuff."

She couldn't think of a reason to dissuade him. And she wanted to see what was on those lists as much as he did.

He stood next to the rolled-down window of the car as she snapped her seat belt in place.

"Grab a nap if you can," he said. "You didn't get much sleep last night. I'll call you later."

As she nodded and opened her mouth to say goodbye, she felt his hands sliding into her hair and his palms cupping the back of her head. Then he ducked his head through the window and settled his mouth over hers. It was a long, deep, very thorough kiss and by the time he let her go, she was trembling.

"It isn't a bad idea," he said softly. "It's a very good idea, Autumn." And then he turned and walked away.

For several long moments, Autumn just sat there, her hands shaking too much to put the car into gear. She took a steadying breath, shoved the gearshift into drive and pulled out into traffic. By the time she drove the short distance home, she was feeling more in control — more determined not to let her attraction to Ben convince her to do something she was sure to regret.

Autumn showered and changed into fresh clothes, rescheduled the single private session she had that afternoon for the following day, then took the nap Ben had suggested.

The sketch artist arrived at ten after three, a young, part-Hispanic man named Jorge Johnson with dark skin and very white teeth. He was a few years older than Autumn and once they got started, she could tell he knew what he was doing.

"Close your eyes," he said. "Sometimes that helps. You might be able to see his face more clearly."

She did as he asked, answered each of his questions.

A round face or more square? How are his eyebrows arched? Are they thin or thick? What is the shape of his eyes? What about his lips?

It took almost two hours to get the sketch done correctly, at least as accurate an image as a dream could provide. It hadn't occurred to her how unclear the man's face actually was until she tried to describe him. She didn't even know the color of his eyes and aside from the blond hair that didn't show in the black and white sketch, the face she had described looked fairly average.

"No tattoos?" Jorge asked. "No distinguishing marks of any kind? A scar, maybe? Or a birthmark?"

She only shook her head. "Somehow he seemed more distinct in my memory. Someone you would remember, but he doesn't look that way here."

"Maybe we've got something wrong."

She bit her lip, studying the image they had worked over all afternoon. "I don't think so." The drawing looked right, yet she couldn't help feeling a little disappointed.

Jorge finished the sketch, then neatly penned the words: Caucasian, blond, approximately five-foot-nine to five-foot-eleven, medium build, late thirties to mid-forties.

"I'll have some copies made," he said, "and make sure Mr. McKenzie gets one and also Pete Rossi."

"Why don't you leave the sketch here? There's a Kinko's two blocks down and Ben is coming over sometime tonight."

"If that's what you want." The young artist took the sheet of paper off his easel and set it on top of the counter. "Let me know if you think of something that doesn't look quite right and I'll change it for you."

"I will, Jorge. Thanks."

For the next half hour, Autumn stared at the picture, trying to think why the man looked different in the sketch than in her dream. Whatever it was, it was subtle enough that she couldn't figure it out. The picture would have to do, at least for the present.

It was early evening when Ben called and Autumn hated the way his deep voice made her stomach flutter. He arrived at her apartment a little after seven, as soon as he could get away from work. He had changed into jeans, a yellow, short-sleeved pullover and a pair of brown loafers. He looked tired, his dark hair less than perfectly combed. A slight frown creased his forehead.

"Tough day?" she asked as he walked through the door. He was carrying a manila file, probably the list of registered vehicle owners.

"A-1's got a new trick," Ben said, speaking of his sporting goods competitor. "They're trying to lease that old building down in the Pioneer Square district, right across from our store. Christ, those guys are a pain in the ass."

"What are you going to do?"

"I'm not sure yet. Whatever it is, I'm not going to sell them my stores."

But it was obvious he was worried. She knew he'd worked hard to build his company. He didn't want to give it up and she didn't blame him.

She reached over and plucked the sketch up off the counter. She'd gone to Kinko's and had three copies of the original made, then had smaller prints made, reduced from the larger one.

"What do you think?"

Ben's tawny brown eyes swung toward the image, the golden depths burning with a ferocity that should have scorched the paper. "So that's the son of a bitch."

"Near as I can recall."

"Not much to remember, just an average-looking Joe. Hard to imagine he's a pedophile."

"Maybe he isn't. Maybe he just wanted a daughter and Molly fit the bill."

A muscle tightened along his jaw. "I guess we can always hope."

She turned away from the grim look on his face. "How about a glass of wine? You look like you could use one."

"Thanks, I could."

She poured them each a glass of chardonnay and set one of them down on the breakfast bar in front of Ben. He placed his file next to the glass, opened it and took out several sheets of paper.

"This is the list of every '66 Chevy Chevelle Super Sport registered in Washington State in the years 2001 to the present. I've gone through and tracked the ownerships. Some have stayed the same, some of the cars have been sold — a few more than once."

She surveyed the list. "Looks pretty daunting."

"Yeah, but if we start with just the white ones — ermine, it was called that year — only eleven show up on the list."

"That sounds manageable. Of course, we have no way of knowing which of those cars might be the one that was driven the day

Molly was taken."

"Or even if that car is registered in this state," Ben said. "But we have to start somewhere."

"We have to hope the guy still owns the car and looks like the man in the sketch."

Ben scanned the list of names and addresses that covered the period. "According to the DMV, of the eleven white Chevelles listed, eight are still owned by the people who owned them in 2001. I'll take a copy of the sketch to Pete and we'll start first thing tomorrow morning."

"Washington's a pretty big state."

"Pete's making the out-of-town calls. Since I've still got a company to run, I'm making the calls closer in."

"I'm going with you."

He didn't argue. "You've seen this guy . . . or at least you dreamed about what he looked like six years ago. You're Molly's best chance."

He looked over at the sketch, ran a finger over the fine lines drawn at the corners of the man's eyes. "Maybe between the three of us, we'll come up with something."

It took Pete Rossi two days to travel the distances between the four white-Chevelle owners in the outlying areas of the state. He came up empty-handed.

None of the owners Rossi interviewed matched Autumn's sketch. If the house sat in the mountains, there were no blond women inside — at least not as far as Pete could tell.

Ben and Autumn made the four calls closer to home. One of the car owners was a woman, but not one of those in Autumn's dream. One was a retired colonel, one an airline pilot, one was a nineteen-year-old boy who had gotten the car as a graduation gift. None were the man Autumn had seen in her dreams.

"I guess we start on the cars that were sold," she said as they climbed back into Ben's Mercedes after reaching another dead end.

"I guess." He pulled out the list. "There are only three more white Chevelle's listed. All three were sold between 2001 and now but we have the names and addresses of the previous owners and none of them live far from Seattle."

The first owner was an old man in his late eighties even little six-year-old Molly could have knocked out. The second owner was a short, silver-haired, bearded high-school mechanics teacher who didn't remotely resemble the blond man and didn't recognize his picture. The last person on the list no longer lived at the residence address, which was a run-down rental house in Tumwater not far from the old Miller brewery.

"Let's go talk to the guy who bought the car," Ben said. "He lives just down the road in Olympia. Maybe he'll recognize the man in the sketch as the previous owner."

As they pulled up in front of the address listed, a simple, ranch-style tract home, they spotted the Chevelle parked in a carport at the side of the house, but the vehicle was yellow with a black landau top, not white, as stated on the DMV registration.

"I guess the list was wrong on this one," Ben said.

"Well, it's a Chevelle and we're here." They climbed out and made their way up the sidewalk to the front door.

The owner, a man named Riley Perkins, was a retired insurance salesman who had moved to the Pacific Northwest in 2002 and bought the car that year. He was vastly overweight and nearly bald, but smiling and proud of his classic car and not shy about answering their questions.

"According to the vehicle registration," Ben said to him, "your car is supposed to be white."

"Well, it was when I bought it. Piece of

junk, I can tell you. But the price was right. I bought it from a guy at a swap meet. He said he needed the money to buy a motorcycle. Talked about getting a Harley. Said he was heading out of state."

Ben held up the sketch. "This the guy?"

"Nah. He didn't look like that at all." Perkins read the description at the bottom of the sketch. "He was blond, all right, but kind of skinny and homely as a mud fence. He seemed sort of wild-eyed — you know, like he might have been on drugs."

He was nothing like the man who took Molly and Ben looked utterly defeated.

"Well, thank you, Mr. Perkins." Autumn took a firm grip on Ben's arm. "We really appreciate your help."

"No problem."

She didn't let go as they left, just led him back along the sidewalk toward the car. "Why don't I drive us home? A girl doesn't get a chance to drive a flashy Mercedes all that often."

Ben didn't argue, which showed how depressed he really was. He gave her the ghost of a smile. "Sure you can handle it?"

"I think I can manage."

They rode mostly in silence all the way from Olympia back to Seattle. Autumn had intended to drive straight to Ben's apartment then walk home from there, but he looked so heartsick she drove to her own place instead.

"You're about to luck out, McKenzie."

He turned those whiskey eyes in her direction, paying attention for the first time in nearly an hour. "How's that?"

"I'm going to cook you dinner. I've got the stuff to make lasagna — if you don't mind the kind with cottage cheese instead of ricotta. Can you handle that?"

He almost smiled. "I think I can manage," he said, repeating her earlier words.

He didn't say more and neither did she as she parked his fancy car in one of the guest spaces under her building and both of them climbed out. As they moved away from the car, Ben's shoulders were a little less straight than they usually were, the purpose gone from his steps.

"That last place we went to today . . ." he said as they walked toward the elevator, ". . . the house was in the mountains. When I saw the car had been painted, I thought for sure . . ." He broke off and swallowed and there was so much pain in his eyes, that Autumn's heart clenched.

"Maybe Pete will come up with something," she said softly. "There are still a lot more cars on that list."

"Yeah, but none of them are white."

"Maybe they were at one time, just like this last one."

"Yeah, maybe." But she could see he didn't believe it. He thought their lead was about to come to a complete dead end.

Unfortunately, Autumn was beginning to feel that way, too.

As promised, Autumn cooked Ben supper: lasagna, salad with a light, balsamic vinaigrette dressing and a bottle of Chianti, which she hoped might lift his mood. Throughout the meal, she was careful not to bring up the subject of their search and what they would do if the car lead faded into nothing.

When dinner was over, he helped her put the dishes into the dishwasher, then grabbed his jacket off the back of a chair.

"I guess I'd better go. Thanks for dinner. It was really great — cottage cheese and all."

"Thanks."

"Tomorrow's Friday. I'll see you in class in the morning." He started for the door, his shoulders slumped in that way she had never seen them before. Autumn knew he would spend the evening worrying about Molly, wondering if she were truly alive and whether or not she was suffering. She watched each of his heavy movements and suddenly couldn't stand the thought of letting him ache that way.

She reached out and caught hold of his hand. "Are you sure you want to leave? We haven't finished that bottle of wine. We could sit around and watch TV."

Ben slowly turned, his gaze sharpening on her face. She could feel the intensity, the heat in those tawny eyes as they slowly moved over her. "If I stay, it won't be to watch TV."

Her heart was beating, thundering inside her chest. She had known what would happen when she touched him, known that although he had banked his desire behind a dull haze of pain, it was there, simmering just beneath the surface.

"Stay Ben . . . please."

He hesitated only a moment, his dark gaze searching her face, then he reached out and pulled her into his arms. His kiss was hot and fierce, greedy and filled with need. He had wanted her before. Tonight he needed her and every kiss, every heated touch, told her just how much.

She was on fire for him by the time he began to strip away her clothes and his own. She didn't resist when he lifted her up, carried her into the bedroom and set her down in the middle of her canopy bed.

He took off his clothes and stood naked, the muscles in his body taut with need. Gazing at her as if she were the most beautiful woman in the world. He was big, she had noticed before, and he was hard with wanting, his shaft jutting forward in silent demand.

He walked toward her, came down over her on the bed, settled himself between her legs. His mouth found hers, moist and hot, his tongue sliding deeply inside. He kissed her and kissed her, then kissed his way down her body and began to suckle her breasts. His tongue circled the hardened tips, making them throb and distend. Making her ache for him.

She was wet. So incredibly hot and wet.

For an instant, she thought about stopping but they had gone too far and it wouldn't be fair to Ben. As her body arched eagerly beneath him, it occurred to her it wouldn't be fair to her either. She wanted this, wanted him. She couldn't remember ever wanting anything so badly.

"Autumn . . ." he whispered, kissing the side of her neck, the rough silk of his voice rolling over her, making her stomach tingle and tighten. "God, I want you."

She wanted him too. Dear God, she wanted him so much. She thought that he would take her, bury his heavy length inside as she ached for him to do. Instead, he kissed her again, deeply and thoroughly, then began to trail hot, moist kisses along her neck and down her body. His tongue circled her navel, lapped at her, and little swirls of heat slid into her belly. His hands sifted through the dark red curls at the juncture of her legs and he began to stroke her.

She had never felt anything like it, never felt the overwhelming heat, the fierce urge to join with a man the way she did with Ben.

She couldn't stop the words. "I need you, Ben. Please . . ."

He claimed her mouth again, but didn't halt the deep, penetrating strokes of his talented fingers. Sliding her arms around his neck, Autumn returned each of his bold, unrelenting kisses, her tongue tangling with his, her senses filled with the taste and scent of him.

She nibbled his ear, gently bit the side of his neck. "Please . . ." she repeated, determined now, eager for the pleasure that was just out of reach.

Ben didn't wait any longer, just raised himself up, eased her legs farther apart and slowly began to fill her. She was tight. It had been years since she had been with a man — and never one as big as Ben.

He must have felt her nerves beginning to build for he leaned down and very softly kissed her. "I'm not going to hurt you. We'll take this slow and easy."

But Autumn didn't want slow and easy. She wanted to feel all of him, every hard inch, and she wanted him now. Lifting her hips, she arched upward. Ben hissed in a breath as she buried him to the hilt.

"Christ, don't move."

"I have to, Ben." And so she did and then so did Ben, finding the rhythm, taking charge, pounding into her until she couldn't stand it a moment more.

Her body tightened, felt as if it were stretched to the breaking point. Then the world spun away and she flew free — her climax swift and sweet, filling her world with pleasure and raising gooseflesh over her skin. Ben didn't stop until she reached another powerful release, then a few seconds later he followed, his body tightening, a deep groan rising in his throat.

For several long moments, neither of them moved. Autumn barely noticed when he lifted himself away from her and settled on the bed beside her. She'd been so aroused she hadn't noticed the condom he was wearing until he stripped it away and tossed it into the trash can near the bed.

The sight cut through her dreamy haze like a splash of cold water. She stiffened.

"Take it easy," he said, running a hand down her cheek. "Everything's just fine."

"I shouldn't have . . . we shouldn't have . . ."

"But we did. And it was amazing."

She started to get up, but Ben pulled her back. "Don't you know it's the guy who's supposed to run for the door when it's over? I'm not going anywhere, Autumn."

He drew her back against his chest wrapped his big body around her spoon-fashion and the tension in her body began to ease.

"We've had one helluva day," he said. "Both of us are exhausted. I ought to let you sleep." He pressed his mouth against the side of her neck and sweet fire washed through her. "But I don't think I'm going to."

And then he was inside her and both of them were hot and moving and another orgasm shook her.

Tomorrow, she thought. *Tomorrow I'll worry about what to do.*

But for now she was sleeping in Ben

McKenzie's arms and it seemed like exactly the right thing.

FIFTEEN

Standing at the base of the forty-foot climbing wall at Pike's Gym, Ben watched Autumn's skillful, precise attack and tried to concentrate on the lesson she was teaching instead of thinking about the hot sex they'd had last night.

He'd made love to her again early this morning, then left before she was awake enough to start listing all the reasons they shouldn't have done what they did and why they couldn't possibly do it again.

He was sure that would have happened if he had stayed. So he'd grabbed his stuff, gone back to his apartment to shower and change and then headed down to his office.

At nine, he'd gone down to the gym on the second floor, certain Autumn would show up for her class and more eager than he should have been to see her. He was only mildly disappointed when she arrived all business and barely speaking to him. Only the occasional color rising in her cheeks gave any indication that she remembered last night as well as he did.

"All right," she said, looking over the group of students gathered in front of the wall. "Everything's set for tomorrow. Has everyone got their gear lined up?"

A couple of students mumbled yes. Courtney Roland, the rangy blonde, gave a no-nonsense nod of her head. Ned Wheaton grinned like a fool.

"We're all really excited about the trip," said Winnie Caruthers, the brunette. "We're supposed to meet in the lobby at eight, right, then caravan out to Snoqualmie Pass?"

Autumn nodded. "The drive isn't far and we can take fewer cars that way. I'll drive. Anyone else want to volunteer?"

"I'll drive," said Ben. His second car was a four-wheel-drive extended-cab pickup, a new GMC he had recently purchased to haul his kayaking gear.

"We can take my car," offered Ned.

"Josh Kendall will be going with us," Autumn said. "As you know, Josh is a certified guide with tons of experience. He's really itching to get you guys up on the rocks."

Ben could think of another, more interesting itch he would rather be scratching with Autumn but he kept the thought to himself. Besides, he was really enjoying the sport and he was as eager as Josh to get outdoors and try some of the moves he had been learning.

They spent the morning session climbing, Autumn working them hard enough to get them ready, but not so much they would be exhausted when they tackled bouldering problems tomorrow. When the class was over, Ben waited until the others had left before he approached Autumn, who was packing up her gear. He was pretty sure what her attitude would be.

"Good class," he said lightly.

"Thanks."

"I thought I'd let you sleep in," he said, trying to snag her attention, which she kept fixed on the canvas bag in front of her. "Give you a chance to get some rest."

Autumn made no reply so Ben caught her hand, which was white with chalk. Her fingers were rough and calloused from climbing the wall and the time she spent on the side of a real mountain. It should have been a turnoff but instead it reminded him how strong she was, the way her finely toned body moved in such perfect rhythm with his.

Autumn pulled her hand away. "What do you want, Ben?"

"I want you to look at me and tell me you don't regret what happened last night."

She glanced up at him for an instant, then looked away. "I don't regret it. Not exactly."

"I suppose that's something."

She did look at him then. "Look, Ben. I've really got to run. I've got a couple of lessons this morning, then I'm driving up to Burlington to see my dad."

"He's all right, isn't he? You said he was released from the hospital —"

"He's fine. I just thought I'd check on him. I've got the afternoon off and it isn't that long a drive." Her russet eyebrows lifted. "Unless you need me to help you make some more of the calls on the DMV list."

"Pete's taking care of it. If he turns up anything, I'll want you to go with me to check it out, but until then there's nothing more we can do and no use worrying about it."

She frowned. "You don't really think he'll find anything, do you?"

They had spoken to every owner of a white Chevelle in the state. There were forty-nine other states. The task was daunting and not very hopeful. "Like I said, Pete's taking care of the Washington list."

"So you're going with us tomorrow?"

"I plan to. I'll have my cell phone with me. Pete can find me if he needs me."

"We might be out of range."

He almost smiled. Instead, he reached over and touched her cheek. "If I didn't know better, I'd think you were trying to get rid of me."

The cat-eyes shimmered with uncertainty. "Look, Ben. Last night was great but —"

"But you aren't interested in a repeat performance. Is that what you were going to say?"

"I just . . . I don't want to get in over my head."

He didn't tell her he was already in way over his head — had been since the first time he had watched her climb that wall. He didn't understand it, wasn't sure what was going on, but something was and he wasn't about to ignore it.

"I won't press you, Autumn. Both of us have a lot on our minds right now, but I'm not letting you pretend what happened between us wasn't special because it was and I think you know it."

She nervously bit her lip. She tried to zip the bag. Her hand was trembling and the zipper stuck. Ben took hold of the canvas tote and closed it for her.

"I've really got to go, Ben."

"You sure you don't want me to come with you? I'd be happy to drive you."

She quickly shook her head.

"Fine. Then I'll see you in the morning."

Autumn looked like a rabbit released from a hunter's snare. He would have asked to see her tonight, but he could tell she wasn't ready and as he had said, he didn't want to press her.

It wasn't until six o'clock that night, as he was sitting behind his desk going over a column of figures on his computer, that he realized he couldn't have seen her even if she had agreed.

Not until his secretary, Jenn Conklin, gave a quick knock on the tall mahogany door and stepped into his office. "It's getting a little late. You haven't forgotten your dinner engagement have you? The country club with Sam and Beverly Styles?"

Christ. He had forgotten completely. He tossed the pencil down on the desk. "I always check my calendar. I guess I had something else on my mind." And Ben knew exactly *who* that something else was.

"You'll have to hurry or you aren't going to make it."

"Thanks, Jenn. You're a gift from God."

Wrapping things up as quickly as he could, he grabbed his suit coat and headed for the door.

"Have fun," Jenn said as he walked past, casting him a know-it-all glance.

How she always seemed to guess which women he had slept with, Ben couldn't say. What she didn't know was that he had no desire to sleep with Beverly Styles, wouldn't have done it the first time if Bev hadn't insisted on coming up to his penthouse for a nightcap after their evening together. Since Sam was a friend, he'd had no notion of seduction, but he wasn't a saint and Bev was an attractive, sensual woman, a divorcée who knew exactly what she wanted.

Well, it wasn't going to happen tonight. There was only one woman he wanted and that one wasn't eager to let him back into her bed.

He sighed as he waited for the valet to bring his car from the underground lot. He'd make the evening as short as possible then go home.

Ben found himself smiling. Tomorrow he'd see Autumn and renew his campaign.

All the way up the freeway to Burlington, Autumn thought of Ben McKenzie.

She hadn't been physically attracted to a

252

man in years, not since Lucas Noland, a climber she had met on a trip to the Colorado Rockies. Luke was handsome and amazingly athletic and they seemed to click from the moment they met. She had briefly recalled her disastrous, month-long dating, one-night disaster with Ronnie Hillson but Luke was a different kind of guy — an honest guy — and she believed she could handle a short-term affair.

She deserved to have a fling, she'd thought. Just this once. She would enjoy the two weeks they had together and expect nothing more from him.

When the trip came to an end, Autumn said her goodbyes to Luke at the airport and flew back to Seattle. *It's over,* she told herself. Yet she couldn't make herself stop waiting for the phone to ring, hoping Luke would call.

He didn't. Not once.

A fling, she had discovered, could be painful.

She hadn't been in love with Luke but she had believed he cared for her more than he actually did. She consoled herself with memories of two glorious high-mountain weeks and vowed not to do anything that stupid again.

So how had she wound up in bed last

night with Ben?

Autumn hissed in a breath. Dear God, the man was the most eligible bachelor in Seattle. His picture was plastered all over the society pages escorting countless women. How could she have been foolish enough to go to bed with him?

But even as she thought of him, she remembered the pain in his eyes, the defeat that weighed him down like a rain-sogged coat. She just couldn't let him go home alone and agonize over his lost little girl.

Or at least that was her excuse.

The truth was that she'd wanted Ben to stay. She had wanted him to make love to her so badly she ached with it.

And she hadn't been disappointed.

Nothing in her experience had prepared her for a night in bed with Ben McKenzie.

She ignored a warm tingling at the memory of slow, heated kisses, hot bare skin and big, talented hands stroking over her body.

Autumn sighed as she slowed and pulled into the driveway of her father's gray-and-white, double-wide mobile home. It sat on five acres a few miles out of town and her dad kept it clean and the property well cared for.

Or maybe these days, Myra kept the inside clean.

Whatever the case, she was glad Max was feeling better. She had spoken to him on the phone every day since the night he had been in the hospital. His continued talk about marrying Myra bothered Autumn only a little. It was his business after all, she had finally concluded.

She wondered if the silver-blond woman would be at the house and found herself hoping she would be. Myra was a good person and a true friend to her father.

If Max married her . . .

Autumn remembered the tears her mother had shed, the hours waiting for Max to come home, the scent of perfume on his collar when he did.

If her dad got married again . . .

Autumn felt sorry for Myra.

It was seven o'clock Saturday morning. The phone had been ringing constantly since six. As Autumn sat at the kitchen table staring down at the photo on the society page of the newspaper, she knew exactly who was calling. Each shrill note made her heart ache and her stomach roll with nausea.

The ceaseless, irritating ring began again and Autumn grit her teeth. She reread the column, which gave a nicely written account of the charity dinner held at the Broadmoor Country Club last night. There were several photos surrounding the article but one stood out above the rest.

A photo of Ben McKenzie in his tuxedo with an attractive brunette named Beverly Styles. The thing that made the picture interesting was the way the woman's arms were locked around Ben's neck. There was no doubt the photo was shot the instant before the two of them kissed.

The phone rang again, a jarring note that pushed Autumn past the hurt and betrayal. She surged to her feet, grabbed the section of the paper with Ben's photo in it, balled it into a wad and tossed it into the trash can.

Dammit, not again! There must be something wrong with her. There had to be, the way she kept believing men were different than they really were, believing she could trust even one of them.

She didn't realize she was crying until a tear rolled down her cheek. Damning Ben McKenzie to hell, Autumn dashed away the wetness, grabbed her purse and headed for the door.

She didn't want to be late getting to the gym, where her group was meeting for their bouldering trip.

If Ben McKenzie had the nerve to show —

Well, she wasn't exactly sure what she would do if he did, but an image clicked into her head of the two of them climbing. With grim satisfaction, she imagined herself letting go of the belaying rope as Ben tumbled off the side of a cliff.

Ben was waiting near the elevators in the lobby when Autumn came up from the parking garage. He stepped in front of her.

"I need to talk to you."

"Get out of my way, Ben."

He released a breath. "I guess you saw the paper."

Autumn shoved past him and continued walking, pretending not to hear him curse.

Ben caught up with her in two long strides, took hold of her arm and turned her around to face him. Across the lobby, her students were gathered and waiting, beginning to notice their approach.

"We can play this out in front of everyone here or you can give me a minute in private so I can explain."

"I'm not interested in anything you have to say."

"I'm giving you a choice. What's it going to be?"

He was a big man and he was determined, but then so was she.

She looked at the group of climbers who watched with growing fascination. "I said get out of my way."

"I'll cart you off over my shoulder if I have to."

He wasn't kidding. She could see it in the set of his jaw. She wasn't about to be embarrassed in front of her students. Autumn grit her teeth, whirled and marched ahead of him down the hall, turning into a lower-level conference room that wasn't being used.

"Good choice," Ben said, closing the door behind him. "I know you're pissed and I don't blame you. But you're going to listen to what I have to say. Once I'm finished, you can decide what you want to do. After that, we're going climbing."

"You aren't going anywhere with me!" She started for the door but he blocked her way.

"Several weeks ago, I agreed to escort Bev Styles and her father, both long-time friends, to an important event at the country club. I'd forgotten all about it until Jenn reminded me at six o'clock last night. I intended to make a short evening of it. I had no idea the paper would be covering the event and I didn't even notice when the photographer snapped that picture of me and Bev."

"But I bet you noticed that kiss." She started moving, but again he stepped in the way.

"I didn't kiss her — she kissed me. If I'd had a clue that was going to happen, I would have stopped her. I took her directly home a few minutes later. I didn't kiss her good-night and I didn't ask her out again — nor do I intend to."

Autumn tried to read his expression. She saw honesty but didn't know if it was real. She raked back her hair, shoving the heavy auburn curls away from her face. "I can't handle this, Ben. I'm not like your other women. Please, can't you just leave me alone?"

He reached out and caught her chin, his hand surprisingly gentle. "I'd leave you alone if I could. I can't seem to make that happen. When I saw the paper this morning, I felt sick to my stomach. I knew what you would think, how you would feel. If you're worried I'll keep seeing other women, I won't. I wouldn't have gone last night if I hadn't already promised Sam."

Autumn said nothing, but her heart was throbbing. She could tell he was upset. Maybe he was being sincere. Although it didn't change anything, it made some of the hurt go away.

"I have to know what's happening between us, Autumn," he said. "Say you'll at least give this a try."

She shook her head. "I can't risk it, Ben." She forced herself to move away from him though she didn't really want to, which made her angry all over again. "My students are waiting. Please let me go."

For a moment he just stood there, then he moved out of her way. She thought he would leave, realize that one wild night was all they were going to have and be on his way.

Instead he fell into step behind her. As they walked back to the lobby, Autumn steeled herself to face the others and pasted a smile on her face. From the corner of her eye, she saw Ben make his way to the rear of the group. Apparently, he still planned to go with them. As a member of the class, he had that right, she supposed.

Autumn braced herself for the day ahead, determined to simply ignore him.

Unfortunately, ignoring a man like Ben McKenzie wasn't all that easy to do.

Sixteen

The morning was overcast with a chill air beneath a leaden sky that wasn't unusual for Seattle. As if the weather gods had read Autumn's mood and knew she needed a lift, by noon the sun had begun to shine through the layers of cloud and the air had warmed to a pleasant degree of cool.

Josh had arrived just before the group departed and was riding with Ben and Courtney in Ben's pickup. Ian and Bruce were riding in Ned's four-door Camry. Matt Gould and Winnie Caruthers were with Autumn.

Taking Highway 90 east to Snoqualmie Pass, they pulled off on the 51 exit and drove under the freeway, parked the cars in the Alpental parking lot, loaded up their gear and headed for the Snow Lake trailhead.

The scenery in the area was spectacular: soaring granite domes, craggy majestic ridges and distant snow-capped peaks. Puffy white clouds lay just below a far-away mountain summit and the deep-green forest rose from the base of the range, climbing up the steep walls until the terrain grew too rocky for the pines to survive.

Autumn led the group a couple of miles up the trail to where it forked, then turned off the Snow Lake path toward a place called The Tooth. The jagged summit was a great all-season climb and Autumn had made it in both summer and winter, but today she was heading for an area of lower rock formations that would serve well for neophytes to develop their skills.

The idea behind bouldering was to free-climb a safe distance above the ground without using ropes or safety devices, just thick foam-rubber mats for protection in case of a fall. The craggy, low granite rocks had plenty of hand and footholds, yet there were problem areas that would prove challenging enough to keep the more rapid learners on their toes.

They had brought their climbing gear as well, and after they practiced a while on the boulders, Autumn planned to have them do some top-roping. She hoped to get the more advanced students like Ned, Courtney and Ben started on some traditional climbing:

roping up and practicing the use of cams and hexes.

As mad as she was at Ben, she was still his teacher and she wasn't going to shirk her responsibilities where one of her students was concerned. Even more than Ned and Courtney, Ben seemed to have a gift for the sport. He was determined to learn and if he continued to develop his skills, he could be an outstanding climber.

They arrived at the area Autumn had chosen, unloaded their gear in the shade of some odd-shaped boulders, dug out their chalk bags and set up their crash pads beneath the rocks she had chosen as their targets. They free-climbed for the first couple of hours, staying low so that no one would get hurt. Top-roping came next: a simpler, safer version of traditional climbing where the rope went from a climber through permanent anchors that led to the top of a route then back down to a belayer.

The climber didn't have to place protection in the rocks; the anchors provided holds for the rope on the way up and down.

After several hours of climbing they broke for lunch, then went back to climbing. Autumn roped up and started up a pitch, a step trench cut into the rough rock surface that had good solid footings and a ledge with a tree anchor not too far up. Courtney belayed her, using good, solid technique, while Josh worked on a nearby chimney with Ben.

Both climbs went well and once they had safely returned to the ground, Autumn sat down in the shade of a big granite boulder and popped the top off a bottle of Gatorade. In the distance, she watched Josh rope up and start working with Ned. She thought that Ben must be with them. She didn't expect to hear the deep rumble of his voice coming from beside her.

"I wish I'd called you last night," he said. "Explained what I was going to do. If I could do it over, I would."

Autumn stiffened as Ben sank down in the shade and propped his broad back against the rock.

"You don't owe me anything, Ben. So you slept with me? So what? You've slept with dozens of women. I'm just one more, no different than the rest."

He turned his head, pinned her with his golden-eyed stare. "That's where you're wrong, Autumn. You *are* different — very different. And I want to see you again."

Autumn tilted her head back against the sun-warmed granite and closed her eyes. Ben wanted to see her. He was sorry for what had happened. He wasn't dating other women.

It didn't matter. It could never work between them.

"You did really great up there," she said when she looked at him again. "You could be a fabulous climber, Ben."

"Coming from you, that's really saying something."

They both knew she didn't give compliments lightly. Ben had incredible talent and he seemed to love the sport.

"Have you heard anything from Pete?" she asked, changing the subject once more.

"Not yet. You were right — we're out of cell-phone range. I'll call him as soon as my phone is working again." He took a bottle of water out of the backpack beside him, twisted off the lid and took a deep swallow. Autumn tried not to notice the way the long muscles in his throat moved up and down but her nipples tightened beneath her T-shirt.

"What's going on with your dreams?" Ben asked. "You didn't dream the night we were together or the night before that. How about last night?"

She sighed, returning her mind to the unpleasant subject. "I think I might have dreamed. If I did, I don't remember. Sometimes it happens that way."

Ben glanced off toward a distant snow-covered peak. She knew he was thinking that if he could be there at night he could help her remember. Thinking that they might come up with another clue.

Autumn took another sip of Gatorade and screwed the lid back on. If Pete Rossi came up empty-handed, her dreams were all Ben had left to help him find his daughter. Autumn had been the one who had gone to Ben in the first place, the one to drag him — against his will — into the search. She was obligated to help him, no matter what it cost her.

She started to tell him that if Rossi didn't find anything, she would consider letting him sleep on the couch as he had done before, but Josh walked up just then.

"You were great, McKenzie. You've got a real knack for this sport. There's an interesting pitch just down the trail a bit. You want to give it a try?"

Ben rose from his place on the ground, dusting off the seat of his khaki shorts and adjusting the navy-blue tank top that showed off his nicely muscled chest.

"I'm game if you are." Following Josh over to the pile of rope and gear they had left near the bottom of a talus field, Ben stepped into his harness and fastened the buckle around his waist, then attached some of the devices he might need.

They moved up the trail, but Autumn could still see them. As they started the climb, she watched Josh's clean, skillful movements over the surface of the rock. She watched him place a piece of protection, hook up his rope, then start climbing again. As soon as he reached the top of the pitch and set his anchor, Ben started up behind him, retrieving the devices Josh had placed to get them both up safely. Lean muscle rippled and tightened as he moved. The sun glinted off the perspiration on his broad back and powerful shoulders.

Autumn admired his strength and growing skill for a moment, then returned to the group climbing low boulders above the thick rubber mats. The day was almost over, the air turning chill. Across the mountains, the sun angled low on the horizon.

They would need to start heading home soon.

Autumn was glad Ben had brought his own car so she wouldn't have to ride back with him.

It was two-thirty in the morning but Ben couldn't fall asleep. Earlier in the evening, he had spoken to Pete Rossi about the last of the DMV classic-car owners. Rossi had finished interviewing the owners and come up with a big, fat zero.

None of the people who owned a '66 Super Sport looked like the man in Autumn's sketch or ever had any connection with anyone who did. Pete had talked to both current and previous owners with the same result.

The logical conclusion — assuming Robbie Hines was right about the make and model — was that the car driven the day Molly was abducted was registered in another state. On Monday, he would have Jenn take charge of mailing and e-mailing copies of the sketch to classic car groups around the country, offer a reward for any information that might be useful and see if they could come up with a hit.

He trusted Jenn to keep the search as quiet as possible. Since they still had no real evidence, he wasn't ready to involve his family. Renewing the search for Molly after all these years would be devastating for Joanne. She had barely survived after it happened. For a while, he had worried she might go as far as suicide. He didn't want her to suffer that kind of pain again.

Lying in his king-size bed, Ben plumped

his pillow and jammed it behind his head. In the last few years, he had finally come to terms with Molly's death. Now here he was, involved again in a hopeless quest to find her.

God, he wished he had never heard of Autumn Sommers and her crazy dreams. It was probably all complete and utter bullshit. He was an idiot to even think any of it might be true.

Ben closed his eyes, willing himself to go to sleep when the phone began to ring.

He reached for the receiver, completely awake now. "Hello . . ."

"Ben, it's Autumn . . ." As if he wouldn't know. "I — I saw him . . . I dreamed about Molly and the other two women but it was different and . . . I — I saw his face. This time, I really saw him!"

Ben's fingers tightened around the phone. "Just sit tight, I'm on my way."

She didn't argue, which told him how upset she really was. Ben hung up the phone, dragged on a pair of jeans and a T-shirt, slid into his tennis shoes and headed for the door.

It didn't take long to reach Autumn's apartment. The instant he knocked, she opened the door. Her face looked pale and she was shaking and it was all he could do not to haul her into his arms. He knew that was the last thing she wanted.

"You all right?" he asked, though clearly she was not.

Autumn nodded and motioned for him to come in. "A little shook up, is all. I made coffee if you want some."

"I could use a cup." It didn't look like he would be sleeping tonight — with or without caffeine — so he accepted the steaming cup she poured and set in front of him on the counter. Her own cup sat untouched beside it.

"Let's go over to the sofa." Picking up both cups, he followed Autumn into the living room, set the cups down on the antique claw-foot table in front of the couch and waited for her to take a seat. She pulled her pink quilted robe a little tighter around herself and sat down. Ben sat beside her.

Autumn raked a hand through her hair. "You know, every time I looked at the sketch I kept thinking that something was wrong but I couldn't figure out what it was. Tonight in my dream, when the blond man walked into the kitchen and I saw him looking at Molly, I realized he had changed more in the last six years than I would have guessed. Maybe he'd appeared in a dream before, looking the way he does now and I just didn't remember. Maybe that's why the sketch looked wrong."

"He looks different now?"

"He looks older, harder. The laugh lines beside his eyes are wrinkles now and there are deep furrows in his forehead. But the thing is, Ben — I've seen this man! Somewhere in the real world, I've actually seen him." She looked up at him with big green, worried eyes. "The trouble is — I can't remember where."

He straightened on the sofa, his senses alert. "You know this guy?"

"No . . . I mean, I don't know him. I just . . . I'm sure I've seen him. I have no idea where. It could have been anyplace . . . a restaurant, a bar, the theater, the gym. It could have been here in Seattle or up in Burlington. God, I wish I could recall."

She looked on the edge of tears so he simply reached out and pulled her into his arms. "Take it easy, baby. You don't remember now, but in time maybe you will."

She tilted her head to look up at him. "We don't have time, Ben. I don't know why, but I feel like time is slipping away."

He drew her closer against him and she rested her head on his shoulder. "We have to stay positive," he said. "The dream has changed, which means it may have given us another clue. We'll work on it. See where it leads."

She nodded and he could feel the soft brush of her hair against his cheek. Ben eased a little away. "We'll start from the beginning, go through the dream frame by frame." Ignoring the little voice that warned that none of this might be real, he reached behind him, pulled a soft wool rose-colored afghan off the back of the couch and draped it over her legs. "We might as well get comfortable. This may take a while."

Autumn told Ben everything she could remember. Molly and the other two women had been in the kitchen when the blond man came home. He looked older than he had before, had aged more than she would have guessed. She had seen that he had pale blue eyes and that they were harder now. And nothing about them was friendly. His hair was cut short and each strand perfectly in place, as if he used something to keep it that way.

"Did any of the women call him by name?" Ben asked.

Autumn shook her head. "No, but he called the older woman Rachael. I remember he said, 'Good evening, Rachael' when he first walked in."

She remembered the kitchen was full of steam and the man got angry when he saw that the table wasn't completely set.

"Supper's almost ready," Rachael had hurriedly explained. She had a thin face, wore no make-up but was not unattractive. She seemed perpetually nervous. Rachael had fixed her gaze on Molly, giving the man another target for his anger. "Ruth burned the bread so you'll have to do without tonight."

He turned those ice-blue eyes in Molly's direction. "You'd better learn, girl. You don't, you'll be taking a walk with me out to my workshop."

Molly's face went pale. "I'm sorry. I — I didn't mean to. It was an accident. I won't do it again."

He grunted. They sat down to a supper of boiled meat and some sort of greens, the man at one end of the table, the women seated around him.

It was the moment he looked down the table at Molly that Autumn recognized the straight line of his nose, the carved cheekbones and slightly hollow cheeks, and realized she had seen him somewhere before.

It was in that moment that she had awakened from the dream.

She felt Ben's hand over hers, giving her

quiet reassurance. "I know I've seen him, Ben. God, why can't I remember?"

She was shaking. She didn't resist when Ben pulled her back into his arms.

"It's all right," he said softly. "None of this is your fault."

Then why did she feel so responsible, feel as if Molly McKenzie's life was somehow in her hands?

They went over the dream again and again, Autumn recalling colors, sounds, words, anything she could remember, and Ben jotting down notes on the pad he retrieved from beside her bed.

"Molly was afraid of him, Ben. We've got to find her before . . ." She didn't finish the sentence. She had no idea what might happen to the young girl or why she felt so certain that it would.

She only knew they had to do something and soon.

Somewhere near dawn, she must have fallen asleep. Autumn awakened with her head resting in Ben's lap, her body curled beneath the warm afghan her great-grandmother had painstakingly crocheted for her when Autumn was a little girl.

As she stirred and began to sit up, Ben

smoothed back a lock of her hair. "You okay?"

"I didn't mean to fall asleep."

"It's all right, I'm glad you did. You needed a little rest."

"What about you? You were up most of the night yourself."

"Yeah, it gave me time to think."

"And?"

"And I want you and Jorge to come up with another sketch. One where the guy looks the way he does in your most recent dream."

"What will you do with it?"

"Have my secretary send it to classic car groups around the country, either by mail or over the Internet. I was going to have her start Monday morning. Now we'll wait until we get the new sketch."

"What else can we do?"

"I want you to make a list of places you might have come in contact with this guy."

Autumn blew out a breath. "God, Ben, it could have been anywhere. I know it wasn't recently. It's a foggy memory at best. I'm thinking it was at least several years ago."

"I still want that list. Maybe just writing it out will jar something loose."

Autumn stood up from the sofa. "I need to shower and dress first. And I think we're going to need a fresh pot of coffee."

"I can handle that." Ben stood up too.

Her robe fell open as she started toward the bedroom, giving him a glimpse of the pink silk nightie she wore underneath. She pulled the robe closed and fastened two of the buttons on the front.

Ben caught her hand before she could escape. "Next time I stay over, I expect you to wear the cute little number you've got on now instead of that baggy T-shirt."

Autumn shook her head. "Staying was a bad idea from the start. It's a worse idea now."

"I told you the truth, Autumn. I didn't betray you with Beverly Styles and I'm not going do it with anyone else."

She turned away, telling herself that she couldn't risk believing him, that it didn't matter anyway. She tried to convince herself and failed completely.

Ben caught her chin between his fingers. "You have to let me stay, Autumn — every night as long as you keep dreaming. You said yourself that time's running out." He let go of her chin. "Whatever you want or don't want from me, I'm asking you to do everything in your power to help me find my daughter."

Her chest squeezed. He was right. When

Ben was there to help her recall the dream, it became clearer and the shadowy pieces emerged from the distant corners of her mind.

She didn't want him to stay. She still didn't trust him and she didn't want to get any more involved with him that she was already.

"Autumn . . . ?" he gently prodded.

She released a weary sigh. "All right, you can stay here at night. It does help me remember. But I want your word you'll keep your distance."

He ran a finger along her cheek. "Like I said, whatever you want or don't want. I'll leave that up to you."

She pressed her lips together. What did she want from Ben? Just looking at him standing there, his hair rumpled and a shadow of beard along his jaw, made her yearn for another hot night in bed with him.

But the more time they spent together, the more intimacies they shared, the more pain she would feel when he left her.

And he would.

Except for her dad, in one way or another, all of the people she'd ever loved had left her. The only family she still had was her dad, an aging aunt and a couple of cousins who lived out of state. Her mom was gone;

her grandparents on both sides had passed away.

Over the years, all of the men she'd dated had deserted her. Not one of them had loved her. Not even Steven, who had wanted a wife and children very badly. She understood now that was never going to happen. Though once she had wanted a husband and family more than anything on earth, that time was past. She didn't want to wind up a single mother, divorced and raising her children alone, or married to a man who chased women all the time like her father.

She just didn't have what it took to hold on to a man. Certainly not one like Ben.

She thought of him as she headed for the shower and heard him rummaging around in her kitchen, grinding beans for a fresh pot of coffee.

As soon as all of this was over, she was saying goodbye to Ben McKenzie and all of the problems he posed.

As soon as all of this was over.

Dear God, when was that going to be?

SEVENTEEN

The weather stayed clear all weekend. On Sunday, Ben drove his truck out to Issaquah to pick up Katie for their scheduled day together. A copy of Autumn's original sketch, the one of the blond man six years ago when he had abducted Molly, rode in the pocket of his jacket. Showing the sketch to Joanne was the last thing he wanted to do, but he had put this off as long as he could.

The time had come when he had to choose — either he believed in Autumn and her dreams or he did not. If he believed her, then he had to believe that Molly was alive. If she was, he had to do everything in his power to find her.

And that meant he had to ask Joanne if there was a chance she had seen this man in the neighborhood the day Molly was taken or maybe at a different time or place. He would do his best not to upset her, to give her the least disturbing explanation he could come up with, but he had to know.

Leaving his pickup parked at the curb, he walked up the path to the expensive custom home he had shared with Joanne for just six months before they decided to divorce. It had been a mutual decision. They simply couldn't go on hurting each other any longer.

Fortunately, in the years since then, their relationship had mellowed, leaving them friends of a sort. They had developed a mutual respect and were determined that Katie wouldn't pay for their failed marriage.

Ben knocked on one of the carved double-doors then waited for his ex-wife to pull it open.

"You're early," she said, stepping back so he could walk past her into the tile-floored entry. The house was spacious and beautifully furnished. Ben wanted them to have the best. "Katie's not quite ready. I'll tell her you're here."

"I came a little early so I could talk to you for a minute alone."

Joanne took another step back at the serious look on his face. "All right. Let's go into the kitchen." At thirty-five, she was still a beautiful woman with shoulder-length honey-blond hair and powder-blue eyes.

For the past few months, she had been seriously dating a man who worked for her father in the banking business. John Cleveland was handsome and smart. Best of all, he seemed to care greatly for both Joanne and Katie. It bothered Ben a little to think he would be sharing his little girl with a second father, but mostly he was happy for his ex-wife and child and grateful that Joanne seemed to have chosen well.

They sat down at the breakfast table in the large, white, very modern kitchen.

"Do you want a cup of coffee or something?" Joanne asked.

"No thanks, I'm fine. What I came here to talk about has to do with Molly."

"Molly . . . ?" she repeated, a slight edge creeping into her voice.

"I hate to upset you by bringing this up. Believe me, I know how painful it is. But I really have no choice."

"I — I don't understand."

"Several weeks ago, a friend of mine spoke to Gerald Meeks. Meeks claims he didn't kill Molly, that he never even saw her. Another man was spotted the day Molly was taken. I need to know if you recognize the man."

Joanne just stared as he reached into his jacket pocket, pulled out the rolled-up copy of Autumn's black-and-white sketch, and laid it out in front of her. "He has blond hair and blue eyes. You can't tell that from the drawing. Does the guy look the least bit familiar?"

Joanne moved her head woodenly to look down at the drawing. For several long moments she said nothing, then her eyebrows drew together. "I might have seen him." She looked up. "What difference does it make? Molly's dead."

"A few loose ends have come up that need to be clarified. Where did you see him? Do you remember?"

"I don't know . . . I . . . there's something familiar about him, but I really can't say for sure."

"He might have come up to you somewhere when you were with Molly."

She jerked toward him. "Are you saying this is the man who took her, not Meeks?"

"It's possible."

She started shaking. "I can't do this again, Ben. I can't."

He reached over and caught her hand. "I only need you to answer this one question. Just tell me where you might have seen him."

She pressed her lips together, closed her eyes for a moment, then opened them.

"At . . . at the sporting-goods store. I think he's the man I saw out in front one day."

"The store here in Issaquah?"

"Yes."

"So you remember seeing him. You recognize his face."

She looked down at the drawing. "I never thought of him again after that day . . . not until this moment."

"Did he speak to you?"

She moistened her lips, nodded her head. "I — I dropped my wallet on my way out of the store. The man picked it up and returned it to me out front. It . . . it was very nice of him . . . at least I thought so at the time." Her eyes sharpened. "You don't think he got our address off my driver's license?"

"It's a possibility." More than that, Ben thought, figuring the man had stolen the wallet in the first place and used it as a means of finding Molly.

"H-he seemed very nice but not the kind of person who makes any sort of impression. I wouldn't have remembered him at all if you hadn't shown me this picture." She looked down at the sketch and her face went even paler. "Oh, God, Ben — he said what a pretty little girl my daughter was."

She shoved to her feet more angry now than upset. "I'm sorry, Ben. I know you think this is important, but the truth is, I don't care who killed Molly. She's dead and gone and I'll never see her again and stirring all of this up isn't going to bring her back."

Ben rose, too. "Take it easy, Joanne."

"I just want to live a normal life, Ben. That's what I want for Katie. Please, don't screw this up for me. Promise me, Ben."

"You've told me all I need to know." He caught her trembling hand, leaned over and kissed her forehead. "We don't have to talk about it any more."

Joanne swallowed hard, then gave a nod of relief. Both of them glanced up at a sound in the doorway.

"We don't have to talk about what, Dad?" Katie came bouncing in, blond hair in a ponytail, wearing jeans and a bright yellow T-shirt.

"Letting you go kayaking with me," he said, shooting a glance at Joanne. "Your mom and I talked it over during the week and we agreed it would be all right for you to go — as long as we stay in the lake and don't go into the river."

"Yippee!" Her arm shot up to emphasize the word and she jumped up and down in a little circle. "Are we going today?"

"Soon as you're ready."

"I'm ready! I'm ready! Let's go!" She grabbed her small blue canvas tote and raced ahead of him for the door.

Ben gently squeezed his ex-wife's shoulder. "There's nothing to worry about, Joanne. I'll take care of everything."

She nodded. When it came to family, she trusted him completely.

It was the only subject on which they ever agreed.

It was early. The office hadn't yet opened. It was Tuesday, the morning after the July Fourth weekend. After a day of kayaking on nearby Lake Washington, Ben and Katie had watched the annual fireworks celebration from the shore.

Ben had returned Katie home, then gone over to Autumn's and spent the night on her sofa. He knew she didn't want him there. She looked wary and nervous — and so damned cute it took enormous self control to stay away from her. Sometime after two, she awakened but her dream was the same one she'd had before and they had gathered no new information.

Last night had been the same. He had purposely gone over late in the evening to give her a little breathing room, though he would rather have taken her out to dinner or just snuggled up in front of the TV.

It bothered him, this unwanted attraction he felt for her, this persistent desire that never seemed to leave. He wanted to be with her, no matter how determinedly she tried to push him away.

Maybe that was it. Autumn was a challenge: a woman he wanted who didn't want him.

Ben wished he could convince himself.

He looked down at the paperwork sitting on top of his big desk. Kurt Fisher had brought him another offer from A-1 Sports, upping the purchase price for the chain by a considerable amount. Kurt also dropped several not-so-subtle hints about the lease A-1 was putting together on property near Pioneer Square, practically next door to Ben's downtown store.

Instead of just refusing the deal as he had before, Ben told Fisher he needed time to consider the offer and of course he would have to have his attorney look it over.

A-1 wasn't the only one who could play games.

Thinking of business, he reached for the phone and dialed his real estate broker, Russ Petrone.

"Any word yet on our proposal?" Ben asked, referring to a plan he was trying to put together to quell A-1's leasing deal.

"Not yet, but I think we've got several parties seriously interested."

"Good. Keep it quiet and keep after it."

"Will do."

Ben hung up and leaned back in his chair. He needed to end A-1's threat and he thought that he might have come up with a way. He smiled, thinking how furious Kurt Fisher would be if his plan actually succeeded.

Ben straightened, the smile slipping away as his mind turned to a different, more important matter. Moving toward his computer, he grabbed his mouse, clicked on the Internet symbol on the desktop, and waited for *Google* to pop up on the screen.

He hadn't been to this particular Web site in years. It was just too painful. He typed in *www.missingkids.com.*

The home page came up, featuring pictures of children who had recently gone missing and offering links to pages that held information on others — a number so high it made his chest hurt.

There was a list of question boxes to be filled in so information on the missing child could be found. Ben started typing. The site asked if the child was male or female, which state the child had been taken from and the number of years he or she had been gone. When he finished, Ben hit the search button, sat back to wait and realized his heart was pounding.

A few seconds later, among a group of seventeen children missing from the State of Washington over the last six years, Molly's photo smiled back at him: her sweet face, finely arched brows, soft mouth and gentle blue eyes.

For several long moments Ben just stared at her beloved features, his throat tight and his eyes burning. He read the information printed on the page though he knew it by heart: Sex, female. Race, Caucasian. Height, 3'8". Hair, blond. Eyes, blue. The information stated the date she had disappeared and that she had been seen leaving in the company of a man in a white car.

He clicked around the site, saw that most of the children who had gone missing some years back had computer-aged photos posted next to their actual pictures and made a mental note to see that done for Molly.

Ben clicked off the site and leaned back in his chair, feeling emotionally drained. For years he had believed his daughter was dead. It was the only way he could go on, the only way he could try to make a life for himself.

Now that had changed.

Joanne had confirmed seeing the man in Autumn's sketch. She believed she had encountered him in front of the sporting-goods store. He only wished they'd had the sophisticated surveillance equipment outside the front door that each store was equipped with now, but they weren't installed six years ago.

Along with Joanne's positive ID and the other bits and pieces of information from Autumn's dreams, Robbie Hines had given them the make and model of the car used that day. Still, they needed more.

Ben reached over and once more picked up the phone.

"You have got to be kidding!" Terri sat across from Autumn at O'Shaunessy's. The place as usual was full, humming with conversation and the faint notes of pop music playing in the background. "*The hunk* is spending every night at your house and he is sleeping on the couch?"

"If you saw his picture in last Saturday's paper, you know why."

"I saw it. So he had a date. Big deal. He's a man, isn't he? What did he say about it?"

Autumn took a sip of her wine. "He said

the evening was arranged a long time ago and that he wasn't going to see her again."

"Well then, what's the problem?"

"The problem is he's Ben McKenzie and I'm just not up to a guy like him."

"So just entertain yourself for a while. Come on, Autumn, you haven't had sex in years. You deserve to have a little fun. Why not have it with Ben?"

Autumn felt the heat creeping into her face.

"Oh my God, you've already slept with him! How was he? Fantastic, I bet! So what's he doing on the sofa?"

"Look, Terri. The last time I had a fling with a guy, it hurt like hell when it was over. I'm not able to keep my distance from a man the way you are. In order to sleep with him, I have to have feelings for him. The more we're together, the more those feelings grow. Then he takes a hike and I'm off the deep end."

"What if he doesn't?"

"Doesn't what?"

"Doesn't take a hike? What if he really cares for you? It's not impossible, you know."

Autumn shook her head. "It wouldn't work. Sooner or later, he'd get bored. He'd want to see other women and I couldn't handle it."

Terri said nothing for several seconds. "You know, Autumn, your old man really screwed you up when it comes to men."

Autumn sighed. "Maybe . . . I don't know. I just know I have to keep my distance."

Which was easy to say and nearly impossible to do. She thought of Ben constantly, replayed the single night she had spent in bed with him a hundred times. And ached to do it again. Every night when he came to the house it was all she could do to leave him on the sofa and go to bed alone.

"What about you?" she asked Terri, hoping to lighten the mood. "Anything going on with *your* love life?"

"Nothing particularly exciting." Terri casually stirred the swizzle stick in her drink. "I ran into Josh Kendall the other day. He was with a girl named Courtney Roland. I guess she's in your climbing class."

"Yeah, she is. She's getting to be a darned good climber. She was with Josh?"

She nodded. "Josh introduced us. She seemed like a nice enough person."

Autumn smiled. "I had a feeling Courtney was interested in Josh. She rode in the car with him and Ben the day we went climbing. They've got a lot in common. I think she'd be great for him."

Terri stirred her drink. "Maybe . . ."

They talked a little while longer, about nothing in particular and thankfully not about Ben, then decided to head down the block to Tony's for pizza. Autumn wasn't seeing Ben tonight. She'd seen him this morning in class but not after. And she didn't intend to see him tonight or tomorrow. Since last Saturday, she had dreamed exactly the same dream every night. Nothing had changed, nothing new had turned up when Ben had questioned her afterward and she was exhausted from lack of sleep.

Hoping she might be able to rest the entire night through, she had asked Ben not to come over and he had grudgingly agreed. Maybe it was the dark circles under her eyes that had convinced him.

Whatever the reason, as soon as she and Terri finished their pizza, Autumn headed home.

Unfortunately, even without Ben there she had trouble falling asleep. In the middle of the night, she dreamed the same dream and awakened in a sweat. It took an hour to get back to sleep. Once she did, it seemed like her eyes had barely closed before the alarm clock awakened her.

She was yawning, padding around the

apartment in her robe when the phone rang.

It was Ben.

"Hi, baby. I didn't wake you, did I?"

A warm little shiver went through her. She hated when he called her that. And she loved it. "I've been awake a while."

"Did you get any sleep?"

"Some. I dreamed, but it was the same as before."

"I really didn't plan to call you today, but something's come up and I need your help."

Her fingers tightened around the phone. "You've found something new?"

"I told you Joanne recognized the guy in the original drawing?"

"Yes, I've been working on the list of places I might have seen him — particularly anything to do with sports or sporting events — but so far I've come up with zip."

"Well, it got me to thinking . . . I'll tell you about it when I see you. By the way, Jorge brought over the updated sketch. I can see what you mean about the guy looking different."

"He doesn't look so nice anymore."

"That's for sure. Listen, Autumn, I need you to go with me over to Bainbridge Island. It might be an overnight trip so pack a bag. What time can you be ready?"

She only hesitated a moment. They were in this together and finding Molly was all that mattered. "I'm finished early today. Only a couple of private lessons. Is noon okay?"

"Perfect. You don't get seasick, do you? Never mind, I've got some patches on the boat. I'll see you at noon."

"Wait a minute —"

But Ben had already hung up. He had new information, he said. She should bring an overnight bag. But why would he be taking her on a boat?

A funny little shiver rose in the pit of her stomach just thinking that she would be seeing him after all, maybe spending the night with him. Crap, the last thing she wanted was to spend more time with Ben. Still, if he had uncovered new information, she wanted to know what it was.

Autumn sighed as she headed for the bathroom to shower and get ready for her lessons. Silently, she cursed the fates for intertwining her life with Ben's.

Ben buzzed the intercom in the lobby of her apartment exactly at twelve o'clock. He came upstairs, helped her slip a light jacket over the pale-blue sweater she wore, then took her overnight bag out of her hand and escorted her back downstairs. He had impeccable manners, which made her wonder about his family and where he had come from. She told herself not to ask. The less she knew about Ben, the better.

When they reached the lobby, Ben held open the heavy glass door and they stepped out onto the sidewalk. A town car waited out front to take them down to the dock where Ben kept his boat, and they slid into the deep leather backseat.

As soon as the car pulled away from the curb, Autumn turned to Ben. "All right, so tell me what's going on."

Ben leaned over and lightly kissed her lips. "I missed you, baby." Before she had time to reply, he started talking as if nothing unusual had occurred.

"After my conversation with Joanne, I got to thinking. We know what this guy looks like, but not a whole lot more about him. I decided to make a call to a friend of mine — Lee Walker. He works at the FBI."

"The FBI? I thought you weren't ready to involve the police."

"I'm not — at least not in the way you're thinking. In high school, Lee and I played varsity football together. There was a time he was my best friend. After graduation, I went off to school at the University of

Michigan and Lee went to Ohio State. Over the years, we kind of lost touch, but Lee called when he heard about Molly and offered to help in any way he could. Yesterday, I phoned him to ask if he could put me in touch with an FBI profiler."

"A profiler? Like on TV?"

He nodded. "I did a little research. What they do is called criminal investigative analysis. Profilers look at all the evidence available, either at the various crime scenes or by going through police files. They put the pieces of the puzzle together and come up with a personality profile of the person involved in the crime."

"I thought profilers were used to find serial killers."

"They are. But they also help on individual homicides, rapes, arson, bombings, even extortion."

"And apparently they also work on child abductions."

"Sometimes they do, though they didn't use one on Molly's case. Lee says statistically most kidnappers either murder their victims or set them free within the first seventy-two hours. Since we're assuming Molly is still alive, I'm hoping this guy, Riker, can give us a little more insight into the kind of person the blond man might be."

"This is a really good idea, Ben."

"Lee says out of thirteen-thousand FBI agents, there are only forty full-time profilers. We got lucky. One of them is currently on Bainbridge Island working on a homicide. His name's Burt Riker. Lee said Riker was swamped but if we could get there, he'd make room for us, either this afternoon or tomorrow morning. I figured if we took the boat, we'd have a place to stay while we waited."

The town car continued through traffic, weaving its way along Magnolia Boulevard toward the marina. The vehicle rolled to a stop and the driver, skinny, young and brown-haired, opened the rear passenger door.

"Thanks, Ted," Ben said as they climbed out. "I'll give you a call when we need a ride back." Leaving either of his cars parked down at the dock apparently wasn't something Ben wanted to do.

"No problem, Mr. Mac."

Ben grabbed his overnight bag along with Autumn's and a leather briefcase she hadn't noticed before. They started toward the marina, Ben using his key to unlock the big steel gate, then headed down the gangway to where the boats were moored. He stopped at the stern of a sleek white cabin cruiser with the name *Katydid* painted on the stern.

"I've owned a boat for years," Ben said. "This one's a newer, larger version of the Riviera I had before. You like boats?"

"Love 'em. My dad and I used to go fishing in the sound." With Ben's help, Autumn climbed aboard. "Of course the motorized skiff we rented wasn't anything like this."

To say the least. The *Katydid* was gorgeous, all white and aqua-blue leather, lots of glass and a stateroom lined with teak wood built-ins. The bathroom — head — was big enough for both a shower and tub.

There was another stateroom with its own smaller bath she saw, and felt a ridiculous pang of regret. Ben was a gentleman. He hadn't brought her there to seduce her — not unless she wanted him to — and she couldn't afford to let that happen.

"Let's go up top and start the engines." He cast her a look. "I guess if you fished with your dad, you don't get seasick."

"Not unless it's really stormy, but thanks for asking."

They climbed a ladder that led to the outside steering station, which was enclosed in clear Plexiglas to keep out the wind but could be unzipped completely when the weather was good.

It was good today, cool though, so Ben unzipped and rolled back a couple of panels and left the others down.

"How long will it take to get to the island?"

"Less than an hour. I've got a friend with a private dock he lets me borrow. He also keeps a car there for his guests to use."

"Sounds like a pretty good friend."

Ben made no reply and it occurred to her that maybe this *friend* was a female. Autumn didn't like the knot that curled in her stomach.

On the top deck of the boat, she sat down next to him. Ben fired up the engines and began to maneuver the big boat out of its slip. As he did everything else, he made it look easy, steering past far bigger yachts, easing by row after row of sail and power boats. It was a lovely day, the crisp sea air tinged with the smell of fish and seaweed and damp, salty spray.

As promised, it took less than an hour to reach the cove on Bainbridge Island where Ben planned to dock his boat. Bainbridge wasn't large, only about twelve miles long and four miles wide. It was lovely, though. Lush with pines and thick-trunked deciduous trees whose branches spread over the roads.

As the boat pulled into the cove, she saw that the inlet lay below a sprawling gray, wood-and-stone house hidden among a dense grove of trees.

"My my, very impressive. So who does this place belong to?"

"Charlie Evans."

"The guy who gives the stock tips on TV?"

"That's him. Unfortunately, he's thinking of selling."

"There goes your dock."

"Yeah . . . unless I'm the one who buys it."

Her eyes widened. "Are you seriously considering it?"

Ben slanted her a glance. "I don't know. It never really occurred to me until now."

He maneuvered the boat into one of three slips in the cove and Autumn tossed the rubber fenders over the side, jumped off and secured the line around the cleats at both ends of the dock.

Ben turned off the engines and came down the ladder to join her. "Anyone told you, you make an excellent first mate?"

"No, but maybe I'll keep an eye out for a job if my current position doesn't pan out."

Ben laughed. "Well, you climbers do know your knots." Learning to tie a rope properly was an important skill for a climber — one that might make the difference between life or death.

Ben pulled out his cell phone, dialed a number he had previously stored, and asked for Burt Riker. "This is Ben McKenzie. Riker's expecting my call." He spoke for several moments, gave his number to the person on the other end of the line, then disconnected. "Riker's out at the crime scene. They don't expect him back until late. He's got my number. Hopefully, he'll call."

"So what do we do in the meantime?"

The corner of Ben's mouth edged up. "I can think of some very interesting ways to spend the afternoon, sweetheart, but I suppose you'd rather take a drive around the island."

Autumn remembered to breathe. "That . . . that sounds great." She managed to smile. "I've only been here a couple of times. Terri and I came over on the ferry but we just prowled around town and then went back to Seattle."

"In that case, I'll give you the five-dollar tour. I'd better take my briefcase. There's always a chance Riker will call."

"What's in it?"

"A copy of the information we've collected from your dreams and the original police report. I'm hoping that's enough."

"Maybe your friend Walker sent him the FBI report."

"I don't think so. I told Lee I wanted this guy to look at the crime scene from a fresh perspective."

"Are you going to tell him about the dreams?" Autumn asked.

"Not if I don't have to. I told Lee. I also told him some of what you've said has been corroborated, enough that I'm willing to pursue the matter. I'm not sure what he told Riker."

They climbed a white wooden staircase that wound its way up the cliff to the house but made their way around to the side instead of going in. A bright red Jeep with four huge all-terrain tires sat in front of a line of five garages.

"One of Charlie's toys," Ben explained. "Fortunately, I get to use it." He knew where the key was so they climbed in and snapped on their seat belts.

Several hours later, after a leisurely tour of Bainbridge Island and a stop for drinks in one of the local pubs to watch the sun go down, they started back toward the house.

The bad news was that Burt Riker hadn't called.

Which meant they would have to spend

the night on Ben's boat.

Autumn's stomach knotted.

EIGHTEEN

"It's getting late," Autumn said as the Jeep made its way along the narrow road winding through the trees. "Maybe we should stop somewhere and get something to eat."

"Good idea." But instead of stopping at a restaurant, Ben pulled into one of the local markets, a small batt-and-board structure with the front door propped open and several cars parked in front.

"A grocery store?" Autumn said.

"That's right. I'm cooking you dinner aboard."

"*You're* cooking? But the morning we had breakfast at my apartment, you said —"

"I said I hadn't had anyone cook for me in years. That's true. After my divorce, I got tired of eating out, so I learned how to cook for myself."

He made her wait in the Jeep while he shopped, hoping to surprise her. It had been a wonderful day, but evening was setting in and during the time she sat in the car, her mood began to shift.

She would be spending the night with Ben. He would be cooking her dinner. They would be drinking wine, enjoying an evening aboard his expensive yacht in a beautiful ocean setting.

She swallowed. All afternoon as they had explored the island, her mind had flashed images of the night they'd made love, of Ben's incredible, gloriously naked body. She remembered the feel of him pressing her down in the mattress, her nipples hard against the muscles in his chest as he moved inside her. She had done her best to block the memories, but they were creeping into her mind again.

For an instant, she panicked. She would make him take her home, tell him she had gotten a call on her cell phone. Something had come up and she needed to get back, a problem with her dad or maybe —

Autumn sighed and leaned back in the seat. She was being ridiculous. Ben hadn't brought her to the island for seduction. After the first time, whenever they had been together he had been a perfect gentleman. She was the one with the problem, not Ben. Surely she could continue to maintain the polite distance he had kept between them all day.

As soon as they got back to the boat, Ben set to work in the galley and Autumn went to change into more comfortable clothes. She had brought loose-fitting lavender plush pants and a matching zip-front jacket in case they needed to stay, and she pulled the garments on gratefully, leaving her jeans and sweater in the smaller cabin, along with her shoes and canvas overnight bag.

Emerging from below, she found Ben busily dicing tomatoes and washing lettuce for a salad. Water boiled in a pot on the small galley stove.

Autumn slid into the dining booth and Ben brought her a glass of Chianti. He still wore his jeans and soft knit shirt but like Autumn, he had taken off his shoes and was padding around the elegant-yet-cozy salon in his bare feet.

Nice feet, she thought with a smile, sun-tanned and masculine, his toenails neatly trimmed. As he prepared the meal, Autumn found herself watching him. With his dark hair, golden brown eyes and solid jaw, he was incredibly handsome.

She loved his body — the lean muscles and wide shoulders, the six-pack muscles across his ribs. Whenever he looked her way, her pulse took a leap. She remembered the feel of his strong hands as he had helped her aboard, remembered the tingle of his arm against her breasts and her stomach contracted.

"Hungry yet?"

"Starving," she replied.

"How about doing the salad while I finish the pasta sauce?"

"Sure." She made her way down the two steps into the galley, barely large enough for both of them to work. For an instant, she stepped in his way. Her breast came in contact with his powerful chest and her nipples contracted. A soft curl of warmth tugged low in her belly.

Autumn stood frozen, staring up into Ben's tawny eyes. She recognized the heat there, the glitter of desire he had kept well hidden until now.

"Ben . . ."

It was steamy in the galley, fragrant with the aroma of garlic and tomatoes and crusty French bread. Ben reached over and turned off the flame beneath the pot of water boiling on the stove.

"Dinner can wait." Then he was kissing her and when she tried to pull away, he wouldn't stop.

"I'm not letting you run anymore," he said

softly. "You want this as much as I do and we both know it."

"You're wrong, Ben."

"I'm right, Autumn." Then his mouth was on hers, moving hotly, wet and fierce, a deep, taking, plundering kiss, his tongue sweeping in, stroking the inside of her mouth. Her legs went weak. Autumn clutched the front of his shirt as he backed her against the wall, his body holding hers immobile, pinning her against his tall frame.

When she tried to turn away, he caught her chin and kissed her until her lips softened and she opened to accept his tongue. For an instant, she wondered what he would do if she tried to make him stop, wondered if he would take what he wanted even if she said no.

The thought should have frightened her. Instead, all she could think was that if he took her, she would have an excuse for getting exactly what she wanted.

Ben ended the kiss before the notion went further. He was breathing hard, his golden eyes burning into her like flames.

"Tell me you want this, Autumn. By God, have the courage to admit it."

She looked into his handsome face. "I want this." Reaching up, she shoved her trembling fingers into his thick dark hair.

"I'm going crazy with wanting, Ben. I want you to touch me all over. I want you inside me."

Ben made a growling sound in his throat and then he was kissing her again and she was kissing him back. Their tongues tangled and mated. He unzipped the front of her jacket and reached inside to cup a breast. She had discarded her bra when she changed and the feel of his calloused hand against her bare skin sent a shiver of longing through her.

He slipped the top off her shoulders, then slid the loose-fitting pants down over her hips. She was left in only her pink thong and he dragged it down too, found her softness and began to stroke her.

Autumn moaned into his mouth.

Ben didn't bother to remove his clothes, just unzipped the fly of his jeans and released himself, lifted her, wrapped her legs around his waist and plunged himself inside her.

"Oh, God, Ben . . ."

"You're driving me crazy," he said against the side of her neck. "I think about you all day. At night, I dream of being inside you." He eased out and drove into her again. He touched her, stroked her, pounded into her until she cried out in release and her head slumped onto his shoulder.

She let out a sigh of pure contentment, but Ben didn't let go.

Instead, he nipped the side of her neck. "Hold on, baby, we aren't finished yet."

Her body tightened in anticipation. Desire sprang to life once more. True to his word, he kissed her deeply and started moving, turning her insides hot with need. His big hands cupped her bottom as his rhythm increased, driving himself harder and deeper, bringing her to a second shattering climax.

They reached the peak together, both of them shaking, their bodies covered with a thin layer of perspiration. Autumn barely noticed when he carried her down the steps to the master cabin and settled her in his bed. As she snuggled beneath the comforter he tossed over her, he leaned down and kissed her softly on the lips.

"I'll wake you when supper's ready."

Autumn didn't argue. She just wanted to lie there, relaxed and content, feeling completely sated and utterly feminine.

Later she would think about what she had done and what she should do about Ben.

"Come on, sleepyhead. Dinner's on the table." Ben held out her clothes and Autumn yawned and stretched and swung her legs to the side of the bed.

"I need to make a pit stop and I'll be right there." She pulled on the soft plush pants and zipped up the matching jacket, went in to use the head then joined Ben at the table. He had set it with white porcelain dinnerware on aqua blue placemats that matched the interior of the boat and refilled their glasses of wine.

"Supper looks fantastic." Autumn's stomach growled at the sight of the lovely pasta in cream sauce piled high with fresh mussels, clams, scallops and shrimp.

"I hope you like it."

What was not to like? The food looked delicious and she dug in with relish, even hungrier that she had thought. Autumn took a sip of her Chianti, which was rich and delicious, her body still faintly tingling from the great sex they'd had. She set her glass back down on the table.

"There's something I've been wanting to tell you."

A dark eyebrow went up. "How much you like it when I take you to bed?"

Her cheeks warmed. "Well, that, too."

His look turned serious. "So what is it you've been wanting to tell me?"

"I think I've figured out why I started having these dreams."

Ben eased back against the padded leather seat of the booth, his gaze fixed on her face. "Why?"

"It occurred to me that when I had the dreams before, back when I was in high school, they didn't start until I met Tim Wiseman. I had known Jolie and Jeff for years — they were two of my closest friends — but it wasn't until I met Tim, the kid who was driving the car the night of the accident, that I started to dream about the wreck."

"Go on."

"It wasn't until twelve years later that I started to dream again. I think there has to be some kind of link between the people involved. In this case, I saw or met the blond man somewhere before I ever knew you. It must have been just sort of in passing because I still can't remember where it was. But I didn't start dreaming about him until I saw you at the gym. You were the link, just like Tim Wiseman. If I hadn't seen both you *and* the blond man, I don't think I ever would have dreamed about Molly. I think I had to come in contact with both of you, the same way I did with my friends and Tim Wiseman."

"I guess that makes an odd sort of sense."

"And I think the event has to be very traumatic — the violent death of three teenagers or in this case, a child who's been kidnapped from her parents."

"If you're right, at least it won't happen to you very often."

Autumn's fingers tightened on the stem of her glass. "If it never happens again, it's fine with me."

They finished Ben's fabulous supper, enjoying the wine and casual conversation. He told her a little about growing up in the Mid-west, about his years in college, that his parents had both passed away and that he still missed them. They avoided more talk of Molly. If luck was with them, they would be meeting the FBI profiler tomorrow and both of them knew it could be a very rough day.

As soon as the dishes were cleared, washed and put away, they headed down to the cabins in the bow of the boat. Autumn didn't protest when Ben opened his door and waited for her to walk past him into the room. She could read the desire in his eyes and a soft ache throbbed inside her. Ben wanted to make love to her again and dear Lord, she wanted him to.

To hell with tomorrow, Autumn thought. If this was a fling, she was going to enjoy every minute of it.

Standing in the narrow space next to the bed, she went up on her toes and kissed him and Ben pulled her down on the mattress.

The big boat rocked softly in the sea. Last night, after another wild round of lovemaking, the rhythm had lulled her gently to sleep. The sun was well up by the time they sat in the booth in the salon drinking rich black coffee and eating cinnamon rolls. Outside the windows, a seagull screeched and wheeled on the wind and the sky was a crystalline blue.

Over the rim of her steaming cup, Autumn looked at Ben. "There's something I've been wondering . . ."

He set his mug down on the table. "About what?"

"Last night . . . when we were in the galley and you first kissed me . . . would you have stopped if I'd really wanted you to?"

Ben's eyes met hers. A faint shadow of beard lined his jaw, which tightened just a little. "If you were any other woman, the answer to that would be easy. I would never force a woman to do something she didn't want to do. Last night . . ." He shook his head. "I wanted you so damned much. I honestly don't know."

But Autumn believed that he would have stopped. Ben was just not the kind of man to force himself on an unwilling woman. That he was being honest about his feelings was refreshing and incredibly flattering.

Ben released a breath. "I brought you here to seduce you, Autumn. That is the flat-out truth."

She couldn't have been more surprised.

"I was determined to have you. I wanted you back in my bed and I was sure you wanted that too. Last night was every bit as good as I thought it would be — hell, it was better than good. It was fantastic. I probably ought to feel guilty, but the truth is I'm glad things turned out the way they did."

She couldn't say she was sorry either. Last night had been the best night of her life.

Ben studied her with his tawny dark eyes. "There's something going on between us, Autumn. You must feel it, too. I don't want you to run from me again."

Her heart was pounding. She had never known sex could be the way it was with Ben. But there was a lot more to consider than the incredible physical attraction the two of them seemed to share. Ben was beginning to sound like he wanted a relationship and that was never going to happen. They were completely unsuited. She could never be enough for a man like Ben and she didn't even want to try. She opened her mouth to tell him that when his cell phone started to ring.

Ben flipped it open. "McKenzie."

She couldn't hear the conversation on the other end of the line, but Ben was nodding and he seemed relieved.

"We'll be there in twenty minutes." He slipped the phone closed and looked at her.

"Riker?"

"Yeah. There's a coffee shop downtown. He'll meet us there in twenty minutes."

Autumn was on her feet in an instant, grabbing their near-empty coffee cups and heading down to the galley, picking up her purse and making her way to the big glass salon door leading out to the deck. They left the boat, hurried along the dock, then climbed the stairway leading up to where the shiny red Jeep was parked. Twenty minutes later, they walked into the Seaside Café near the ferry boat landing.

It was eleven o'clock. Most of the break-fast traffic was gone and it was still too early for the lunch crowd, so it wasn't too busy. In a booth at the rear of the café, Autumn spotted a dark-haired man, slightly balding, wearing a navy-blue windbreaker and a pair of khaki slacks. He was sitting by himself and there was something in the set of his jaw, the way he seemed to notice everything and everyone around him, that made him stand out from the other few patrons in the café.

"Riker?" Ben asked as they approached.

He stood up from his seat in the pink vinyl booth. "Burt Riker. I take it you're Ben McKenzie."

"That's right and this is Autumn Sommers."

One of his dark eyebrows went up at the name and Autumn smiled. "That's *Sommers* with an *O*," she said.

She slid into the opposite side of the booth, leaving room for Ben, who slid in beside her. Riker sat back down and Ben pushed the two manila folders he was carrying across the table. Riker pulled a pair of reading glasses out of his jacket pocket and slipped them on, then began to peruse the information in the files. When the waitress arrived to refill Riker's cup, Ben ordered coffee for himself and Autumn.

It was nearly twenty minutes later when the profiler finally looked up. While he read, neither Autumn or Ben had said a word.

Riker fixed his attention on Ben. "Your friend, Lee Walker, asked me to talk to you as a personal favor. He didn't say much, just that you have information you can't verify but you believe may be valid. He said I probably didn't want to know where you got the leads you're following, so I won't ask."

Autumn felt a faint jolt of relief. No questions about the dreams. One less problem they would have to deal with.

"Assuming the data we've collected is correct," Ben said, "what can you tell us?"

Riker tapped the file. "According to the information in your folder, the UnSub — that's the term we use for an unknown subject — is blond, fair, late thirties to mid-forties, weight one-hundred sixty to one-hundred eighty pounds."

"That's right."

"From the first sketch and your notes, he seems to be a harmless-looking fellow, fairly average. The later sketch gives him a harder appearance, but for the most part his ability to blend in is part of his protection. On the other hand, from the way you believe the abducted child was lured into his car, we can assume the man can be charming. He was able to win the child's trust in a very short time — though there is a chance he had already started to develop that trust at an earlier point in time. Maybe he spoke to her at school or somewhere else."

"Recently my ex-wife remembered him approaching her and Molly in front of the sporting-goods store before Molly was taken."

Riker nodded. "He may have talked to her at other times as well. Molly was abducted on a weekday after school. The UnSub likely knew her schedule. He had been stalking her, figuring out the best time to take her without getting caught."

"So he did his homework."

The profiler gave a nod. "This is not an impulsive individual." He sipped his coffee, set the mug back down on the table. "You believe the girl is currently living with two other women, both of them blond like Molly, so the UnSub's choice wasn't random. He wanted a child with his own fair coloring. It's possible he wanted a girl who appeared to be a child of his own blood, but odds are he is also somewhat of a racist."

"You mean he's some kind of white supremist?" Ben asked.

"Not necessarily a member of an organization but a person of that mentality. There's an encounter described in your notes where the UnSub interacts with the women in his familial group. It says they seemed frightened of him. That's because he's extremely controlling, particularly with women."

"A male chauvinist," Autumn said.

"Carried to the extreme," said Riker. "He doesn't like losing control and he doesn't like disobedience — real or imagined. He will likely become angry or sullen, determined to retaliate by punishing the offender. He rules with an iron hand, but not unfairly. These women are afraid of him, but they are also in awe of him. Women in general are probably attracted to him."

Autumn glanced at Ben. His eyes were hard, his jaw clenched.

"From the plain sort of clothes the women were wearing in the encounter, I'd say he's socially avoidant, an introvert. He keeps pretty much to himself and he expects his family to do the same. Whatever work he does probably involves cash payments and is something he can do on his own, perhaps in his own home."

"What else can you tell us?" Ben asked.

"We know the UnSub has three women in his familial group. The oldest is close enough to his own age that we can assume she was wooed into joining him, not forced. There's a chance he took the fifteen-year-old and got away with it. He took Molly and got away with it. He's arrogant — thinks he's smarter than everyone else. Molly's six years older now, close to her teens, heading into womanhood. There's a chance he'll try to abduct another young child to add to the family unit."

Autumn glanced at Ben. There was a look of controlled fury on his face unlike anything she had seen.

Riker tapped the file. "That is, assuming the information in this file is correct," he added.

"You've left out one piece of pertinent information," Ben said softly. "Do you think Molly and the other girl are being sexually abused?"

Riker leaned back in his seat. "It might seem the obvious conclusion, but I don't think there's enough information in these files to say for sure. It appears the UnSub has some kind of Godfather complex. I think he wants this family he's constructed to see him that way. Whether that involves sex with the younger girls is difficult to say."

Riker closed the file and shoved it back to Ben. "Whatever's going on here, I wish you luck. In the meantime, if I can keep a copy of the latest sketch, I'll have it run through the National Pedophile Registry. If we get a match, I'll let you know."

"Thank you."

Riker slid out of the booth and so did

Autumn and Ben.

"I appreciate your time," Ben said.

Riker looked him straight in the face. "Walker told me the girl is your daughter. I know how hard it must be for you to be objective but you need to do your best."

It was a subtle warning for Ben not to let his hopes get too high, especially since the information he was using might be completely erroneous. He was right and it made Autumn's stomach tighten.

Ben stretched out a hand. "Thanks again."

Riker completed the handshake. "You come up with some kind of tangible proof, you call me."

"I'll do that," Ben said. Autumn heard the bell chime as Riker walked out and the door closed behind him.

Standing next to her, Ben blew out a breath. "That was even worse than I thought."

Autumn swallowed against the lump beginning to build in her throat. Everything Riker had said seemed to hold a kernel of truth. If the blond man was anything like the man the profiler described, he was a monster.

And they were no closer to finding him than they had been before.

Nineteen

They got back to Seattle early in the afternoon. Ben returned to his apartment to change then went down to his office while Autumn went to work at the gym.

She had phoned Josh last night and asked him to take her morning session, then moved a couple of private lessons to later in the day. She walked into the climbing gym and headed straight for Josh, who was working with Ned, Autumn's first private lesson of the day. She reminded herself to stay focused, that she was being paid to do a job.

It wasn't that easy to do. She knew the toll the profiler's words had taken on Ben. He'd been worried before. Now that he knew the sort of man they were dealing with, he was hanging on to his control by a thread.

"I swear if we find this guy," he had said

on the trip home, "I'm going to tear him to pieces."

"We're making progress, Ben. You have to believe that. You've got to stay focused on finding Molly."

His jaw tightened. "I know."

But again, they were running out of leads. Flyers and e-mails containing the blond man's sketch had been sent to classic car clubs across the country. A number of calls had come in describing men who looked like the man in the sketch, but Pete Rossi's follow-up had led nowhere. Maybe Riker's search of the pedophile registry would turn up something. As Autumn watched Ned skillfully climbing the wall, she said a silent prayer that it would be so.

"He's getting really good, isn't he?" Josh stood next to her on the mat in front of the wall. He was belaying Ned, since the guy was so big. Autumn could do it, but Josh was heavier, more Ned's weight, which made it far easier and he was already there working out on the wall.

"He's got incredible talent." Autumn admired Ned's grace of movement as he reached the top of the wall. His red tank top stuck to his broad back, which glistened with perspiration. He paused for a moment to catch his breath, then made his way carefully back down the wall.

"You did great," Autumn said when he reached the bottom. "Now take that bundle of rope, loop it over your shoulder and do it again."

Ned just grinned. The bundle weighed twenty-five pounds. For traditional climbing, the total weight of rope and equipment could weigh as much as fifty. Since she was so small Autumn used the very lightest gear, which for some reason always seemed to cost the most.

She watched Ned start his assent, silver earrings glittering, dark, muscular legs moving with dancer-like rhythm, using hand and finger jams in the man-made cracks in the pseudo-granite face of the wall. He hauled his big, lean-muscled body upward, clinging to the wall like a fly on a window pane, and she found herself thinking of Ben, who was also amazingly good for an inexperienced climber.

"Ned and I are going up to the mountains this weekend," Josh said, breaking into her thoughts, his legs braced apart in case Ned lost his footing. "Courtney too. Why don't you come along?"

Autumn cocked an eyebrow in his direction. "I heard you and Courtney were dating. I like her. She's a great girl, Josh."

He smiled in a way that made him appear almost shy. "Yeah, Court's a lot of fun. Good climber too."

Ned reached the top of the wall and started back down, taking his time, making each step count. He was determined to learn. No shortcuts for Ned.

Autumn understood. She had been that way herself.

"So you want to come along?" Josh repeated.

"I wish I could, Josh. I really do, but I'm kind of busy right now."

"Yeah . . . You know, I didn't think I was going to like him . . . Ben, I mean. But I do."

Autumn had felt the same way. "I like him, too," she said, trying to keep erotic images of last night out of her head.

Josh continued, "But he's still Ben McKenzie. When he's working out in the gym, women come up with all kinds of excuses just to talk to him. He runs in the fast lane, Autumn. You're not like that. I'm afraid you're gonna get hurt."

Her stomach started churning. She was rarely in the gym at the same time as Ben, but she could still remember Terri drooling over him, calling him *the hunk*.

"I know you're right. It's just . . ."

"Yeah, I know. Sometimes we're just attracted to the wrong people."

He was talking about Terri. He was dating Courtney Roland but Terri was the one he truly wanted. Or at least believed he did.

She thought of Ben. She hadn't been up to his office since the day she'd been firmly escorted out. She wasn't sure she would be welcome there and even if she was, she didn't really want to see him.

Josh's words had crystallized the thoughts rolling round in her mind. She needed to keep her head where Ben McKenzie was concerned. Still, she wasn't ready to give him up — not yet.

As Terri had said, she deserved a little fun. Why not have it with Ben?

Autumn ignored the little voice that called her ten kinds of a fool and went back to working on the wall with Ned.

By the time Ben finished at the office, it was dark. Jenn and the rest of his staff had gone home at least two hours ago. He'd had a lot of catching up to do after being away nearly two days and he still wasn't quite done. Because he was staying with Autumn, before he'd gone to work he had stopped at his apartment to change and pick up clean clothes. Now it was getting late and he didn't want Autumn to have to wait up for him.

Autumn. Ben almost smiled. She was the best thing that had happened to him in years. And the worst. The pain and heartbreak her dreams had forced to the surface made each day more difficult than the last. She had given him hope that Molly was alive, that his little girl was out there waiting for him to find her.

But what if she wasn't? What if all of this was for nothing? What if she was alive and they couldn't find her? She would remain as lost to him as she had been since the day she disappeared.

Just thinking of what Molly might be suffering made his insides clench into a knot.

He took a deep breath and pictured Autumn's face in his mind. Whenever he felt the lowest, he would see her sweet smile and beautiful tilted cat-eyes.

He was falling for her, he knew. It was the worst thing that could possibly happen, but he couldn't seem to help himself. Christ, he had no idea where her dreams might lead. Molly might be long dead, just as the police believed, and all of this just a series of crazy coincidences.

But Ben no longer believed that. Somewhere along the way, he had become convinced that his little girl was alive and he was desperate to find her. Molly had to come first. He didn't have time for a woman in his life right now.

And yet there she was, irrevocably in the middle, *Autumn,* the only person who could help him find his daughter.

Ben sighed as he walked along the sidewalk in the darkness on his way to Autumn's apartment. It was Friday night and Seattle was coming to life. He could hear the faint notes of jazz coming from one of the clubs. Laughter bubbled from a group of young women in very short skirts standing outside the neon-lit doorway. As he crossed the street, he caught a glimpse of a departing ferry's lights on the water in the bay.

On a normal Friday before all of this had begun, he would be out till late with whichever woman he was seeing that night. Afterward, he would take her back to his penthouse where they would probably have sex, then he would take her home.

He didn't like to wake up with a woman in the morning. There was nothing to say that hadn't been said the night before and he had too much work to do.

At least he had felt that way until he'd met Autumn. In the past few weeks, he had come to realize how much he missed the pleasures of an evening at home and the joy of waking up with a woman you cared about snuggled in your arms.

He had been that kind of man once. He had loved being married, loved being a husband and father. After losing Molly, all of that had changed.

Maybe thinking of his daughter had stirred old memories. Or maybe it was just Autumn. Whatever it was, it was frightening and wonderful at the same time. If only he had time to explore his feelings, to find out if there was something there they could build on.

He couldn't. Not until they found Molly.

If they found her, he thought darkly and pushed the buzzer in the lobby of Autumn's apartment building.

Autumn was sitting at the table in the small dining area when the doorbell rang. Ben had called earlier, so she knew he was going to be late. He was always thoughtful that way.

"Hey, baby," he said as she pulled open the door. Leaning down, he pressed a soft kiss on her lips and a charge of sexual heat went through her.

It was insane. It was only a simple kiss.

"Tough day?" she asked, trying to sound

nonchalant.

Ben set his overnight bag on the floor. "Mostly I worked on getting that A-1 lease deal stopped." Ben reached out and caught her hand, brought it to his lips and kissed her palm. A sizzle of electricity zipped through her. "How about you?"

She tried to pull her hand away but he wouldn't let go so she gave in and let him lead her back over to the dining table. Several pages out of her yellow legal pad were spread across the top.

"I spent the evening going over the lists of places I might have seen the blond man."

"Since you didn't call, I gather it didn't work."

"No, but . . ." Autumn grinned. "I came up with this fabulous idea."

One of his eyebrows arched. "Which is . . . ?"

"We hire a hypnotist. We get someone to put me in a hypnotic trance and maybe I'll remember where I saw him. I've seen it done on the cop shows on TV and it works like a charm."

"Unfortunately, this isn't TV."

"I know, but it's worth a try, don't you think?"

Ben pondered the notion. "Might just be. I'll put Jennifer to work on it Monday."

"Too late. I've got a guy lined up to come over at eleven in the morning. Tomorrow's Saturday. You don't have to go to work. I was thinking you could be here to listen in case I said something important."

"I was planning to go into the office . . ."

"It might work, Ben."

He smiled. "I suppose work can wait. If you're game, we'll see what you come up with."

They talked a bit about the idea of using hypnotism as a memory stimulus, but as time passed the conversation grew more and more stilted and the looks that passed between them, more and more heated.

Ben stood up. "I think it's time we went to bed." He reached out, caught her hand and urged her to her feet. Autumn made a funny little squeak as he lifted her into his arms and carried her into the bedroom.

They made love as passionately as they had on the boat and after the second time, Autumn drifted into a deep, trouble-free sleep.

Autumn's eyes popped open and she snapped bolt upright, her heart hammering madly from the shock of her latest dream. The clock on the nightstand read two forty-five a.m.

"Oh, God, Ben!"

He reached over and clicked on the lamp next to the bed. They were using a small tape recorder now and it sat on the night-stand. The morning after, they transcribed whatever new information, if any, Autumn had received.

Ben reached for the palm-sized machine and turned it on. "Slow down. Tell me what you saw."

"I — I can't believe it. It was just . . . just like Riker said." She looked up at him. "There's another little girl, Ben. She's there in the house with the others."

Ben frowned. "It's pretty coincidental, don't you think, that you would dream about another little girl right after you talked to Riker. Are you sure this didn't happen because he mentioned it, put the thought into your mind? The power of sug-gestion can be extremely strong."

She raked back her heavy auburn curls with a shaky hand. "I don't know, I . . . I don't think so, but maybe . . ." She looked up at him. "Until the very end, it was just like the other dreams. The women were in the kitchen cooking supper. Then the blond man walked in. The conversation was ex-actly the same until they started to sit down at the table and the man asked where Mary was."

"Mary? That was the little girl's name?"

She nodded. "He was talking to the older woman — the one he calls Rachael. Then he said, 'Rachael, where's Mary?' "

"What did Rachael say?" Ben asked softly, the tape whirring quietly in the background.

"Rachael said Mary was being punished, she wasn't going to get any supper until she learned to answer to the name she had been given."

"So Mary's not her real name, just like with Molly. How old was she?"

"I think . . . somewhere between five and seven. She looks just like Molly when she was that same age."

"What happened next?"

Autumn closed her eyes and allowed the dream to resurface in her mind. "The little girl walked from the other room to the kitchen door. She stopped and the blond man stood up. He said he would deal with Mary. That she was old enough for a visit to his workshop in the garage. That's when I woke up."

She looked at him and tears welled in her eyes. "Oh, God, Ben, what if the dream is real and he's abducted another little girl?"

Ben turned off the tape recorder and

pulled her into his arms. Autumn clung to his neck, her cheek pressed against his. She tried not to cry but tears began to leak from beneath her lashes and roll down her cheeks.

She didn't know how much more of this she could take. How much more either of them could handle.

When in God's name would all of this be over?

She felt Ben's hands moving gently up and down her back, easing the tremors running through her.

"It's all right, honey. It doesn't do any good to cry. Believe me, I know."

Autumn silently nodded. She held on to him a moment more, then dragged in a shaky breath and eased away. "I think it was real, Ben."

The sigh he released sounded weary. "As real as any of this, you mean."

"Yeah . . . as real as a dream can be."

He shifted to the side of the bed and stood up. He pulled on the dark brown terrycloth robe he had brought with him the last time he had spent the night. "I want to go over everything you saw one more time and I want to replay the tape."

"All right."

"I think we need a pot of coffee."

"Good idea." Autumn reached for her

335

pink quilted robe and walked past him out of the bedroom into the kitchen.

"We've got to talk to the police," Ben said, trailing along behind her. "We need to know if a child who fits the description of the one in your dream has come up missing in the last few months. It would have to be fairly recent if Mary isn't ready to accept her new name."

"That's what I was thinking."

"I'll call Doug Watkins in the morning. See what I can find out."

"If we tell the police the truth, they won't believe us."

"Doug's a pretty good guy," Ben said. "I think he might do us a favor."

"If a child was abducted, it couldn't have happened anywhere around here or we would have seen it on the news. Maybe he kidnapped her in another state."

"Could be. Hell, maybe he lives halfway across the country and we've been looking in the wrong place all along."

Autumn shook her head. "Maybe, but I don't think so." She padded over to the cupboard and pulled out a bag of fresh ground coffee. "I saw him once, remember? I travel some, but I have a hunch it was somewhere not that far away."

"You never know — maybe your hypnotist

will help us figure it out."

She glanced over to where he stood next to the breakfast bar. He looked worried and exhausted. "I hope so," she said. "God, I hope so."

The hypnotist, Peter Blakely, turned out to be a man in his forties. Handsome, Ben thought, with streaks of silver in his light-brown hair, blue eyes and a pleasant smile. He looked completely normal, beige slacks and a blue, short-sleeve Izod pullover, nothing at all like the weirdo Ben half-expected him to be. There was even a trace of upper-class British accent in his speech.

"Thank you for coming, Mr. Blakely," Autumn said as he walked into the apartment.

"I'm just Peter. I prefer to be on a first name basis with my clients."

"That's fine with us. I'm Autumn and this is Ben."

Ben shook hands with Blakely.

Autumn smiled. "I explained on the phone a little of what's been happening and what we're trying to do."

"You would like to recall a meeting you had with a particular person some years back."

"That's right."

Ben led Blakely over to the table to look at the sketch. "This is what he looks like."

"At least that's the way he looks in the dreams I told you about," Autumn explained. "It's important we find him. Unfortunately, I can't remember where I saw him."

She managed another smile but Ben thought it looked strained. He knew she was tired after sitting up for hours last night going over the tape and her recollections of the dream, but once they had gone back to bed, making love had helped them both fall asleep. He'd awakened early, sporting his morning hard-on, but knowing how exhausted she was, he didn't reach for her. Instead, he simply lay there enjoying the feel of her small body pressed up to his and let her sleep.

"So how do we begin?" she asked Blakely, returning Ben's attention to the matter at hand.

Blakely took a quick glance around. "Why don't we go into the living room and you can lie down on the sofa. There are dozens of different techniques, of course, but I prefer to start with a quiet, relaxed atmosphere. Ben, will you please pull the curtains?"

He walked over and pulled the drapes.

Earlier he had phoned Detective Watkins at the Issaquah police department. He hadn't spoken to the man in years, but he needed to enquire about the possibility of another missing child. He discovered the detective had been promoted and now worked out of the East Seattle precinct, which was good since it was right there in the city.

Watkins wasn't in. The detective didn't work weekends unless he was on a case, the dispatcher said, so Ben left his name and number. Hopefully Watkins would call him once he got the message.

"Do you have a CD player?" Peter Blakely asked.

"Right next to the TV," Ben said.

The hypnotist handed him a disc and Ben walked over, slid it into the player and pushed the play button. The soft sounds of water rippling over rocks drifted into the living room, giving the place a calm, soothing atmosphere. As Autumn stretched out on the sofa, she seemed only a little nervous.

It didn't hurt, after all.

Ben almost smiled. As tired as she was, she would probably just fall asleep.

"All right, Autumn, are you comfortable?" Blakely asked.

She yawned in answer. "Very comfortable."

He flicked on what looked like a small penlight, held it so the beam moved in an arch on the wall. "I want you to let your eyes follow the light and listen as I speak. Are you ready?"

"I'm ready."

"I'm going to count backwards from one hundred. Before I get to one, you will be deeply asleep but able to hear exactly what I say." The light arched slowly back and forth on the wall. "One hundred, ninety-nine, ninety-eight. You are relaxed and comfortable. Your eyes are beginning to close."

Her body seemed to subtly relax.

"Ninety-seven, ninety-six, ninety-five, ninety-four. You are growing more and more sleepy, barely able to keep your eyes open now."

The light moved in a slow, steady rhythm and her body sank limply into the sofa.

"Ninety-three, ninety-two, ninety-one. Your eyes are closed. You are deeply relaxed now. Can you hear me, Autumn?"

"Yes . . ."

The penlight went off. "Ninety, eighty-nine. You are very deeply asleep, Autumn, and as you lie there, you are going to think back in time." There was a deep, soft cadence to Peter Blakely's voice, a mesmerizing rhythm that seemed to pull gently at the muscles in Ben's body as well as Autumn's. He found himself beginning to get sleepy, shook his head and sat up a little straighter in his chair.

"There is a man . . ." Blakely said. "A blond man you have seen many times in your dreams. You know his face. At sometime in the past, you encountered this man somewhere, perhaps even met him. Can you see him?"

"Yes . . ."

"Is he there with you now?"

"Yes . . . He just said . . . 'hello'."

Ben's heartbeat quickened.

"What else is he saying?"

"Nothing . . . he is just being . . . friendly."

"Where are you?"

"Burlington."

Ben's whole body went tense.

"Where in Burlington?"

"In the . . . sporting goods . . . store."

Blakely flicked Ben a glance, then returned his attention to Autumn. "Do you know the name of the store?"

"Burlington . . . Sports."

Blakely spoke softly to Ben. "You know it?"

Ben nodded. "It's an old place that's been there for years."

The hypnotist turned back to Autumn. "Tell me what's happening."

"I'm there with . . . my dad." She moistened her lips. "We're buying . . . some . . . camping gear."

Ben's pulse roared. Max Sommers had been there that day. Maybe he would remember the man. Maybe he even knew him.

"What is the blond man doing?"

"Buying a . . . camp stove."

"Does he say anything else?"

"No, only . . . 'hello'."

Blakely shifted a little in the chair he'd pulled up next to the sofa. "Do you know the date?"

A small frown tugged between Autumn's eyebrows. "It's . . . summer." She moistened her lips. "Dad and I are going . . . climbing. I'm visiting him for the . . . weekend."

"Is there anything else you can recall?"

"The man . . . seemed nice. I thought . . . it would be nice if I could meet someone like him."

A chill ran down Ben's spine. The profiler had said the man could be charming, that women were attracted to him. The thought of Autumn anywhere near the bastard made Ben's blood run cold.

"You did very well, Autumn," Peter Blakely continued. "Now I'm going to start counting, beginning with the number one. By the time I reach five, you will be wide awake and able to remember everything we've said. One. Two. Three. Four. Five."

Autumn's eyes slowly opened. She sat up on the sofa and looked straight at Ben.

"Burlington," she said. "I saw him in Burlington."

TWENTY

As soon as Peter Blakely left the apartment carrying a check made out to him by Ben, Autumn dialed her father. Max had been with her the day she had seen the blond man. Maybe her dad had seen him again, maybe he even lived there in Burlington.

She hadn't mentioned anything about her dreams to Max. She was afraid he would think of the last time it had happened and how distressed she had been and she didn't want him to worry. Now she was frantic to talk to him to see what he might recall. The phone rang and rang but there was no answer. Finally, the message machine kicked on.

"Max and Myra here. Leave us a message."

So they were officially living together now. *Interesting.* Things between her father and Myra had begun to move fairly rapidly since the time he had spent in the hospital.

"It's Autumn, Dad. It's important I talk to you. Give me a call. If I'm not at home, call me on my cell." She hung up and turned to Ben. "He isn't there."

"So I gathered."

"Now we're waiting for two return calls. I hate waiting, don't you?"

"We've got our cells. It's past lunchtime. Let's get out of here for a while, go get something to eat."

"Good idea." They'd had coffee and a Bisquick coffeecake she had whipped up earlier that morning, but that had been hours ago. They headed downstairs then walked over to The Shack, a nearby café, for sandwiches and a bowl of soup.

They were almost finished with the meal, sitting in one of the three small booths at the back of the shop drinking coffee and sharing a piece of cheesecake, when Autumn's cell phone rang. She didn't recognize the caller ID number.

"Hey kiddo, it's your old man."

"Dad, where are you?"

"Me and Myra are in Reno. We're on our honeymoon. We just got hitched!"

"Dad!"

"Yup. Alaska Air's got a direct flight down and we just hopped on and right-quick we were here. We were planning to call you tonight with the news."

Several strange emotions went through her: doubt, worry, disbelief and denial were only a few. "You got *married?* But you said —"

"I told you I was going to make Myra an honest woman." He said something to Myra that Autumn couldn't hear and both of them laughed. "This is the happiest day of my life."

The joy in his voice began to reach her. He really did sound happy. Maybe he would be. She really hoped so.

"Congratulations, Dad. I wish you both the very, very best."

"Thanks, darlin'."

She mouthed across the table to Ben that her dad had gotten married and he seemed surprisingly pleased.

"Good for him," he mouthed back.

"Say hello to your new step-mama," Max said and handed Myra the phone.

"Hi, Autumn honey. I'm so happy."

"I'm happy, too," Autumn said, wishing she meant it a little more. The two of them talked for a while, Autumn again expressing her best wishes. "Ben sends his congratulations, too."

"You better grab that one, sweetie. He's a real peach."

Her insides tightened. She wasn't grabbing anyone and especially not Ben.

Fortunately, Max came back on the line. Autumn blocked the thought of her dad having sex with Myra and the stress it might have on his heart.

"There's just one thing, Dad, before I let you get back to your honeymoon."

"What is it, darlin'?"

"Dad, I need you to think about a trip we made up into the Cascades a few years back. I'm not exactly sure what year, but it was in the summer and we were going camping. Before we left, we stopped at the sporting-goods store and bought some equipment — a new tent and I think I bought a sleeping bag. Do you remember, Dad?"

"Not offhand."

"It's really important. There was a man there, a blond man. He said hello to us."

"Hello? That's it? You expect me to remember some guy in the sporting goods store who said hello?"

She sighed into the phone and shook her head at Ben. "It was just a long shot. I thought you might have seen him sometime since, maybe even got to know him."

"Sorry, honey. I think I remember the

camping trip, but the guy doesn't ring any bells."

"Well, thanks, anyway. You two enjoy your honeymoon. We'll celebrate when you get home." She disconnected and stuck her cell phone back into her purse.

"No luck?" Ben said.

"My dad's the only one who's getting lucky."

Ben chuckled. "I like your father. He makes the most out of life. We should all do that."

Autumn didn't answer. She couldn't help wondering how much her dad would make out of his life with Myra. One woman had never been enough for him. Why should that change?

She sighed. Maybe now that he was older he would be different.

Autumn wished she could convince herself.

Since it was the detective's weekend off, the department phoned Doug Watkins at home. Ben McKenzie was a powerful man in Seattle and the police still remembered the kidnapping from six years ago. The good news was that Watkins now worked in the city, at the East Precinct up on Twelfth Avenue.

Ben and Autumn were waiting for his arrival when the front door swung open and her friend, Joe Duffy, walked in. Joe worked out of the Virginia Street precinct, so she was a little surprised to see him.

"Hey, hot stuff, what are you doing here? Someone burgle your apartment?"

"No, thank God."

He frowned. "Is that pervert still hanging around the school? If he is, we need to —"

"We're here to see Doug Watkins," Ben interrupted, sparing Autumn the necessity of lying again.

Joe flashed him a look. His ruddy complexion appeared even redder than usual, his sunburn probably a result of a recent climbing trip, Joe's favorite way to spend his off-duty time. "You're Ben McKenzie, right? Josh Kendall mentioned you were taking Autumn's classes. You getting into climbing?"

"I've always been interested. I'm enjoying it so far."

Joe cast Autumn a glance then turned back to Ben. "If you don't mind my saying, I hope all you're doing with Autumn is taking classes."

"Joe! For heavens sake!"

"I think that's Autumn's business, don't you?" Ben's tone held a hint of warning.

"Maybe. But the lady is a friend of mine and she's not like the rest of your women. Treat her right, McKenzie, or you'll answer to me."

Instead of getting angry, Ben just smiled. "It's nice to know Autumn has friends who look out for her."

Autumn wished she could drop through a hole in the floor. "You'll have to ignore Joe," she said to Ben, casting a hard look at her friend. "Being a cop, sometimes he gets a little overprotective."

The detective studied Ben a moment more, taking his measure in some way. "When Autumn thinks you're ready, maybe we'll all go climbing some weekend."

"I'd like that," Ben said, looking as if he meant it. Joe nodded, then took off down the hall, waving over his shoulder at Autumn, satisfied it seemed, at least for the present.

"I'm sorry," she tried to explain. "Joe's really a very nice guy. I have no idea what got into him."

"He cares about you. There's nothing wrong with that." Ben's gaze followed Joe down the hall then he turned as Detective Watkins pushed through the glass front doors.

Watkins spotted them and headed in their

direction. "Ben. It's good to see you." He stuck out his hand and Ben shook it.

"You too, Doug. I'd like you to meet a friend of mine, Autumn Sommers." Ben's mouth faintly curved. "That's Sommers with an *O*."

Watkins smiled. "Nice to meet you, Autumn."

"You too, Detective."

With the formalities over, Watkins led them down a hall tiled with linoleum through a door to an empty conference room, a small, bare space with a metal table and chairs seating four. A framed Ansel Adams black-and-white photo of Yosemite at dawn was the only decoration in the room.

"I'm sorry to drag you in on a weekend," Ben said, waiting for Autumn to take a seat then taking one himself.

"It's all right." Watkins smiled. "The kids were fighting and Vickie's mother is visiting. I was glad for an excuse to get out of the house."

Ben chuckled.

"So what's this about a missing kid?" Watkins was short and stout, late thirties, muscular, with a shiny, shaved head. He looked tough, yet there was something in his face that said he could keep an open mind.

"I've been trying to think of where to begin, Doug — the truth is so damned hard to believe. But I think it's the only choice we've got."

"The truth is generally the best approach," Walkins drawled with only a trace of sarcasm.

Ben started talking and with Autumn's help finished nearly half an hour later, explaining about the dreams, the blond man and Molly and the facts they'd been able to confirm. They told the detective about the classic car and tracking down the owners, relayed Autumn's brief meeting with the blond man in the sporting goods store, which had also been the kind of business where Joanne had seen him.

When they finished, a skeptical Detective Watkins leaned back in his chair. He ran a hand over his bald head as if he still had hair. "Just when you thought you'd heard it all . . ."

"Yeah, I know what you mean," Ben agreed darkly.

"So aside from all this stuff about dreams that might be real and the fact you think your daughter could still be alive, what you're basically asking me to do is find out if a blond girl who roughly fits the same description as Molly has recently been abducted."

"That's about it. Before we left the house, we went on the Internet and pulled up *miss ingkids.com.* There were six hundred and six victims listed missing nationwide in the last year. That in itself is daunting, but some of them don't have photos and I'm not sure the site is completely up-to-date. Odds are it would have happened somewhere in the western region but we don't know for sure."

Watkins seemed to mull that over. He took a deep breath and slowly released it. "All right, for old times' sake, I'll make a run at it. See if we can at least narrow down the list of possible victims matching your description."

"That'd be great."

The detective stood up. So did Autumn and Ben. "I'll get back to you by the middle of the week."

"I appreciate this, Doug. I can't tell you how much."

"Do me a favor. Don't say anything around here about kidnap victims showing up in dreams."

A faint smiled touched Ben's lips. "No problem."

"No offense," Watkins said to Autumn.

She smiled. "None taken."

■ ■ ■ ■

Autumn and Ben left the station and headed back to her apartment. The sun had slipped behind a thin layer of clouds and the temperature was falling. A damp breeze stirred the hair at her temples and Autumn pulled her sweater a little closer around her shoulders.

"I've been thinking . . ." She walked beside him across the lobby and Ben pushed the elevator button.

"Seems like we've both been doing a lot of that lately."

"Those names the women are using . . . if they aren't their real names, they must have some meaning, some reason they were chosen."

"I've been wondering about that myself."

"The thing is, Riker said this guy has a Godfather complex. Rachael, Mary and Ruth are all biblical names."

When they arrived at the twelfth floor and stepped out of the elevator, Ben took the key out of her hand. He opened the door then waited for her to walk past him into the condo.

"It hadn't really occurred to me, but maybe you're on to something. This guy could be some kind of religious nut. A zealot of some sort."

"That could be good, right? If he's a religious man, maybe he isn't the kind of guy who would molest young girls."

"Depends on the religion, I guess. It didn't stop David Koresh down in Waco, or the guy who took Elizabeth Smart."

Her shoulders sagged. What a nightmare this had to be for Ben.

"We'll find her, Ben. We won't stop until we do."

He looked at her and pain crept into his face. "You know what I keep thinking? If I hadn't stopped looking, maybe we would have found her. Maybe if I hadn't given up —"

"Stop it, Ben. You thought she was dead, just like everyone else including the police and the FBI." Autumn reached out and laid a hand on his cheek. "The hard truth is, she might be. All of this could just be some crazy hallucination. You think *I* don't think about that?"

The burn of tears rose at the back of her eyes. Ben moved closer, drew her into his arms.

"This isn't easy for either of us," he said softly. "I know that."

For a moment, Autumn rested her head

against his shoulder, enjoying the comfort of his embrace. On a shaky breath, she eased back to look at him. "You can't change the past, Ben. And I can't afford to have doubts."

He nodded. "You're right. We just have to keep going. That's the best we can do right now."

The best thing for her and for Ben.

The best hope for Molly.

It was early Sunday morning. The dream had been the same last night, the blond man and the women, Molly and Rachael and little Mary, the newest member of the clan. Autumn was only slightly tired this morning. After they had talked about the dream, Ben's lovemaking had helped them go back to sleep.

"We need to go to Burlington," she said. "Show the sketch to the people who work in the sporting-goods store, see if anyone recognizes his picture."

"I know." They were padding around her apartment, drinking coffee, just finished with a breakfast of scrambled eggs, sausage and canned biscuits with honey and butter.

"Unfortunately, Burlington Sports is closed on Sundays." Autumn carried the empty plates over to the sink. "It's still a small town. They don't stay open till nine every day the way your stores do."

"Ah, yes . . . I remember those good old days fondly." Ben finished the last of his coffee then carried his cup to the sink. "I called earlier, got their answering machine. I couldn't go today at any rate. It's my day with Katie, remember? We're going to the lake." His gaze found hers. "I was hoping you might come with us."

Autumn nearly lost her grip on the plate she was washing. "You aren't serious."

"Why not? We can't go to Burlington until tomorrow and we won't hear from Watkins until sometime in the middle of the week. I'd really like you to come. I think you'd like Katie and I know she'd like you."

Autumn bit her lip. This was the last thing she'd expected from Ben. She knew how private he kept his personal life. Why was he asking her to meet his daughter?

"I don't know, Ben . . ."

"I'll tell you what. You go kayaking with me and Katie, and next weekend we'll go climbing with you."

She flicked him a glance. *This weekend, next weekend.* She was already in way too deep with Ben. If she didn't watch out, she was going to fall in love with him and he was going to break her heart.

And getting over him would be a helluva lot harder than getting over Steve Elliot or Luke Noland.

"Come on, be a sport," Ben said. "You're teaching me to climb. I'll teach you how to kayak."

It did sound like fun and she had always wanted to try the sport. Surely she could keep her head on her shoulders a little while longer.

What the heck. If you're gonna be a bear, be a grizzly, Max always said.

She grinned. "All right, I'll go." She was wearing jeans, sneakers, and a T-shirt. "What gear do I need?"

"Grab your fleece sweater, just in case. We'll swing by my store and pick up a helmet in your size and whatever else you might need."

She didn't argue. Ben was practically forcing her to go. He could damn well pay for her gear. She felt the tug of a smile. Besides, she had a feeling she was going to like it.

Autumn ignored the little voice that said she liked pretty much everything about Ben.

Twenty-One

They loaded Ben's pickup, stopped to get Katie, then headed for the lake. Autumn could have picked Ben's daughter out of a crowd. He had said the girl looked a lot like Molly when they were the same age. At ten years old, Katie had the same blond hair and gentle blue eyes, the same delicate features.

She was a very pretty little girl who, according to Ben, took after her mother, though Autumn could see a bit of Ben in the determined set of her jaw as they lifted the kayaks out of the truck bed, as well as the quietly assessing glances Katie cast in Autumn's direction.

"Are you my dad's girlfriend?" she asked while Ben was digging the life vests out of the back seat of the truck.

"No, we're just friends."

"He's never brought one of his friends with him before."

Autumn managed a smile. "Then I'm flattered. I guess he figured it was okay for you and me to meet. Maybe he was hoping we might get to be friends, too."

Katie watched her guardedly. "Do you like sports? Dad says you do."

"I love sports."

Ben walked up just then. "Autumn's a fabulous rock climber, sweetheart. One of the best in the state."

The girl's blue eyes widened. "Wow! I've seen those guys up on the mountainside, hanging down off the boulders. Do you do that?"

"I do." This time Autumn's smile came easy. "I love it. My dad taught me. It's really a lot of fun."

"What about kayaking?"

"Never tried it. Maybe that'll be fun, too."

Katie grinned. "It's awesome! My dad's teaching me, just like yours did."

"Well then, I have a feeling you've got a very good teacher."

"Dad's won lots of trophies and stuff. He doesn't compete anymore, but he's still the best."

She thought of making love with Ben and bit back a smile. "Your dad's really good at a lot of things."

She looked up to see Ben watching her

and there was a tilt to his lips that said he knew exactly what she was thinking.

"I'll take that as a compliment," he said.

Autumn blushed. "Are we ready?" she asked brightly, hoping to steer the subject in a safer direction.

"Kayaks are in the water — all but yours, Autumn. Katie already knows how to get into a kayak. She also knows how to get righted if you happen to turn over and how to get back inside if you fall out. Sweetheart, why don't you show Autumn how it's done?"

With the kayak sitting on dry land, Katie showed Autumn how to get in, then they worked on how to self-rescue. When Ben was satisfied Autumn could handle it, they were ready to go.

"All right," he said. "Let's get this boat in the water."

They had already put on their PFDs — personal flotation devices — so they were all set. The lake was placid today, just a few ripples along the shoreline, that moved out across the surface and finally disappeared. A green-headed mallard and his lady watched them curiously, bobbing in the water not too far away, and a seagull careened in the wind overhead. A warm July sun shined down and the air smelled of pine and loamy earth.

With the kayaks in the water, Ben reviewed the best way to get in and how to use the paddles.

"I've canoed with my dad," Autumn said, "so I should be okay with that."

"Great. We're using SOTs. That means Sit-on-Tops. They're the easiest to master when you're learning. Some of the guys are switching over to them completely."

She cocked a brow. "But you're an old-school kind of guy."

"How'd you guess?"

But Ben was old-fashioned in a lot of ways. He was always a gentleman, except in the bedroom where he turned into a total caveman. He used just the right amount of male dominance to make the sex good, but also knew when to let her lead — the perfect combination as far as Autumn was concerned.

Apparently, her body agreed. Thinking about being in bed with Ben made her nipples tighten. Thank God, she had on a life vest so no one could see.

"If everything goes well today," Ben said to Katie, "maybe your mom will let us try the kayaks in the river. There's a nice easy stretch that feeds into the lake not far from here."

"I think she might let me. John tells her all the time that it's better for parents to let kids be kids."

Ben had told Autumn John Cleveland was the man Joanne was dating, a nice guy who worked hard and had a good career with the bank.

"So you like him?" Ben asked.

Katie looked down and shuffled her feet. "Yeah, I do."

Ben reached over and caught her chin, lifted her face so that she looked up at him. "You don't have to be ashamed of liking someone, sweetheart. I'm glad your mom has met someone nice."

Katie seemed relieved. A big grin spread across her face. "Are we ready to go yet, Dad?"

"We're way past ready. Let's get moving."

By the end of the day, Autumn was comfortable in the kayak and really enjoying herself. It was great being out on the water again. She hadn't realized how much she had missed those canoe trips with her dad.

All in all, it was a terrific afternoon, though as the day came to an end, she began to notice something odd between Katie and Ben. As much as he obviously loved his daughter, Ben kept a certain distance between them. Autumn thought perhaps it was just his way, but he wasn't that way with her — in fact, he was getting far too close.

She couldn't help wondering if Molly's disappearance hadn't played a role in his relationship with Katie. From what she could tell, Ben always lived up to his obligations where Katie was concerned, but never went further. She couldn't help feeling a little sorry for the child, who looked up at her dad with big, adoring eyes and dropped occasional hints about them spending more time together.

Ben always managed to navigate the minefield leaving no hurt feelings, but still . . .

"Well gang, I think it's time for us to go home," he said as the afternoon came to a close. "Katie, you were fantastic. You're gonna be a real pro one day. Autumn, you did great for your first time on the water."

"Yeah, Dad — she was terrific!"

Autumn grinned. The ten-year-old had already won her over completely. Maybe it was because Autumn felt so close to Molly and the sisters looked so much alike. But Katie was sweet and kind and like her dad, a very good athlete. Maybe somewhere down the road, Autumn would teach her to climb.

She shoved the thought away. Once they found Molly, her relationship with Ben would be over. There would be no reason to continue to see him. Odds were he would be tired of her by then anyway.

Autumn felt a sad little quiver in her stomach and forced her attention back to Katie.

"I have to admit it was really a lot of fun," Autumn said. "I love being out on the water."

"Me, too." Katie reached out to catch her hand. Autumn laced their fingers together and when she glanced at Ben, she saw that his expression had softened.

Autumn smiled at Katie who grinned, carving a tiny dimple into her cheek, then spotted a woman walking toward them. She was wearing a yellow bikini on a tall, curvy, darkly tanned body and had long, honey-blond hair.

"Ben McKenzie! Is that really you?"

Ben smiled. "I'm afraid it's me, all right."

The woman reached him just then, leaned over and planted a light kiss on his lips. "You are a sight for sore eyes. How long has it been?"

"I haven't competed for at least four years. It's been that long, I guess." He turned. "Charlie, you remember my daughter,

Katie, and this is Autumn Sommers. Autumn, this is an old friend of mine, Charlene Brockman. Everyone calls her Charlie."

"Nice to meet you," Charlene said, but quickly returned her attention to Ben and started reminiscing about old times.

Katie leaned closer. "Charlie's a champion kayaker. She travels to competitions all over the world. You've probably seen her on TV."

She was too sinewy, too athletically built to look like a movie star but Charlie Brockman came close. As she and Ben conversed, Charlene stood a little too close and touched him with an ease that said they knew each other well — *very* well. Autumn could feel her face getting hot with jealousy with every word.

"Well, we'd better get going," Ben finally said.

Charlie turned to Autumn. "Nice meeting you."

"You too," Autumn said, wishing she had never laid eyes on the woman. As she watched the tall, leggy blond walk away, her stomach did a sickening roll. It was obvious she and Ben had been lovers. And there were dozens of others just like her.

"You all right?" Ben asked as Katie headed for the truck ahead of them with an armload of gear.

"Fine." She released a breath and wondered if he could tell how much the encounter had disturbed her. "As you said, we'd better get going." She started picking up gear, but Ben caught her arm.

"If you're worried about Charlene, don't be. I haven't seen her in years, not since I stopped competing in the sport."

"It's nothing to me if you have."

His hold subtly tightened. "Bullshit. You're jealous, even if you won't admit it. Charlie and I dated for a while, but that was a long time ago."

"It doesn't matter."

"It does matter. Dammit, Autumn, in case you haven't figured it out, I'm crazy about you. I'm not interested in Charlene Brockman or anyone else. The only woman I'm interested in is you."

She fought to hide her surprise. Ben was crazy about her? It didn't make sense. She wasn't movie-star gorgeous or a world-class athlete. She cast a last fleeting glance at the leggy blonde. "You might think that way right now, but I'm sure soon enough . . ."

Ben's jaw hardened. "Are you really that insecure? Do you doubt your appeal so much you can't see how much you have to offer a man?"

Her heart was pounding. She was embarrassed he had come so close to the truth and was not about to let him know. "Maybe I just doubt there's a man on this earth who could ever be satisfied with one woman — no matter who she is!" She started marching back toward the truck, then drew hard on her control when she saw Katie standing next to the passenger door.

Autumn forced herself to smile. "I think we've got everything, hon."

"Maybe Dad will stop for pizza." She tossed a hopeful glance at her father, who walked up beside them just then.

Ben's jaw still looked hard. "Not today, sweetheart. Autumn's got to get back home."

It was tempting to run for the safety of her apartment, away from Ben and the danger he posed. But the downcast features of the little girl next to the truck ended the notion.

She turned to Ben, lifted an eyebrow in challenge. "I think I can manage time for pizza. I know a great place not far from here where we can go."

Ben's dark gaze locked with hers. She couldn't decide if the expression he wore was anger or triumph as he turned and strode for his side of the truck.

■ ■ ■ ■

Ben drove Autumn home after sharing a pizza with Katie and went back to his own apartment. Autumn figured he was still angry over the argument they'd had. Or maybe he had already begun to grow tired of her.

Her stomach twisted into a knot. It was ridiculous. She knew what men were like and Ben was worse than most.

Still, she missed his lean, powerful body lying beside her in bed, missed their passionate lovemaking, missed waking up next to him in the morning.

She saw him Monday in class, wearing his usual tank top, his chest and shoulders newly tanned from their day at the lake. She wanted to drag him down off the wall and take him home with her. Wanted him back in her bed.

She didn't tell him that.

Ben stayed a moment after the session, long enough to tell her they would have to postpone their trip to Burlington until the following day.

"A problem's come up at work," he said. "We won't be able to go until tomorrow."

"Why don't I just go up there myself? It's

not that far and I'm used to the drive."

Ben shook his head. "No way. I want to be there. I've got questions I want to ask. Besides, there's always the chance this might actually lead to something important."

He left without saying more and he didn't come over that night. She dreamed the same dream, then lay awake for hours, disturbed by the dark, familiar images, missing Ben and wondering if their brief affair was over.

Determined to keep her mind off Ben, Autumn met Terri for lunch at The Shack on Tuesday. The place was packed this time of day. The faux butcher-block tables were crowded with shoppers and locals. They sat at one of the booths in the back, where it was easier to talk and the fifties music playing in the background wasn't so loud they couldn't hear.

"So how's the search going?" Terri ate a bite of her salad then followed it with a drink of iced tea. Both of them had ordered grilled-chicken Caesars, a specialty of the house.

"Nothing new since the dream changed last week. Now that we've talked to the police about the other little girl, Ben and I are really hoping something will turn up. So far we haven't heard, but they promised to let us know if they found anything."

"That sounds promising." Terri dug into her salad, looking as pretty as always, her dark hair shining and her blue eyes brightened by her long thick lashes. She took another sip of tea and set the glass back down. "I can't believe your dad got married. God, that is the last thing I would have imagined him doing."

Autumn forked a chunk of lettuce. "You can say that again."

"You think he'll be true to Myra? I wonder if he's been faithful since they've been together."

"I doubt it. He was never faithful to any woman before."

"You know what they say — a leopard doesn't change his spots."

"That's what they say." Autumn fought not to think of Ben.

"So how's *your* love life? I gather you and *the hunk* are still an item."

Autumn shrugged. This was the part of the conversation she had dreaded, but Terri was her friend so there was no way to avoid it. "We're enjoying each other. We're having a fling, just like you suggested. As far as the sex goes, it couldn't be better." Except that Ben hadn't been in her bed for the last two

371

nights. It shouldn't have bothered her. It wasn't as if they were living together. Still, he seemed to be avoiding her and she didn't understand why.

"What about the rest of the relationship?" Terri asked.

"There is no *rest*." She toyed with her salad but didn't take a bite. "It's a fling, remember? We sleep together." *Or had been.* "Ben goes to work and so do I. The balance of the time we try to unravel the puzzle that's driving both of us crazy." She dug into her salad, anxious to change the subject. "What about you? Anyone new in the cross-hairs?"

Terri glanced away, fiddled with her fork. "Not really. I ran into Josh Kendall the other day. I was thinking . . . I don't know . . . maybe it was time he and I went out."

Autumn frowned. "Josh is seeing Courtney Roland. I thought they were getting pretty involved."

Terri flipped a lock of dark hair over her shoulder. "Well, it isn't like they're engaged or anything. Josh hasn't really known her all that long."

Autumn studied her friend's pretty face. "You've never had any interest in Josh before. Why has that suddenly changed?"

Terri just shrugged. "Josh was always just there. I guess I never really thought about him as more than a friend."

"But now that he might be interested in someone other than you, you don't like it. Is that about it?"

Terri sat up a little straighter on her side of the booth. "Josh has been in love with me for years. You know it and so do I. He's kidding himself when it comes to this girl. He doesn't love her and I don't want to see him get hurt."

"So you're going to save him from himself."

"More or less."

"And what happens to Josh when you get tired of him?"

She picked at the last of the salad on her plate. "Maybe I won't get tired of him. Maybe he'll be the guy I've been looking for all my life."

"And maybe he won't be and you'll break his heart just like all the others." Autumn shoved back her half-finished salad, her stomach queasy with worry for Josh. "Don't do it, Terri. For once, think of someone besides yourself."

Terri set her fork back down on her plate. "That's a terrible thing to say. Besides, I'm thinking of Josh — whether you believe it or not."

Autumn reached over and caught her hand. "We've been friends a long time, Terri. I know you require a lot of male attention. Most of the time it's harmless. But Josh is different. There's no question you can have him if you want him. The only real question is, do you want to hurt someone who's been such a good friend? Think about it."

Terri sighed and leaned back in the booth. "All right, I'll think about it. But remember, Josh is old enough to decide for himself what he wants."

Autumn just nodded. In a way, Terri was right. Sooner or later, Josh had to figure out what it was he really wanted — a brief fling with Terri or a serious relationship with Courtney Roland.

Autumn caught herself, realizing in that instant that she was in a similar position with Ben. They were having an affair. It could never be anything more. How could she criticize Terri or Josh for doing that same thing?

"I guess you have a point. You know I love you both whatever you do." She slid out of the booth. "I'd better get going. I'm meeting Ben and we're heading up to Burlington to show the sketch around."

"I'll keep my fingers crossed."

"Thanks, Terri." Autumn leaned over and hugged her. "Talk to you soon."

She headed for the door and spotted Ben's Mercedes double-parked out front. She knew he was as anxious as she to get on the road for Burlington.

She just prayed, for both their sakes, they would find something when they got there.

TWENTY-TWO

Autumn hurried out of The Shack, crossing the sidewalk to where Ben's car idled next to a van parked at the curb. He leaned over and opened the door. Autumn slid into the passenger seat and Ben pulled out into the traffic, turning toward the freeway heading north.

"How was lunch?" he asked.

"Great. Their chicken Caesars are always delicious and it was good to catch up."

Ben just nodded. As they drove along the highway, he seemed quieter than usual, slightly withdrawn as he had been since their argument at the lake. Autumn kept her thoughts focused on Molly and tried to ignore the churning in her stomach that warned her something was wrong.

"You brought copies of the sketch?" Ben asked as the car cruised along the freeway at nearly eighty miles an hour. Ben did everything with gusto and that included driving his sexy silver car.

"I had extra copies made. I had the size reduced to eight-and-a-half by eleven so we could pass them out if we wanted."

"Good idea."

She glanced at him from beneath her lashes. She couldn't miss the tautness in his shoulders, the tension in the long muscles in his thighs. He glanced her way, his gaze running over her from top to bottom, lingering for a moment on her breasts. She was surprised to see the heat, the desire burning in those golden brown eyes.

Autumn sucked in a breath. Her heartbeat shot up and her palms went damp. Ben might be angry, but he still wanted her.

Something loosened in her chest. Their affair wasn't over — not yet. She nervously moistened her lips, suddenly restless, a familiar tautness building inside her. She tried not to think of the last time they had made love, tried not to wish he would pull over to the side of the road and take her right there in the backseat of his car.

"You keep looking at me that way and we aren't going to make it to Burlington — at least not until after I stop at the local motel."

Her cheeks flushed. It was humiliating for a man to know how much she wanted him.

"We have work to do," she said, sitting up

a little straighter, clamping her legs together to calm the ridiculous pulsing. "We don't have time for that."

He didn't smile or say any more. Sex might be on his mind, but so was finding Molly. And she thought there was something more. She wished she knew what it was.

Neither of them spoke for the balance of the journey, not until they turned onto the off ramp and headed for downtown Burlington. The town was originally an old logging camp but the years had taken their toll, leaving the buildings in need of repair and a number of them vacant.

They parked the car on the street and walked along the road to the sporting-goods store, one of the older structures in town and in dire need of care.

"Ready?" Ben asked as they reached the front door.

Clutching copies of the sketch in her hand, she nodded.

Ben pushed open the door and they stepped into the interior, which looked better than the outside, with wide-planked wooden floors and molded-tin ceilings. They asked for the manager, a Mr. Cline, who turned out to be in his forties, slightly rotund, with a mop of silver-touched hair.

"You wanted to see me?"

Autumn handed him a copy of the sketch. "We're trying to locate this man. We were hoping you might be able to help us find him."

Cline's gaze fixed on Autumn. "You look familiar. Have I seen you in the store before?"

"My name is Autumn Sommers. My dad and I used to come in quite a bit. Max Sommers? He still lives a little ways out of town."

"Of course! Now I remember. You're Max's daughter. Your father is a very good customer."

Ben stepped into the conversation just then. "As Autumn said, we're hoping you might be able to help us find this man. Autumn saw him in here a few years back. He may be a regular customer. We thought maybe you or someone in the store might know who he is."

The manager took the copy Autumn held out to him and studied the face in the sketch.

"He has blond hair and blue eyes," she added. "He's about average in height and weight."

"I'm afraid I don't recall him offhand." He glanced up. "May I ask the reason you're trying to find him?"

"There's a chance he's involved in the

kidnapping of a child, perhaps more than one."

Cline frowned. "I should think, if that were the case, the police would be the ones asking questions."

"We're hoping to persuade them to help us," Autumn said. "We believe this man may be involved, but we need proof."

The manager shook his head. "I don't know . . . There's the question of customer privacy."

Autumn reached out and caught his arm. "The little girl who's missing is Ben's daughter. Please, won't you help us?"

The manager looked up at Ben, pity in his eyes. "Let me keep a few of these. I'll ask around. Maybe someone will remember him."

"That would be great."

"Let me speak to Andrew before you go. He's worked here off and on for years." Ben and Autumn followed the manager over to what appeared to be the store's lone employee. Unfortunately, Andrew had no recollection of the man in the sketch. Disappointment settled over them both.

"I'm sorry, I truly am." Cline hung onto a small stack of copies. "I wish we could have been of some help. Maybe, as I said, one of our customers will recall him."

"How about former employees?" Ben asked. "People who have worked here and left? Maybe they would remember him."

"I can give you the names of the few who have worked here part-time."

"Thanks," Ben said. "We'd appreciate that."

"There aren't many, of course. Burlington is a very small town."

They left the store with the employee list in hand, leaving numbers with Cline where they could be reached if the blond man made an appearance in the store or if anyone remembered seeing him. They went into stores up and down both sides of the street but the result was the same.

"I'll have Pete Rossi follow up on these other names. Maybe one of the ex-employees will remember something."

"Maybe."

But neither of them actually believed it was going to happen. Burlington appeared to be another dead end.

Ben spent Tuesday night at home, as he had the last three nights. He needed time to think, try to construct his next move in the search for his daughter.

And he needed to consider his disturbing feelings for Autumn.

He had told her the truth at the lake. He was crazy about her. He couldn't remember the last time he had felt this way about a woman, wanting to be with her every minute, dreaming about her, aching to be inside her even when they had just made love.

It was frightening.

Especially when it was clear Autumn didn't feel the same way about him.

Oh, she wanted him, all right. The sexual attraction between them sizzled with invisible sparks whenever they were together. As he sat propped up in bed, an old Robert Ludlum novel open on top of the covers, merely thinking about her made him hard.

The sex was amazing, but the cold fact was that Autumn wasn't looking for a long-term relationship. Her few affairs had left her wary and uncertain of men. She was afraid of getting in too deep, afraid it wouldn't work out between them and she would wind up getting hurt.

Well dammit, so was he.

Ben sighed as he sifted through his uncertain thoughts. For an instant, it crossed his mind that the safer route would be to end the relationship before Autumn did and *he* was the one who got hurt.

The notion was fleeting. Ben McKenzie

wasn't a man who gave up on what he wanted without a damned good fight and in that moment it occurred to him that Autumn Sommers was exactly what he wanted — exactly the woman he needed. Whatever happened, wherever their search for Molly led them, Autumn had become an important part of his life and he would do whatever it took to keep her there.

It wasn't time to give up on her yet.

Just like it wasn't time to give up searching for Molly.

Ben set the book aside, then reached over and turned out the lamp. But as he lay in the darkness, aching for Autumn, thinking of Molly, he couldn't fall asleep.

After their return from Burlington, Ben had again declined to spend the night at Autumn's apartment and this morning he had missed her climbing class for the very first time.

All her fears surfaced. He was tired of her. It was over between them. Ben didn't want her anymore. She tried to steel herself, told herself she'd known it would come to this sooner or later, but the sick feeling in her stomach wouldn't go away.

When her cell phone rang in the women's locker room as she changed out of her climbing clothes, her insides tightened even more.

"Doug Watkins called," Ben said simply. Though his tone was strictly business, a warm tremor ran through her. "He wants to see us down at the station."

"What time?"

"As soon as possible. You still at the gym?"

"I was just leaving."

"Good. I'm calling from my office. I'll meet you in the lobby."

Autumn hung up, left the locker room and headed for the elevator. Her pulse was still thrumming from the sound of Ben's voice and she wanted to kick herself for the anticipation swirling through her.

Ben was waiting when she walked through the elevator doors. For several moments, he said nothing, just stared at her as if he hadn't seen her in years, as if he wanted to eat her up with a spoon.

"I've missed you."

Her eyes widened as he pulled her into his arms and very thoroughly kissed her, ignoring the startled looks of the women who walked out of the elevator behind her.

By the time the hot kiss ended, her knees were shaking, her stomach floating. "Come on," he said, taking hold of her hand. "We need to get moving."

They headed for the stairs leading down to the parking garage and climbed into Ben's Mercedes. He started the engine and drove the car out into the street.

Autumn leaned back in the deep leather seat. "So I guess you were busy this morning," she said, just to keep her mind from straying to that kiss.

He nodded. "I hated missing the lesson but we're about to do a master lease on that building across from our store near Pioneer Square — the one A-1's been trying to get their hands on. My real estate agent has been working his ass off to line up tenants for the property before A-1 can sew up their deal."

She relaxed a little. He had been working, not trying to avoid her. Still, she couldn't help wondering where he'd been spending his nights. "That's great, Ben."

"I'm getting really tired of those guys. I think it's time I did something besides just sit around and let those jokers try to ruin me."

"Any ideas?"

"A few. I've got great people working for me. Be interesting to see what we can come up with."

They talked a little more about the leasing deal as Ben wove his way through the line of cars moving along the Seattle streets, making his way toward the police station on Twelfth Avenue. The mid-morning traffic had slowed, but the shoppers were out full-force, milling up and down the sidewalks, their shopping bags stuffed to overflowing.

As the car neared the precinct, all talk of business ended. Molly was on their minds and the little girl, Mary — if she actually existed. Ben parked the car and they went inside the building and up to the front desk. Almost immediately, they were led down the hall to the same sparsely furnished room they had been in before.

Doug Watkins joined them a few minutes later. "Thanks for coming in."

"What have you got?" asked Ben.

Taking an envelope from beneath a stout arm, Watkins pulled out a stack of pictures and spread them out on the table. There were five color photos of little blond girls with blue eyes.

"These kids are all between five and seven years old," he said to Autumn. "Do any of them look familiar?"

Autumn could feel the dull beating of her heart. Were all these children recently abducted? Was one of them little Mary? She moved closer and began to carefully examine each photo one by one. All of the girls looked a little like Mary, with the same blond hair and blue eyes, the same delicate features.

Autumn's shoulders slumped as she reached the final picture. "I'm afraid Mary isn't here."

"You sure?"

She nodded.

The detective cast her a final glance, then surprised her by pulling a second set of photos out of the envelope. Collecting the first set, he placed the second set on the table. "How about these? Do you see her here?"

"Have all of these little girls — ?"

"Please take a look and tell me what you see."

Autumn looked down at the photos. Again there was the blond hair and blue eyes, a slight difference in years, but still they looked a lot alike. She leaned closer. There was something about the photo second from the end. . . .

Autumn picked it up. Her hand trembled as the features became clear in her mind. "This is Mary. This is the little girl I see in my dreams."

"You're sure this is the one?"

"As sure as I can be. I've been dreaming about her for almost a week, but I don't get

387

that long a look at her before I wake up."

"But you think it's her?"

"I'm almost certain it is."

Watkins let out a long-suffering sigh. "Her name is Ginny Purcell. She's seven years old. She went missing two months ago from her home in Sandpoint, Idaho. Disappeared right out of her own backyard. There's an alley behind the house. Best guess, the guy just drove up and somehow persuaded her to get in his car. No witnesses, no one heard anything. She just disappeared."

"That sounds a lot like what happened to Molly," Autumn said.

Watkins made no reply. "The rest of the photos are just pictures of kids we collected. We needed to give you an objective test. Unfortunately, you passed with flying colors."

"Unfortunately?" Ben repeated.

"Yeah. I'm not exactly sure where to go with this information — if you know what I mean."

Ben nodded. "I know exactly what you mean. But the fact remains, Autumn's ID fits in with the rest of the suppositions we've made so far. And Idaho and Washington aren't that far apart. We think the guy is some kind of sportsman. Autumn remembered seeing him shopping for camping gear, so he's probably into being outdoors. Idaho is a sportsman's paradise. He could have been there doing whatever it is he does and in the process come across little Ginny."

"Sounds reasonable." Watkins collected the second set of photos, all but the one of Ginny Purcell, and slid them back into the envelope. "Could be he lives in Idaho, maybe moved there after he abducted Molly — assuming any of this is real, of course."

"I don't think he's there," Autumn said. "I saw him in Burlington a couple of years after Molly disappeared. And I just have this feeling he's here in Washington. Somewhere up in those mountains."

"Burlington is the gateway to the North Cascades," Ben added. "Maybe the guy is a climber."

Autumn bit her lip, the possibility running through her head as it had a number of times before. "I've never seen him among any of the climbing groups or on any of the trips I've taken. I don't think that's it."

"Let's back up a step," Watkins suggested. "Let's assume he's an outdoorsman, not necessarily a climber but maybe a fisherman or backpacker or maybe a hunter — an outdoor kind of guy. That would explain his presence in Idaho and also in Burlington. Right?"

"Right," Ben said.

"Get me a copy of that sketch you had made. I'll have it sent out to all the sporting-goods stores in both Washington and Idaho. We'll see if anybody recognizes him."

"Great," Ben said. "We've been to the store in Burlington and asked around the area, but no one there remembered him."

"Maybe we'll have better luck."

"Maybe," Ben said.

Autumn could see his hopes rising. They had the police working with them now. If they found Ginny Purcell, they would also find Molly. Or at least that's what Autumn hoped.

"I'd like to show this sketch to the Purcells," Watkins said. "But to do that I'd have to bring in the Idaho police. That means telling them this is a guy you saw in a dream. That'll go over like a lead balloon. We've got to approach this very carefully if we're gonna get any results."

"We'll talk to the Purcells ourselves," Ben said. "I've had a daughter kidnapped. I imagine they'll be willing to speak to me. And like I said, Idaho isn't that far away."

"Good idea. You have any trouble getting them to see you, call me. And let me know if you get anymore information — no matter how you get it. Okay?"

It was obvious the detective was referring to Autumn's dreams. Getting more information that way was both hopeful and at the same time scary.

"Will do," Ben said. "Keep us posted, will you, Doug?"

"You know I will." He extended his hand. "I hope this works out for you, Ben."

"I hope it works out for all of us."

TWENTY-THREE

"When are we going to Sandpoint?"

Ben flicked a glance at Autumn, who sat in the passenger seat as he drove away from the police station. "I'm thinking we could head up there Friday after work. I'll call the Purcells to see if they'll agree to talk to us on Saturday morning."

He caught her gaze in the mirror above the dash, saw the faint crease settle between her eyebrows.

"I read in the paper the Heart Association is having an important benefit Friday night," she said. "The paper listed you as one of the people on the guest list."

"I plan to give them a big donation and cancel. The money's all they really want and this is a lot more important." He cast her a glance. "So leaving Friday works for you?"

She nodded.

He wove the Mercedes through the traffic, cutting neatly in and out, enjoying the automobile's performance and getting a secret kick out the high mileage that stuck it a little to the greedy bastards in the oil business.

"When's your next appointment?" he asked, his thoughts returning to Autumn, from whom lately they rarely strayed.

"I only had one private lesson this morning. I'm finished for the day."

He smiled. "Isn't that a coincidence? I'm finished too." He didn't turn onto Second Avenue toward her apartment as she probably expected him to, but kept driving toward the destination he had in mind.

"Where are we going?"

"My place. I've never taken you there. If you want to know the truth, I liked being at your house better."

"Why?"

"I don't know exactly. It always just feels so cozy." *And you're there,* Ben thought. He had slept poorly the last few nights without Autumn lying beside him. But he had needed time to consider, to work things out in his head.

Now he saw things clearly, saw that whatever happened, no matter how tough it was to handle, he wanted Autumn to be with him, wanted her to be part of his life.

He was risking a broken heart, he knew.

Likely, she would run from him, push him away and never look back.

But Autumn was worth the risk.

Besides, he didn't intend to lose her. All was fair in love and war and he was willing to play dirty if he had to.

Ben pulled into his underground parking space, helped her out and escorted her over to his private elevator.

"Impressive," she said as the heavy door rolled open to reveal an interior done in mirrors and polished dark wood.

"I guess it is. I like being able to go in and out on my own schedule."

She was curious now, he could tell. He was a little afraid his expensive penthouse apartment would be slightly overwhelming but he wanted her to get used to it. He wanted her to accept the idea of sleeping in his bed.

He went hard as an image of the tiny butterfly tattoo on her tight little behind rose into his head. Inwardly, he cursed. All he had to do was think of that tattoo and the blood surged into his groin.

As the elevator made its ascent to the twentieth floor, Ben slid an arm around her waist and drew her against him. The single advantage he had was that little Ms. Autumn Sommers liked sex as much as he did —

maybe more. And they were fantastic together.

His plan was to spoil her for any other
man and he meant to start today. Ben
smiled as he took her hand and led her out
of the elevator into the marble-floored foyer
of his condo. When she stopped and stood
staring in awe at the beautiful view, he
tugged on her hand.

"Come on. I'll show you around." He
would give her the tour, all right. And a
whole lot more when they ended up in his
bedroom.

They started in the living room. It was
sleekly modern, with polished dark wood, a
thick ivory carpet and matching sofas. A
few of the objects on the tables were actually purchased by him but most of the
artwork and expensive sculptures were just
there for decoration.

"It's really beautiful, Ben."

"Not exactly cozy, the way yours is. A
decorator did it for me. Maybe someday I'll
change it. Make it more livable."

She glanced his way but didn't say anything. They toured the kitchen, which was
state-of-the-art with stainless-steel appli-
ances and dark wood cabinets. He could
tell she liked it even though the design was
modern, but then what woman wouldn't?

The dining room was impressive, with mahogany furniture and more great views. The guest bedroom came next, nicely done with simple lines and a few Asian accents. Guest bathroom, powder room, his study and finally his bedroom.

"That's the biggest bed I've ever seen."

"Oversized king. It's a pain in the neck to find sheets." And damned lonely at times. His bedroom was a little more relaxed than the rest of the house, his closet neat but not ridiculously so, his shoes out of order and a pair of sweat pants folded but lying on the floor. He liked the warm down comforter on his bed and the overstuffed chair next to the window. He tugged her over to it. "Nice view, don't you think?"

"Fabulous."

From the bedroom they could see out over Elliott Bay and on a clear day all the way to the islands. The view of a deep-blue sea stretched for miles today. The best part was that the way the building sat, even with the curtains open nobody could see in.

He turned Autumn around and very thoroughly kissed her.

Instead of kissing him back, she eased away. "If I ask you a question, will you tell me the truth?"

"I've never lied to you. I don't intend to

start now."

"Did you sleep with another woman during the time we were apart?"

It bothered him that she felt she had to ask. "No. I told you up at the lake I wasn't interested in anyone else. I just needed a little time to sort some things out. I probably should have told you."

"What kind of things?"

"My feelings for you, to start with."

"Oh," she said and glanced away, looking as wary as he had ever seen her.

"Want to know what I figured out?"

She nervously bit her lip and he knew right then that telling her he was falling in love with her would be exactly the wrong thing to do.

He grinned. "I figured out that we're fantastic in bed and though we have a lot of extremely important things going on in our lives right now, we ought to take advantage of the attraction as often as possible." He reached for her, caught her face between his hands and captured her lips in a deep, burning kiss.

This time Autumn didn't resist. She kissed him back as if she wanted to climb inside him, as if her body ached for his as much as his ached for hers. She was back on familiar ground. The sexual attraction they shared she could handle. She wouldn't let herself fall in love — or at least he thought that was her plan.

If the way to a man's heart was his stomach, the way to this woman's heart was good hard sex. And he was just the man to give it to her.

Ben kissed her and kissed her and had her out of her clothes before she seemed to realize what was going on. In a minute she was naked and so was he. More drugging kisses as he urged her up on the bed, onto her hands and knees.

"Ben, what are —"

"I've been aching to have you this way." He came up behind her, smoothed his palm over her butterfly tattoo, caught her hips, positioned himself and filled her, heard her swift intake of breath, then a soft, throaty moan.

He wanted her and he let her know it, driving deep, taking her hard, pounding into her again and again. The tiny pink butterfly on her ass seemed to taunt him, forced him to fight for control. He tightened his hold and she arched her back and beads of perspiration broke out on his forehead.

It wasn't until Autumn reached a shuddering climax, her small body trembling and whimpering his name, that he finally let himself go. His muscles clenched in a powerful climax even more fierce than hers.

Easing her onto her side, his erection still inside her, he nestled her spoon-fashion against him and just lay there soaking up the feel of her in his arms. He smoothed damp auburn curls back from her temple and nuzzled the side of her neck.

They spiraled down together, luxuriating in the sweet afterglow. Then reality began to creep back in.

"I spoke to Pete Rossi this morning," he said, still toying with a lock of her soft russet curls. "He's coming over a little later this afternoon. We're going to talk about what else we can do to find this guy."

"Maybe he'll have some good ideas."

"I thought about asking Rossi to drive up to Sandpoint to talk to the Purcells, but I think we'd have better luck going ourselves." It occurred to him that in the past few weeks they had both begun using *we* instead of I. He wondered if Autumn had noticed.

She rolled onto her back. "The Purcells are more likely to be helpful if they talk to someone who has lost a child himself."

"That's what I think, too." He found her breast, cupped it, began to run his thumb over the end and felt it tighten. "We've got an hour or so before Pete gets here. I thought after our meeting, we'd go get something to eat." He gently abraded her nipple and she squirmed. "We can spend the night here or at your place, whichever you want."

He said it casually, as if it were a given. As if every night from now on he would be sleeping right beside her — which he fully intended to do.

Autumn ran her fingers through the hair on his chest and when he rose up over her, she guided him inside her. "I think my place would be better," she said, nibbling the side of his neck.

Inwardly, he grinned. "If that's what you want, baby." And then he kissed her and started to move.

Pete Rossi showed up for his appointment at four o'clock. He was a big man, as tall as Ben but heavier through the chest and shoulders. Autumn thought he looked like an ex-football player, without the usual mid-forties paunch. He was still fairly attractive, though he was beginning to lose his hair.

Introductions were made and they sat down at the round table in Ben's study.

"We're heading for Idaho on Friday," Ben said, jump-starting the conversation. "Watkins came up with a missing girl who fit the description we gave him and Autumn identified her as the girl she'd seen in her dreams. Her name's Ginny Purcell and she was abducted in Sandpoint, Idaho."

Rossi looked over at Autumn. "This whole thing has been quite a stretch for me," he said. "But like I told Ben, if my daughter was missing, I'd do whatever it took to bring her home. Seems to me you've been pretty right-on so far. No reason not to keep going as long as we keep coming up with leads."

"The cops are mailing the sketch to sporting-goods stores in Washington and Idaho," Ben said. "Maybe someone will remember the guy. Maybe even know who he is. We're talking to the Purcells. Unfortunately, if that doesn't pan out, we're out of airspeed and altitude."

"Yeah, I kind of figured. I spoke to a friend of mine . . . works for CBS News here locally. He's got a friend with a connection to that TV show, *Missing.* You know the one I mean?"

"I've seen it," Ben said.

"So have I," said Autumn.

"This friend — his name's Lloyd Grayson — thinks maybe we can get the sketch of the blond man on TV. He figures the producers might go for it, since it's such an interesting angle — the dream thing, I

401

mean. We'd have to tell the whole story, though. You need to decide if you're ready to deal with that."

Autumn looked at Ben, who was frowning. His family would find out he was searching for Molly, that Ben had come to believe she might still be alive. From what he had said, his wife was trying desperately to make a new life for herself. The last thing she wanted was to stir up old grief. And there was Katie to consider, as well as what the kids at school might do with a story about her father searching for a missing sister based on something as crazy as a dream.

To say nothing of the trauma they would all be forced to suffer again if Ben didn't find her.

"As much as I'd like to take advantage of the show," he said, "I don't think it's time yet. Let me talk to the Purcells. If they recognize this guy, maybe we can get the producers to show the sketch based on the Purcells and Joanne both having seen him before the abductions took place. That should make him a person of interest at least. If that happens, I'll deal with Joanne and Katie and the rest of the family. Until then, let's hold off."

Rossi nodded. "All right. We'll wait. You

go to Idaho and I'll head north. The last place this guy was seen was Burlington, right? Even if it was a couple years ago, it's a place to start. I'll travel north as far as Bellingham then work some of the smaller towns in the surrounding areas. I'll take copies of the sketch and show them around to see if I can find anyone who knows who he is."

Ben nodded. "Sounds good. Let's talk again on Monday."

At the time, Monday seemed a long way away.

The long drive to Idaho through the middle of the towering Cascade Mountain Range, across the wide swath of agricultural land in the center of the state, to the cow town-turned-city of Spokane and on up to Sandpoint might have been pleasant if thoughts of Molly and little Ginny hadn't been so heavy on their minds.

Ben took the 90 Freeway east, the fastest route. Still, the over three-hundred-mile journey left them exhausted by the time they reached the quaint little town of Sandpoint just fifty miles south of the Canadian border.

It was one of those all-American towns being rapidly discovered by tourists thanks to a world-class ski resort at the edge of the town. It boasted a main street lined with old-fashioned buildings, many of them converted to charming restaurants and cozy boutiques, and a beautiful lake as a back-drop.

Ben got a room at the Best Western, which wasn't fancy but had a gorgeous view of Lake Pend Oreille and the surrounding mountains. Tired from the drive, they ate at the restaurant in the motel and went to bed shortly thereafter.

Autumn didn't dream that night, or if she did she didn't recall. She should have been comforted, but instead she was worried. What if she didn't receive any more infor-mation? What if something had happened to Molly?

She didn't say anything to Ben, but she was sure he was wondering that same thing. Over coffee and pastries in the restaurant off the lobby, he asked about it.

"You slept straight through last night."

"It happens, you know. I don't always dream."

"No, but you usually do when you're with me."

She sighed, raked back her hair. "I know. Maybe I was just so tired I didn't wake up."

"I suppose that could be it."

They finished the light breakfast and headed off to their ten o'clock meeting with the Purcells. Their house sat on Pine Street in an older downtown residential neighborhood lined with trees. It was an old, white, wood-frame house with a big covered porch out in front. Like the house where Molly was abducted, it wasn't far from the grammar school and Autumn wondered if that had somehow factored into the abduction.

"Well, this is it." Ben rang the bell and a minute later, Mr. Purcell answered the door. Jack, he said to call him, was a man maybe thirty years old with a bad complexion and sandy hair, stepped back and invited them inside.

"Long drive all the way from Seattle," Jack said as they walked into the living room.

"Pretty, though," Ben said, "if you like incredible scenery, which I do." Introductions were made and they went into the kitchen and sat down at a round oak table. Laura Purcell stood at the counter next to the stove when they walked in. She was somewhere near Autumn's age, late twenties, with blond hair. She was way too thin and her hand trembled as she set mugs of coffee in front of them on the table.

"I'm Autumn and this is Ben," Autumn

said, hoping to put the woman a little more at ease.

"I'm Laura. It's nice to meet you."

The kitchen was simple, like the rest of the house, with Formica countertops and linoleum floors. As they had passed through the dining area, Autumn had noticed the old-style, built-in leaded-glass cupboards. She figured the place was at least sixty years old, but well cared for and immaculately clean.

"Do either of you take cream or sugar?" Laura asked. "I've got some Coffeemate in the cupboard."

"That would be great." Autumn watched the woman moving woodenly around the kitchen, as if she were barely holding herself together. Autumn could only imagine what Laura Purcell had been suffering: the horror of losing her little girl, the terror of imagining what might have happened to her and what the child might be enduring even now. Laura finally took a seat next to her husband.

"I know what you're going through," Ben said, speaking gently to both of them. "I lost my daughter, Molly, six years ago. She was a year younger than your little girl, Ginny, at the time."

Jack Purcell's long fingers gripped his coffee mug. "I'm afraid I still don't understand why you're here. You mentioned your daughter on the phone. What does your child's disappearance six years ago have to do with mine?"

Autumn reached for the manila folder she had set down on the table. She flipped the file open and shoved the sketch of the blond man toward Jack Purcell.

"I wish the drawing were better. I wish it could be in color, but this is the best we could do. The man is blond, average in height and build. He has light-blue eyes."

Ben pointed to the sketch. "This man spoke to my ex-wife a few days before my daughter went missing. We need to know if he looks familiar . . . if this is someone you or your wife might have seen before your daughter disappeared."

The couple glanced at each other, then began to study the sketch, passing it back and forth between them.

"We believe this man may have had something to do with both girls' abductions," Ben added. "He might even be the man responsible. Is there any chance either of you have seen him?"

Laura Purcell looked at her husband. "I — I can't be sure. There's really nothing about him that stands out, but . . ."

Autumn leaned forward. "But what, Mrs. Purcell?"

"But I think this might be the man who helped us chase a bear away from our campground up at the lake. It was a Girl Scout overnight trip — Brownies. It was two weekends before Ginny disappeared." Her eyes welled with tears. "He seemed like such a nice man."

"Let's talk about that day," Ben said, trying to keep Laura focused. "Who else was there?"

She inhaled a shaky breath. "Well, there were two adult troop leaders and six girls. We were just about to have breakfast when a black bear wandered into camp. The girls were yelling, throwing things, trying to scare the bear away. The man ran over from the camp next to ours waving his shirt and shouting at the bear. When the animal saw him, it turned and ran away."

"Did this man talk to you or any of the girls?"

"Not really. He just said that from now on we should be sure to bundle up any food and haul it up in the trees, but we told him we were leaving right after breakfast. He said that he was just glad he could help." She frowned.

"What is it?" Autumn asked.

"I just . . . I remember he pointed at Ginny and asked if she was my daughter and I said yes. He said he could tell because both of us were so pretty." She started crying then and her husband settled an arm across her shoulders.

"I hope you understand . . . my wife has been through a great deal in the last two months. Both of us have."

"Believe me, I understand."

"Is there anything else you need?" Jack asked.

"I just need to know if there is anything more you can tell me about this man or where we might find him."

Laura looked up, blew her nose on a tissue her husband handed her. "He was just a camper, you know? Someone enjoying the outdoors, just like we were. I think he was there by himself. I — I do remember seeing him earlier that morning. I remember thinking he must be extremely athletic. He was jogging, you see, running up and down these very steep hills. I remember he had his shirt off and there wasn't an ounce of fat on his body. He looked extremely fit."

Ben glanced over at Autumn. "Anything else?" he asked.

"No, I . . . that's all I recall."

"Thank you, Mrs. Purcell," Autumn said,

rising from her chair. "You've been extremely helpful."

To Jack, Ben said, "I need the names and
addresses of the people on the camping trip,
the other leader and the girls."

"You really think this might be the guy
who took Ginny?" Jack asked.

"I think there's a chance. So far we don't
have enough evidence to prove it. We need
to see if the rest of the people who saw him
think he's the man in the sketch."

Purcell disappeared and came back with a
list of the members of the local Brownie
troop and their addresses. He put a check
in front of the people who went on the
overnight trip.

"Thank you," Ben said, accepting the list
as Jack Purcell walked them to the door.

Laura Purcell came up beside her husband. "Please . . . if you find out anything,
anything at all . . ."

Ben nodded. "I'll let you know, I promise."

The door closed behind them. Autumn
took a deep breath. "You really think he was
the guy at the campground?"

"I'll have Rossi get up here and interview
the rest of the people on Jack Purcell's list.
We'll see what the others have to say.
Personally, I think it was him. I think he
spots a certain little girl and his predatory

urge kicks in. Maybe it doesn't happen for years, but then something triggers it. Or maybe now that Molly's older, he was on the prowl. All of the girls are blond and blue-eyed. All of them pretty. He spots his victim, carefully makes a plan to abduct her and so far he hasn't come close to getting caught."

"He's smart and athletic. That fits with his interest in the outdoors."

"I'd say so."

"Smart people still make mistakes."

Ben's jaw clenched. "Let's hope he's made one this time."

They started the long drive back to Seattle. Autumn tried to relax and enjoy the scenery, but it wasn't that easy to do. Ben was as tense as she was. During a pit stop, he called Pete Rossi on his cell.

"How's the search going?" Ben asked.

Pete must not have found anything because Ben said, "That's too bad. Listen, I've got a job for you. I need you to head up to Sandpoint." He went on to explain what they had found out when they talked to the Purcells and that he wanted Pete to try to verify Laura Purcell's ID of the man in the sketch.

"We get it confirmed, we'll have something

to take to the police besides the face of a man in a dream."

Ben hung up and leaned his head back against the headrest. "Rossi thinks we should pursue the *Missing* TV angle. I told him to go ahead and call this guy, Grayson, and set things in motion."

"Even if the producers go for it, it'll take a while to do the show."

"Which will give me time to handle my family." He kept his eyes on the road, and didn't seem to notice the pine-covered mountains that lined the highway leading south, back to the turnoff onto the 90 Freeway.

"I feel sorry for the Purcells," he said. "I know what they're going through. I wish I could have given them at least a little hope."

"There's no way you could, not yet. It might just make things worse for them in the long run."

That was the truth. If they never found the girls, false hope only made the pain more severe. Autumn gazed out the window as the car moved along the highway, pulled around a slow-moving truck on an uphill grade, then settled back into the sparse traffic.

In the mirror, Ben's gaze met hers. "What does she look like . . . Molly, I mean? Now that she's so much older."

Autumn's heart twisted. She knew how terrible this was for Ben, searching for his daughter all over again, terrified he wouldn't find her.

"Well, she's twelve now, no longer a little girl, so her features are more grown up."

"Not quite twelve," Ben corrected. "Not till August first."

"That's right, I forgot." She closed her eyes and tried to conjure the image she had seen so many times in her dreams.

"She still looks a lot like Katie. Her lips are a little fuller, her cheekbones a little more pronounced. She's on her way to becoming a teenager, so she's lost the baby-ish appearance of a child. I think you would recognize her as your daughter, though. You wouldn't have any doubt."

The muscles in Ben's throat moved up and down. "God, I want to bring her home."

"We're getting closer, Ben. Closer all the time."

But they still had no more idea where to look for her than they'd had before.

Autumn knew it and so did Ben.

TWENTY-FOUR

Autumn was sleeping in Ben's big bed. It was amazingly comfortable: the mattress deep and luxurious, the expensive cotton sheets as smooth as silk. Still, as roomy as it was, they both slept on the same side, Ben's muscular body pressing against her, one of his hair-roughened legs thrown over hers. She caught the faint scent of cologne and man, turned her head toward him and burrowed a little deeper into the pillow.

She wasn't sure how he had managed to convince her to stay at his condo when they got back to the city instead of going back to her place, but she was there, content from his lovemaking, drowsy and on the edge of sleep.

She shouldn't have stayed, she knew. It was just plain stupid to get so deeply involved with a man like Ben. He was a wealthy playboy who attracted the most glamorous women. For now, he needed her.

She was crucial to finding his daughter. For the moment their lives were entwined, but eventually — one way or another — that would end. She told herself when the time came she could handle it. She was a survivor. She always had been.

She listened to the rhythm of Ben's deep breathing and her eyelids grew heavy. She drifted into a bottomless, trance-like sleep. Sometime in the late hours of the night, she started to dream.

In her sleep, she frowned as the images took shape in her mind, different than any she had seen before. Even the house was different, though she could still see mountains somewhere in the distance. She was in the living room. There was an overstuffed sofa and chair, both covered with fringed, brown-flowered throws, a cross-stitched sampler hung on the wall and an antique armoire set in the corner. She could see the dining room. A Duncan Fyfe mahogany table was covered with a lacy white crocheted tablecloth. There were six matching chairs.

Sounds began to reach her, voices, though she couldn't make out what they were saying. Furniture moved upstairs, scraped across the floor. A lamp smashed into an upstairs wall. Then a woman screamed, her

415

tone high-pitched and frightened, nearly hysterical.

A shiver ran through Autumn's body as the screams grew louder, more intense. Then somehow she was there in the upstairs bedroom. Two men wearing ski masks stood over the terrified woman who lay sprawled on the bed. She was injured, clutching her chest, oozing bright red blood onto the sheets. Autumn could see drops of scarlet on the butcher knife in one of the hooded men's hands.

Autumn twisted on the mattress, biting back a scream herself, suddenly thinking of Molly, terrified that she was the young woman on the bed, that she was the one being attacked. Then she saw the woman's face. She had blond hair but her eyes were dark.

Not Molly. Not Molly. Not any of the women in the house of her dreams. Autumn wanted to weep with relief. She felt the tears leaking from the corners of her eyes, but there was still the terrified woman facing her attackers and Autumn did not awaken. The man with the knife moved toward the bed and the woman let out another piercing scream. He lunged toward her, drove the knife into her a final time, dragged it upward. And then all went still.

No . . . ! Autumn whimpered in horror as the men backed away from the bed. In her mind she saw a young woman in her early twenties in a short, blue nightgown, her eyes wide open, staring up at the ceiling, her mouth agape, frozen in a final soundless scream.

Autumn twisted on the bed, fighting to wake up, moving her head from side to side. "No . . . *No . . .*" Her heart was pounding, her body clammy with sweat. As the men turned and started for the door, she couldn't see their faces, but in the holes exposing their mouths, she saw them smile.

Autumn's eyes flew open and she started to scream.

"Autumn! Autumn for God's sake wake up!" Ben caught her shoulders, roughly shook her. "It's a dream, Autumn! That's all! It's just another dream!"

She turned toward him, looked up at him with glazed, tear-filled eyes and threw her arms around his neck. "Oh God, Ben, oh, God, oh God."

His chest constricted. She'd been dreaming and she was terrified. His hands started shaking. He didn't want to know what she had seen. "Was it . . . was it Molly? Did . . . did something happen to Molly?"

417

Autumn hurriedly shook her head. "No, no, not Molly. Oh, God, Ben, they killed her. I saw it. I saw them kill her with a butcher knife."

"Take it easy." He took a breath himself, drew on his control. "You said it wasn't Molly. If it wasn't her, who was it? Who did you see get killed?"

"I don't know. I've never seen her before."

"Was it the blond man who did it?"

"I couldn't tell. There were two of them and they were wearing ski masks. They were . . . they were in a different house, not the house where Molly lives . . . somewhere else."

"All right, just calm down." Advice he was trying to take himself. "Take a deep breath and let it out slowly." She did as he instructed. "Better?"

She nodded.

"All right . . . now tell me exactly what happened in the dream." He wished he had the tape recorder but the one he'd bought sat on the bedside table at Autumn's.

"They stabbed her." She pressed her lips together and closed her eyes, but tears leaked from beneath her lashes. "Twice, I think." She looked up at him and teardrops rolled down her cheeks. "They were . . . they were smiling, Ben. They murdered her and left her there and they were smiling."

Ben drew her closer, held her till her trembling body finally stopped shaking.

He smoothed back strands of her hair. "Maybe it was just a dream. You didn't know the people. You said nothing was the same. Maybe this wasn't anything to do with Molly or the rest of your dreams."

"I saw mountains . . . through the window in the living room. It wasn't where Molly lives but I think it was somewhere near."

He eased her a little away, then reached down and grabbed his robe off the foot of the bed and wrapped it around her naked shoulders. "Start at the beginning. Take it very, very slow."

For the next few minutes, he listened patiently as Autumn described the brutal murder of a helpless young woman and the two men who had committed the crime. The woman was blonde and there were mountains in the distance.

Coincidence? He prayed that it was, prayed that this had nothing to do with their search for Molly, but it was impossible to convince himself.

They were both too wide-awake to sleep. He needed to make notes, to get everything down on paper, so they went into the kitchen. Autumn was still wearing his robe, which dragged along on the floor and completely engulfed her small frame.

Ben tried to clear his head and keep his thoughts focused. Autumn's dreams seemed to involve both the past and present — and in the case of the teenagers fifteen years ago, the future. If there had been a murder the story would be in the newspapers or eventually would be.

Sitting at the table in the kitchen, he made careful notes of what she said, wrote down the date and time the dream had occurred and the other information she gave him. There wasn't all that much. It occurred to him that in the past she had dreamed the same dream over and over and prayed this time it wouldn't happen, that she wouldn't have to suffer the brutal murder again and again.

They went back to bed just as the sun was beginning to crest the mountains east of the city. Both of them were exhausted. There was no way to know if the dream was real and nothing they could do about it, even if it was.

It was Sunday morning. He was scheduled to pick up Katie that afternoon. They were going to the movies. He intended to keep his plans and hoped he could convince Autumn to go with them. He would choose a romantic comedy, something as far from the horrors she had witnessed in the night as he could possibly find.

He held her until she finally fell asleep, then closed his eyes and tried to follow her into slumber. He tried not to let his mind stray to dark thoughts of murder and young blond women and what it could mean to his lost little girl.

They slept until nearly noon. Autumn showered while Ben made coffee. He carried a cup in to her when she was drying off. She still had the overnight bag she had taken to Sandpoint so she slipped into her jeans and a clean, light blue, short-sleeved blouse.

She felt sluggish and tired even though she'd slept far later than usual. She tried not to think of the nightmare she'd had but it haunted her. As soon as Ben brought in the newspaper, she searched it front to back, looking for any mention of a young woman who had been murdered.

"There's nothing in there," she told him. "Maybe it hasn't happened yet."

"Maybe it isn't going to. Maybe the dream was a result of being under so much stress. That's one of the reasons people dream, you know. To help deal with the problems in their lives."

"Yeah, like watching someone murdered is going to relieve my stress."

His mouth edged up. "That's not exactly what I meant."

She sighed. "I know. Maybe it was just my imagination. If I don't have the dream again, I'll be more inclined to believe it."

"Let's hope you don't." He dragged part of the paper away from her, across the kitchen table where they sat drinking coffee and looking out at the view. He flipped to the theater section and began searching for a movie. "I'm taking Katie to the show this afternoon. I want you to come with us."

"Not today, Ben."

He caught her hand. "You had a rough night, baby. You need something to do besides sit around and worry. We'll pick a comedy, something fun to watch that will take your mind off last night."

She shook her head. "I need a little time to myself. You and Katie go on. I need to go home, be by myself for a while."

Ben looked at her hard. "I'm staying with you tonight — in case you dream about the murder."

"I've got your tape recorder. I'll make sure I use it. I'm hoping this was a one-time thing, that it wasn't really real."

"I'm hoping that too." He got up from his chair, walked over and settled his hands on her shoulders. "Tell you what, I'll check in with you later, okay? See how you're feeling."

She nodded. "All right."

"In the meantime, I'll drive you home on my way to pick up Katie."

She bit her lip, still feeling restless and tense. "I'd rather walk. I need the fresh air."

She could see he wasn't pleased. She stood up, made her way back to his bedroom to get her overnight bag, then grabbed her purse and headed for the door.

"I'll talk to you later," she said.

Ben walked up behind her, turned her into his arms and gave her a quick, hard kiss. "Try to get some rest. I'll call you."

She left him standing in the foyer. Tall and dark and so handsome it made her heart hurt just to look at him. In that moment, she realized she was more than half in love with him and terror filled her.

Dear God, somehow she had to stop herself from falling any deeper. Had to put an end to what was meant to be a brief affair, a fling.

She rubbed her arms as she walked along the sidewalk back to her apartment. It occurred to her that she'd only been gone twenty minutes and already she was missing Ben.

She wandered the streets for a while, went down to the Pike Street market and bought some fish for supper, a few fresh vegetables and a mixed bouquet of bright-yellow flowers. Her arms were full when she got home. She set her overnight bag and shopping bags down by the front door and began to dig into her purse for her house key when she realized the phone was ringing.

By the time she got the door open, the ringing had stopped. An instant later, her cell phone started to jingle. She pulled it out of her purse and flipped it open.

"Turn on your TV," Ben said. "Hurry."

Still holding the phone, she raced for the remote and pressed the power button. "What channel?"

"CBS. They've interrupted the scheduled programming for breaking news. I saw it a few minutes ago. I'm on my way over." Ben hung up and Autumn fixed her attention on the screen.

Her insides were churning. As soon as she saw the house and the mountains in the distance behind it, she knew what the report would be about. Her legs turned to rubber and she sank down onto the sofa.

"Earlier this morning a young woman's body was found in the upstairs bedroom of this small house in Ash Grove, Washington." The camera zoomed past the young reporter to a house in the distance. "Sometime around midnight, the victim was brutally attacked and after a valiant attempt to fight off her assailant, died of multiple stab wounds. Her name has not yet been released, but authorities say her husband, an insurance agent, was away from home on business when the murder took place. At this time, no suspect has been apprehended and so far authorities have found no motive for the crime."

Autumn fought to catch her breath and bring her pounding heart under control. Her head was still spinning when Ben began to hammer on the door.

"Autumn! Let me in!"

Her eyes filled with tears as she pulled the door open and Ben swept her into his arms.

"Oh Ben."

"It's all right, baby. It's all right."

Autumn clung to him, her arms locked around his neck. She moved her head but her throat was too tight to speak. She didn't object when Ben lifted her up and carried her over to the sofa, sat down and cradled her in his lap. For long moments, he just held her.

"It's okay," he said, smoothing back her hair. "Everything's going to be all right."

But everything wasn't all right. It hadn't been for weeks, not since the dreams had begun.

Autumn trembled, then dragged in a shaky breath. "I wanted it to just be a dream."

"I know, honey." He pressed his cheek to hers and held her a moment more, then eased away. "We've got to tell Doug Watkins. The police think there's only one man. We need to tell them there were two."

"They'll figure it out. There's bound to be evidence. Maybe they already know."

"You were there. You saw what happened. You might be able to tell them something that will help them find the killers."

She swallowed past the knot in her throat, let out a shuddering breath. "I know you're right. I just . . ." She closed her eyes and leaned into him. "Knowing it's real makes it worse."

Ben squeezed her hand. "I know. Dammit, I wish we knew why you had that particular dream."

"None of it makes any sense. Why did I dream something like that — something so different from the others?" She lifted her head off his shoulder and looked into his face. "We've got to go up there — up to Ash Grove. Until now, all the dreams have been connected. Maybe the blond man was one of the killers. Maybe he lives right there in town. We've got to show the local police the sketch, see if they recognize him."

He eased her off his lap, down beside him on the sofa. "I'm going to call Doug, ask if he can meet us at the station. You think you're ready to handle it?"

"Do I have a choice?"

He reached out and cupped her cheek. "I'll be with you all the way. Just remember that. We're in this together."

Autumn clung to the thought as they walked to the door.

Detective Watkins was waiting at the police station when Ben and Autumn got there. Without a word, he led them down the hall to what Autumn had begun to think of as the Ansel Adams room.

Ben didn't bother to apologize for bringing Watkins down on his day off. "I imagine you've seen the news."

"The murder? I've seen it. It's been on every channel." He looked over at Autumn. "Don't tell me you've got information on the murder?"

"She dreamed about it last night," Ben explained. "She saw the woman get killed."

Watkins blew out a breath, ran a hand over his shiny bald head. "I need a cup of coffee. You two want some?"

"I'm fine," Ben said.

"I could use a glass of water," said Autumn.

Watkins disappeared and returned with a bottle of Aquafina for Autumn and a paper cup filled with thick black coffee for himself.

"All right, start from the beginning." He sat down in a chair across from them. "What time did you have this dream?"

"Sometime around two o'clock," she said. "That's about the usual time it seems to occur."

"So the murder had already been committed."

"Apparently so. I wasn't sure if what I was seeing was going to happen or already had. It seems to happen both ways. I was hoping it wasn't going to happen at all."

He sighed. "But it did."

She didn't answer.

Ben shoved the notes he'd taken across the table. "This is what Autumn told me when she woke up. I wrote it down as closely as I could. She couldn't possibly have known any of this at the time since she

428

was with me."

Watkins sipped his coffee and grimaced at the bitter taste. "All right, let's take this one step at a time." He held on to the notes but didn't read them. "Tell me everything you saw in your dream."

Autumn took a steadying breath and began to describe the terrible events. She tried to stay unemotional, tried not to feel the woman's terror, but it was nearly impossible to do. She picked up the bottle of water, but her hands were shaking too badly to crack off the lid.

Ben pried it from her fingers and opened it for her. Autumn took a long drink of the icy water, grateful the detective had brought it.

"So that's about it," she said. "I never saw their faces. I couldn't get a good enough look at the men's eyes to tell what color they were, but I remember as they left the room, they were smiling."

Watkins frowned. "Smiling? Are you sure?"

She nodded, swallowed. "I could see their mouths through the holes in their masks. I remember the way it made me feel — sick inside, you know?"

The detective grunted. "I can imagine." Though he had been scribbling on a pad throughout, he reached for Ben's notes. "I need to make a copy of these."

"Go ahead," Ben said.

Watkins left with the notes and brought them back a few minutes later. "I don't know what to say, how to handle this. I'll just do the best I can."

"We're going up there," Ben told him.

"No way. You can't do that. You can't get in the middle of a police investigation."

"Unless you plan to throw us in jail, we're going. This is all somehow connected to Molly and that little girl in Idaho. By the way, Laura Purcell recognized the guy in the sketch. He was camping next to her Brownie troop up at the lake."

"Man, this is a wild one."

"We've got to roll with it, Doug. So far everything Autumn's given us has checked out."

"Yeah, but we've still got no idea where to look for the bastard."

"Yes, we do," Autumn said. "He's in those mountains near Ash Grove. Maybe he lives right there. This dream has to be related to the others in some way."

"It's possible the blond man was one of the men who murdered that woman," Ben said.

"And if he is and you're up there getting

430

in the way of an ongoing investigation —"

"We won't do anything that might jeopardize your case. We just need to take a look around and ask a few questions."

"All right, but you had better watch your back. There's a dead woman involved in this now. You go up there asking questions, someone might not like it."

They left the office and started making plans for the trip. "This is liable to take a few days," Ben said. "Can you clear your schedule?"

"I'll call Josh and ask if he'll take my classes. The pay is good for the private lessons so he'll probably be glad for the extra money."

"I never thought of that. If this starts costing you money, I'll be glad to —"

She sliced him a glance. "I don't want your money, Ben."

He looked like he wanted to argue, but didn't. He was beginning to understand her. She was extremely independent and she wanted to keep it that way. Surprisingly, Ben seemed not to mind. Of all the men she had dated, he was the only one she could think of who really allowed her to be herself.

Steve Elliott had wanted her to change her into his ideal woman. Luke Noland hadn't made the effort to know more about her than how good a climber she was. Ronnie Hillson just wanted to get laid.

"What about Katie? What did you tell her yesterday when you cancelled your day?"

"I told her something important had come up. I said I'd make it up to her during the week. Since I almost never miss one of our dates, she was okay with it."

Autumn and Ben both went back to their apartments to pack their bags, enough to last for several days. Ben arrived for the trip in his pickup.

"It's got four-wheel drive," he explained. "And it's a lot less conspicuous."

Autumn thought that considering they were dealing with child abduction and murder, the less conspicuous the better.

TWENTY-FIVE

Ash Grove wasn't easy to find. It was little more than a wide spot along a two-lane road leading north off scenic Route 20. There was a run-down gas station, a mercantile that sold groceries, a café with a handicraft shop that catered to what few tourists ever found their way up there, and the Ash Grove Motel.

Most of the houses in the area sat on large pieces of land, Ben noticed, which was the reason no one had heard the murdered woman's screams. Her name, Priscilla Vreeland, had finally been released to the news media and Doug Watkins had grudgingly given them the property address, a route number they found painted in black letters on a mail box tilting precariously over the narrow road. The light blue stucco house sat at the end of a long gravel driveway off the main road behind a cluster of pine and sycamore trees, nearly out of sight, which would have aided the murder and getaway.

"How do you think we should handle this?" Autumn asked. "We can't just pull up in front of the house and start asking questions."

Ben smiled grimly. "I think maybe that's exactly what we should do."

Turning the pickup into the driveway, he drove toward the robin's-egg-blue house. It was gable-roofed, with what appeared to be a couple of bedrooms upstairs. He recognized the yellow tape strung across the front door, designating the place as a crime scene. He'd seen it in a hundred TV shows. Two cars were parked in the open space in front of the house, a sheriff's patrol car and a plain brown newer model Buick. Probably the medical examiner, who, in an area like this, could be any person with forensic training, from a dentist to a mortician, under special contract with the county. Fortunately, at least for the moment, the TV camera crews were gone.

Ben parked near the perimeter, out of the way, and both of them climbed out. They headed for the deputy sheriff standing guard outside the front door, a young man with wheat-colored hair, deep-set eyes and youthful features.

"Any suspects yet?" Ben asked.

The deputy gave them an assessing glance. "Is there something I can do for you?"

Ben pulled the rolled-up sketch out of his pocket. "We're looking for the man in this drawing. We were hoping someone from around here might know who he is. There's a chance he lives in the area."

The deputy's nearly white eyebrows pulled together. "Pretty average-looking guy. Hard to tell from this. Could be a lot of different people."

"Anyone in particular you can think of?"

"Blond hair, blue eyes," he read. "Average height and weight. Like I said, could be a lot of people. Why are you looking for him?"

"He's a person of interest in a child abduction case. Two of them, actually. One two months ago, one six years back."

The deputy studied the sketch, then handed it back. "Sorry. Can't help you." He looked up. "You got some reason for thinking the guy might be an area resident?"

"We know he's a big outdoorsman or at least we're pretty sure. Rumor has it he may be holding the girls somewhere up here in the Cascades."

"Rumor?"

"Leads we've tracked down." It was a lie but easier than trying to explain the truth.

"What's your interest? You a private detective?"

"One of the missing girls is my daughter."

The deputy's youthful features softened. "I wish I could help you, I really do."

Funny thing was, from the uneasy look on the young man's face, Ben thought there was a very good chance that Deputy Cobb, the name on the silver tag on his pocket, might be able to do just that.

Ben handed the deputy one of his business cards. "We'll be checking into the local motel. If you think of anything, you can find us there."

"You may have trouble getting a room. Lots of media folks around."

"Yeah, I figured." They got the last of six small rooms, tossed their stuff onto the sagging double bed and flipped on the TV.

"Thank God they're hooked up to satellite," Ben said, using the remote to click through channels until he found a news broadcast.

"In the bizarre murder of a young woman in rural Warren County," the reporter said, "it now appears the attacks were perpetrated by two men instead of one, as police originally believed." The newsman went over the latest facts, which were few, and began to rehash what both Ben and Autumn already knew. Ben clicked off the TV.

"At least they know there were two of them," Autumn said.

"Yeah, but not much more." It was getting late. Even in summer, dark set in quickly once the sun dipped behind the high mountains. They had driven up late in the afternoon, wanting to tackle the curvy road into the canyon while it was still light enough to see.

"You hungry?" Ben asked.

"Not really, but I guess I could eat."

"Good. That's what you need to do. Tomorrow we'll start digging around, see what we can find out."

"Let's take the sketch with us and show it to some of the people in the café."

They headed out, walking the short distance along a narrow road that was paved but had no sidewalks. The Grove Café was about half full. A couple of families, a pair of leather-vested bikers, some media types who were waiting like vultures for the next trickle of news and a guy and girl with sunburned faces Ben figured for backpackers.

There were great hiking trails in the area. Ben had kayaked the river running through the canyon and backpacked the trail over Cascade Pass.

"I climbed up here a couple of summers ago," Autumn said as they sat down at one of the heavy pine tables. "Josh and I came to climb Angel's Peak, which is only a little farther down the road, but it started to rain and it's a tough climb to begin with. The weather turned nice the next day, but we were already into another area."

They each unrolled the paper napkins that held their silverware then reached for the menu, a scratched plastic holder that enclosed the usual dinner fare and the specials of the day. A waitress arrived in a black skirt and white blouse. They ordered hamburgers, always the safest bet, though Ben was tempted to have the meatloaf and mashed potatoes. The woman called in their selections, including a couple of Diet Cokes, then returned with plastic glasses full of water.

"Your order will be up pretty soon," she said.

Ben pulled out the sketch. "We're looking for someone . . . maybe you could help us." He read her name tag. "Millie, is it?"

"That's me." She had short, frizzy blond hair and a face full of wrinkles, which made her look older than she probably was.

"We're trying to find the man in this sketch. We think he might live around here."

She looked down at the drawing.

"It's an estate matter," Ben added. "There may be an inheritance involved."

It was the story they'd come up with on their way to Ash Grove, a tale they would tell the locals, if not the police.

The waitress frowned. "Pretty much an average lookin' fella. Says he's got blond hair and blue eyes. A lot of people around here look like the guy in this picture."

"Anyone in particular?"

"Well, Isaac Vreeland looks a little like him. He's the poor fella whose wife was murdered."

Ben cast Autumn a glance. "Terrible about that. Do the police have any idea who did it?"

"Not so far."

"Is Mr. Vreeland back in town?" Autumn asked. "After what happened, surely he isn't staying at the house."

"He got back right after they found the body. Once the police got through talkin' to him, he left with his cousin, George. He's got family all over up here."

Millie left to wait on other customers. She seemed to know a lot of them, stopped to gossip with those she knew and some she didn't. The woman could be a well of information, Ben thought, if he could manage to keep her talking.

She brought their Cokes and set them down on the table.

"So, Millie, what do you think happened up there? Doesn't seem like Ash Grove would be the kind of place a woman would get murdered."

The waitress set her hands on her very generous hips. "Coulda been some scum off the highway, I guess, but the fact is, Priscilla'd been askin' for trouble. She shouldn't have married Isaac in the first place. She didn't belong up here. Folks in these parts didn't like her much."

"Why not?" Autumn asked.

"Folks here got their own ways, their own beliefs. Prissy Vreeland was always tryin' to change things, tellin' people what to do."

"What kind of things did she try to change?" Ben asked.

"Family things. Church stuff." Millie whisked herself away to refill a customer's coffee cup before Ben could ask more. Besides, he had a feeling he'd gotten all he was going to get.

"What do you suppose she meant?" Autumn asked.

"I don't know."

Millie arrived with their greasy hamburgers, which smelled delicious.

"Would it be okay if I left you a copy of the sketch? Maybe someone will recognize the guy. Like I said, it's an estate matter. Could mean a good bit of money for him."

Millie took the sketch. "I'll put it up on the bulletin board. Folks know to look for things there."

"We're staying at the motel, if someone needs to find us." Ben handed her his card. "Or they can call me on my cell phone."

They ate their hamburgers and drank their Diet Cokes, Autumn's appetite better than Ben had expected. He paid the check, then they headed back to the motel. He'd told Autumn about the pistol he'd brought along. Guns were sold in all his stores. He'd made a point to learn how to use them and because of his business, he had a permit to carry. He wasn't really expecting trouble but a woman was dead. It was better to be safe than sorry.

"There's something about this place . . ." Autumn said as she slipped into a sexy lavender nightgown that made him think about something besides murder. "I'm not sure what it is, but it's like . . . like there's something we aren't getting."

"Yeah, I know what you mean." Ben took off his jeans and shirt but left on his boxers. They were sleeping down the street from the scene of a brutal killing. Neither of them felt comfortable naked.

"I think you should take a sleeping pill," he said. "You need to get a good night's sleep and you won't if you're dreaming about a woman being murdered."

Autumn shook her head. "I can't do that. I might learn something that could help the police — or something that could lead us to Molly."

Ben ran a hand through his hair. "Dammit, I don't like this. Not one bit."

"No, but you know I'm right."

He gave up a sigh and climbed into bed, reached over and drew back the covers. "Come on. I think we both need to get some sleep." He nestled her against him, her head resting against his shoulder. They were tired and uneasy and neither of them felt like making love. Instead they closed their eyes and tried to fall asleep.

It was sunny in the room when Autumn's eyes slowly opened. She couldn't believe it. Once she'd fallen asleep she had slept the entire night through without dreaming. It had happened before of course, recently, in fact. Still, sleeping right down the road from the scene of the murder she had witnessed the night before, it was amazing she hadn't suffered the nightmare again.

She heard the doorknob rattle and realized Ben was already up and dressed. He shoved his key into the lock and opened the door, juggling two foam cups of coffee.

Autumn leapt out of bed and caught the top cup just before it toppled over.

"Nice save." He smiled. "Thanks."

She looked up at him. "I didn't have the dream, Ben."

"Yeah, I figured that out when I woke up and it was morning."

"I wonder what happened."

"Who knows? None of this makes any sense. But we've got to presume your theory's correct and all the dreams are related."

"Which means the murder is also related. What do you think we should do next?"

"We need to get a look at Isaac Vreeland. If we get lucky, he'll turn out to be the blond man in your sketch."

"If he is, where are the girls? The news reports didn't mention any children. I got the impression the Vreelands had only been married a couple of years."

"Millie said Priscilla Vreeland wasn't well-liked. Unless the killing was random, someone disliked her enough to murder her."

"Who, I wonder?" Autumn said. "And why?"

He took the lid off his black coffee and took a sip. "Isaac Vreeland is staying with one of his cousins. Let's find out where the cousin lives and go see him."

It wasn't difficult to find George Vreeland. The TV crews were stalking the husband of the murder victim as if they were on a big-game hunt. The story of a young woman so brutally murdered seemed to have caught fire across the country.

Ben pulled his pickup out of the motel's gravel parking lot behind a CBS van and followed it up the winding canyon road. Several turns later they pulled up in front of a simple, single-story house where a group of media people had gathered. Ben and Autumn wandered over to join them.

"Has Vreeland made any sort of statement?" Ben asked one of the reporters, a skinny guy craning his neck to see.

"Not yet. He's due to come out in ten minutes."

They settled in to wait and fifteen minutes later a blond man came out to face the yard full of reporters.

Isaac Vreeland looked like the guy in the sketch. His cousin, who walked out after him, also looked a little like the guy in the sketch.

Neither one was the man in Autumn's dreams.

"So much for getting lucky," Ben said.

They listened to the victim's husband's statement and his plea for any information on the murder of his young wife, then watched him disappear in tears back inside the house.

"Well, that did us a lot of good," Autumn said.

"Come on, let's take a drive. There are a couple of other rural communities in the area. We'll show the sketch around, ask some questions, see if anyone knows anything. Before we head back, we'll stop at the sheriff's station in Beecherville, see what the authorities there have to say. And I'd like to speak again with Deputy Cobb."

They spent the day making stops, one after another, showing the sketch to anyone who happened to be around. None of the rural communities had more than a single business or two. One had a gas station, another a grocery store of sorts. One had a post office and café. There was the occasional seasonal motel. This time of year, a few places had stalls set up to sell items made from the area's natural resources: pottery, wood carvings and various other handicrafts.

One of the communities in the area was Beecherville, the farthest town east. It was located on the opposite side of the pass, which was closed from the west in winter.

Though Beecherville had actual city services, parks and schools and a volunteer fire department, it was still small, with a population on the sign that read eleven-hundred and two.

"If he lives in the area," Autumn said as Ben pulled into a parking space in front of the local sheriff's station, "he's picked a good place to hide. I've never talked to so many I-don't-know-anything people."

"You're right. If they do know something they aren't saying — not even if it might mean money for someone."

Ben helped Autumn down from the truck and they went inside the narrow brick building. There was only one sheriff's car parked out front.

"May I help you?" An older woman moved toward the counter. Her gray hair was pulled back in a bun and she didn't wear a trace of makeup.

"I need to speak to whoever's in charge," Ben said.

"Sheriff Crawford's in from Warren today, but I'm afraid he's extremely busy, what with the murder in Ash Grove and all. He was up there all morning. He's here now, but he's on the phone."

"Tell him we have information that may be pertinent to the murder."

The woman's eyes rounded. "I'll tell him." She hurried away, wearing a loose-fitting dark-brown dress that fell well below her knees, a pair of thick support stockings and sturdy brown shoes. During the day, Autumn had seen other women dressed in an equally plain manner and she couldn't help thinking of the waitress's comment about *church stuff.* She'd noticed several churches in town as they drove through. One in particular caught her eye. *Community Brethren* the sign out in front read.

The woman returned to the counter. "The sheriff will see you. Please follow me."

They pushed through the low swinging door at the end of the counter and made their way into an office at the rear of the building. Sheriff Crawford stood up as they walked in, a heavyset man with iron-gray hair, a belly that tipped over his belt and sideburns that needed trimming.

"Lottie says you've got information on the murder," Crawford said without preamble.

447

"What's your name?"

"Ben McKenzie. The lady is Autumn Sommers."

The sheriff tossed her only the merest glance, one that gave her the impression he didn't think all that much of women. "So what information do you have?"

Ben unrolled the sketch. "This man has been identified as being at the scene of two child abduction cases — one six years ago, one just two months back. There's a chance he may live in the area."

The sheriff looked down at the sketch. "What makes you think he's connected to the Vreeland murder?"

"Nothing conclusive, just a couple of leads we've been following that led us up here."

The sheriff eyed him with suspicion. "What's any of this got to do with you?"

"My daughter was one of the kidnap victims."

"That so . . ?" Sheriff Crawford studied the sketch, read the description on the bottom, then rolled it up and handed it back to Ben. "You think this fella might be involved in a murder but you don't have any proof, just these so-called *leads* you've been following."

"That's right. We were hoping you might help us find out who he is."

The sheriff shrugged his beefy shoulders. "Could be anyone. Lots of fair-skinned folks in these parts. Norwegians settled here way back, came here for the logging."

Ben tapped the rolled-up sketch. "So he doesn't look familiar?"

"Not particularly. What's a kidnapping got to do with murder?"

It was Autumn who answered. "We don't know, Sheriff. We just thought the incidents might be connected."

"Hmm, I don't know anything about any child abductions and so far the murder is still under investigation. So if that's it, I guess your business here is finished."

"I guess it is," Ben said, his jaw a little tight. "At least for the moment."

The sheriff's mouth thinned. "If I were you, I'd think about heading back to where I came from. Folks in these parts value their privacy. They don't cotton to people sniffing around, poking into their personal business, asking questions."

"Is that some kind of warning?" Ben asked.

"Matter of fact, it is. I'm warning you to stay out of a Warren County murder investigation. You don't, you're asking for trouble."

Ben said no more, just settled a hand at Autumn's waist and urged her toward the

449

door. As they climbed back into the pickup and snapped their seat belts in place, Autumn suppressed a shiver.

"Nice guy," she said.

"I can see why he's the sheriff. He fits in perfectly with the rest of the know-nothings up here."

She almost smiled. "Are we going back home?"

"Not until I talk to Deputy Cobb. Since he doesn't appear to be here in Beecherville, he's either in Warren or still in Ash Grove. Odds are, they'll be wanting to keep an eye on the crime scene. We'll go over there again tomorrow morning."

"You think you might be able to get him talking? So far we haven't had much luck in that regard."

"It's worth a try. I got the feeling he knows something we don't and he seemed a little more inclined to talk than most of the people we've spoken to." Ben fired up the engine. "Let's get something to eat and then head back to the motel."

Twenty-Six

With the road so narrow and curvy, it was a fairly slow drive back to Ash Grove and dark had set in by the time they arrived at the aging, fifties-era, flat-roofed motel. Autumn was tired and frustrated and she knew Ben felt even worse. They didn't talk much, just undressed and got into bed. When Ben kissed her goodnight, things started to heat up.

A round of sweaty sex left them drained and sated and able to fall asleep. Autumn tried not to think how much she enjoyed their lovemaking, enjoyed being with him. It was frightening, her growing attachment to him.

I'll deal with it when this is over, she told herself, burying the thought beneath the more urgent problem of finding Molly.

Autumn wasn't sure what time it was when a rustling sound in the room broke through her sleep. Her eyes flew open at the

451

feel of a man's hand clamping around her throat, turning her scream into a muffled croak.

Next to her, Ben shot up in bed, his hand reaching for the drawer next to the bed where he had put his automatic pistol.

"I wouldn't do that if I were you." A man dressed completely in black stood over him, pointing a gun at his head.

There were two other men in the room, the one pinning her to the mattress with a chokehold on her throat, the other at the foot of the bed, aiming a gun at her heart. Instead of ski masks as the men had worn during the murder, they were wearing handkerchiefs tied over their noses and mouths like a trio of Wild West bandits. The subtle difference gave her hope they weren't Priscilla Vreeland's killers, but it didn't keep her heart from slamming into her ribs.

"Don't make any sudden moves," the guy next to Ben warned. "You do and one of these guns might go off." Autumn could barely see the man in the darkened room, but she could tell he was taller than the others and very thin. "You wouldn't want anything to happen to your lady friend." He glanced over to his cohort at the foot of the bed. *He's young,* she thought, but wasn't quite sure why. To make the point, the younger man shifted his aim to Autumn's head and Ben's whole body went tense.

"How did you get in here?" he asked, his back against the headboard, the covers bunched around his waist. "What do you want?"

"We're just here to deliver a warning," the tall man said. Apparently he was the leader.

"That's right," agreed the man with the chokehold on her throat. "We don't need outsiders up here sniffing around, prying into Brethren business. The woman down the street . . . she found out what happens to people who meddle in other people's affairs."

"You killed her?"

"Not us," said the younger man. "But we aren't surprised it happened."

"You don't want something like that to happen to you or your lady," warned the leader. "Take my advice — leave Warren County and don't come back."

Autumn managed to swallow, then sucked in a breath as the man holding her reached down and jerked back the covers. She was naked and trembling and a scream lodged in her throat. Ben came up off the bed like a tiger, the muscles in his arms and shoulders bulging, his chest heaving as he went into battle mode. The cocking of the pistol pointing at Autumn froze him there on the bed.

"Easy . . ." the leader warned.

"Nice . . . very nice," said the man beside her, leering at her over the top of his mask.

"Women up here know their place," said the leader. "We got no patience for those that don't."

The blunt hand moved away from her throat, releasing her, but the gun at the foot of the bed didn't waiver. Autumn reached down and yanked the sheet back up to cover herself.

"This time no one gets hurt," said the tall man. "Next time you won't be so lucky."

They were gone as silently as they had entered the room, closing the door quietly behind them.

Ben pulled open the drawer and drew out his pistol, then leaned over and pulled Autumn into his arms. "Christ, are you all right?" The tension in his muscles remained. Autumn couldn't seem to stop trembling. She nodded and blinked against the burn of tears.

"Take it easy. It's over now."

She took a shaky breath. "I'm . . . I'm all right."

"No chain," Ben said, staring at the door. "And only one lock. The manager must have given them a key."

"We . . . we can't stay here. We aren't safe with a door we can't even lock."

"We'll leave as soon as we talk to Deputy Cobb." Ben moved his hand and the pistol glinted in the thin ray of moonlight that streamed in through a crack in the curtains. "This is a 40 millimeter Springfield. It's pretty much state of the art." His jaw hardened. "They come through that door again, they'll be in for a surprise this time."

Autumn made no reply but a shudder ran down her spine.

Ben cursed. "With the reception we've been getting around here, I should have figured something like this might happen."

"There's no way you could have known."

He made no reply, just leaned back against the headboard, the gun still gripped in his hand. "I'm wide awake. Why don't you try to get some sleep?"

Autumn got up and turned on the TV, put the sound on low. "Let's find an old movie," she said. "I think we're both done sleeping for the night."

Ben almost wished the bastards would come back. Every time he thought of the son of a bitch who'd assaulted Autumn and leered over her naked body, he wanted to kill him.

He'd brought his pistol for protection. He hadn't been prepared for the assailants to have a key to their room.

The TV's harsh glow lit the motel room. He and Autumn watched until first light, barely aware of what show was on, then dressed, packed their overnight bags and headed over to the coffee shop. Neither of them were hungry, but he could use a cup of coffee and he wanted to give young Deputy Cobb time to get to the crime scene at the Vreeland house.

He figured there was a good chance the officer would be there. The story was still big news and Ben didn't think the sheriff would want anyone out at the house tromping over whatever evidence might remain.

If the deputy was there, Ben had a little information of his own to offer — mainly the fact that more than a few people in Ash Grove believed the murder was some sort of retribution. Their reference to the Brethren confirmed his suspicion that the church figured heavily in what had occurred. He wondered what terrible offense Priscilla Vreeland had committed to get herself killed.

He wondered if Sheriff Crawford was a member of the Community Brethren Church or if he actually gave a damn about the murder of Isaac Vreeland's young wife.

They finished their coffee, then went back to the motel to check out. Conveniently, no one was working in the office. The room was already paid for, but he'd wanted to ask how three armed men were able to simply unlock the door to unit six and walk into his motel room.

"I had a feeling the manager wouldn't show up," Autumn said.

"Yeah, at least not for a while. Probably figured, after what happened we'd be gone before breakfast."

"I wish we could be."

"Let's go up to the house and see if Deputy Cobb is there."

She nodded, let him take hold of her arm. She'd been quieter than usual all morning and her face was a little pale, missing its usual sunny glow. She'd been scared last night. In truth, so had he.

A woman had just been murdered. For an instant when he'd awakened and seen the men, he'd thought the same thing was about to happen to them.

As he climbed into his truck, his hand tightened around the steering wheel. He had never felt so damned helpless in his life. If it hadn't been for Autumn, there was no way in hell he would have just sat there and let three masked men point guns at him. He would have done *something,* even if it was wrong.

He turned to look at her as he shoved the key into the ignition. "Listen, about last night . . . I wish I knew what to say that would make you feel better. I let you down, I know. I should have protected you. I —"

"You didn't let me down." She reached over and touched his cheek. "We had no way of knowing those men would be able to walk right into our room. If you hadn't reacted exactly the way you did, one of us might have been killed."

He released a weary breath, trying not to think of the way the bastards had manhandled her. "I hate what they did to you. I'd like to put my hands around that bastard's throat the way he did yours. I'd squeeze the bloody life out of him."

"It's all right. So they saw me naked. It wasn't your fault and both of us are alive."

"That's a point, I guess." The pickup rounded a corner and moved farther up the hill. "Still, I don't like the idea of anyone but me lusting over your beautiful body."

Autumn finally smiled.

"As I look back," Ben added, "I don't think they had any intention of committing murder."

"No, they just wanted to scare us to death. If that was the plan, it worked for me."

He clenched his jaw. "I hope I run into the bastards somewhere else. I've got a message I'd like to give *them*." He rounded another corner. They were almost at the turnoff.

"The important thing is to figure out how they're connected to all of this," Autumn said. "I don't think they were involved in the murder. When I compare them to the killers I saw in my dream, there's something about the way they look that doesn't fit. Maybe their size or the way they moved, I don't know."

"I don't think they did it. They wouldn't have let us live if they had."

Autumn said nothing, but her face went even paler than before. Ben figured she was remembering Priscilla Vreeland's brutal murder.

He slowed the truck to make the turn into the driveway and as they neared the house, spotted a gold and white sheriff's patrol car and Deputy Cobb leaning back in a wooden chair on the small front porch.

Autumn noticed the tension creeping into Ben's shoulders. When she glanced up the driveway, she understood. "He's here."

"Thought he might be."

"Now if he'll just talk to us."

The deputy stood up, tall and lanky, wheat-colored hair showing beneath the flat brim of his brown uniform hat. As Ben pulled into the yard and turned off the engine, Deputy Cobb came down the wooden steps and met them before they reached the front porch.

"I see you're still here. Any luck finding the guy you're looking for?"

"Not so far. No one's being particularly helpful. Matter of fact, some of the locals went to a lot of trouble to keep us from finding anything out."

"People are pretty private round here."

"So we gathered. Last night we got a warning in no uncertain terms to stop asking questions and leave the area while we still had the chance."

The young man straightened. "That so?"

"Three men broke into our motel room."

"Actually," Autumn amended, "they had a key."

Cobb's gaze sharpened. "You had a break-in last night? Were either of you injured?"

Autumn showed him the red marks on her throat while Ben filled him in on the details of the assault.

"They referred to themselves as the Brethren," Ben said. "I saw a church with that name in Beecherville. You know anything about it?"

"That'd be the Community Brethren. The congregation — the Brethren — are a powerful group in this area."

"You a member?" Ben asked.

Cobb shook his head. "My family only moved up here about ten years ago. Most of the folks in the area have been in these parts for a lot longer than that."

"How about Sheriff Crawford?"

"Crawford, the mayor of Beecherville, more than half the people in that area belong to the church."

"Must be a pretty tight-knit group."

"*Real* tight-knit."

"The men who broke into our room said Priscilla Vreeland got what she deserved," Ben said. "It isn't the first time we've heard that sentiment. You mind telling us why the Brethren might feel that way?"

The deputy glanced around as if he were afraid someone might see him. "I'll tell you. It's not exactly a secret. But I'd appreciate it if you didn't say where you heard it."

"Fair enough."

"Priscilla Vreeland met her husband, Isaac, in Portland a couple years back. He's

461

in insurance. I suppose he was there on business. The members discourage marriages outside the church, but I guess Isaac was in love. He and Priscilla got hitched and she joined the church, but . . ."

"But . . ?" Autumn prodded.

"But there are things about this particular church she couldn't go along with. She started speaking out, said it wasn't right and tried to encourage some of the members to stand up for their rights. Twice she turned a report into the sheriff's office that she was assaulted. She couldn't identify the men and they were never apprehended."

"So what is it about this church that Priscilla didn't approve?" Ben asked.

The young man glanced around, but the area was quiet, not even a car on the distant road. "They practice plural marriage. According to the Brethren, they're just following the Lord's plan, leastwise to their way of thinkin'."

"I can't believe it," Autumn said. "Plural marriage is illegal in this country."

"Maybe so, but no one's ever been able to stop 'em. The Brethren legally marry one wife, then take the others to wife in private ceremonies that aren't recorded. There's no law against living with more than one woman."

"I've read about this happening up in Utah and down in Arizona," Ben said. "Fanatics who claim God gave them the right to marry more than one woman."

"That's what their leader says. He's the head of the inner circle, the high mucky-mucks in the church. They call themselves the Brotherhood of Lazarus. Some of the members claim they can personally talk to God."

"What's their leader's name?" Autumn asked, still trying to digest the fact that the men in the church had multiple wives.

"Samuel Beecher. His family founded Beecherville back in the late 1880s."

"From what I've read," Ben said, "the men marry very young girls and incest is often involved."

"Like I said, no one's been able to stop it from happening. The women are raised to accept their lot and that's what they do. Priscilla Vreeland never had a chance. Those women weren't about to change the way they live. That's just the way it is."

"So two of the Brethren murdered Priscilla to keep her from trying to persuade their women they didn't have to go along with the status quo."

"Could be." Deputy Cobb glanced back at the house. "No matter how bad it looks, people in these parts are mostly law-abiding citizens. They don't like violence and they don't cotton to murder. We find the men who did it, they'll go to jail. Odds are, in time we will."

Ben stepped back and extended a hand. "Thank you, Deputy. You've been a real help."

Cobb accepted the handshake. "You want to file a report on what happened at the motel?"

"Not today," Ben said. "Maybe some other time."

They left the deputy in front of the house. Autumn let Ben help her into the pickup, then waited for him to climb in. As they drove back down the gravel driveway, his jaw looked as hard as the face of Angel's Peak, looming over the canyon in the distance.

Ben's gaze caught hers. "Tell me you don't think Molly was taken to become some religious nut's wife."

"I don't know. But it seems . . ."

"It seems what?"

"You mentioned Elizabeth Smart. Well, that's what happened to her."

"Elizabeth was in her teens. Molly was only six when she was taken."

Autumn looked over to where Ben sat

rigidly behind the wheel. "You're right. It probably has nothing to do with Molly."

But she didn't think he believed it and neither did she.

As soon as they reached an area where Ben's cell phone worked, he pulled onto the shoulder of the road and dialed Pete Rossi's number.

"Pete, it's Ben. I need everything you can find out about a group called the Brotherhood of Lazarus. They're connected with the Community Brethren Church. They're into plural marriage, Pete. Their leader is a guy named Samuel Beecher. Find out about him too."

Ben hung up the phone and pulled back onto the road. "If he's touched her, I'm going to kill him."

TWENTY-SEVEN

Autumn lay next to Ben, staring up at the canopy over the bed in her condo. Ben was asleep. He was exhausted and terrified for his daughter. He hadn't heard back from Pete Rossi. There hadn't been enough time.

She turned her head on the pillow so that she could see his face. Such a handsome face, beautiful, masculine.

Every day that face grew a little more dear to her, a little more beloved. She had never felt about a man the way she felt about Ben, had never let a man get this close. Not even Steven Elliot.

Her heart pinched. She was falling deeper and deeper in love with him. She had known she was in very grave trouble the moment she had awakened at the motel and seen the men in the room, one of them pointing a gun at Ben's head. As frightened as she had been, she was even more frightened for Ben. She was falling head over heels and it was exactly the wrong thing to do.

She told herself to lock away her feelings, that she didn't have time to deal with whatever she felt for Ben. That would have to wait until after they found Molly.

And they *would* find her, she vowed. They hadn't come this far to fail. She would give Ben back his daughter no matter what price she might have to pay.

She lay back against the pillow, her eyelids drooping, her body heavy with fatigue. As tired as she was, she was afraid to fall asleep, afraid of what she would see in her dreams. The muscles in her neck and shoulders ached from her struggle with the man in the motel room and her eyes felt gritty. Still, she fought to stay awake for even a little while longer. Maybe if she was tired enough, she wouldn't have the dream.

It was a little after midnight when she lost her battle with exhaustion and finally fell asleep.

At half-past-two, she began to dream.

She was back in the house where Molly lived, in the steamy kitchen with the long wooden table and the old-fashioned lamp hanging over it. Molly was there, along with Rachael and the little girl the women called Mary. But the blond man wasn't with them

467

and it wasn't dinner time, as it had always been before.

The hands on the old oak clock above the kitchen door read four in the afternoon. Autumn watched as Molly climbed up on a chair next to the table.

"I just need to mark the hem," Rachael said, "then we'll be finished."

Molly made no reply, just stood there staring down at her feet, encased in low-heeled sturdy leather shoes. She was wearing a high-waisted dress, her small breasts just beginning to bud beneath the fabric. The gown came to her ankles. White cotton with small pink flowers embroidered across the bodice and around the bottom of the skirt.

"We've only got a little time left," Rachael said.

"I know." Molly moved and Rachael tugged on the dress.

"You're fidgeting, Ruthie. I told you to stand still." She folded the hem up and marked it with a pin. "You want to look pretty for him, don't you? You want him to be pleased?"

"I guess so."

Sarah, the teenage girl, toyed with her dress, a printed cotton that came well below her knees. "I never please him, no matter what I do."

"That isn't true." Rachael jabbed another pin into the hem of Molly's dress.

"It is so true." Next to the chair, Sarah turned and smoothed a hand over her stomach, and Autumn's heart began to hammer wildly.

She bit back a scream as she shot up in bed and Ben came awake beside her. She swallowed as he reached for her hand. She could still see the swollen outline of Sarah's body — the roundness of the baby she carried in her young belly.

Ben sat in his office.

After Autumn's latest dream, he'd made himself go to work. He had to get away, had to do something besides think of Molly. If he didn't, he was going to go crazy.

He spoke to his attorney, Marvin Steinberg; his vice president, Jerry Vincent; his financial officer, Bill Simpson; and also John Yates at Russell-Bingham, the small investment banking firm that had agreed to represent them. Russ Petrone had managed to lease, then sublease, the building near his store in the Pioneer Square district, stifling A-1 for a while, but it wasn't enough. He was tired of A-1's constant threats and determined to do something to stop them. He and his staff had been working hard to solve the problem.

Ben almost smiled. So far his ducks were lining up in a very nice row.

He had just finished talking to Yates when Pete Rossi phoned. Pete rattled off the info he'd managed to dig up on the Community Brethren Church and the Brotherhood of Lazarus, most of which Ben knew. Except that Samuel Beecher had been arrested on charges of sexual contact with a minor as well as conspiracy in an alleged forced marriage of a teenage girl. Both charges were dropped for insufficient evidence, Rossi said. No one would testify against him. And then the girl disappeared, probably packed up and shipped off to another plural family somewhere else.

But Beecher had fallen under the Washington State radar and at this time remained there.

Ben tried not to think what the information might mean for Molly.

"I haven't gotten into Beecher's personal life," Pete continued. "I'll start digging and get back to you."

"The sooner the better," Ben said.

He left the office, his mind still on overload, went down to the climbing gym and spent a couple of hours on the wall. He'd been doing that fairly regularly since he had started Autumn's classes. He'd even taken a couple of private lessons from Jess Peters, a climber who worked at his downtown store. He and Jess had made a couple of afternoon trips up into the mountains to practice. Maybe he was hoping to impress Autumn, he wasn't completely sure. Whatever the reason, he was really coming to like climbing and he wanted to give it his all.

It was late in the day by the time he got back upstairs to his office. He started in on the stack of paperwork he'd been avoiding all week that now looked like a good way to keep his mind from straying to places he didn't want to go.

It was the call from Deputy Cobb that took him by surprise. Jenn buzzed him on the intercom and told him who was on the line. He steeled himself before he picked up the phone. Jenn knew the whole story now and as he should have expected, she was doing everything in her power to keep him sane and help him find his daughter.

"McKenzie."

"It's Deputy Cobb. I figured you'd want to know as soon as possible. An arrest was made this afternoon in the Vreeland murder case."

His chest tightened.

"It'll be big news when it hits the airways

but the information hasn't yet been released."

"Who was it?" Ben asked.

"The Beecher brothers — Samuel Beecher's sons, Joseph and Jedediah. They said they spoke to God and he told them to kill Priscilla Vreeland."

Ben leaned forward in his chair, his mind spinning. "Where are they now?"

"In custody at the city jail in Warren."

"I need to talk to them."

"I don't think the authorities will let you."

"I've got to try. Thanks, Deputy. I really appreciate the call."

"I figured it might be . . . you know . . . something that could help you find your daughter. I'd be grateful if you'd keep my name out of it though. I'd sure like to keep my job."

"Your name won't come up. You have my word." Ben hung up the phone and sat there for several moments, digesting the deputy's information. Then he dialed Autumn.

"I'm going up to Warren. They just arrested the two men who murdered Priscilla Vreeland."

"Oh, my God."

"Joseph and Jedediah Beecher — Samuel Beecher's sons. I don't know how I'm going to convince the police to let me talk to them, but I've got to find a way. I'll call you when I get back."

"No way. If you think you're going up there without me, you're crazy. I'm coming with you."

"Not this time. You got hurt before. I'm not taking any chances something like that might happen again."

"I'm going, Ben. Either I go with you or I drive up there by myself."

He clamped down on his jaw. He knew her well enough to know she wasn't making an idle threat. "Dammit, Autumn —"

"I mean it, Ben."

He sighed into the phone. "Fine. I'll pick you up in twenty minutes."

"I'll be waiting in the lobby." She hung up before he could say more. He should have known she would want to go. It just wasn't her way to sit on the sidelines.

For the first time that day, Ben actually smiled. That incredible grit of hers was only one of the reasons he had fallen crazy in love with her.

Ben was late. Since he was always on time, Autumn began to worry. Pacing back and forth across the narrow, tile-floored lobby of her apartment building, she looked out at the street. She didn't see Ben's truck and checked her watch for the umpteenth time. She was reaching for her cell phone to see where he was when it started to ring.

She recognized his number and flipped open the phone. "What's happened, Ben?"

"Damn truck won't start. I think I may have left the inside light on last night. Triple A's on the way but I don't have time to wait. We can take the Mercedes, but —"

"Let's take my car. Like you said, it's a lot less conspicuous. I'll pick you up in five minutes."

She headed down to the parking garage, unlocked the car and tossed her overnight bag into the back, on top of the bag of climbing gear she always carried. A few minutes later, she pulled up in front of the ritzy Bay Towers, spotted Ben on the side-walk and pulled over to the curb.

He leaned into the window on the pas-senger side. "Want me to drive?"

"It isn't that far. You can take over once we get there."

Amazingly, he didn't argue, just got in and leaned back in the seat. The set of his shoulders and the tight line of his jaw betrayed the tension humming through him.

"I didn't think it would go down this way," he said.

She pulled the car up onto the freeway.

"You figured the law would cover for them."

"After meeting Sheriff Crawford, I figured it could happen."

She flicked him a glance. "I wonder if one of the brothers is the blond man."

Ben sighed. "In a way I hope he is. In another way . . ."

"In another way, you don't want to wish that on Molly."

He didn't answer, but she knew it was what he was thinking.

She merged her little SUV in with the traffic and headed north, out of the city.

"That last dream you had . . ." Ben said. "I've been thinking a lot about it."

"So have I."

"Sarah was pregnant."

"That's right."

"She was young, you said. No more than fifteen."

"That would be my guess."

"So he's sleeping with her and she's only a kid."

"We don't know for certain the baby is his."

"But you believe that's the way it is. You figure he's sleeping with Rachael, too."

Autumn didn't reply. She thought exactly that. "There's something else, something that's been nagging me. Rachael said they only had a little time left. She said, 'You want to look pretty for him, don't you? You want to please him?' "

"So?"

"I keep seeing the dress Molly was wearing." She chanced a quick look at Ben. "You told me her birthday is August first. That's only a couple of days away."

Ben straightened in his seat. "Go on."

"Molly is going to be twelve years old. In some places that's old enough to be married." She didn't want to say the rest out loud. She knew what it would do to Ben. But time was running out. "It looked like a wedding dress, Ben."

"What?"

"Not the modern kind, but an old-fashioned dress like women wore in the past . . . like a lot of women in the church seem to wear."

Ben's face went bone white. "Jesus," he said. *"Jesus."*

"If he's planning to marry her on her birthday, we've still got time to stop it. All we have to do is get his name and then we can find him. And I think the Beecher brothers may very well know the answers to both of those questions."

Ben made no reply but his features looked etched in stone. Autumn, drove a little too fast all the way to the off-ramp then pulled onto the two-lane road heading east. The Warren County seat was in the small town of Warren, a ways south of Route 20, about fifteen miles east off Interstate 5.

As they pulled into town, she spotted the county courthouse, one of those old-fashioned buildings with a rotunda, sitting in the middle of a nice grassy square. The police station was next door, a modern structure that seemed out of place in the quaint old logging community.

Autumn pulled up in front of the station and turned off the engine. "Well, did you figure out how to convince the police to let us talk to the men?"

Ben's mouth barely curved. "No, I didn't. I cheated. I called someone who could convince them for me."

One of her eyebrows arched up. "Who's that?"

"Burt Riker at the FBI. I told him our sources had led us to the kidnapping of a young girl in Idaho, which led us to the scene of the Vreeland murder. I told him we needed to talk to the brothers who had been arrested for the crime, that we believe they have knowledge that might prove useful in finding my daughter."

"And he went for it?"

"I think he's intrigued. He made the call to Warren, at any rate. Since kidnapping's a federal offense, if we come up with anything, the feds will jump in. The police are letting us speak to Jed Beecher. Apparently, he's confessed to the murder and willing to talk about it. His brother, Joseph, has lawyered up."

The police station hummed with activity, though the brothers' arrest for the murder had not yet been released. It soon would be. Autumn hoped she and Ben were long gone by the time the little town was over-run by the media.

Ben checked in with the stocky sergeant behind the front desk, who steered them to a police lieutenant named Frazier. It was obvious the man wasn't happy the FBI was sticking its nose into his investigation.

"Apparently you've got friends in high places, McKenzie," said Frazier. He was tall, dark and not the least bit handsome. "Follow me and make it brief. You've got fifteen minutes."

Autumn followed the lieutenant, Ben right behind her, toward the rear of the station into a building adjoining the main structure, through a barred entrance that slid open to admit them then closed with an unnerving clang. Lieutenant Frazier led them into a grim room furnished only with a table and chairs. There was a mirror on one wall, one-way glass, Autumn was sure.

"Like I said, fifteen minutes."

Frazier left and Ben and Autumn sat down on one side of the table. A few minutes later, the door opened again and a young man — shackled hand and foot, thin with very short blond hair — made his way into the chamber.

Ben rose as Jed Beecher slowly dragged himself over to the table.

"Cops said you wanted to see me."

"That's right." Ben cast a sharp look at Autumn, who studied Jed Beecher and slowly shook her head.

Ben sat back down, barely masking his disappointment. "We're looking for some-one," he said. "I think you may know him. I'm hoping you might be able to help us find him."

"Why should I?" Beecher moved a shack-led foot, making a rattling sound beneath the table.

"Because your life is pretty much over. Maybe if you help us, God will cut you some slack for the crime you committed."

"I didn't commit a crime. I just did God's will. He spoke to me and Joseph, told us exactly what to do."

"God told you to kill Priscilla Vreeland?"

"That's right."

"Seems to me it was God who said 'Thou shalt not kill.' "

"He's the Almighty. He doesn't have to explain himself. He commands and we follow. Besides, she was warned — more than once. She just wouldn't listen. She was trouble from the day Isaac married her. He and my father argued over her all the time."

"Your father argued with Isaac Vreeland?"

Beecher nodded. "He's my cousin."

Ben reached into his coat pocket and pulled out the sketch of the blond man. "Your cousin looks a lot like this man. Is this your brother, Joseph?"

Beecher made a quick perusal and shook his head. "No."

"Take another look. I think maybe you know him."

Vreeland studied the sketch. In a blink, recognition dawned and his features turned guarded.

"It's not Joseph," Ben continued. "But you know who he is."

Beecher's shoulders stiffened. "What do you want with him?"

"Who is he?" Ben pressed.

Jed Beecher shrugged. It was clear he

knew and equally clear he wasn't going to say.

Ben's jaw clenched. Reaching across the table, he grabbed the front of Jed's orange prison shirt and jerked him out of his chair. "This man abducted my daughter. Tell me who he is!"

Beecher's lips curled. "She belongs to him now. Her life with you is over."

Ben shook Beecher hard. "Tell me his name, goddammit!"

The door slammed open and two police officers rushed it. "You're finished in here, McKenzie. Get out before you wind up in a cell next to his."

Ben let go of Beecher's shirt. For an instant, his hand fisted so hard it shook. He took a deep breath and Autumn could tell he was fighting for control. "We need to find out who this man is," he said to one of the officers.

Both officers glanced at the sketch. "Don't know him. Now, like we said, you're through in here. Get out before we haul you out."

Ben reached toward Autumn, who linked her fingers with his and gently squeezed. Her heart ached for him. They were close and yet still so far away. Ben led her out of the room, down the hall and out of the building.

"We won't get any more help from the local police," he said darkly.

"It doesn't matter. We'll find him some other way. We know he's one of them. We know he lives somewhere up in those mountains."

"She's not even twelve years old, still just a little girl. I can't stand to think of him hurting her."

"We'll find him, Ben, I swear it."

Ben looked down at her, his eyes haunted. "The question is, will it be too late?"

Twenty-Eight

"We've got to go back up there." Adrenaline still pumped through Ben's veins. "Up to Ash Grove. We've got to find someone who knows who this man is and make them talk."

Walking next to him toward the car, Autumn just nodded. If she was afraid of what might happen once they got there, Ben couldn't see it.

Nothing's going to happen, he vowed. *Not this time.* His Springfield was tucked away in his canvas duffle and if he had to, he would use it.

"Let's talk to Isaac Vreeland," Autumn suggested as they reached her SUV, Ben making his way to the driver's side this time. "Beecher said Isaac and Samuel fought over Priscilla all the time. By now he's been told about the Beecher brothers' arrest. Now that he knows who murdered his wife, maybe he'll be willing to talk."

Ben slid behind the wheel, adjusting the

seat to fit his tall frame. "Good idea. Let's go."

They were halfway down Highway 20 on their way back to Ash Grove when Ben's cell phone rang. He picked it up from the center console and answered it. Pete Rossi's voice resonated from the other end of the line.

"How'd it go?" Pete asked. "You find the blond man?"

"Jed wouldn't talk but it was clear he recognized the guy in the sketch."

"Yeah, well, guess what? Jed and Joe aren't the only Beecher brothers. The older brother's name is Eli. He lives in a wide spot in the road called Shadow Point. It's a few miles north of Ash Grove. I'm trying to come up with a photo as we speak."

His pulse was leaping. "Call me if you get a match."

"Will do. Where are you?"

"Heading back up to Ash Grove."

"Be careful. These boys play rough."

No kidding, Ben thought, remembering the bloody murder at the Vreeland house and the men who'd broken into their motel room that night.

"Don't worry — I've got Autumn to watch my back." He flashed her a reassuring smile as he closed the cell phone.

"Well?" Her green eyes were wide and filled with hope.

"Samuel Beecher's got another son. His name's Eli and he lives near Ash Grove. Rossi's getting the info on him now."

Autumn sat up straighter in the seat. "It's him, Ben. It must be. If Eli's the blond man, it would explain why I dreamed about the murder. The dream led us to Joseph and Jedediah Beecher. Now Jed Beecher's leading us to Eli."

"Let's hope you're right."

Ben took the curves as fast as he dared and still keep the car on the road. Autumn pulled out the map and finally found the pale lettering for Shadow Point. "The dot's so small I didn't notice it before. Must not be much of a place."

"Yeah, I got that impression from Rossi."

Within the hour, they had reached the two wooden structures that were all there was of Shadow Point, a bait shop and a one-pump gas station and market that made a Circle K look like a Wal-Mart.

Unfortunately, once they got there, they were out of cell phone range.

"Rossi can't reach us." Ben pulled up in front of the gas station and turned off the engine. "There's no way to know if Eli Beecher's our man or where to find him."

Autumn cracked open her car door. "Let's take the easy way and try asking. Maybe we'll get lucky."

The bell rang as Ben pushed open the door to the tiny store for Autumn. In the cramped interior shelves were sparsely stocked with candy, aspirin, cereal, milk, flour, sugar and a few other staples. There was no coffee on the shelves, Ben noticed, and no cigarettes.

Autumn fixed a bright smile on her face and made her way up to the counter toward a heavyset man with a long gray beard who was dressed in worn bib overalls.

"Hello. We were hoping you might be able to help us." Her smile remained in place though Ben figured it took no small amount of will. "We're looking for a friend of ours, Eli Beecher? We got the directions to his house wrong. I guess we didn't write them down correctly. Would you happen to know which way it is?"

The man scratched the chin buried in his fuzzy gray beard and amazingly began to smile. "Easy to get lost in these parts. Eli's just up the hill. Take the first road to your left and keep goin'. You'll see his house on the right, around the second curve."

Ben's heart raced. He could read the same excitement in Autumn's eyes, though for the store-owner's sake, she carefully kept it out of her voice.

"Thank you. Thank you very much."

Ben followed her out of the tiny store, trying to ignore the adrenaline pumping through his system and the tension in his neck and shoulders.

"This could be it," he said. Moving around to the rear of the SUV, he opened the back, dragged his duffle toward him and pulled out his Springfield automatic.

"I'm not taking any chances. If my daughter's in that house, I'm getting her out — one way or another."

He expected Autumn to argue, to tell him it was dangerous to overreact, but she didn't. Ben got into the car and so did she. Setting the gun on the console beside him, he reached over and started the engine.

As the SUV rolled out of the gravel parking lot, Autumn studied Ben's profile. There was a glint of steel in those dark brown eyes she had never seen before. She could only imagine what he was thinking, the fear he was feeling for his daughter.

The hope she really was still alive.

The car climbed the hill, throwing up dust as it rolled over the unpaved road. As they rounded a curve and the house came into view, Autumn noticed the mountains behind it. They looked somehow familiar, though in her dream she had never seen them from this angle.

"I think this is it, Ben. It feels right, somehow. I think this is the place in my dreams."

Ben made no reply, but she could see his jaw clench. He pulled the car into a dirt parking area in front of the lawn. They got out and closed their car doors.

Ben stuck the pistol into his waistband at the back of his jeans. "I'd rather you stayed out of this, but I need to know if you recognize Beecher or maybe one of the women."

"You couldn't keep me away."

He nodded, his expression grim. He led her up to the door and knocked on the wooden frame. The house was batt-and-board, a simple, one-story structure, painted white and well maintained. Dark-green shutters hung at the windows. Next to the house a separate garage and what Autumn suspected was Eli's workshop sat a few feet away.

They waited anxiously on the porch. Ben knocked again. A minute later, a slender blond woman, tall, with deep-set blue eyes, pulled it open. She was wearing a simple housedress and sturdy leather shoes. Autumn recognized her in an instant as the older woman in her dreams.

She forced herself to smile. "Hello, Rachael. My name is Autumn. I was wondering if Eli might be home?"

As soon as she said the name, Ben shoved his way into the house. "Molly! Molly, it's your father. Molly!"

"Who are you?" Rachael tried to block Autumn's entry into the living room. Autumn slammed her foot against the door to keep it open. "What do you think you're doing?"

Autumn shoved past her into a living room filled with handmade pine furniture and a rock fireplace sat at one end. Through the door into the kitchen, she saw the long wooden table in her dreams. "We need to speak to Eli. Where is he?"

Ben turned back to Rachael. "Where's Eli? Where's my daughter, Molly?"

"You . . . you must be mistaken. There's no one here named Molly."

Footsteps sounded on the carpet in the hall. Autumn turned, recognized Sarah, watched her waddle into the room. She was even more pregnant that she had appeared in the dream.

"Eli's not here," the girl said, her gaze

wary. She nervously toyed with a strand of shoulder-length blond hair a darker shade than Rachael's.

"Where is he?" Autumn asked. Before she could answer, another face she recognized appeared in the doorway — little seven-year-old, Ginny Purcell.

"Go to your room, Mary!" Rachael commanded.

"It's all right, Ginny," Autumn soothed as she carefully made her way toward the child, her heart squeezing at the frightened look on the little girl's face. "We've come to take you home."

Ginny bit her lip, eased farther into the room, then ran over to Sarah and clung to her skirt.

"You don't have to be afraid anymore, Ginny," Ben said, his gaze softer now as he moved toward the child, then went down on one knee in front of her. "Your mommy and daddy have been so worried. They've been looking everywhere for you. They'll be so glad to have you back home."

The little girl looked at him and tears filled eyes as blue as the other two women's. "Rachael said my mama and daddy were dead."

Ben speared the woman with a glance that could have cut through steel. "Rachael's wrong, sweetheart. They're very much alive and they miss you very very much."

"I want to go home," Ginny said, sniffing back tears, burying her face in Sarah's skirt.

"We're going to take you home, honey, just as soon as we can." Ben came to his feet, his attention shifting back to Rachael. "As of now, Eli's cozy little household is finished. I want to know where my daughter is. The girl you call Ruthie. Tell me where to find her."

Rachael's chin firmed. "I have no idea what you're talking about."

Sarah ran a hand over Ginny's fair hair. "Eli took Ruthie and went into the mountains," she told Ben.

He took a slow deep breath and Autumn realized how hard he was fighting for control. "You're Sarah," he said.

"Yes . . . How did you know?"

"It's a very long story," Autumn said gently, working as hard as Ben to stay calm. "Are you . . . are you Eli's wife?"

Sarah flicked a glance at Rachael who shook her head in warning.

"I'm having his baby," the young girl answered.

Ben's tone remained soft. "Sarah, I came here to get my daughter. Her real name is Molly. Eli kidnapped her from our home when she was only six years old. Can you tell me where he took her?"

"Shut your mouth, Sarah," Rachael warned. "If you don't you know what Eli will do when he gets home."

Sarah bit her lip and suddenly looked every bit as young as Autumn was certain she was.

"He won't hurt you," Ben promised. "I won't let him. Eli isn't going to hurt anyone ever again."

Sarah still looked uncertain. "He'll beat me. If I tell you where he's gone, he'll whip me. He likes to do that. He likes hurting people."

Ben's jaw hardened. "If he touches you, I'll take a whip to him myself. I'll protect you, Sarah. I give you my word. I'll do whatever it takes to keep you safe. Tell me where he took my daughter."

"Sarah . . ." Rachael warned, her mouth a thin line.

"He took her up to his cabin — the sanctuary. That's what he calls it. It takes three days to get up there. You have to climb the trail to the summit of Angel's Peak."

"I know the trail," Autumn said. "I spent a week up here one summer climbing with my dad. The trail isn't too bad, since it zigzags back and forth across the mountain, but it takes a while to reach the top."

"The cabin is off on a trail to the left, just before you reach the top," Sarah said.

"Why is he taking her there?" Ben asked.

"He's going to marry her, just like he did me. Ruthie will be twelve tomorrow. Eli says that's old enough for a woman to know a man in the way God intended."

Autumn thought she'd been prepared for this, but her stomach rolled with nausea and she had to fight back tears. She glanced over at Ben, saw the terrible look on his face.

"We've got to stop him before he reaches the cabin," he said.

"When did he leave?" Autumn asked Sarah, who cast a glance at Rachael who stood stiffly resigned.

"Yesterday. He wanted to be there exactly on time. He plans to have the ceremony tomorrow evening, on her birthday. After that she'll belong to him and he'll . . . he'll . . ." Sarah bit her lip and looked away.

"It's all right, honey," Autumn said gently. "This is all going to be over very soon."

"I was thirteen when he married me. I tried to get him to wait another year for Ruthie, but he said he was tired of waiting, that she was old enough now." Her eyes shimmered with tears. "He's my husband, the father of my baby. His dad is my mother's brother. I don't want to hate him, but I do."

Autumn's heart went out to her. She could only imagine what it must have been like for a child of thirteen to be forced into a sham of a marriage, to have sex with a man she barely knew.

Autumn reached out and gently squeezed the young girl's shoulder, aching for what she had endured. "It's all right, Sarah. Everything is going to be okay."

"Do you have a phone up here?" Ben asked.

"There's one in Eli's shop," Sarah said. "But we aren't allowed to use it."

He turned to Autumn. "We need to call the authorities, get them out here to take care of these girls. I'll call Burt Riker and let the FBI know we've found Ginny Purcell. I'll also call Doug Watkins, tell him what's going on and see if he can get the police to chopper in. If they get here quick enough, we can stop Beecher before he reaches his cabin."

Autumn shook her head. "There's no way, Ben. The whole mountain is completely covered by forest. The trail to the top is the only way in. It's steep and totally hidden among the trees. There's no way a chopper could get in there."

Ben ran a hand through his hair. "Then I'll go by myself. You stay here and wait for the police and I'll pack some gear and start after him. If I push hard all night and all day tomorrow, there's a chance I can catch up with him before he reaches his cabin."

"You can't start up the trail in the dark — it's too dangerous! You'd never make it! You've got to wait till morning and I'll go with you."

"If I wait, there's no way I can catch him in time."

"It's the only thing you can do, unless . . ."

"Unless what?"

"There *is* another route to the top. My dad and I climbed it once, but you don't have the experience."

"You climbed Angel's Peak?"

"Not the face — the weather wasn't good enough. We took a secondary, slightly easier route to the top." Her heart started pounding. If they could make the climb, there was a chance they could get to the cabin before Eli. "We made the ascent in about ten hours, all the way to the top. There are a couple of pretty tough faces, but maybe —"

"No maybes. I can make the climb if we can get the gear. It's a long drive back but we sure as hell can't free-climb a mountain like that."

Autumn grinned in spite of the circumstances. "My gear's in the back of the car and I always carry an extra harness and equipment for a second climber. You never know when you might get the chance to take a hill so I like to be prepared. The gear may not be as fancy as the stuff you've been using, but I keep it up-to-date. It's safe and it'll do the job."

For an instant, Ben grinned back. "I knew there was a reason I fell in love with you. Let's take a look. If we've got what we need, as soon as the cops arrive, we're out of here."

Autumn ignored the *I fell in love with you* part of Ben's speech. There wasn't time for speculation as to what that might mean, wasn't time to react or worry about what she should or shouldn't do.

They had a climb to make, a tough, grueling trip up the east face, all the way to the summit of Angel's Peak and she wasn't sure Ben had the technical skill to make it.

"I've been climbing some with Jess Peters," he told her, reading her thoughts. "Whenever I got a little spare time. I've grown pretty comfortable working with the equipment and being on the side of a mountain."

"Jess is a really good climber." She was more than a little impressed, slightly relieved and a little more optimistic. "But you haven't been climbing very long. It's dangerous, Ben. Are you sure you want to risk it?"

"You have to ask?"

In truth, she didn't. Ben loved his daughter. Now that they'd found the house and the women, it was clear Molly was alive. If they didn't get to her in time, God knew what depraved sex acts Eli Beecher had in store for her. They had to get to the cabin before Beecher had time to reach it and there was only one chance of that. A slim chance, based on a climbing scenario where nothing went wrong.

So far in the dozens of trips she'd made over the years that had never happened.

Twenty-Nine

The *whop-whop-whop* of a chopper announced the arrival of the Warren County sheriff's department. Considering the terrain the department covered, the helo was probably kept on ready alert. Beefy Sheriff Crawford ducked beneath the blades and met Autumn and Ben in the front yard of the house. A second chopper began its descent before they had the chance to begin a conversation, this one marked with the letters *FBI* on the side.

Autumn was only a little surprised to see Burt Riker step out and make his way toward them, careful to stay low as the long helo blades began to slow.

"I didn't figure you'd come in person," Ben said, shaking Riker's outstretched hand. "But I'm really glad you did. You'll find Ginny Purcell inside, along with two other women. I told you everything I know on the phone. Eli Beecher has my daughter and you know the plans he's got for her."

Riker nodded, his expression hard. "We'll have a team on the mountain in the next fifteen minutes, heading up the trail. They'll catch him, Ben. They'll bring her back to you."

"They'll have to stop at dark, which means they'll catch him but not in time. Autumn and I are climbing, taking the east-face route. We can make it to the cabin before Beecher gets there."

Riker's lean profile angled toward the range of mountains in the distance, taking in the rugged terrain, granite outcroppings and heavily forested slopes. "You're involving yourself in FBI business, to say nothing of the risk you're planning to take. I should probably stop you but I'm not going to."

Ben nodded. "I appreciate that."

They had already sorted through the gear to make sure they had everything they needed and that it was all in working order. The route started at the base of Angel's Peak, off the main road on the far east side of the mountain. They would drive in as far as they could, hike in to the base at first light and then start making the climb to the summit, using the route Autumn had taken before. The climb was difficult but not impossible, a mixture of hiking and climbing that required more stamina than skill.

Except for the Pinnacle and an even tougher spot called the Devil's Wall. The wall was a granite outcropping, an overhang that blocked the ascent near the top, an obstacle in their path that had to be surmounted to reach the summit.

Autumn had conquered the Devil's Wall on a previous climb, but had badly bruised an ankle on a rocky crevice and gotten a number of ugly cuts and a handful of nasty scrapes along the way. She had narrowly missed a twenty-five-foot plunge to the end of the rope Max was belaying. She hoped to hell neither she nor Ben took a serious fall on their climb to the top.

Autumn surveyed the mountain in the distance. The weather was pleasant now, but this far north a rain storm could hit without warning or it could turn cold. She had a fleece jacket in her gear bag. Since Ben hadn't brought any outdoor gear along, he raided Eli Beecher's camping stash out in his workshop, most of which the man had taken with him. An old jacket hung on the wall, a little tight across the shoulders for Ben but it would do.

The shop smelled of sawdust and there were several works in progress: a pine sofa and chair, a hand-rubbed coffee table. From what Sarah told them, Eli earned a small but adequate living from making furniture. It was an all-cash business he could run from his house. It looked as if Eli did finely crafted, very solid work, which fit Riker's profile, demanding a good deal of himself as well as the people around him.

Sarah also told them she and the two younger girls were being home-schooled. Rachael taught them the basics, with the occasional help of a neighbor woman. The family rarely went to town except to attend church and almost never invited friends over. It was obvious Eli liked to keep his women close at hand and under his domineering rule.

It was getting dark. Way too late to begin the grueling climb to the summit. She and Ben planned to spend the night in the SUV, then set off before dawn.

Though Riker had taken over the crime scene, he didn't ask where Sarah got the blankets or the bread and cheese she brought to Autumn and Ben. Promising to give the FBI agent a formal statement later, they left the authorities to deal with the girls, and Rachael — apparently wife number one. There was evidence to be collected in the kidnapping of two children and also in the matter of the sexual assault of an underage girl.

Autumn leaned back in the seat of the car while Ben took the wheel. The ride to the trailhead seemed to take forever along the curvy road through the pitch-dark forest, up to the end of the road. They parked there, then curled up together in the cramped back of the SUV, pulling the borrowed blankets over them for a little warmth.

Neither of them slept well in the cramped interior, just off and on, maybe an hour or two. They were too wired to sleep, too worried. But the climb would be difficult enough in the daylight and they couldn't risk failure.

Too much was at stake.

As the first purple-gray morning light seeped over the horizon, they slung their gear onto their backs and started up the trail. They would make the hike up to the base in the near-dark, packing two lengths of rope and the tools they would need for the ascent: harnesses, cams, hexes, carabiners, chalk bags, helmets and whatever else might prove useful. Packed among their gear Autumn carried a lightweight pair of binoculars and Ben carried his Springfield automatic.

If Eli Beecher proved to be as ruthless as

his brothers, they figured it was a good idea to have a weapon.

Moving swiftly over a narrow trail mostly obscured by a heavy summer growth of vegetation, they made the two-and-a-half-mile trip to the base of the mountain in record time. The sun was just cresting the tall peaks to the east, a thin streak of yellow that soon became a glowing orb. The ground was still wet, the rocks slick, and water beaded on the leaves of the earth-hugging plants. But near the bottom, the slope was not that steep and they were able to keep their footing.

The mountain itself, Angel's Peak, rose into the sky like the ancient volcano it was. Being far off the usual tourist paths, it wasn't a common destination. Part of the land around it was national forest, some of it Bureau of Land Management land, and there were a few private parcels that had started as gold mining claims back in the late 1870s.

Autumn figured the cabin for one of those, a place high up on the mountain where someone had hoped to find gold and make his fortune.

The real wealth was in the view.

She paused for a moment at the base as they strapped on their harnesses. Early-morning light in the mountains was amazing. It backlit the horizon and gave the vast, towering peaks a magical glow that made them seem almost enchanted. The landscape looked endless and deserted; the hazy mist floating over the ground made it appear surreal. Near the craggy peak that was the summit, a smoky ring of clouds encircled the mountain, only the topmost point escaping the wispy white blanket.

Autumn returned her attention to the task at hand, exchanging her hiking shoes for her climbing slippers. The extra pair she kept in the car had once belonged to Josh. The shoes were nicely broken in and fit Ben fairly well.

"Ready?" he asked, anxious to get underway.

"I'm ready."

Ben nodded, his jaw set with determination. Neither of them knew what problems they might encounter along the route. They only knew that whatever obstacles arose, they had to overcome.

Ben's daughter needed him.

They couldn't afford to fail.

THIRTY

Ruth Beecher climbed the trail in the early-morning light, walking behind the man, trudging, for the third day in a row, up the mountain path leading to Eli's sanctuary in the woods. For the past two nights they had slept in sleeping bags around a small campfire. If she hadn't been with Eli, it would have been fun.

But she didn't like the way Eli had been looking at her lately, the way he made her feel. For years, he had ignored her, except to assign chores or punish her for something she did wrong. Now that she was older, things had changed. His eyes seemed to follow her wherever she went. He stared at her as if she had something he wanted. And once they reached the cabin, it was going to get worse.

Ruth knew about the sanctuary. Sarah and Eli had been married there two years ago when Sarah had turned thirteen.

Now he wanted to marry Ruth. Instead of being his ward, as she had been for the last six years, tonight — on her birthday — she would become Eli's wife.

Her stomach churned. She wished her birthday would never come. She wasn't exactly sure how Eli knew what day it was but maybe she had told him when she was a little girl, back when she remembered things like that. Or maybe he just knew. He had known her parents, he said. He'd told her they had sent him that day to her house, the day she had gotten in the car with him. They told him to take care of her because they didn't want her anymore.

Ruth barely remembered that day or the parents she'd once loved, hardly remembered anything at all before Eli and Rachael and her home in the mountains. She wasn't his daughter, she knew. He had always made that clear. She guessed it must be true about her parents not wanting her because she still lived with Eli and Rachael and her real parents never came for her.

For years she prayed they would. At first she could even remember their faces, but Eli told her she had to forget them. He was her family now, he and Rachael.

Then Sarah had come. Ruth had loved Sarah from the moment she walked into the house. She was always so sweet and smiling, at least when Eli wasn't around. She was his second wife, she said. Sarah told her once that she hadn't wanted to marry Eli but her father and mother said it was the right thing to do. That the leader of their church, Samuel Beecher, had spoken to God and he had commanded that Sarah marry his son. And so she did.

Sarah was having a baby now. Ruth wasn't quite sure how that happened. It was a forbidden topic in their house. But she knew it had something to do with sleeping in the same bed with Eli.

Sarah had tried to explain the things a wife had to do for her husband, how she had to sleep with him and let him touch her, but Eli had heard them talking and he had gotten angry. He had whipped Sarah for speaking of private matters and Sarah had cried.

Ruth had cried too. She didn't want to marry Eli. She didn't want to marry anyone, though she wouldn't mind having a baby. She didn't like the idea of being fat, but having a baby to cuddle and care for, having a little girl or boy to love sounded good to Ruth.

Since she had come to the mountains, she couldn't remember ever having anyone to love, except for Sarah. She kind of hoped she and the little girl that Eli had brought home one day might get to be friends, but Mary was always so frightened she just stayed off by herself. Ruth wondered if she had been as frightened as Mary when she had first been brought to the house.

"Hurry it up, girl. And watch where you're walking. You don't want to break a leg up here, do you?"

For an instant, Ruth thought the idea had merit. If she couldn't reach the sanctuary, Eli couldn't marry her. He couldn't touch her, do the things she was afraid to imagine he might do.

"I said, get your skinny backside up the trail. We've got a lot of ground to cover if we want to get to the cabin by nightfall."

"Yes, sir," Ruth said. "I'm coming."

But she was praying they wouldn't reach the cabin at all.

Autumn wedged a hex into a narrow crevice, then attached a carabiner and hooked her rope through it. Once the rope was in place, she slid a hand into the chalk bag around her waist, then reached up toward a thin slice of granite protruding from the rocky face, providing a sturdy grip for her fingers. She swung her leg up, hooked a heel and hauled herself up. Another few feet and she reached the end of the pitch, a narrow ledge where the three-inch trunk of a pine tree protruded from the side of the mountain, the perfect place to anchor herself as Ben made his climb up the pitch.

She watched him moving upward, the tightening of muscle over bone, the movement of suntanned skin across his shoulders, the flexing of the long muscles in his thighs and calves. A fine sheen of perspiration coated his body and she could hear his labored breathing as he reached for a handhold, then found a foothold and used his legs to push himself up.

He looked magnificent, tall and masculine, every woman's fantasy, and she couldn't help thinking how much he had come to mean to her.

She shook her head. Her time with him grew closer to ending. It didn't matter. She would do whatever it took to help him. His needs were more important than her own. She loved him that much.

The words slammed into her with the force of a blow, almost knocking her off the side of the mountain. She was in love with Ben. Not a little in love, she realized. But desperately, passionately in love and when this was over, her heart was simply going to shatter.

She sucked in a shaky breath, then slowly released it, letting the calm settle in. Now was not the time to think of her feelings for Ben. Now was the time to think of Molly. The little girl was in terrible danger and they were the only ones who could save her.

She looked down the mountain at Ben, watched him maneuver the rope, reach down and retrieve the tool she had placed as he climbed higher. His job was to pick up the protection they used to make the climb and at the top of the pitch return the tools to the first climber — in this case, her.

As soon as he reached where she sat braced against the wall, her legs propped against the trunk of the tree, he positioned himself, providing an anchor for her as she prepared to climb the next pitch.

She checked her map, then stuffed it back into her pocket. "At the top of this, we get to hike a bit. Give us a chance to catch our breath before we start climbing again."

Ben just nodded. Autumn could only imagine how hard it was to concentrate when he was so worried about his daughter. But so far he was doing an outstanding job, making it appear he had climbed a dozen peaks just like this one.

The morning slipped past, the air drying, becoming a little warmer. So far they were right on schedule. There were half a dozen more difficult pitches, including the Pinnacle, before they reached the Devil's Wall. She looked over at Ben, saw that he was anchored and ready to belay her, and started to climb the next pitch.

Ben watched those small, powerful legs moving confidently up the route in front of him. Her skill was remarkable, the graceful movements of hands, arms and legs that searched out the tiniest grips and footholds and skillfully placed the protection they needed to stay safe, choosing the most expedient path. She was helping him reach his daughter, doing everything in her power to make sure he got to Molly before Eli Beecher could hurt her.

For Autumn there was no half way, no room for failure. From the beginning, she had been that way. She had never backed off, never given up, just kept moving forward. No woman had ever been there for him the way Autumn was and he had never loved her more than he did today. She was everything he wanted in a woman and so much more. Strong, loyal, beautiful, passionate and a dozen other qualities he couldn't begin to name.

Whatever happened, no matter the outcome, when this was over, he was going to ask her to marry him.

He wished he were more certain that she would say yes.

"You ready?" she called down to him and he realized she had reached the top of the pitch.

He waved and called back to her, "Ready!" Then started to climb the route she had prepared for his ascent.

Oddly, as bad as the situation was, as worried as he was about Molly, the climb was a thrill. There were times he found himself looking down at the world from a thousand feet up on the side of a granite slab. The views were spectacular, like nothing you could experience from the ground. Jagged, craggy distant peaks reached into the sky, some still topped with a dusting of snow. Deep green forested valleys spread out beneath him, cut by thin ribbons of water like threads of gleaming silk.

What he didn't like was the precious time that was ticking away as they made their way, inch by grueling inch, toward the summit of Angel's Peak.

The hours were slipping away. Even after they got to the top, they would have to locate the cabin — and pray Eli Beecher hadn't had time to get there ahead of them.

Burt Riker stood next to Doug Watkins in the front yard of the Beecher house. It was almost noon.

Last night, Rachael and Sarah had been taken into protective custody. By now, little Ginny Purcell had been reunited with her parents, who had flown into Seattle this morning for the teary reunion. The child had been emotionally abused by her abductors, but she had suffered no sexual or serious physical abuse. She was with her parents again and in time, the trauma of the kidnapping would fade.

It was nice when the good guys won one.

Riker almost smiled. The Purcells had Autumn Sommers and Ben McKenzie to thank for the return of their child.

And maybe some of the credit went to the stout detective with the shaved head who had taken a chance and helped them. Doug Watkins was there at the scene today because he had been involved in the Molly McKenzie abduction case six years ago and because he had information pertinent to the current situation.

"So let me get this straight," Riker said to him, continuing the conversation they had already begun. "You're telling me the Sommers woman helped McKenzie track down Eli Beecher through a series of dreams — is that right?"

The man was obviously uncomfortable with the subject, as he had been since the discussion began. "That's the way it looks. Apparently, this dream thing happened to her once before, back when she was in high school. When the same thing started to happen again, she went to McKenzie and eventually convinced him to renew the search for his daughter."

Riker grunted. He had worked with a psychic once and had a bit of luck but nothing like this. "Well, it got them this far so I guess there must be something to it."

Watkins seemed eager to change the subject and Riker let him. "When will your team reach Beecher's cabin?"

"The team on the ground — not until tomorrow at best. But we're putting another chopper in the air. They'll be looking for a place to set down or drop a team in from above, someplace that'll give them faster access to the cabin."

Watkins nodded. "You . . . ahh . . . said the dream part of this conversation was off the record. I don't think Ms. Sommers would want her story spread all over the media. Those guys would hound her to the ends of the earth to get that kind of news."

"They won't get it from me. This is going to go down as a case of a father's persistence. His determined six-year search for his daughter. How he put old clues together and uncovered new ones. How his search led him to Ginny Purcell."

"Yeah. I just hope he also finds his Molly and that she's unharmed."

"So do I," Riker said. He stared off at the distant mountain. "So do I."

The middle of the day grew hot, but they had dressed lightly, knowing the physical exertion would be enough to keep them warm. As the afternoon began to wane, the temperature started dropping. It was going to be colder than it was this morning, which Autumn thought might be good because it would keep them awake and alert.

They were pushing themselves too hard, she knew, both of them nearing exhaustion, the last thing a climber wanted to happen before he reached the top. They had made it up the Pinnacle with only a few minor scrapes and when Ben joined her at the top of the pitch he had actually grinned.

"That was something," he said.

"You're something, McKenzie." Leaning

over, she kissed him hard on the mouth, then turned and started climbing again before he could react.

She headed up the mountain with renewed determination though her muscles had begun to scream. The good news was that they had come to a heavily vegetated slope they could hike up instead of climb, which gave them a chance to rest a bit and check their gear before they tackled the next pitch then faced the Devil's Wall.

Half an hour later, they were there, standing at the bottom of a sheer granite face with an overhang near the top.

Ben peered up at the massive slab of rock. "Man, this baby is a monster."

"Yeah, you could say that."

"You said you took a beating when you climbed it before." He stared up at the wall. "I can see how that could happen."

"Some of the rock near the top may be loose. We need to be careful so we don't pull a chunk down on top of us."

"I'll keep that in mind," Ben said dryly.

They were wearing helmets. Autumn preferred to climb without one unless the terrain had a lot of loose rock or crumbling sandstone, but there wasn't room for error in the climb they were making. And this was a place that was dicey at best.

"Once we get past the wall," she said, "we're mostly in the clear. We should be able to make the rest of the climb without much problem." *Should* being the key word.

At the base of the wall, they each checked their harness, then worked the rope into position. Autumn took a deep breath, steeled herself and started to climb the first pitch, which was longer than she liked, requiring a great deal of rope before she reached the indention in the granite, a thin ledge that would provide a safe place to anchor herself for Ben's climb up the wall.

Though the cloud around the mountain had lifted half an hour ago and the weather was clear for the moment, the mist had left some of the shady rock surface wet and slick. Before she finished setting her third piece of protection in place, a cam wedged into a wide crack in the rock, her grip slipped off the stone and her toe-hold broke free, catapulting her into thin air. It was only a six-foot fall, since her second piece of protection had been firmly placed, but her breath caught just the same. She didn't like that moment of being out of control and hanging out over a thousand feet of nothing but air.

Ben held her steady, as if he had belayed her a thousand times. She repositioned herself on the rock and started climbing again but she couldn't help worrying about him tackling the slick rock surface.

She set the cams and hexes close together, giving them both a little more insurance if another fall occurred, and finally dragged herself up to the top, using a heel hooked on the rock to haul herself over the edge. She took a few deep breaths to steady herself, found her footing, set her anchors and settled in to support Ben's climb.

He was near the third cam when he reached for a handhold above him and his foot came loose. His other hand, wedged in a narrow crack, scraped free, loosening a big chunk of rock as he started to fall. One of the cams she had set jerked out of the crack and another, larger boulder tilted forward and started to fall.

For a single heart-stopping instant as the huge piece of granite crashed down the mountain, Autumn watched in sheer terror, certain Ben was about to die.

Ben swung out over a vast canvas of nothing, then plummeted backward, his helmet cracking hard against the solid rock surface. The granite protrusion fell sharply away from beneath his feet and for a second time he swung free, barely avoiding a massive chunk of rock that came loose from above and bounced down the mountain, then careened out over the vast expanse of nothingness below.

Braced on a ledge above him, Autumn held him steady as he swung back and forth, trying to find purchase with his feet, trying to get a secure hold on the damp, slick rock in front of him.

Finally, he managed to right himself and secure his position, wedge his hand into a crack and hold on. A little at a time, the strength began to seep back into his muscles and bones. He didn't realize he was bleeding till he felt something wet running into his eyes, wiped it away with the back of his hand and saw it was blood. He pulled out a small cloth towel from his pack and blotted his face, then reached into his bag for some chalk to dry his hands.

For the first time, he really understood that your climbing partner held your life in his hands — or in this case, hers. He had found the perfect partner in Autumn, Ben thought with the hint of a smile.

"That was definitely an e-ticket ride!" he called up to her as he prepared to climb again, but it was only for her sake since his heart still hammered like hell. His first movement upward alerted him to the throbbing in his ankle. As he reached for a handhold, he felt a sharp sting where the skin had ripped off his fingers, felt the burn of the cuts on his knees and shins.

Ben muttered a dirty word. They were almost there. He didn't need any more aches and pains. He didn't have time for bruises and blood. Taking a deep breath, steadying himself, Ben continued to the top of the Devil's Wall.

THIRTY-ONE

"It won't be long now," Eli said. "We're almost there."

A shiver ran down Ruth's spine. It was going to be dark soon. Eli had said they would get to the cabin before night came. She was tired. Her ankle hurt where a spot rubbed at the back of her boot. She wanted to ask Eli to stop so that she could rest, but he hiked a lot and he didn't seem to get tired at all. In fact he seemed eager to get there.

Ruth thought she knew why.

Once they reached the cabin, Eli would say the words that would marry them and then she would have to say them and then she would be his wife. Her stomach rolled with nausea. She was getting more afraid with every step up the mountain. Sarah had said that once they were married she would have to take off her clothes and let Eli look at her. Let him touch her, do anything he wanted.

Ruth's eyes filled with tears. For an instant, she considered running away. Then she glanced around, saw nothing but a thick green forest of towering pines, dark, ominous shadows and impending darkness. She would never find her way back down the mountain on the overgrown trail. There were bears out there, and cougars and crawling things she didn't want to think about. She could only imagine what else.

There was nowhere to run, no way to escape.

"Hurry it up, girl. You'll need to change once we get there, put on your weddin' dress. You women like that sort of thing."

She wanted to tell him she didn't care about wearing a wedding dress. She didn't want to get married at all. Instead she kept silent. If she cried or argued, she would only make him angry. Whatever he planned to do to her would be worse if he got mad.

Through the trees up ahead, the hazy outline of a building came into view. As she got closer, she could make out the shape of a small house made of logs.

Eli's cabin. A sob welled up in her throat. They were there. There was nothing she could do to stop it from happening. As she walked behind Eli along the trail, Ruth began praying to a God who never listened that somehow she would be saved.

"It has to be here somewhere," Ben said, searching the dim light that was all that was left of the day.

"It's here," Autumn told him. "The trail takes off to the left of the main trail near the top and that's where we are now."

"Then why can't we see it?"

"Because it's getting dark." Autumn turned to search again the rapidly darkening woods.

Both of them were battered and bruised and exhausted. Ben had a fist-sized bruise on his shoulder. His ankle throbbed with every step he took; his hands were scraped raw and bleeding. But they had made it to the summit.

Unfortunately, it had taken longer than they had expected and once they got there, they hadn't been able to find the damned, godforsaken cabin. Ben was beginning to panic.

"Time to dig out that flashlight you brought," Autumn said. "I think we'd better put it to use."

He set his pack down on the trail and got out the light, turned it on and flashed it through the heavy growth of trees in the forest.

"Wait a minute — turn the light back off."

"What is it?" Ben switched off the beam, leaving them in what had become total darkness.

"Just before the light went on, I thought I caught a glimpse of another light over that way." She pointed in that direction, moved along a game trail that led through the trees. "There! See it over there?"

There was only a faint yellow glow in the darkness but as they moved along the trail, he could see it was lantern light muted behind the curtains in the window of a cabin. A thin plume of smoke drifted up from a small rock chimney on the roof.

His chest tightened. They'd found it — Beecher's *sanctuary.* He wanted to rush to the door. Knock it down if he had to. He wanted to get to Molly to protect her from whatever horrors Eli might be doing to her at that very moment. He forced himself to stay calm.

"That's got to be it," Autumn said softly.

"Yeah." Ben tossed his pack down again, reached in and pulled out his Springfield automatic. He raised a finger to his lips and motioned for Autumn to follow him. As they drew near the log house, he could hear voices inside.

"Now, don't you look pretty?" It was a man's voice, deep and a little husky.

Ben heard a soft, child-like whimper and it cut right through him.

"There's no need to be ashamed of what God gave you," the husky voice said. "There's no room for shame between a man and his bride. Now toss away that dress and get up on that bed."

Ben's whole body tightened. He told himself to hang on to his rage. That he had to be careful. He couldn't take the chance of Molly getting hurt.

"You hear me, girl?"

"I don't want to, Eli."

"You'll do as I say. You'll take your rightful place as my wife, just like you were meant to. Now get up on that bed before I have to take a switch to you."

Anger rose inside him, so hot for a moment it blurred his vision. He fought for control even as he raised the pistol and wrapped both his hands around the grip.

"Easy," Autumn whispered. "You need to think of Molly. Make sure she's out of harm's way."

He released a slow breath and nodded, fighting every instinct to crash through the door and tear Eli Beecher apart limb by limb. Reaching for the door latch, he quietly lifted the handle. He wasn't surprised to find the door unlocked. Eli Beecher was a man of supreme ego. It never occurred to him anyone would try to stop him from doing exactly what he wanted.

Ben stepped back and kicked open the door. "Freeze right where you stand!" Two handed, he leveled the gun at Eli's chest. Molly stood next to him in a pair of white cotton panties, trembling all over, her cotton dress clutched against her small breasts.

"It's all right, sweetheart," he said, trying to keep the fury out of his voice. "You're safe. Everything's going to be okay."

His chest squeezed in a mixture of rage and pain, love and a joy so fierce he blinked against a quick burn of tears. He would have known her anywhere, recognized the fine pale arch of her brow, the sweet curve of her lips, the soft blue of her eyes.

"Molly, I'm your father. I've been looking for you since the day Eli Beecher stole you away from your home. I've come to get you. Move away from Eli where you will be safe."

Molly's frightened gaze fixed on his face. She made that same little whimpering sound and his heart constricted.

"It's all right, angel. Just move away from Eli. I don't want you getting hurt." But he wanted to hurt Eli Beecher. His grip on the pistol tightened. Ben wanted to kill the man for what he had done, for what he planned to do.

Molly's hands shook as she raised the dress, turned and slipped it on over her head, then let it fall down around her ankles.

Next to her, Eli's gaze darted around the cabin, looking for a means of escape.

"Don't even think about it, Beecher. You want to stay alive, you won't move an inch."

Molly's eyes lifted to Eli's face and Ben could read her uncertainty, the fear she must have lived with for years.

"It's all right, Molly," Autumn said softly. "Your father has come to take you home."

"My name is Ruth."

"I know, sweetheart," she said. "That's what Eli told you, but your real name is Molly. Does that sound familiar? Molly McKenzie?"

"Move away from him, Molly," Ben said. "Come over here where you'll be safe."

With a last glance at Eli, she made a faint, tentative movement, but before she could take a step, Eli grabbed her and pulled her in front of him, slamming her back against his chest and clamping his arm around her throat.

"I'll squeeze the life out of her — I swear

I will. Put the gun on the floor and back away."

"I'll kill you where you stand, you son of a bitch." Ben raised his aim, pointing the barrel straight at Eli's head. "I'd like nothing better than to see you dead."

"You won't shoot me. Not in front of the girl." His arm tightened around Molly's throat and she began to claw at him, fighting to get enough air into her lungs. He was a strong man, the arm around Molly's throat roped with muscle. Ben wanted to tear him to pieces.

"I can break her neck like a twig," Eli warned, his stranglehold tightening even more. "You want that, McKenzie? Put the gun down now."

Ben's fingers tightened around the trigger. It took sheer force of will not to squeeze. But a head shot might hit Molly. A leg shot might not keep Beecher from breaking her neck. And thinking of the other Beecher brothers and what they had done to Priscilla Vreeland, Ben believed there was every chance the bastard would do it.

Un-cocking the pistol, he set it down on the wooden floor a few feet in front of Eli Beecher. He wouldn't let Beecher reach it. If he did, they might all wind up dead. But he needed to buy a little time.

Beecher inched forward and bent down, dragging Molly with him as he groped for the weapon on the floor. Ben watched him, waiting for his chance. Arm outstretched, for a split second Eli wavered. Molly shoved hard and broke free of his hold and Ben leapt forward tackling Beecher and knocking him backwards onto the floor.

Ben hauled back a fist and slammed it hard into Beecher's face. Another blow had the bastard reeling. Beecher blocked a third punch and landed a solid blow to Ben's jaw, rolled on top of him and hit him again. Ben blocked the next blow, rolled Beecher beneath him and threw a roundhouse punch that slammed Beecher's head against the floor with the thud of a ripe melon.

Pinning Beecher beneath him, Ben began to use his fists, delivering blow after blow, his mind a blur of fury and pain. Again and again, his fist smashed into Eli Beecher's face. Blood flew and Beecher's body finally went limp but Ben just kept hitting him.

Molly made a strangled sound that Ben barely heard and Autumn ran to her, pulled the girl into her arms. "It's all right, Molly. Stop it, Ben! It's over!"

Fury muted her words. He drew back his fist and punched Beecher again.

"Ben, stop it! You're scaring your daughter!" Her words reached him, as she had known they would. Molly had suffered enough. He wouldn't be the cause of more pain. He pulled his next punch, his arm trembling with the effort, and pushed himself to his feet, leaving Eli Beecher unconscious on the rough wooden floor planks.

Molly stared at him, her blue eyes huge and uncertain. She was wearing the dress Autumn had described, the long, embroidered white cotton gown she had seen in her dreams.

"Are you . . . are you really my father?" She was trembling, but there was something in her eyes. His heart clenched as he recognized the glimmer of hope.

A lump rose in his throat. "Yes, sweetheart, I am. I've been looking for you for so long. I love you so very much." Ben started toward her, stopped when he saw her shrink against Autumn. "You don't have to be afraid, angel. I would never hurt you. And Eli's never going to hurt you again. I promise you, this time you'll be safe."

As she should have been before. He pushed the guilt away. He'd been dealing with that for the past six years. It was time to look to the future.

Molly's gaze held his and it was as if he

could see inside her, the way he had when she was a little girl.

"Eli said my father and mother didn't want me. Rachael said they were dead."

"They wanted you to think that but it isn't true. We just couldn't find you." He blinked, fighting the pain, trying to hold back tears.

Her eyes, the soft blue he remembered, remained on his face. "There was a man once . . . he called me angel. We had tea parties and he carried me around on his shoulders. Rachael said I should forget but I never did."

Ben swallowed past the lump in his throat. "I'm glad you didn't. You were always my angel. You always will be."

Molly's gaze shifted to Autumn. "I feel like I know you. Are you my mother?"

Autumn smiled and discreetly brushed away a tear. "My name is Autumn. I'm a friend, someone you met in a dream. Your mother doesn't know we've found you. She's going to be so happy to have you back home. And you have a sister named Katie. You're really going to love her and I know she'll love you." Autumn wiped away another tear but several escaped down her cheek.

Ben's heart squeezed hard. He looked at Autumn and thought how much he loved her, thought that no matter how long he lived, he could never repay her for the gift she had given him in returning his lost little girl.

Molly looked up at him. "I don't have to live with Eli anymore? I don't have to marry him?"

"No, sweetheart." Ben's words came out gruff as he pushed them past the ache in his throat. "From now on you just get to be a little girl — my little girl. Like you were before."

Molly moved toward him, stopped just in front of him. Very tentatively, she reached out a hand and touched his cheek. Ben's eyes slid closed but he didn't make a move. His heart was beating, thundering inside him, telling him to pull her into his arms. Still, he stayed where he was, afraid he would frighten her, determined she would never be frightened again. "I love you, Molly. I love you so much."

She stared at him through eyes he knew as well as the ones he saw every day in the mirror.

"I prayed to God that He would send someone to save me," she said. "This time He heard my prayer."

He tried not to think how many times she must have prayed to go home but no one

532

had ever come for her.

"What . . . what about Eli?" she asked turning to look down at him.

Ben's jaw hardened. He forced himself not to think of the pain he had seen in her blue eyes and spoke instead to Autumn. "We need to tie him up. In the morning we'll head down the mountain. In the meantime —"

The sentence died on his lips, cut off by the earsplitting sound of a chopper. A blinding light pierced the windows of the cabin as a helicopter circled overhead. An instant later, the door burst open and three men wearing FBI vests, guns drawn, crashed into the room, dropped from the chopper, Ben figured, somewhere close to the cabin.

Ben was damned glad to see them, even if their arrival was a little late.

The men spotted Eli Beecher, bloody and unconscious, and began to holster their weapons as they realized the scene had already been secured.

"I take it you're McKenzie," one of the agents said, young, dark-haired and eager. "Everybody here okay?"

Ben nodded. "That's Beecher. He isn't dead, I'm sorry to say. He just looks that way."

"We'll take care of Beecher." The young

agent smiled. "You just take care of your family."

His family. Two of the people he loved most in the world.

"Then again, it looks like you've been doing a pretty fair job of that already."

Ben looked over at Beecher. "He's lucky I didn't kill him." Would have if Beecher had given him the slightest excuse. But there was Molly to think of.

And Autumn.

It wasn't time to speak to Autumn about the future, not yet, but soon the time would come. He just hoped he meant half as much to her as she meant to him.

He returned his attention to his daughter. "Are you doing all right, angel?"

Molly watched the agents handcuff Eli, haul him to his feet and out the door.

"Is Eli going to jail?" she asked.

"Yes, Molly. For a very long time."

"If I go home with you, what will happen to Sarah? Who's going to take care of her and the baby?"

She had always been loving, even as a little girl. He wanted to hold her so badly. He needed to reassure himself she was really alive and there with him now. "We'll make sure Sarah and her baby get everything they need, okay?"

One of the agents walked back in, carrying a handheld radio. "The pilot got lucky. He located a spot not too far from here that was wide enough he could set the chopper down. He's waiting for us there. One of the men can show you the way whenever you're ready to leave."

Ben turned back to Molly. "Everything's going to be all right," he said. "I promise."

"Okay."

"Let's get out of here." He couldn't resist catching her hand to lead her out the door. When Molly didn't pull away, hope blossomed inside him. She was his little girl and in time she would know how much he loved her.

It was a beginning.

A new beginning with Molly was a gift from God — and Autumn Sommers — Ben never thought he'd have.

Thirty-Two

Autumn sat across from Terri Markham at O'Shaunessy's. She hadn't seen Ben in more than two weeks, not since the night they'd been choppered off the top of Angel's Peak.

He'd called every few days, which didn't surprise her. In the weeks they'd searched for Molly, they had become good friends. And there was the debt Ben felt he owed her for helping him find his little girl. That's the way he would think of it, she was sure. Ben was an honorable man. Honorable and caring, among the many other qualities she had come to admire in him.

The reasons she had fallen so deeply in love with him.

Her heart squeezed. Dear God, she missed him.

Autumn looked across the table at Terri. Her friend hadn't said more than a couple of words since they had climbed up on the

536

stools at the small round table.

The ghost of a smile curved Terri's lips. "You're thinking of Ben."

"Actually, I'm trying not to think of Ben." She sighed. "Unfortunately, it isn't all that easy." She took a sip of the Cosmo she had ordered instead of the white wine she usually drank.

"You're in love with him, aren't you?"

Autumn ran a finger through the mist on the side of her glass. "I tried not to be. It didn't do any good."

"How does Ben feel?"

"I don't know. Right now his most important concern is his daughter."

Terri shook back her thick dark hair. "Yeah, it must be tough trying to put things back together with Molly after so many years."

"He's making progress. That's what he said when he phoned." She took another sip of her drink and changed the subject. "What about you? You look a little down in the mouth today. What handsome male has managed to get you brooding over him? It's not an easy thing to do."

Terri took a drink from the frosty, long-stemmed glass in front of her. "Actually, I was thinking about Josh."

"Josh Kendall?"

Terri nodded. "I asked him out but he turned me down. I didn't tell you. My ego wouldn't let me."

"You asked Josh out on a date?"

"I called him, invited him out to dinner. I told you I was going to — or at least I was thinking about it. Josh agreed. We were supposed to go out that Saturday. I picked a place I thought he'd like, you know, something not too sophisticated. I figured that would be best."

"Josh can hold his own pretty much anywhere. His family's got plenty of money. He just doesn't enjoy that kind of thing very much."

"Yeah, that's what I figured."

"So what happened?"

"That Saturday morning, he phoned me. He said he'd changed his mind, that he was seriously dating Courtney Roland. He said he'd finally figured out what he wanted in life." She looked up, a soft, sad smile on her lips. "Apparently, it wasn't me."

Autumn couldn't believe it. Josh had been in love with Terri for as long as Autumn could remember. "I'm proud of him, Terri. I know that isn't what you want to hear, but it's true."

"I know. In a way, so am I. Josh finally figured out what's important, that finding someone you love who truly loves you is what really counts. I only wish that would happen to me."

Autumn reached over and caught her hand. "I think you're on your way — I really do."

Terri smiled. "I kind of think so too." She took a sip of her drink. "So what about you? Have you figured out what it is you really want?"

I don't want to feel like this. I don't want to ache for Ben, to think of him every minute and miss him every hour of the day. She shrugged her shoulders. "I had my fling. Now it's over. I'm resigned, I suppose. I still feel like shit."

Terri laughed. "You're in love with him. If he's in love with you —"

"I told you — I have no idea what Ben feels for me. Mostly, I think he feels grateful."

"Yeah, I imagine he does."

A noise came from behind them. Autumn turned at the sound of a familiar deep voice.

"I'll always be grateful for what you did, Autumn." Ben stood beside her, his dark eyes soft on her face. In the noisy room, she hadn't heard him walk up to the table. "But gratitude isn't all I feel for you. I'm in love with you, Autumn. I have been for a very long time."

Autumn's heart twisted. It wasn't true. She didn't dare let herself believe it. "I — I suppose you might think something like that. Love and gratitude . . . they can get mixed up in your head. In time —"

"Time won't change the way I feel. I love you and I want you to marry me. I didn't plan to ask you standing in the middle of O'Shaunessy's but I heard what you said and I can see that if I don't ask now, I might not get another chance. I love you. Say you'll marry me, Autumn."

Autumn stared at him as if she couldn't have heard him correctly. Part of her had longed to have him say those words. Another part thought of her father and mother and how terrible their marriage had been, thought of Steven Elliot and how she had been stupid enough to believe he loved her and wound up with a broken heart. She remembered how women loved Ben and how he was sure to get tired of her and move on to someone else.

Tears filled her eyes as she stood up from the table and looked into his beloved face. "I can't marry you, Ben. It would never work out. Surely you can see that." She cast a desperate glance at the door. "I have to go now. I have to leave." And then she was running, brushing past busy tables, hurrying toward the door leading out to the street.

She could hear Ben calling her name from somewhere behind her, but she didn't stop. Tears blurred her vision, but she just kept running, frantic to escape. As she raced along the sidewalk, she was terrified Ben would follow, but when she glanced back, she saw him standing on the corner staring after her, a grim look on his face.

It was over. She had known it the moment they had left the tiny log cabin on Angel's Peak. It was over — even if Ben wasn't ready to accept it.

Ben jammed his hands into the pockets of his jeans and watched the woman he loved running for her life to escape him. He hadn't seen Autumn in what seemed like forever but was only a little over two weeks. There had been so much to do, so much to take care of.

As soon as he had arrived back in Seattle with Molly, he had phoned Joanne. He'd asked to speak to John, afraid of what the shock of finding Molly alive might do to her mother. He had trusted John to gently break the news, to warn Joanne that Molly had been found and that Ben was bringing her home.

Joanne had been weeping when she finally came on the line.

"Is it true? Tell me it's really true."

"It's true, Joanne. I'm bringing our little girl home." He went on to explain that Molly had few memories of the family she had been stolen away from, but in time that would change.

"She'll need our help," Ben said. "Along with Katie's and John's." *And Autumn's,* he had thought.

He looked up the crowded street, watched her disappear among the throng of people on the sidewalk, knew she was making her way back to the safety of her condo. He should have known she would run. She was afraid to trust him with her future, afraid to take a chance on making a life with him.

Afraid to believe in happily every after.

Ben wasn't afraid. The only thing he was afraid of was that Autumn wouldn't be able to trust him enough for their marriage to work. That was the reason he had let her go. He needed her to be sure of him, certain of his commitment to her and the future they would make together.

It was the only way their marriage could succeed.

Ben sighed as he started along the street on his way back to his apartment. He would give her some time, let her mull over what he had said, then try again.

He wasn't about to give up — not yet. But neither could he marry a woman who wasn't able to trust him. And there was only so much he could do.

He remembered the incredible confidence it had taken for her to guide him to the top of Angel's Peak. If only she had that kind of confidence in herself as a woman. If only she knew how much he needed her, how much he loved her.

If only Autumn realized that with her in his life, he would never stray.

Two days passed but Autumn didn't hear from Ben. By now, he had surely come to his senses, realized how foolish it was for a man like him to think of marriage. Ben could never be happy with only one woman. Why should he be, when women threw themselves at him on a daily basis?

Sitting in her condo, Autumn stared dully out at the city. It was raining today, damp, dark and dismal. Exactly the way she felt.

God, loving someone hurt. She ached with a physical pain that crushed down on her like a heavy stone and yet she knew if she weakened it would only get worse. She told herself eventually she would get over it.

Relationships ended all the time.

And in truth, they had never had a real relationship. A wild physical attraction to each other, yes. But aside from that, they were just two people thrown together in a desperate situation, two people searching for a lost little girl.

Autumn thought of Molly and a brief, sad smile touched her lips. Molly and Katie were wonderful children. Being part of their lives would be a privilege.

She couldn't risk it. Katie had suffered one broken home. Molly had known even worse.

She dragged herself up from the sofa, barely able to make her feet move toward the kitchen. A good strong cup of tea would make her feel better. In less than a month, school would start and working again was bound to help keep her mind off Ben.

She was reaching for the teapot when the intercom buzzed. "It's your pop," said a familiar voice coming from the lobby. "Let me in."

She pressed the button to admit him though she didn't really want to see him. A few minutes later, Max walked into the condo.

"Where the hell have you been?"

She couldn't look at him. Didn't dare. "Hi Dad."

"I asked you a question." He was furious. She hadn't seen him this angry in years.

"I . . . ah . . . I've been a little under the weather."

"Is that so? I've been calling for the last five days. You never returned even one of my calls."

"Like I said —"

"That's a load of bull and we both know it. What happened between you and McKenzie? It was all over the news, you and him finding his daughter. You two break up?"

She set the teapot on the stove and turned on the heat, hoping he wouldn't notice her hand was trembling. "I guess you could say that."

"What happened?"

She turned to face him. "Look, Dad, I appreciate your concern, but this really isn't any of your business."

His mouth flattened out. "Well, little girl, I'm making it my business. I've never seen you look at a man the way you looked at Ben. I figure you're bad in love with him. Thing is, I think he's in love with you just the same. Now tell me what the hell is going on."

She tried not to tear up, but she couldn't help it. "I fell in love with him, Dad. I didn't mean to. God, I tried so hard not to."

"What about Ben? Looked pretty lovesick to me the night he brought you up to the hospital."

She shook her head, swallowed past the lump in her throat. "He thinks he loves me, but . . ."

"But what? The man ought to know if he loves you or not."

"He's grateful, Dad. I helped him find Molly. He feels like he owes me."

"More bullshit. Why'd he stop seeing you?"

"He didn't. I mean, he was busy at first with his daughter, but then . . . well, I stopped seeing him."

"Why, for the love of Pete?"

"Because he asked me to marry him."

The teapot whistled, cutting off whatever tirade Max started to make. He scratched his gray head. "I'm confused here, little girl. If Ben asked you to marry him, why the hell are you crying?"

"Because I can't do it. I can't marry a man like Ben."

He blew out a breath. "I guess I'm missing something here. What the devil's wrong with him? Seemed like a fine enough fellow to me."

Autumn squared her shoulders, looked him straight in the face. "Ben's a lot like you, Dad. Women love him and he loves them. I could never be enough for him."

Max frowned. "Tell me this ain't because of me and your mother."

She glanced away. "I know how men are, Dad. They can't be faithful. It isn't in their nature."

Max's busy eyebrows came together. "Well, you've had a belly full of losers, that's for sure. But if a man loves a woman — really loves her — it isn't hard to be faithful."

She snorted a laugh. "Yeah, sure."

Max caught her hand, led her into the living room, sat her down on the sofa, then took a seat in the overstuffed chair. "I never thought to say this. I didn't want to hurt you. Now I see it has to be said."

She looked up. "What is it, Dad?"

"I never loved your mother. I know that sounds like a terrible thing to say, but it's true. Kathleen was a fine woman and she deserved a whole lot better than me but the fact is, I was never in love with her. We were both a little reckless and while we were dating, Kathleen got pregnant. We got married because it was what our families wanted. I tried to be a good husband but something was missing right from the start. I was a young man then, as lusty as they come. For years I carried on, before and after your mother died."

"You never cared about her feelings. You knew how much it hurt her, but you didn't stop."

"I tried. I couldn't seem to help myself. Not until I met Myra. For the first time in my life, I fell in love. I always kind of played down my feelings for her when I was with you, but the truth is, I'm crazy about the woman — was right from the start. I love Myra and I've never cheated on her. I never will."

Autumn stared at him, more than a little surprised.

"What I'm trying to say is when the right woman comes along, if a man loves her with all his heart — he would never do anything to hurt her. If Ben loves you that much, grab onto him and never let go."

Her heart was pounding, thumping away inside her, beating with something she recognized as hope. Was it possible? Her father had changed, become a faithful husband. But Ben was younger. Could he be happy with just one woman? Could she trust him with her future? With her heart?

"You hear what I'm sayin', honey?"

Autumn blinked and a tear rolled down her cheek. "I hear you, Dad. But how will I know if he loves me enough?"

"You ask him. And when he answers, you look him straight in the eye."

She nodded and managed a tentative smile. It seemed like a good idea. Her heart couldn't hurt any worse than it already did. "Okay, I'll ask him."

Max reached over and patted her hand. "That's my girl. And don't you wait too long. A man in love don't have a lot of patience."

Autumn chewed her lip. If she was going to do this, she had better do it soon. Ben had never been a patient man.

Ben sat behind the desk in his study. It was a weekend but he had work to do. They were closing the deal on A-1 Sports, doing a stock takeover that would end with him owning the controlling portion of the company.

Earlier, he had declared his intent to make an open tender offer for A-1 stock at above-market prices. The company was undervalued, he had discovered. There were several pieces of real estate A-1 owned that had gone way up in value but the increases weren't yet reflected in the books.

He had made a run on the company and succeeded in taking over the majority of the stock — putting an end to the threat A-1 posed once and for all.

And making himself a good bit of money in the process.

If he hadn't been in such a foul mood, Ben might have smiled. The deal was about to be completed and though it had required a considerable amount of work, at least it had helped keep his mind off Autumn.

Keeping busy had helped, but the waiting was driving him crazy.

Ben shoved to his feet. He was tired of staying away from her; he had waited long enough. He was going to talk to her, get things straight between them once and for all.

Grabbing his jacket off the back of a chair, he headed for the door just as the intercom sounded, signaling a visitor at the elevator in the parking garage. Wondering who it could be on a Saturday, he reached over and pushed the button. He was amazed to hear the sound of Autumn's voice.

"It's me . . . Autumn. I . . . um, I was hoping we could talk. If . . . if it's not a bad time."

As if he wouldn't know the sound of her voice. As if there could be a bad time.

"I'll buzz you in." He strode down the hall to the entry, then paced nervously as he waited for the elevator doors to slide open. Autumn walked into the room in a gauzy flowered skirt and mauve sweater, sexy yet sweetly feminine. His heart clenched so hard it hurt.

"Hi," he said, suddenly at a loss for words.

"Hi."

God, she looked good, her hair in shiny auburn curls around her face and wearing a hint of make-up, nothing at all like the determined woman she had been on the climb to the top of the mountain. The combination of soft femininity and hidden strength stirred his blood and made him ache with desire for her.

"Would you like something to drink?" he asked, trying to force his thoughts in a different direction and hoping she said yes because he could use a stiff drink himself.

When she nodded, he headed for the bar hidden behind the mahogany panels in the living room. "White wine?" he asked over his shoulder.

"Yes, that would be nice."

He poured himself a Scotch on the rocks and took a sip, then brought the glass of wine over to where she stood. Their fingers brushed and the familiar electricity sparked between them. Autumn looked a little surprised.

"You didn't think the physical attraction would be there anymore?" His gaze ran over those soft, full lips, and he wanted to kiss them, sink into them. He remembered her tiny butterfly tattoo and thought how much he wanted to take her to bed.

"I don't know," she said. "I guess I thought the attraction had probably — you know — faded."

He took a sip of his drink. It seemed like forever since he had been inside her. "You thought it was over between us. You figured once we found Molly, we were finished. Is that about right?"

"Well, yes, I suppose I —"

"We aren't finished Autumn. Not unless that's the way you want it."

She turned away, carried her wine glass toward the massive expanse of windows that overlooked the sea. "How is she? How's Molly doing?"

"She's doing great. She and Katie are nearly inseparable. A few of her memories are returning. Both Joanne and I are helping her remember whatever we can. And she's seeing a very good child psychologist.

I think it's going to be easier than we imagined."

"I hope so." She sipped her wine.

"You said you wanted to talk."

She turned toward him, her eyes big and uncertain. "I came to ask you if you meant what you said at O'Shaunessy's."

He reached out and touched her cheek. "I meant every word."

"You said you loved me. I need to know how much."

In a heartbeat he knew what she was asking; he had come to know her so well. Would she be enough for him? Could he be satisfied with only one woman?

He had never cheated on Joanne. He wished he'd told her that. He took her wine glass, set it down on the table and caught both her hands.

"I love you so much every hour we're apart is killing me. So much I can't allow myself to think how much it's going to hurt if you won't marry me. You mean everything to me, Autumn. I want to share my life with you. I want to have kids with you. I desperately want you to be my wife."

When she opened her mouth to speak, he held up his hand. "But I need to know something in return. Since you're here and asking me these questions, I'm going to assume you love me too. If you do, I need to know how much. I need to know if you love me enough to trust me, to know deep in your heart that I would never hurt you."

Her eyes filled with tears. "I love you more than life, Ben McKenzie. When I saw you fall off that mountain, I thought I was going to die myself."

"Can you trust me not to hurt you? To be the kind of husband you deserve?"

Something shifted in her expression, seemed to settle deep inside. Her posture slowly relaxed. "I trusted you with my life. I still do."

Ben drew her into his arms, bent his head and very softly kissed her. "Marry me."

Autumn looked up at him and the tears in her eyes slipped down her cheeks. "I'd love to marry you, Ben." She went up on her toes and kissed him and then she smiled. "But do we have to wait for the honeymoon?"

Ben laughed in sheer relief. The desire he'd been fighting tore free. "Not on your life."

He meant to carry her into the bedroom, make slow, passionate love to her. Instead, he took her there on the sofa in the living room, just shoved up her skirt, pulled down her sexy thong panties, opened his jeans and entered her with a single thrust.

"God, I missed you so much."

Twining her arms around his neck, she opened herself a little wider, took him a little deeper. "I missed you, too. I love you so much, Ben."

The words poured into him, released him in some way. He tried to hold back but he couldn't wait any longer, just kissed her deeply and began to move. He was so damned hot for her. It was always that way with Autumn. She met each of his movements, giving and taking, demanding all he had and more. She was his match in every way and as he drove into her, as they reached the crest together, he had never felt more certain of the future.

He was home at last. He had found his daughter and begun a new life. His soul had been resurrected when Autumn led him up the summit to Angel's Peak.

EPILOGUE

One year later

They were moving. A penthouse was no place to raise a family, Ben said, and Autumn was part of his family now. The girls were with them every other weekend and several days a week after school so they needed a more suitable place to live. Charlie Evans had officially decided to sell his Bainbridge Island home and Ben had bought it. The place wasn't too far from Autumn's teaching job at Lewis and Clark or Ben's Pike Street office. It was roomy enough for the girls — and more children when they came.

The house was lovely. A big, sprawling ranch house, gorgeous, yet homey. Autumn had been working with a designer to insure it had a sophisticated but comfortable air, a masculine study for Ben and a sunny room, filled with Victorian antiques for her.

Katie and Mollie loved the house. They

were darling girls, so sweet and loving, so dedicated to each other. Molly was seeing a child psychologist named Dr. Mince, who was helping her come to grips with the trauma she had suffered. She was behind in school, since Rachael believed that some of the subjects she should have been taught were a waste of time for a girl, but Ben had hired a tutor and Molly was catching up quickly.

Katie was spending a lot more time with her dad, which made her happy and brought them closer than they had ever been before. Autumn was teaching the girls to climb and Ben was teaching the whole family to kayak.

Added to all of that, Autumn's reccurring dreams had stopped completely. The Beecher brothers had pled guilty to the murder of Priscilla Vreeland and were serving life sentences without parole. Eli Beecher's trial had been briefer than expected. He had been found guilty of kidnapping, as well as a long string of other charges that would keep him in prison for most of his life. An interesting fact about the car had surfaced. One of Eli's cousins had owned the battered classic car, loaned it to Eli, then sold it to Riley Perkins, the insurance man, and bought himself a Harley. Robbie Hines had been correct.

Autumn smiled. No more ugly dreams — and Ben's incredible lovemaking — kept her sleeping like a baby.

The door opened and her handsome husband walked into the penthouse. Today was the last day they would spend there.

"You ready? Time to head for the boat. Katie and Molly are jumping up and down, anxious to leave."

Autumn smiled at Ben. "I'm ready. I was just thinking how lucky I am."

Ben walked over, wrapped his arms around her, drew her back against his chest and kissed the side of her neck. "I'm the lucky one. I've got my girls and I've got you. I'm the luckiest man on earth."

Autumn smiled. Ben always made her feel treasured. Apparently, Max was right. When a man really loved a woman, he let her know it. She didn't have to worry about being enough for him. She *knew* that she was.

"You're right, we'd better get going." Reluctantly, she left his arms. "Your girls have about as much patience as you do — which is practically none at all."

"I waited for you to make up your mind about marrying me, didn't I? Believe me, that took a boatload of patience."

Autumn just laughed. She took his hand and let him lead her out of the penthouse.

Ben thought he was lucky — and truly he was. He had his daughter back home and he had Katie and both of his girls adored him. He had a wife who would walk over a bed of hot coals for him.

Still, when she looked at Ben and saw the love for her shining in those warm brown eyes, Autumn knew who the lucky person was.

She was so lucky. Molly said a thank-you prayer to God every day. She was with her real family again — her mom and Katie, her mom's new husband, John, and her dad's pretty wife, Autumn. She loved them all and they seemed to like her.

At first when she'd come to the fancy house where she was supposed to live, she had been so scared. She didn't know the lady in the elegant clothes named Joanne who said she was her mother, and barely remembered the man who claimed to be her father. At night, she would wake up crying, but her sister slept in the bed next to hers. Katie would hear her and climb into bed beside her and then she would be able to sleep.

Once her dad had heard her when she was staying in his apartment and he had come in and scooped her up onto his lap. He had settled her there and just held her and it didn't feel funny at all like it would have with Eli.

"You're my daughter and I love you," he had said. "Nothing is ever going to change that. You don't ever have to be afraid again."

She'd looked up at him and called him Dad for the very first time and he got a funny glitter in his eyes.

She loved all of her parents and she loved Katie. She didn't really remember her, but it didn't matter. They looked just alike and they liked the same things, even the same foods, like devil's food cake with thick chocolate frosting. Molly didn't much remember her mom and dad either, though when they told her stories about when she was a little girl and showed her pictures, she pretended sometimes that she did. It made them so happy and seeing them that way made her happy, too.

She didn't cry anymore — only when she dreamed about Eli, but then Autumn would be there in her dream to tell her everything was okay and remind her that she was safe. And the nightmare would go away.

And Sarah and the baby came over a lot. Sarah was living in a home for young girls that Autumn had found for her. She was studying to get her high school diploma and thinking she might even go to college. If she did, Dad had promised to pay for it.

Molly loved Sarah and the little blond, blue-eyed baby named Matthew Benjamin. But then she loved everything about her life since her dad had saved her that night on the mountain. She would never forget the way he had crashed through the door and seen her with Eli and beaten Eli to a pulp.

He had done it for her. God had heard her prayer and sent him to save her. Every once in a while when she looked at her dad, she thought of that night and felt this funny little tingle of love for him.

"Come on, Molly! Everyone is waiting!" It was Katie. They were going boating this afternoon. Both of them loved the water. They loved kayaking and swimming and now Autumn was teaching them to climb.

"I'm coming!" Grabbing her beach towel, she raced along the dock. Autumn and Katie were already aboard, but her dad was waiting to help her onto the deck.

"Time to get going, angel." He called her that a lot. It was one of the few things she remembered from her childhood — her dad calling her *angel.* He held her hand until she was safely aboard, then smiled at her in that soft way he did, climbed aboard himself and made his way up to the wheel to steer the boat out into the harbor.

Molly looked up at him and waved. Katie giggled and Autumn smiled.

Molly felt so lucky. The luckiest girl in the world.

FROM THE AUTHOR

Hope you enjoyed *The Summit,* the second in my paranormal romantic suspense series that began with *Scent of Roses.* These are stories about ordinary women who have extraordinary experiences, as so many of us have had. I hope you will look for *Season of Strangers,* the third book in the series, and that you also enjoy it.

Until then, all best wishes and happy reading, Kat

ABOUT THE AUTHOR

Kat Martin is a *New York Times* bestselling author of over thirty-five historical and contemporary romance novels. To date, she has more than ten million copies of her books in print and has been published in seventeen foreign countries, including Sweden, China, Korea, Russia, South Africa, Argentina, Japan, and Greece. Kat and her husbandd, author Larry Jay Martin, live on their ranch in Missoula, Montana.